DESCENT INTO HELL

The ship lurched to one side suddenly. Bullets tore up through the floor on all sides, and as the Huey began to bank hard to the left, a gaping hole appeared in the floor of the craft. A split second after Brody realized what was happening, the RPG detonated, knocking him partially out of the hatch.

His monkeystrap kept him from being belched out into Void Vicious, however, and as smoke filled the cabin he realized the small of his back was soaked wet with his own blood from dozens of minute shrapnel wounds.

The crew chief lay across the hole in the floor, dead. His throat had been sliced open by a fist-sized chunk of flying metal. The downdraft was trying to suck him out through the hole, but his body was too stocky. Brody watched blood cover the floor of the Huey in the time it took him to stumble through the pile of crimson-coated brass and regain his footing. Then the ship was rolling onto its side, and the blood was all over the front of him too as it took to the air and sprayed out the hatch like a bucketful of red paint being thrown through a window.

The intercom was out, but Brody heard the AC clearly as he yelled to the pilot beside him, "Hold your breath, slugger —we're goin' down!"

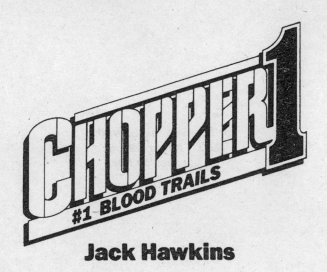

CHOPPER 1

#1 BLOOD TRAILS

Jack Hawkins

IVY BOOKS • NEW YORK

For Sergeant Nik-Uhernik,
who's "still in Saigon"
...but shouldn't be.

Ivy Books
Published by Ballantine Books

Copyright © 1987 by Butterfield Press, Inc.

Produced by Butterfield Press
133 Fifth Avenue
New York, New York 10003

Library of Congress Catalog Card Number: 86-82545

ISBN 0-8041-0006-3

Printed in Canada

First Edition: February 1987

BOOK 1
RAIN FOREST GHOSTS

CHAPTER 1

He loved the licoricelike taste of gunsmoke lining his throat.
But Brody was having trouble keeping his balance as the shifting pond of brass cartridges piled up around his boots. He
leaned into the M-60 machine gun hanging from a canvas strap
in the middle of the hatch, keeping his trigger finger taut.
Smoke clouded his vision for an instant as fifty rounds roared
down into the rain forest forty feet below. Then the gunsmoke
was sucked out of the hatch by rotor downblast as the helicopter
banked hard to the right, and he lost sight of the black-clad
guerrillas. Brody could not hear the empty brass cartridges
clattering across the metal floor of the Huey because of the
headset, but his mind recreated the sensation from countless
past missions. The clinking din could mesmerize a less-disci-
plined soldier. Brody had known three newbies—rooks in The
Nam—who'd slipped on the four-inch-long objects and flown
out the hatch into what the grunts nervously referred to as Void
Vicious: that blinding green carpet of hostile flora below that
reached up awkwardly with gnarled claws and never let go if it
snatched you. Void Vicious was jungle hell bad news. Numba
Ten with a clip of tracers on the Chart of Misfortunes.

"Choi-oi!" Brody's gun hand flew off the Hog—every door
gunner worth his salt called the hatch-60 a "Hog" if he didn't
name her for a whore down in Saigon or some round-eye back
in The World who'd sent him a Dear John—and clamped onto
the hatch frame as the chopper banked to the left. His dog tags
flew out in front of his face, fluttered in the sticky air an instant,
then bounced off his chin as the craft leveled. *"Choi-fuckin'-
oi!"* His voice rose for the benefit of the two pilots up front,
though they wouldn't be able to hear him over the rhythmic
whopping of the rotors overhead.

The AC sensed Brody's irritation and glanced back. Instant
mindmeld, Fletcher called it, for neither man could lock eyes
through the black visors. A metallic hiss filled Brody's ears as
the aircraft commander spoke over the intercom. "Sorry 'bout
that, Treat. Still hangin' in there? We're takin' hostiles from the

2

whiskey."

No sweat. Brody didn't bother with words but flipped a thumbs-up as he watched baseball-sized tracers arc up at them from a clearing's edge to the west. Glowing bright green, the ground-to-air rounds seemed to hover in front of the hatch a moment, trying to keep up with the chopper, then abruptly fall away, leaving lancelike plumes of smoke to mark their path.

"LZ in zero-five," the pilot warned as he brought the gunship around and descended through the mist. Brody kicked open an ammo can and fed a fresh belt of 7.62 into the Hog. Cursing himself silently for not having the big gun primed already, he tested the dual web belts around his waist. Satisfied with the improvised security blanket holding him aboard, he leaned into the M-60 again.

The chopper dropped a dozen feet between breaths as he directed ten- and twenty-round bursts at the edge of the clearings where gold flashes, dancing pixielike in the blue mist, marked an obvious NVA machine-gun nest. Brody poured everything he had into the target grid beyond the Hog's smoking muzzle, beginning the game. Could he take out the nest before the AC unleashed the ship's nose cannons? And then Brody remembered. He was a sub gunny today. He didn't know these men. Not personally. Not like Zack and Krutch, Larson and Fletcher. This AC wouldn't know how to play the game—or would he? Was it really any different from ship to ship, crew to crew?

The Huey bucked slightly, and Brody had his answer as dozens of grenades popped forth from the front of the craft. He could follow the peach-sized 40mm projectiles with the naked eye as they shot forward, and he eased up on the Hog's handles as the first detonations catapulted two North Vietnamese infantrymen head over heels out of their foxhole.

"Lucky shot, honcho-san," Brody clicked-in to the intercom as he leaned back, wiping the sweat from his eyes.

The AC glanced back, an ear-to-ear grin taunting him. He didn't reply over the intercom, but Brody read his lips: "Nice try, trooper."

He would have to note the man's name tag after the mission, when they got back to base. *If* they got back.

A zipperlike string of holes suddenly stitched through the

3

belly of the fuselage, knocking over a pile of Saigon phone books in the middle of the floor. The craft trembled under the assault but remained aloft.

The noise had sounded more threatening than the actual results: like someone below pounding the Huey's underbelly with a baseball bat as hard as he could. A glowing green tracer ricocheted about in the cabin as a half dozen bullets tore up through the roof.

"Definitely a hot LZ, gentlemen," someone was muttering sarcastically over the intercom as the craft broke from its abort hover and slipped behind a line of treetops.

"That's a Roger," came the reply from one of the other birds. "Got *bookoo* sunshine leakin' through our topside like a sieve. Ten new windows and counting . . ."

"Cut the chatter, Holy Man."

Brody recognized the major's voice as a huge shadow fell across the land, and he glanced up through the clouds floating in over the battlefield. Somewhere up there circled Gibb's C&C chopper. " 'Command and Control,' my ass," he muttered under his breath.

"Bad guys all along that canal down there," another voice cut in.

"I see 'em . . . ."

"That's where all your hostile bang bang's comin' from . . . to your sierra-echo . . . ."

"I said I see 'em," the AC in front of Brody replied dryly, and the nineteen-year-old door gunner took this as his cue. He swung around, scanning the sea of elephant grass to the southeast as the Huey whirled about. At the same moment Brody fired, a lone AK round struck the visor of his helmet, ripping the headgear off and flinging him backwards. The lifeline kept him on his feet, wrenching his back as the torn helmet rolled down the pile of brass and out the opposite hatch.

Lady Death! Crump's haunting words of the night before screamed in Brody's mind as a salty fluid filled his eyes. *"Lady Death gonna sneak up and kiss you on the lips,"* Crump had warned when Brody and the others refused to go AWOL with him. *"When you least expect it, white boy, she gonna snatch you down into the jaws of death, and it ain't gonna be no trick for Treat . . . it gonna be 'welcome to a world of hurt, suckah!'"*

4

Brody ran his fingers through his soaking blond hair, forcing it back out of his eyes. He was drenched in sweat again, but not his own blood—not this time. He wiped his mustache with a backhanded swipe of his bruised knuckles, then gripped the Hog in both hands and screamed his fury. Rounds poured forth with a deafening roar, saturating the field of reeds below. Brody yelled again, laughing now at the omens and the signs he'd seen after each monsoon downpour and at the simple insanity of his present situation. Daring Lady Death to rise up from the depths of the rain forest again, "Come on, cunt!" he challenged, blasting away nonstop, ignoring the M-60 barrel as it began to glow despite the rotor downblast. "Show Brody what you got!" He stumbled in the piles of shining brass, but the lifeline kept him on his feet, and his finger never left the trigger. "Strut your stuff, you rice paddy slut!"

The helicopter dipped between two rows of trees, dropping closer to the earth: twenty. . .fifteen. . .ten feet. "Death from above, you bitch!" Brody locked eyes with a squad of startled Vietnamese as the Huey burst forth through a clutter of palms. The blink of an eye later, all six enemy soldiers lay dead, their torsos shredded by the merciless shower of lead. One had been completely severed at the waist. Brody broke into a Death's-head grin as he watched the hips, shuddering atop stiff legs, fall back as if in slow motion—just the way he envisioned a towering aspen felled by a lumberjack in the forest. He was laughing like a maniac as rounds continued to chew into the enemy position, scattering limbs about the jungle floor. "Say hello to Buddha for me, babies!"

"You okay back there, Whoremonger?" a faraway metallic voice clicked into his private little hell. Brody's grin warped into an irritated frown.

Conditioned somehow to respond automatically, he merely nodded as he surveyed the carnage below, eyes bulging. His mind spoke a harsh whisper, *Numba One, honcho-san: Things couldn't be better in zap-'em-back-to-Buddha zone! Stand by for a body count. . . .*The Whoremonger's gun hand rose slowly, forming the usual thumbs-up. How did he know our name? A voice laughed from the depths of memory as the Huey's nose dropped slightly and slid to the left, probing for more hostile fire.

5

Brody did not glance over a shoulder at the pilots—his mind's eye already saw them shaking their heads at his antics. Instead, he focused on the four slicks swooping down between his Huey and the gunship laying out cover fire on the other side of the clearing. Two helicopters landed at the same time—their troopers jumping down off the skids, M-16s blazing, even before the birds touched down. Then the third. Brody watched a bright flash tear a section of fuselage from the tail of the fourth chopper. Black smoke poured from the ten-inch cavity as the craft whirled around, out of control. Nose heavy, the Huey straightened out and skimmed the tops of the trees as its rotors struggled to drag it up through the muggy heat blanketing the LZ. Brody watched it labor between two leaning palms without disgorging its human cargo.

Instinct told him where to point the Hog. Ten months straddling choppers into the Asian bush had honed skills only a point man could appreciate: The M-60 barked an unceasing stream of lead that split trees and bone.

Another burst of rounds crashed up through the Huey—this time from the opposite wall. A splinter of lead ricocheted off the pile of discarded ammo cans, stinging his elbow like a bee. *Like the big gold-and-black ones they used to sneak up on and pound into the dandelions with their fists back in California near Garden Grove...the ones grandmother warned held enough venom in them to out and out kill little mischievous boys* ....But the bite was minor—probably didn't even rate a Purple Heart—and the sting felt good. It woke him to the swirl of emotions and strength and power chasing after them out there, tearing at the craft's skin, *trying to reclaim him!* It started the flow again, the adrenaline rush—the legal "high" he and the other gunnies professed they lived for.

"Stallion-Lead, this is Colt-Lead...." Static conversation on the VHF frequency drifted about in the background of his thoughts like dusk creeping down through tombstones. "We're experiencing loss of hydraulics...pulling out...." The rapid-fire discharges from the M-60 drowned out much of the transmission. "...Back to the Tea Plantation...."

"Roger your last, Colt."

The Hog jammed without warning—just as Brody was beginning to feel "one" with the weapon—and he flipped open the

6

cover latch, tossed out the mangled links, and slammed a fresh belt of ammo down in one fluid movement.

A platoon of NVA Regulars was sprinting through the trees at the edge of the canal, zigzagging toward the clearing with the sun at their backs. They were passing right below Brody's chopper as they concentrated on the GIs on the ground and ignored the metallic dragonfly hovering overhead. Guerrillas at the head of the platoon began heaving Chi-Com stick grenades at the Americans.

The blasts that followed sent shock waves up through the shifting layers of gunsmoke clinging to reeds at the edge of the clearing, but Brody did not feel the craft buck and shake. His forearms, jarred up and down by the Hog's discharges, became a flesh-toned blur as he frantically sent wave upon wave of tracers down at the enemy. He swung the big gun back and forth as the barrel began to glow again. All his concentration was focused on stopping as many Vietnamese as was possible, using the only tool of war he had at hand. He wasn't chasing glory—all he cared about was killing.

Five, then six Vietnamese were pounded into the ground by the rain of lead. Brody burst into tense laughter as a trio toting satchel charges was cut down, their gunpowder-packed rucks exploding with a billowing white cloud that quickly hid any survivors.

"*Mo' fuck!*" Brody muttered, gritting his teeth. He'd taken to imitating Crump, the Division's resident militant. Crump was insisting lately that the troopers call him Abdul Mohammed. Brody didn't care much for all the African heritage and fist-waving crap, but there was something he liked about Crump. "Descend, *damnit*," Brody muttered into the intercom as smoke engulfed the contingent of North Vietnamese below. "Blow that gray gauze outta my kill zone so I can really bring smoke down on those dink sons of—"

"No can do, Whoremonger." The AC was almost giggling as he swung the Huey around, climbed fifty gut-flopping feet, then backed off. "Sharkskinner is movin' in on our starboard. Already told him he could pop a couple pods on ol' Charlie. . . ."

"Well fuck me 'till it hurts," Brody grumbled in protest after clicking off the intercom without responding. He'd missed the

7

exchange with Sharkskinner completely. He leaned out the side hatch until the Bell AH-IG prowling across the far side of the clearing came into view. "God-damned Cobra jocks." The words oozed from between grim lips, but Brody's eyes were quickly lighting up, and he couldn't fight the grin for long as the sleek gunship, only thirty feet above the shimmering sea of elephant grass, passed slowly through a wall of smoke. The sharks' teeth painted boldly across the sides of its "snout" looked so mean and menacing that Brody felt himself growing hard as the first projectile dropped from the right stub wing of the craft and ignited.

Trailing a plume of silver smoke, the two-point-five ripped into the ground with a deafening roar even before it really got going. Long-dead bodies from the NVA platoon were thrust like rag dolls into the air, limbs riding the concussion for a moment, then abruptly falling back to earth, inanimate objects, unreal. Shadows hiding at the edge of a nightmare.

"Get some!" Brody thrust one fist out the hatch in admiration. His left hand clutched the dog-tags chain around his neck, but he was not rubbing the tin flap that held his name, service number, religious preference, and blood type in search of good luck. His fingers moved across each individual bead, the way a nun might caress her precious rosary, seeking out the bits and pieces from past chopper crashes dangling between knots of bamboo twine: a half-inch sliver of tail rotor from a shoot-down in the Delta, a chunk of shrapnel taken from the belly of a Huey dropped by Soviet-made AA slugs near Danang, a melted splinter of Plexiglass from the window of a gunship he'd watched burn into the red clay between hills outside Pleiku . . . . His lucky charms. Souvenirs of his adventures with the U.S. Army's First Air Cavalry Division. Constant reminders of the dues he'd paid to dance with Lady Death in that exotic, Oriental nightspot called Vietnam. Painful mementoes of the buddies who hadn't been so lucky. . . the men who no longer counted the days until their Tour 365 was up. . . the warriors who went back to The World in body bags and government-issue caskets. . . troopers whose souls, he was convinced, would haunt these miserable rain forests forever.

The dull pop of rotors slapping at the air pulled his eyes to the aft. Another gaggle of slicks was bringing more Air Cav troopers into the landing zone.

Brody watched the Cobra on the far side of the clearing dart about the tree line like a carefree hummingbird, searching out nectar. While the pilot in his own craft held their Huey stationary, waiting to pounce if Sharkskinner drew ground fire, the Cobra unleashed sustained bursts from dual XM-21 mini-guns every few seconds at suspected NVA hideouts. At a rate of 6,000 rounds per minute, leaves, and even some limbs, were torn from the forest wall that rose a hundred feet all around them. With every fifth round a glowing red tracer, Sharkskinner was putting on quite a show. Resistance had tapered down to a few solitary snipers as the LZ became saturated with flamethrower-equipped GIs. Now and then a North Vietnamese holdout, left behind by the communists on a suicide mission to protect the main unit's retreat, was knocked from the treetops by Sharkskinner.

A death shroud of smoke was quickly concealing all activity down in the clearing, and dust from the rotting jungle floor rose in fine wisps to make matters worse.

"Light up some zips, Mister Zippo!" Brody's attention was focused on one of the soldiers manning a flamethrower, but the trooper—a stocky teenager with a baby face and gorilla's physique—did not torch the tree line. The last thing they needed right now was a forest fire in never-never land. The Foxtrot Tosser would be saved for any tunnel discoveries later.

"Sharkskinner, this is Python-Lead, over...." Brody's attention returned to the last Huey still on the ground when he heard the calm but tension-laced voice crackle over the net. Already, four more choppers were circling beyond the tree line, waiting to come in. "Go, Python-Lead...."

"On our whiskey, Hark-Lead! Contact on our whiskey! Those palms with the L.A. part to 'em. Straight down the middle: a couple dinks with something *big*!"

Brody could hear the sound of lead smacking against the target Huey's skin in the background, like a ball peen hammer against an empty gas can.

Sharkskinner was already swooping in for the kill. "Got 'em in my cross hairs, Python-Lead. Hold onto your—"

The last of his transmission was covered by the roar of multiple explosions as the gunner riding in tandem below the Cobra

9

pilot fired the ship's 40mm cannons.

Brody strained, but he could not see the snipers in the tree-tops—not until two Vietnamese and three rifles dropped out of the palms. One soldier was screaming, but it was all a silent movie to the men in the gunships. Multiple explosions was the background music as blood poured from cavities at the edges of the sniper's chest, where both arms had been severed. But he was dead before he hit the ground.

Sharkskinner moved in close to the tree line now—so close the tips of his rotors cut off several branches like a powerful fan snipping away flower petals. Puffs of blue smoke appeared in front of the Cobra as its mini-guns went to work again, stitching a specific palm tree from top to bottom then back up again.

"Bingo!" Sharkskinner's voice cut-in to the radio net calmly and confidently as the third sniper was knocked from his perch, arms and legs flailing during the fall. But the body was headless.

"Score another commie for Mommy." An anonymous comedian blew a kiss over the FM band.

"Tally-*ho!*"

The Cobra's nose rose slightly, and the craft ascended above the treetops, then banked sharply out of sight, leaving the remainder of the escort to Brody's Huey.

"I don't know how you do it, Sharkskinner," one of the slick pilots whispered over the air in awe.

But Sharkskinner was gone, headed back to Camp Holloway for more ammunition and fuel.

"He was killing before killing was cool," an unknown fan answered for him.

Sharkskinner's got his shit together, Brody's lips moved silently with the thought as he listened to the Cobra's distinctive rotor pitch fading in the distance. The door gunner was both jealous and impressed. Impressed because it wasn't often he was treated to such a show of mini-gun marksmanship from the air. Jealous because it might not happen again. It wasn't often he rode escort like this. He was usually gunny aboard one of the birds that landed. "Damn." He started to get antsy, well aware they'd soon be heading back to camp, insertion and mission accomplished. Time to play was running out. He ate this escort duty up, but the enemy had beat feet when Cobra was set loose

10

in the jungle—there was nothing left to go after with his Hog. "Patience, my ass. . ." He brought out the binoculars as the Huey contined to circle the landing zone. "I'm gonna kill something."

Escort duty was usually reserved for the Cobra gunships. Groups of half a dozen or more Hueys ferried six to ten troops each into predetermined landing zones, while the two-man, predatorlike Cobras buzzed the LZs, hunting for any Cong or NVA lucky enough to survive the preinsertion arc-light bombing runs and artillery, and brave enough to face wave upon wave of helicopters that followed. But sappers had knocked out a whole gaggle of the experimental Cobras that week, and escort duty of late had fallen to some of the newer-model UH-lC Hueys, which were more maneuverable than the older slicks, but not as fast or powerful. The cargo became ammo instead of infantrymen, both hatches were jury-rigged with dual M-60s, and Brody was having the time of his life.

It was 1965, Brody's Indian August, and the Airmobile war was being brought to Vietnam with both enthusiasm and great expectations by the armchair warriors at MACVs Puzzle Palace. The 173rd Airborne Brigade had officially been the first U.S. Army Airmobile unit to see action in The Nam, two months earlier, but now the First Cav had arrived with over 16,000 gung-ho warriors and 400 helicopters, intent on pounding Charlie, the North Vietnamese Army, and Ho Chi Minh himself into the red dust of the Central Highlands.

The Air Cav would introduce themselves to the enemy at Ia Drang Valley, southwest of Pleiku, and set up a "tent city" of some ten thousand o.d. dwellings at a place dubbed "the Tea Plantation." The First Cav's choppers and crew took over "the Turkey Farm," a vast field between Camp Holloway and New Pleiku, and five miles north of the main grunt encampment.

The North Vietnamese had been harassing U.S. Special Forces camps in the Ia Drang area, until the arrival of the First Cavalry Division. Now most were slowly working their way west, to the Cambodian border. It was the American commanders' job to intercept and annihilate them before they crossed that invisible line into sanctuary.

Brody set the binoculars down. He sat on a pile of Saigon phone books (they protected the family jewels from ground fire

11

better than flak jackets, and sitting on helmets could get uncomfortable after a few hours) and rummaged through his flight bag until he found the head.

Halloween was fast approaching, and his brother had yet to come through for him on the werewolf mask request. Yes, he could just see those goofy guerrillas on the ground doing a double take when he fired down on them, screaming and yelling and cursing and carrying on like a graveyard ghoul straight out of hell. But baby brother had not come through for him. At least the U.S. Mails had not.

So Brody went and did the next best thing. Nobody could accuse *him* of not getting into the Halloween spirit! The dedicated door gunner paid an unauthorized visit to Pleiku City and spent a few piasters—less than a single greenback—in a souvenir shop catering especially to foreign devils. Tucked down behind an off-limits whorehouse in a back alley running parallel with the main drag, Brody found the prize he was looking for, the headgear that would be the envy of every door gunner and chopper jock north of Saigon!

He slipped the hollow, stretched-out head over his own, careful not to scrape his cheeks again with the bottom neck scales the way he had the first time. Then he grasped the M-60 handles menacingly, flexed his arms until the biceps bulged, and froze as if posing for a picture.

An eerie hissing sound filled the crew's intercom headphones. The copilot whirled around with a start, mistaking the noise for a leak in the fuel cells. His mind's eye envisioned a string of bullet holes from some anonymous rifleman on the ground.

But what he actually saw was a huge snake's head leering back at him from atop an unmoving door gunner's torso. "What the fu—"

The crew chief glanced over his shoulder too. The sight of a giant python staring back at him with green marbled eyes did not seem to phase the career combat soldier. "Whoremonger, you crazy, mindless fuck . . ." He locked eyes with the face grinning behind fully extended jaws and bristling snake's teeth. "You tryin' to tell me somethin', boy?"

Brody hissed into the intercom again as the rotors above beat out their deafening yet hypnotic clamor. "Just thought I'd get into some of the local customs, chief. It *is* the Year of the Snake, you know. Thought I'd mix Halloween this month with a little—"

"Ain't no time to be goin' native on us," the AC interrupted with a crack in his voice as the ship lurched to one side suddenly. Bullets tore up through the floor on all sides, and as the Huey began to bank hard to the left, a gaping hole appeared in the floor of the craft. A split second after Brody realized what was happening, the RPG detonated, knocking him partially out the hatch.

His monkeystrap kept him from being belched out into Void Vicious, however, and as smoke filled the cabin he realized the small of his back was soaked wet with blood from dozens of minute shrapnel wounds.

The crew chief lay across the hole in the floor, dead. His throat had been sliced open by a fist-sized chunk of flying metal. The downdraft was trying to suck him out through the hole, but his body was too stocky. Brody watched blood cover the floor of the Huey in the time it took him to stumble through the pile of crimson-coated brass and regain his footing. Then the ship was rolling onto its side, and the blood was all over the front of him too as it took to the air and sprayed out the hatch like a bucketful of red paint being thrown through a window.

The intercom was out, but Brody heard the AC clearly as he yelled to the pilot beside him, "Hold your breath, slugger, we're goin' down!"

A terrible grinding sound tore at his eardrums, drowning out all other sound, and the rotor smashed through the roof of the craft, cutting the crew chief's body in half as the Huey tumbled down through the trees.

Except for two strips of metal connecting the turbines to the tail rotor, the helicopter had been severed nearly in half. The cockpit windows shattered and collapsed as a huge tree branch lanced up through the nose of the Huey, impaling the copilot. The limb punched through his chest in a shower of blood and exited between his shoulder blades as the chopper plummeted to earth.

Brody felt his stomach rising as the warrent officer was carried backward toward him, the branch filling the cabin. Blood gushed from his mouth, but his expression would be forever hidden—the black visor was still in place.

The cockpit flattened out under the weight of the cabin and tail boom as it struck the ground, and Brody's ears were filled with the screams of the AC as he was slowly crushed beneath all the twisted, settling metal and Fiberglass. He glanced past the dead copilot toward the opposite hatch. The door gunner who was crouching there only a moment earlier had vanished. The frame was smeared with blood. Vines and bushes filled the opening, packed tight. The bile was in his mouth now, but he had no time to pause and empty his guts on the dead. No time to drop to his knees and close his eyes and vomit—purge all that he'd just seen from his soul.

That morning's rations exploding from his lips, Brody scrambled over the bodies of the men he knew only by nicknames. The soles of his jungle boots trampled across someone's chest as the still-spinning tail rotor ripped down toward him like a wild buzz saw.

He dove through the hatch, rolling across a soft blanket: the dead and rotting rain-forest floor. Dust from an endless carpet of mushrooms engulfed him, and he began coughing and gagging as the Huey exploded. A fireball rose toward the triple canopy blocking out the sun overhead, but it did not set the jungle aflame; the leaves and trees...everything was too wet.

Brody glanced back at the squashed helicopter. He made the sign of the cross as the hydraulic reservoir and swash plate assembly began to hiss and crackle. "We'll come back to get you, brothers," he vowed under his breath, then turned to run deeper into the trees.

A rifle was suddenly leveled at his chest, but the Vietnamese behind the trigger was screaming in terror and sprinting back into the forest, abandoning the weapon—*Brody was still wearing the python's head!*

A discharge sounded several feet away, and bark flew from the tree beside him before the door gunner realized he was unarmed. Another burst of AK rounds showered leaves and a dead gibbon down on him—the NVA private's sergeant was not so naive or superstitious.

Brody dropped to earth and began low-crawling through the ivory carpet of mushrooms. He had no choice, he had to get back to the slick.

14

CHAPTER 2

Over a dozen combat-hardened jungle fighters from the crack 33rd NVA Regiment had circled the downed gunship before Brody made it even halfway back to the crash site.

Fire had yet to consume the Huey. In fact, the flames had lessened considerably. *We musta been flyin' on fumes*, Brody decided as he watched the North Vietnamese soldiers poke and prod bodies, severed body parts, and already shredded mushrooms with their bayonets. *And them fuckin' fumes went up in that fireball* . . . .

Brody's vision was beginning to blur as he slowed to watch the NVA. The throbbing between his temples increased, and for a moment he seemed to black out. But his eyes flew wide open again before his chin even pressed flat the plants beneath him. At first he feared shock was setting in, that he was now paying for the loss of blood, the trauma of the crash. He started to move his hand, to search for any sign of more serious wounds, well aware the adrenaline rush would mute all pain for a while longer. But Brody froze. Any movement could signal his presence—there were now more NVA moving past on both sides of him, separated by about one hundred meters. He watched them advance through the reeds in their brown, long-sleeved uniforms, rifles at port arms as they glided by, legs hidden in the surrealistic mist. Some wore pith helmets—he could see the little red star even at this distance.

Another wave of pain swept over him, and Brody's head dropped onto the rotting jungle floor. Exhausted by the simple effort of trying to control his breathing, he could barely keep his eyelids parted. All activity outside the grid of his tiny, personal space in that vast rain forest became a blur. He was positive Treat Brody was dying. A leech was burrowing into his nose, and some army ants were running circles around the outer edge of his ear—no, now they were wrestling, fighting and tumbling over each other, deeper into his ear, yet he was powerless to move. When they tired of battle, they would bite through his eardrum and gnaw into his brain—he just knew it.

Something slithered between his legs, slowed now, and was moving toward his face—a python attracted to his mask, perhaps? He wanted to fling the dried-out cranium as far away as possible, but now the creature was moving back down his frame...over his one good testicle...chewing on the canvas lip of his boot.

Something else bit him on the elbow, and Brody felt a sudden surge of strength that came with terror. His eyes popped open again, but he was not staring face-to-face with a python or a boa. Not even a two-step krait viper, which was indigenous to Southeast Asia, kept to the bamboo, and could kill a man in sixty seconds. Victims of its deadly bite were lucky to walk two more steps after being struck, hence its name. Brody was forever having nightmares about the damn things, nightmares that hadn't started until he patted his Viet housegirl on the rump one day and she threatened to slip a krait viper up his pants leg when he was sleeping. When he was defenseless. He would never forget the dead-serious expression she wore that day.

No, it was not a scaled serpent that greeted the semiconscious door gunner, but mushrooms. White and gold mushrooms stretched out through the trees as far as the eye could see. And that was when it hit him—the mushrooms were poisonous!

Now that he realized he wasn't going to die from his wounds, that he was suffering from mushmouth and still had a chance at survival, the whole game changed. The odds were shifting a bit.

Brody was no fool. He knew he could slip into the wreckage and sneak out a rifle, if, in fact, there were any left with stocks, hand grips, or barrel guards that hadn't melted in the fire. He doubted he could make it into the tree line without being heard. In the past, he had always been envious of bigger men than he. To be six-foot-six and two-forty was a dream he'd nurtured since ordering all the Joe Weider courses in high school. But "Mama's little weed" had stopped growing at five-foot-eleven, and no amount of banana splits could push him over 170 pounds. Today, though, he'd give anything to be shorter and smaller than any of the Vietnamese swarming into the crash site. Five-foot-two would do nicely, thank you.

The air beneath the triple canopy began to vibrate. Leaves fell like green rain from branches intertwined a hundred feet

16

overhead. The ground seemed to tremble slightly as a helicopter hovered briefly above, out of sight. But then the chopping, beating sensation faded, and the craft was gone.

Brody glanced over his left shoulder slowly. No more soldiers were coming from that direction. He was lying in a sort of shallow gulley, where trees had thinned out so there was a good four or five feet between trunks—as opposed to the shoulder-to-shoulder crowding that encircled the freak depression where their Huey happened to crash. If he could just roll to the left, into the dense brush at the edge of the ravine and wait for an SAR crew to jerk him out.

Brody placed both hands against the fungus under his chest, push-ups style, and started to rise up out of the fungi when a cold point of steel rubbed the back of his skull almost tauntingly. He knew immediately the object was a bayonet. "No move, Joe, or. . .*fini*. . .you. . . ."

He had never heard such an icy, horrifying voice before. Brody froze.

The NVA soldier was standing in his blind spot on the right. And now he heard movement through the crisp, crunching leaves on his left.

"*Moc len,*" the soldier directed. "Ge' up, Joe."

Brody would have to act fast. Before the man called out to his comrades. And before the creature wrapped around his ankle chewed through his boot. Death by gunshot—even bayonet—was preferable to a fatal reptile bite, as far as he was concerned.

Kicking out suddenly with his free leg, Brody tried to snap the soldier's leg with a heel jab to the calf, but the Vietnamese was agile. He stumbled backwards but managed to keep his footing as the American rolled over, python mask intact.

The expression on the NVA sergeant's face was one of bored indifference—to find a GI facedown in the mushrooms beside a downed gunship was nothing out of the norm apparently—but then his gaze shifted to Brody's leg and he started backing away. His lower jaw dropped as a milky substance shot up and struck him in the face.

Neck scales flaring, a King Cobra's head rose off the ground to shoulder height and turned toward the second Vietnamese. Hissing like an enraged tomcat, the twenty-foot-long serpent tightened its coils around Brody's leg but otherwise ignored the

17

door gunner.

The NVA sergeant, blinded by the poison spat into his eyes by the snake, stumbled backwards onto his haunches. He began yelling for assistance in rapid-fire Vietnamese as the private brought an AK-47 to his shoulder and took careful aim at the angry reptile.

Brody opted for the only clear avenue of escape. The cobra was too big, its head too far away from him to stab out with his survival knife. Besides, the dagger was strapped to a calf sheath, and any movement in that direction only invited a visit from fang city. He rolled to the right as fast as he could, slapping at the snake and pounding its head into the mushrooms the way he and his cousins had smashed killer bumblebees into dandelions an ocean away and a lifetime ago. He slapped with all his might until his leg burned, and he somersaulted so swiftly through the trees the move would have inspired a standing ovation from Mr. Koshak, his old gym teacher back in The World.

Brody rolled and slapped and rolled some more until he bounced off a tree trunk and hopped into a crouch. The snake had released him. He drew his survival knife and threw it at the NVA private. But the soldier was already sprinting into the trees, pursued by the bewildered and enraged cobra, and the blade missed.

The American Spec-4 charged toward his blinded adversary as soldiers surrounding the Huey raced toward them. Scooping up both the light Vietnamese and his automatic rifle, Brody headed into the thickest outcropping of trees he could find. His prisoner, soaked in sweat and with tears streaming down his face, began to struggle. Brody stumbled, dropped the sergeant, and punched him unconscious. He drew a Chinese made revolver from the NVA's web belt and fired off the entire cylinder at their pursuers, completely forgetting about the AK slung over his shoulder, then threw the prisoner's limp body over the other shoulder and continued deeper into the rain forest.

"Grenades," he muttered. "If I only had some frags. You got any Chi-Coms, pal? Not in the talkative mood, eh?"

Brody's boots snagged on a wait-a-minute vine, tripping him up. "Asshole. . ." He decided it would be better not to hold a one-sided conversation. "Gotta conserve energy. . .gotta. . ."

18

The dense foliage suddenly gave way to another clearing choked with mist that swirled about but couldn't seem to escape. A few scattered tree trunks were all that remained in this eerie slice of the rain forest.

Brody froze in his tracks. Three South Vietnamese soldiers, stripped naked except for their uniform caps, sat around the largest trunk, their backs against the bark. Squinting, he could see that ropes held the men immobile.

One trooper, beaten about the face, appeared unconscious. Another, his eyes tightly shut, screamed up at the branches overhead every few seconds without warning. Brody could not see the third soldier very well.

"Phuong dong!" he yelled, breaking from the tree line. "East! Which way is east?" He raced toward the tree trunk, letting the NVA sergeant roll off his shoulder.

Brody's smoking jungle boots, smeared with dust, executed an impressive shift into reverse as he came upon the Bengal tiger feeding on the third soldier's chest cavity. "Ohhh, *Lord*ie!" The hushed exclamation was involuntary as he backed away quickly. The big, striped cat, its head twisted to the side as it gnawed on the trooper's exposed ribcage, glared up at Brody when he spoke. It emitted a roar of territorial warning— this slab of meat would not be shared!—and Brody felt every sweat gland on his body burst.

"No problem...no sweat, kitty-kitty," he continued, backing away and raising his hands with fingers spread and palms toward the animal, the AK dangling from both wrists on its sling. Startled, the tiger's hind end slid around while the forepaws kept a secure grip on the mutilated carcass. "I'm gone ...I'm history! Beatin' feet right now, Mr. Bengal. Beatin' feet back to Bangkok, where ol' Round-Eyes belongs, yes sir!" His mind was racing frantically the whole time. What was a lousy EM to do? This was no time for heroics.

Behind him, the sound of more NVA soldiers crashing through the jungle grew louder. They were right on his heels.

"Aw, fuck me 'till it hurts, bwana-san...." His peripheral vision had caught the blur of orange, gold, and black stripes emerging from the tree line behind the cub Bengal.

Three more man-eaters.

Roaring in unison, the tigers charged.

Two thoughts flew through Brody's mind as he rushed back toward the tree line from which he'd just emerged: Death by hot lead was preferred to death by tearing incisors and ripping fangs; and if he could make it into the sagging line of palms before the soldiers reached the clearing, perhaps he could roll into a pile of dead leaves, or into a gulley stream, or beside a rotting log. His mind envisioned the tigers leaping through the "green line" after him only to crash into the charging Vietnamese.

Discharges shattered his wishful thinking. Soldiers were already kneeling between the trees, rifles rising to their shoulders. But it was not the communists who had fired.

Brody, dropping low out of instinct, whirled around as a dead Bengal slid on its haunches through the dust past him. Another tiger was airborne, paws out, claws extended, leaping through the mist at him, wide golden eyes locked on his throat when another flurry of discharges sliced through the din of echoes and knocked the big cat out of the air.

Blood from the three holes in its chest splashed across Brody's face before he could shield his eyes, and the lifeless carcass smashed into him the same instant he caught sight of the tall man emerging from the opposite edge of the clearing.

"Colonel!" The combination greeting and warning left his throat more like a violent discharge as the Bengal's body rolled him along through twigs and leaves, the air knocked from his lungs.

Brody quickly pushed himself up from beneath the bloody cat. He stared in disbelief at the giant apparition appearing from the mist. Tarzan the Apeman his rescuer wasn't.

But Col. Neil Buchanan, dressed in a khaki safari suit, pith helmet, and knee-high riding boots, was a character straight out of Hollyweird nonetheless.

20

CHAPTER 3

An entire platoon of American soldiers appeared behind Buchanan as Brody shouted warning about the Vietnamese, but the colonel was already waving his men forward through the clearing. Clad in regulation jungle fatigues, flak jackets, and helmets, the Cav troopers charged past Brody, firing into the tree line with M-16s leveled at the hip.

The Vietnamese never returned a single shot. They had been too shocked by the sudden appearance of the great white hunter and were melting back into the rain forest without a fight.

Brody did not watch the GIs pursue them into the trees. His eyes were glued to the last tiger scrambling over the body of its mate and retreating through the reeds, a blur of stripes as its hind quarters slid back and forth across the slippery mushrooms.

Col. Buchanan had been staring at Brody curiously for several seconds, and now he started toward the army specialist. He ignored the tiger cub, still gnawing at the bound Arvin and oblivious of the deadly goings-on all around it, except to mutter a directive at the buck sergeant walking behind him, "Stick that pussy in a duffel bag and take him—or her—back to the Tea Plantation."

Buchanan stopped a few paces in front of Brody, raised the 30.06 to his shoulder, and pointed it straight at the enlisted man's face. Brody distinctly heard the safety mechanism click off despite the clamor of a dozen Americans chasing twice as many guerrillas through the trees—at least his mind insisted he'd heard it. "Always did want a stuffed King Cobra hanging from the wall of my CP back in—"

"Colonel!" Brody realized he was still wearing the hollowed-out snake-head, and he flung it off, high into the air. "It's *me,* sir! Treat Brody! Specialist 4th Class Brody! Seventh of the First! *Echo* Company, sir!"

Buchanan started laughing, raised his rifle into the air, and pulled the trigger. The firing pin slammed forth onto an empty chamber. "Ha! Specialist *Brody!*" The colonel threw his hunt-

21

ing rifle to an aide as another lieutenant handed him an M-16. "I thought I recognized those blond locks beneath the green gills."

"Scales, sir," one of the aides corrected him with a whisper, "and it was...appeared to have been a python head he was wearing, sir, not a—"

"Uh, sure, Winston—whatever makes you happy: *scales.*" Buchanan glanced over at the tall, slender lieutenant with a mild look of irritation, then his eyes took to scanning the tree line. "What brings you to this neck of 'the woods,' anyway?" The Brooklyn accent was so out of place it brought an uncontrollable smile to Brody's face.

A small squad of men slowly appeared behind the colonel. Mostly black Americans, the soldiers worked in pairs, one in front of the other, connected by poles suspended over their shoulders. Hanging from the poles were two dead tigers, a huge tree monkey, and an assortment of wild hogs. Buchanan laughed inwardly. He was surprised none in the shit detail were loaded down with ivory.

"The CO asked you a question, Specialist!" one of the lieutenants snapped.

"I was just wondering what you were doing in 'this neck of the woods,' sir."

"The colonel asks the questions around here, Soldier!" Lt. Icy Eyes began, but Buchanan waved him silent.

"It's okay, Winston."

"I thought...we *all* thought you were on thirty-day leave to Cockbang Thailand, sir, Kingdom of Siam, Land of the Most Beautiful Women in the World," Brody interrupted. "What with you just extending for another combat tour with the Cav and all."

A flurry of shots and screams in the distance punctuated his remark, and Buchanan gazed off into the jungle in the direction of the skirmish, concerned about his men.

"The colonel finds his relaxation in the tropical jungles of Southeast Asia," Winston replied dryly, "not the claptraps of the Orient."

"I can speak for myself, Lieutenant." Buchanan's eyes dropped to where Brody still sat on the ground, and the colonel moved forward, reaching out. Brody took the hand, flushing

22

with embarrassment as the CO yanked him to his feet. "Big-game hunting has always been a passion of mine, son," he revealed with an almost fatherly smile, bullet-gray eyes twinkling. "And Vietnam has all the best predators, you know."

Brody wasn't sure what the colonel meant by that, but memories of a story he'd once read, in which unarmed men were set loose on an island owned by a sharpshooting madman, came to mind. He smiled again as two privates appeared at the edge of the clearing, carrying, of all things, elephant tusks.

It was true, though. Buchanan *did* have a reputation for turning up in the middle of a raging firefight, sporting his pith helmet, safari suit, and a confused, what's-going-on-here visage.

The CO was no buffoon, however. And he was not the kind of commander who ordered his men into battle against overwhelming odds unless he was there to lead the charge personally. He refused to implement strategy and alter the course of campaigns from the safety of a rear-echelon bunker. Buchanan often circled high above field operations in a C&C chopper, directing the battles himself. The brass back at Disneyland East frowned on some of the Bull's antics, often condemning his daredevil adventures privately, but refusing to complain on the record—the man had friends in high places. But why all the colorful heroics? many of them wondered.

After all, Neil Buchanan had nothing to prove. He'd won the top banana in Korea, a Congressional Medal of Honor, only two weeks after earning a battlefield commission from corporal to lieutenant during some of the most intense fighting near Inchon. But war was his world, and Nam was where it was at. It was the only war he had right now, and he was damned well going to fight it right. Buchanan was one of the few old timers who didn't dismiss Indochina as just another nuisance between the two real contests: World War II and World War III!

"What's the story on this character?" He was standing over the blinded NVA sergeant. The Vietnamese had regained consciousness and was sitting with his back against one of the tree trunks. His eyelids were swollen shut. Blood oozed from their inner slits.

"You wouldn't believe it, sir." Brody almost laughed aloud, recalling his narrow escape from the huge snake.

Lieutenant Winston was beside Buchanan like a shadow.

"What did you *do* to this man, Soldier!?" he demanded accusingly.

Brody fought the urge to rush up and confront the butterbar, nose to nose. "I didn't *do* anything to him, *sir.*" He continued walking in the direction of the EM "porters" standing silent and semi-defiant at the jungle's edge. "A king cobra spat venom into his eyes."

"A *who* did *what?*" The lieutenant slammed his palms onto his hips with incredulous vigor while Buchanan just cleared his throat knowingly.

"Get this prisoner bound and gagged. And stick a blindfold on him too," he told the buck sergeant. Brody ignored them both, spotting Disciplinary Problem No. 1, Abdul Mohammed, on the shit detail.

He slung his captured AK-47 over a shoulder and grasped the black soldier's fingers quickly, beating him out of a "soul brother's dap"—which Brody hated watching and refused to participate in—and maneuvering the clasp into what the door gunner felt was a normal handshake. Mohammed frowned and rolled his eyes skyward. Brody's smirk grew. Treat liked Mohammed but he wasn't sure why. Perhaps it was because every statement the black GI made was carefully structured jive that, no matter how hard the militant tried, came out sounding nearly as hilarious as something Rodney Dangerfield would dream up. And the Whoremonger was ol' Rod's Numba One fan.

Mohammed was tall and bone-skinny despite serious daily workouts at dusk. He was never without his teakwood Malcolm X likeness, fashioned in the subliminal form of a clenched fist. Slightly larger than a St. Christopher's medal, the medallion had been purchased in Saigon's soul alley during one of his AWOL stints and was worn on his dog-tags necklace. The buck privates hadn't bothered to wear the actual dog tags since a trio of drill sergeants booted him out of Infantry AIT. Brody had to shake his head: The dude was forever wearing jet-black sunglasses—even in the dark, it seemed—and had spent time in the LBJ stockade for refusing to remove a BLA patch from his flak vest as well as other uniform violations and UCMJ infractions. Mohammed claimed to be thirty-one years old. He looked twenty-five at the most on a bad day, but Brody knew the kid was midway through the vulnerable years: nineteen.

24

Mohammed pounded Brody's shoulder with his free fist before dropping one of the elephant tusks. "Say, my man!" His chin lifted rebelliously from years of practice. "What the boojiggers a mo-fuck no-account skate like you doin' in Great Whitey's domain? Stalkin' to club Tarzan and rape Jane, or you one of them white bread perverts 'oose into butt-humpin' baboons?" He pointed across the clearing at the grunt staring down at his dead monkey. The question was asked with a straight face, and though Brody could not see Mohammed's eyes now because the sunglasses had dropped back in place, the aspiring Black Panther seemed to be gazing over Treat's shoulder, unable to ignore all the carnage surrounding the three tree trunks. Or was this busted-back-to-E-Nothing just displaying his routine nose-in-the-air defiance?

"Well, I'll tell ya, ya old spook 'n' puke jungle bunny. . . ." Brody launched into his best Duke impression.

"*Yah!* What the hell *are* you doin' out here in the middle of Bumfuck Egypt?" Lt. Winston was suddenly beside him, glaring straight through Mohammed, then shifting his eyes back and forth between the private's unpenetrable sunglasses and the valuable tusk of ivory he'd allowed to become stained with mushroom juice. Mohammed let out a loud sigh. His head fell back and shook from side to side, expasperated . . . reminding Brody of a certain blind rock-and-soul singer back in The World. It was a wonder Mohammed's shades didn't fly off into the trees.

Brody turned his face away so the lieutenant wouldn't spot the grin. "I was gunny for a slick outta the Turkey Farm today, sir," he said. "Workin' escort for an insertion at LZ Tango. Charlie hit us with an RPG. The bird went down 'bout half a klick in that direction." He pointed at the overgrown trail Buchanan's platoon had chased the retreating NVA down.

"You were the only one who made it out?" he asked skeptically.

"To the best of my knowledge. Crew chief bought the farm on the way down. AC and peter pilot KIA on the spot, sir. The other door gunner disappeared into Void Vicious while I was busy with the Hog. I don't know if that was before or after we stacked it up."

"Hhmph." The lieutenant rubbed his chin thoughtfully.

Without further questioning, he turned and strode back toward Buchanan to report.

"*Hhmph*," Mohammed scratched his own chin, imitating Winston. "What a royal pain in the rectal cavity."

"No shit." Brody ground his teeth. If there ever was a soldier he wished would stumble over a tripwire...

"They gonna give yo white ass an ArCom, minimu, fo this." Mohammed was still rubbing his chin, but this time he appeared to be genuinely in deep thought. "Yo' baby! No doubt 'bout it. Maybe even a star—silver, I'd say. Yah, you rate a Silver Star, Bro-fuck."

"I didn't do nothin' anyone else wouldn't of." Brody kicked a couple of mushrooms over with an aw-shucks shrug of his shoulders.

"You didn't do *anything*," Mohammed corrected him.

Brody's mouth hung open. "Since when is a jive, monkey-faced illiterate like you going around correcting—"

"You captured a North Vee*yet*namese NCO, General." Mohammed's features remained emotionless as he ignored the taunt. "That's big time, even in *this* nigger's book." He leaned closer to Brody. "Now tell me, my man"—Mohammed flashed a bright, ear-to-ear smile—"Why didn't ya just waste ol' Luke the Gook?"

Brody laughed out loud. "You shoulda seen the poor fucker, Abdul...."

"Call me 'Elijah,'" Mohammed corrected him again.

"Oh, right..." That was what the African culture "student" was insisting on this month. "...The zip had me dead to rights. I mean, I was bein' damned near devoured by this python—"

"Cobra," Mohammed was correcting him a third time, based on what he'd overheard Brody telling the CO.

"Oh, right—whatever...anyway, this king cobra was humpin' my leg like a horny puppy when ol' Luke sneaks up on me. Thought my ticket was canceled for sure, you know? Only the dink didn't see the snake—not until it was too late anyway."

"So Señor Serpent rears up all the sudden like and hacks a throatful of venom into the slope's face? You really expect me to believe that, Whoremonger?"

"I shit you not, bro...." Treat wanted to swallow, but his throat had gone dry. He knew Mohammed wouldn't let anyone

26

but another black man call him brother. "And that's the way it was...." Brody's voice dropped an octave as he imitated a network news anchor back in The World.

Mohammed's smile faded, and he glanced over at Buchanan. Without elaborating on the sudden change of attitude, he turned and stalked off to rejoin the other busted-back-to-El buck privates, muttering, "Ain't no white boy *my* brother, chump— that's fo' damn sure!"

"What officer's wife did you get caught ravaging to warrant shit detail again?" Brody sought to keep the exchange going.

"Got more white meat waitin' for me back stateside than I can handle," he replied loudly, for all the others to hear. The shit detail was mostly black, but also a mixture of all the races. "Don't need no snotty officer's wife hangin' from my haunches, though this nigger *do* have a waiting list of *cock*casian cunt back in the rear." He glared at a soldier with a Confederate flag decal across the side of his helmet.

"Oh. Well, pardon my perniciousness."

Mohammed turned to challenge Brody's mild sarcasm. "Actually, I failed another urinalysis, Treat." Lowering his voice, he dropped the jive for a moment. "Kind of hard to resist this high grade, kinky quality Asian weed, you know? Besides, I kinda like carrying the colonel's pigheads around for him."

Brody wasn't into the dope scene. He felt it was a waste of scrip, time, and talent. And in The Nam, it could prove to be deadly. "Keeps your worthless ass outta the fryin' pan." He forced a smile, deciding not to rub it in. Brody loved riding gunships into battle and despised the skates who avoided chopper duty, but somehow it was just too hard to avoid or pass up a verbal duel with Mister M.

"Right on, brother." Mohammed slipped but just shook it off. Lt. Winston was back, motioning for the men to get ready to move out.

"Well, back to breakin' your backs for bwana." Brody flashed the thumbs-up.

Mohammed returned the gesture. "Better than bustin' my balls for a country that don't give a damn 'bout us, Treat. Take ten, bud. Be a REMF for a week—you earned some time off. Go on up and get yo'self some Pleiku pussy and maybe go AWOL for a while 'til you get the smell of death off your skin.

27

You deserve it. And you'll be back. What can they do if they catch you, send you to Viet-fucking-Nam? Leave bein' a hero to the hicks." His thumb flipped in the direction of the soldier flying the Confederate flag on the side of his steel pot.

Brody nodded and turned away but did not smile. Mohammed was full of shit. As usual. Brody loved The Nam and his contribution to what was happening in the Highlands. They were making history here, and he was a part of it. So what if their commanding officer was acting a bit eccentric of late?

He didn't know that much about Indochina, and he really didn't give a hoot about stopping communism. All he knew was that it felt good to ride a foot above the treetops at a hundred and fifty miles an hour, the hot, tropical air pulling your locks back like a sex-starved nymph set free after a month in a monkeyhouse. It felt good to hang out the hatch and fire the Hog down at warriors who were actually shooting back. *It felt great!* He lived for the adrenaline rush that came with firing ten thousand rounds down into the hostile rain forest. Never before had he experienced such...such *job satisfaction*. Yes, that had to be the term. Okay, so he was only making a lousy hundred bucks per month. Chickenfeed, compared to some Wall Street executive, granted. But he'd work this job for free, the twelve-hour-plus shifts thrilled him so!

"Keep the faith, Treat!" he heard Mohammed call out, and he knew the militant had a clenched fist raised, but he didn't look back. Abdul, or Elijah, or whatever name he was going by that week, could be a real minority migraine, but Brody didn't think the man's 'hatred' was all that sincere that he was a genuine radical. Brody was convinced it was all just a game, a release valve, a methodical scam to vent his frustrations and survive this hell in the tropics they called a Tour 365. Mohammed had learned several rocket attacks ago that death knows no colors. Snipers fired at you no matter what shade your skin was; the sappers usually attacked at night, and "white boys" made better targets in the dark than "brothers." Mohammed once had even been pulled out of a crossfire by two rednecks whose Mississippi accents, according to the civil rights activist, were sure signs there was probably a white robe or two lurking in their family tree. In June, a white soldier died in his arms when a monsoon downpour had rolled through and grounded medevac slics, and Mohammed had shed tears of both sorrow and rage over the helpless feeling in his gut. The dead soldier never had a chance anyway—one rarely survives a thumper round to the chest—but Mohammed refused to accept that, and carried the guilt around, like scars across his soul, to this day.

"Fine job you did here. Brody, is it?" Col. Buchanan's voice intruded into his thoughts, and Treat realized he was standing beside the officer and staring down at the NVA sergeant.

"Y-yes, sir," he stammered uncertainly. "Gonna put you in for a DFC, Specialist Brody." Buchanan lit up a cigar, slapped Treat on the back, then offered it to him.

"No thanks, sir." Brody couldn't take his eyes off the Vietnamese's face. The man's eyelids had swollen to the size of apples and were just as red. "Don't smoke."

"Mind you, I'm not really sure what transpired here today really rates a DFC, young man." Buchanan chuckled. "I mean, it seems to me the damn snake did all the work!"

Brody forced a laugh himself but grimaced as the medic treating the prisoner pressed a straight razor against one of the eyelids.

Blood and pus squirted forth, sprinkling across Brody's trousers below the knees. "Aw, fuck me 'till it hurts," he muttered.

Buchanan cocked an eyebrow at him but dismissed the remark just as quickly. "I just want to see how them clerk-and-jerks back in Pleiku City word-up the citation!" He erupted into more laughter and slapped Brody on the back again.

"I'm sure our boys in MI can coax some intel...some *good* intel outta your prisoner here." He glanced over at the two dead Arvins tied to the other side of the trunk. The South Vietnamese captive who'd been rescued by Brody's arrival was all smiles, ignoring his coutnerparts' fate as he gutted one of the tigers in preparation for skinning it. The colonel would get two more trophies of this brush with death to go next to the other predator skins on his CP walls. "And I'm sure that Arvin over there'll have quite a tale to tell when he's reunited with his buddies, too!

"You'll need a lift back to camp," Buchanan continued. "Our jeeps are three klicks in that direction." Half the original escort platoon was returning to the clearing, their faces soot covered, a wild, satisfied look in their eyes. A master sergeant held up nine fingers, signaling the body count to the colonel. "So saddle up, soldier." Buchanan wrapped an arm around Brody's shoulder, fatherlike.

"Mind if I beat feet back to the site where the bird went down, sir?" An expression of mild worry creased his grim features.

"I've already got a team in the area searching for that MIA." Lt. Winston had appeared out of nowhere.

"It's not that, Colonel," Brody did not really acknowledge the junior officer's presence, "there's a couple things back there I wanted to. . .retrieve. . . ."

The smile returned to Buchanan's face, and he reached forward and lifted the Spec-4's dog-tag chains from his chest, admiring the bits and pieces collected from past chopper crashes.

"Go ahead, Soldier." He nodded approvingly, a trace of envy in his eyes. "Go back out there, and. . .*get some!*"

CHAPTER 4

It was with a certain flair and style bordering on pomp-and-circumstance that Treat Brody rode back into camp at the head of Col. Buchanan's convoy two hours later. Several North Vietnamese bodies strapped across jeep hoods, the circus had returned to town. And Specialist 4th Class Brody was prepared to bask in the much-deserved limelight. But a sight fifty meters outside the "Turkey Farm" perimeter, down the hill from the main gate, captured his attention. Brody outranked the pale, ruddy-complected driver—an FNG slicksleeve—and ordered him to pull out of the convoy, the planned, grand entrance after his heroic shoot-down totally forgotten.

Brody quickly slipped the python head back on when he spotted a helmetless, tall, and lanky soldier standing at the edge of a cluster of several other First Cav troopers, flak vest wide open and trousers unbloused. "What's cookin', Snakeman?"

Private First Class Elliot Fletcher recognized Brody's crash-site charm necklace instantly. "Why, Treat!" He rushed over and wrapped an arm around the survivor, unable to take his eyes off the reptilian face-lift. "We heard you crashed and burned, boy. Crashed and fuckin' burned to a crisp! How much you want for the boa snout?"

"Yah, I'm fine, thanks." Brody slipped the mask off, revealing a disappointed expression. "The *python* head is not currently for sale. What's the clusterfuck all about?"

Fletcher, his light-brown flattop drooping along the edges from the humidity, shrugged and led Brody over to the group as a helicopter set down without fanfare fifty meters away.

Five or six Americans formed a semicircle around three captured enemy soldiers. The Vietnamese, clad only in baggy GI shorts, were blindfolded, with their hands tied behind their backs. Two sat in the dust as a Chieu Hoi scout interrogated the third.

The group of combatants was standing around what appeared to be a giant oven-baked 'stick-man' who'd been squashed flat into the middle of the concrete-hard, dirt-packed road. Two MP jeeps sat parked off to the side, behind the GIs. "Truong Ju-ju snatched those three Cong motherfuckers comin' out of a tunnel just beyond the tree line there—can ya believe it?" Fletcher shook his sunken, sunburned cheeks from side to side. "They're not talkin', but Ju-ju hasn't started kickin' 'em around yet, neither." A look of anticipation suddenly danced in his eyes as he removed mirrored sunglasses and grinned.

"I'd say they're NVA, Snakeman, judging by their haircuts." Brody referred to the bushy-on-top, shaved-on-the-sides style all three Vietnamese exhibited.

"Whatever." Fletcher's Southern accent flowed in all its glory now with the simple, three-syllable word as he spat into the clay at his feet. Both men watched a small puff of orange dust rise from the trapped ripple of disgust. "A dink is a zip is a target to me, brother—no matter how you wanna cook it up

31

and dish it out."

Brody glanced over at Fletcher with a dumbfounded expression but didn't press the matter. He watched Truong Ju-ju unleash a torrent of unintelligible Vietnamese down at the closest prisoner without noticeable results. The enemy soldier just kept his shoulders hunched up against his earlobes and his groin protected by his knees. The scrawny man trembled but displayed no other reaction to the barrage of nonstop questions and pidgin-English profanity.

"What about the slab of blood-and-guts in the middle of the roadway there?" Brody watched Truong Ju-ju slap one of the prisoners, rip away his blindfold, and point at the remains flattened across the roadway. He pointed over at the Huey, then back at the mutilated corpse again.

"I heard the MPs saying it's what's left of some South Vietnamese soldier who accidentally got splashed flat by an ARVN tank, but Ju-ju's tellin' the prisoner the body belongs to another communist who wouldn't talk either—so he threw the bastard out the side of a gunship at two thousand feet. Truong Ju-ju always was a bit of a storyteller." Fletcher laughed.

Brody felt a sick grin curl his lips against his will. "Poetic license to the max."

"*Mind*fuck to the max." A passing soldier who'd overheard their conversation threw in his two bits.

"Whatever." Fletcher replaced the sunglasses before glancing over at Brody. "You know my motto: 'Fuck the Geneva Convention, then fuck *your* housegirl 'til my balls ache.'"

"My house 'girl' is pushin' eighty, Casanova. But you're welcome to follow her home to her hut, if that's what really turns your crank, prevert."

Fletcher snickered and resumed watching the roadside interrogation. "I think I'll pass, sport."

Brody sucked in a lungful of air as Truong Ju-ju suddenly kicked the nearest prisoner over onto his side then screamed at all three Vietnamese to rise to their feet.

"What's going on, Snakeman?"

"Don't know, Whoremonger, but Zack thinks these dinks are responsible for our six KIAs yesterday, and tensions are high. Ju-ju knows it. He wants answers, and he wants them today."

Brody cringed at the nickname "Whoremonger." It had been

his unit "tag" for going on ten months now—ever since, while joking with an in-processing clerk-and-jerk at battalion, he'd written on the future assignments dream sheet that his immediate goals involved screwing one virgin in every country of Asia before he went back to The World. "Haven't you heard?" the clerk had replied. "Ain't no cherry girls *left* in the Orient!" Brody had chuckled accordingly and responded that he'd settle for any lady of questionable virtue who'd sew it back up for him, and the word quickly preceded him to his unit: The man was more perverted than *most* door gunners—guard your backsides when bending over to retrieve fumbled soap bars in the shower room. Penciled into the maiden-name slot on his 201 File was the legend "Beware the Whoremonger." And it had stuck, fortunately. Brody himself did not help matters any when he was escorted to the unit that first day after a predawn raid on an off-limits whorehouse in An Khe.

Truong Ju-ju was dragging the most hard core of the prisoners toward the chopper, its rotors still rotating lazily through the thick, muggy air as the crew chief prepared to tie the blades down.

A staff sergeant was yelling at the AC and peter pilot as they jumped down onto the Huey's skids. Frowning, they didn't bother to argue but just shrugged their shoulders and climbed back into the craft as other soldiers, prodding with their rifle butts, urged the two remaining prisoners toward the gunship.

"Come on." Fletcher grabbed Brody's arm. "Roller-coaster time. Let's go along for the ride. I just *gotta* see this."

Brody did not protest. He knew all these men and felt at ease with them, yet he had to make a concentrated effort to ignore the voice of warning crying out. The Whoremonger stared at the upside-down steel pot hanging from Fletcher's web belt. An assortment of colorful, multi-hued serpents of the nonvenomous variety slithered about through the letters from home stuffed into the seldom-used helmet. Brody counted seven different snakes as they walked over to the chopper pad. Fletcher had a weird passion for the creatures, hence his nickname.

Two soldiers climbed up through the side hatch of the Huey and reached down to take custody of the prisoners as they were hoisted into the gunship. The peter pilot had yet to assume his position beside the aircraft commander. He stood over the two grunts instead, voicing concern. "What's the destination?"

"Yah," added the crew chief, a huge NCO with six months as a door gunner in the Delta under his belt. "We got nothin' from the Charlie Tango on youz guys!"

"Improvise, gents." A short but stocky Asian-American appeared on the chopper's skids. With ruggedly handsome features marred only by a drooping, untrimmed Fu Manchu mustache, he whipped a casual half-salute on the helicopter crew. They'd obviously just returned from a mission. The craft was empty except for piles of empty brass on the cabin floor. And PFC Lawrence S. Lee, known affectionately to the men as "Jap," knew he had to work fast. "These assholes are the low-life ratshit responsible for downing those two Hueys yesterday!"

"What!?" The AC had taken his seat behind the controls but stared back over a shoulder now.

"That's right, Lawless! Snakeman and the Whoremonger caught 'em dead to rights comin' out of a tunnel less than a klick outside the wire. Both of 'em were totin' LAWs too!"

"American-made?" The peter-pilot's eyes went wide. "What do you think?" Lee was already climbing aboard.

Warrant Officer Lance "Lawless" Warlokk pulled the trigger that fired-up the craft's engines. "Well, ordnance and evidence changes everything!" He flashed an ear-to-ear smile, then pulled on his chicken plate and APH-5. "Hop aboard, doggie-legs!"

Lee was soon reaching down to pull the other two prisoners in through the hatch and impatiently waved Brody, who seemed to be lingering uncertainly at the edge of the tarmac, up to the gunship.

Treat stared back at Lee, hesitating, and his mind replayed the flicker of Warlokk's expression. The men were a study in contrasts, yet deep inside they both nurtured the same desires for glory, the same immediate goals: locate and terminate *Charlie.*

Lance Warlokk, called "Mister" by the NCOs who respected him and "Lawless" by the grunts he ferried into battle, flew Cobra assault choppers as well as the Huey slicks. A headful of blond hair offset numerous half-inch scars along one side of his face when charming the local village maidens, who were easily

34

mesmerized by his deep, sky-blue eyes. But Warlokk—the men often joked about his last name, wagering it was not *really* his last name but the result of a chopperjock jotdog's legal change —preferred to keep it shaved short, though he was notorious for showing up at fire missions sporting absurd Mohawk styles or even Beatles' bowl-cuts when it did go untrimmed. Usually clean-shaven, he had roared into LZs before wearing a Santa Claus beard or Ho Chi Minh goatee, complete with uncooked *pho* soup strands. Short like most whirlybird pilots, his fore-arms seemed as thick as his biceps. When he smiled, only one side of his face granted cooperation—the half that hadn't been disfigured by shards of cockpit glass blasted into it by an RPG the monsoon before. But Warlokk managed to capitalize on the mishap. Brody even thought the pilot's looks were strangely improved by the dozen or so razor-thin marks, and the camp followers found his corner-of-the-eye wink captivating.

Private First Class Lee's charm was also deceptive. Though his talents at womanizing the Highlands' populace were near legendary and the local ladies often found his dark, sinister eyes irresistible, trouble always erupted when they heard a bud-dy call him "Jap." Seems the Viets had a few bad experiences with the conquerors from Tokyo some time back. And as all soldiers of misfortune know, Asian women rarely forgive and *never* forget.

"Come on, Whoremonger!" Fletcher was screaming across whirlwinds of dust fanning out beneath the helicopter's madly flopping rotors. Treat glanced up at the gleaming ballast weights molded into the ends of blades that measured fifty feet tip to tip, then, bent over and holding his helmet in place, he hustled up to the skids at the last second and clambered aboard as the tail lifted off the ground. "Time to take Luke the Gook up for a little 'Truth or Consequences!'"

Truong Ju-ju was already screaming into a prisoner's ears, though Treat was not sure the Vietnamese could be heard above the rotors' teeth-jarring clamor. Ju-ju had obviously picked the weakest-looking prisoner for the initial series of questions—an older NVA with a grim frown beneath his blindfold was hand-cuffed to a three-inch creweye protruding beside the hatch Hog. Ju-ju screamed and stomped up and down until the veins along his neck began to bulge, but after five minutes, the most he

35

could get out of the communist teenager—Brody judged his age to be between eighteen and twenty—was a jerky nod in the negative.

Ju-ju made a motion to Lee then began dragging the prisoner on his haunches over to the hatch.

The peter pilot was not watching his instrument panel or anything else in the cockpit. His chin seemed glued across his shoulders as he stared back at the Chieu Hoi scout's method of obtaining information. "Ju says to take her up over Void Vicious now, if you would. Two thousand barefeet or so should do, sirs, right above the dead man's zone."

The peter pilot did not acknowledge at first. He did not glance over at his AC for guidance. His visor was flipped back, and the troopers in the cabin all saw the frightened look of indecision in his eyes. It was a face that said, "Okay, I'm a newby ...I've only been in-country a couple weeks, but this *is not the way things are done!*" He refused to watch his career fly out the hatch with their prisoner. He would not be a party to murder! This was homicide, plain and simple and, by God, it just was not justified!

"Fifteen hundred to two thousand oughta do it," Lee repeated calmly, allowing the mandatory clarification. He did not blink as he stared at the junior warrant officer. His face was emotionless. The way his lips came together after he spoke, bored and uncaring, told the peter pilot a hundred things. *We do this a dozen times a week* topped the unspoken list.

"No!" the twenty-five-year-old pilot responded finally. Lee broke eye contact as soon as he sensed the FNG was going to erupt and turned his back on the gut-colored momex flight suit.

"What?" Fletcher flew past Lee and slid to a stop abreast of the cockpit's split aft shield. The nose had dipped, indicating a dive, but Brody knew they were actually ascending—and ascending rapidly. The load was light today: five troopers with no rucks or bandoliers, and three dispensables. "What did you say?"

The peter pilot leaned back but did not back down entirely as this mad-dog grunt squared off with him, nose-to-nose. "I *said* we're not participating in any...unauthorized executions...is that clear?" He did not notice the AC was smiling as the Huey leveled out above Void Vicious: that dangerous span below two thousand feet where small-arms fire from the ground was accurate and the treetops seemed to radiate a mysterious power that would snatch a gunship from the skies and drag it down into the brutal jaws of the jungle. "If you want to interrogate these prisoners. . .well, *that's* fine, but—"

"But, *sir!*"

"But there better not be any —"

"Sit back and shut the fuck up, Harry." The man with LAWLESS stenciled across the back of his helmet eased the peter pilot into his station with the back of his hand.

"But Warlokk—"

"*Mister* Warlokk to you, newby. Now sit back and enjoy the ride—that's an order." Lawless was banking hard to the right, out over the South China Sea.

Harry stared down at the lazy, hypnotic whitecaps disturbing a glasslike span of turquoise below. "But—"

"These troopers broke me in *rikky-tik*. They taught me everything I need to know," Lawless exaggerated. "Just like they're gonna break *you* in someday." Harry didn't seem to notice the gunship was slowly descending again.

In the back of the cabin, Truong Ju-ju was hard at work at his craft. With the back of his hand, he slapped the prisoner twice—not hard enough to hurt him, just hard enough to get the man's attention, to keep his adrenaline surging. "Now tell me your cell leader's provincial status," he directed in Vietnamese. "We already know his name. Just confirm his status. Or out the window you go, Lucas." He switched to pidgin-English, smiling over at Brody: "And I no think we over Kan'as an'more, Toto!"

Brody just shook his head from side to side in reply. Ju-ju never used the label "Luke," always "Lucas." Everytime the scout said it, Whoremonger thought of *The Rifleman* television series, for that was how Ju-ju liked to fire his M-16: rapidly, and with only one hand—using the pistol grips like a handgun.

Fletcher erupted into laughter and slapped Ju-ju on the back. The prisoner, memories of the flattened Vietnamese in the roadway no doubt fresh in his mind and resigned to a high-altitude demise no matter how he answered, kicked out blindly, yelling *"Du di me!."*

Brody had to restrain the laugh this time. Too bad Moham-

37

med wasn't here. *Du di me* was the Vietnamese equivalent of *Yo mama!* Definitely fighting words.

Truong Ju-ju backed out of the thrashing prisoner's reach, straightened up, and placed his hands on his hips. *"Dien cai dit,"* he muttered under his breath. *Crazy ass.* Behind him, beyond the hatch outline, two leaf-pattern Phantoms swooped past in the distance, waving their wings at the gunship crew before disappearing high in the clouds rolling in off the ocean.

Raising his voice, the scout chose a different question. "We already know the 32nd, 33rd and 66th North Vietnamese Regiments are working this area." Ju-ju had switched back to Vietnamese again. "Which one are you and your two limp-wristed *girl*friends there assigned to?"

"Su bo!" the prisoner spat out blindly. *Fuck your ancestors!* Words to die by in a country where people *worshiped* their dead ancestors.

"Lang di." Ju-ju kicked the man lightly, just to let him know where he was standing. *Shut-up.*

"Bu bui toi di." *Suck my penis.*

"Lang di tep!" Ju-ju brought the M-16 down off its shoulder sling. *Shut-up!*

"Hon dit to di!" The prisoner flashed a taunting, defiant grin at the ex-communist. *Kiss my ass.*

"Suc may, tet congo!" Ju-ju yanked back the rifle's charging handle. A sharp metallic *twang* echoed about the cabin interior as a live round was forced into the chamber. "Nebbah happen...*punk!*" He rammed the end of the flash suppressor against the prisoner's temple.

The NVA was now leaning halfway out the hatch, the sole of Ju-ju's jungleboot against his chest, the wind and the rotor downblast pasting his sweat-slick hair back. He winced slightly when the cool steel muzzle pressed deeper into his flesh. But the sneer remained intact.

"Di am phu." His teeth gnashed with hatred. *Go to hell.*
"Lang di nhai!" Truong Ju-ju flipped the rifle's safety selector to AUTO mode, and Brody envisioned the prisoner catapulting backwards out the hatch in a burst of crimson against the sunset, his limbs twitching to a Colt rock 'n' roll ballad.

"All GI in 'dis *Hew*ey die before leave Vee*yet*-Nam!" the prisoner declared in broken English as it appeared imminent he was

38

about to bow out of the picture. "You kill me...I come back...*haunt* you, *bic*? All GIs *fini!*"

Ju-ju didn't seem upset by the threat. He'd been cursed before. And by better men than this clown. *"Xin loi!"* He lowered his M-16 and booted the prisoner out the hatch.

Brody had never heard such a chilling, spine-tingling scream before as the Vietnamese dropped backwards out of sight. The peter pilot nearly abandoned his station, the incident so unsettled him.

Brody knew he would never forget the prisoner's soul-ripping scream—not as long as he lived. He wondered why it had ended so abruptly, and not drawn itself out, as he'd thought it would—the way he pictured such an event in his mind...like in all the movies, when jumpers leaped from New York bridges. And then he wondered what thoughts had gone through the guerrilla's mind as he lost that last contact with his fellow man and plummeted down through space.

Truong Ju-ju was rushing past the next closest prisoner who was already, in rapid Vietnamese, babbling away everything he knew. The Chieu Hoi scout latched onto the oldest, most experienced guerrilla and began shaking him. "You die, *du ma!* You die today, for sure! You want put voodoo curse on Truong Ju-ju, too?" He spoke in English. And more for the benefit of the Americans around him, more to bolster his own image and reputation among the troopers of the First Cav than to impress the tight-lipped communist at his feet. "Well, sorry 'bout that!"

Ju-ju dragged the NVA over toward the hatch, and that was all it took. He broke into tears, all courage and defiance dissolving, and cooperated with ear-splitting answers to questions that hadn't even been asked yet. Statements about those strategic issues that obviously interested Truong Ju-ju were blurted out nonstop for a good five minutes straight as the scout scribbled choice tidbits of military intelligence across the palm of his hand with a ballpoint pen. Brody's own eyes locked on the unfolding drama within the cabin and not the shifting scenery outside.

When the prisoner finally paused to catch his breath, Ju-ju grabbed him around the throat and dangled him halfway out the hatch. The Vietnamese screamed in horror for several drawn-out seconds, and when the rotor downblast nearly ripped his blindfold away, Ju-ju pulled him back in a little bit, frowning.

Brody couldn't understand that; he was sure that were the prisoner to suddenly gaze down, wide-eyed, into so many countless meters of open space, his confession rate would escalate considerably.

Truong Ju-ju slapped the communist's cheekbone and yelled what Brody was positive was the prize-winning question. The prisoner hesitated, and Ju-ju flew into a fury, slapping him around some more. He grabbed the smaller man by the elbows, lifted him off his feet, and began to swing him in and out of the open hatch, counting loudly from one to three.

"Mot...hai..."

The North Vietnamese screamed out the necessary coordinates, and Ju-ju's face lit up proudly. He glanced about the cabin, the excitement in his eyes revealing he smelled a bonus and perhaps even a promotion coming out of this sky-high session as his arms continued to swing back. *"Ba!"* he said, and he heaved the prisoner out the hatch with all his might.

"Truong, *no!*" Fletcher was rushing across the cabin toward the scout. Brody found Snakeman's words and movements strange as the scene seemed to shift in a terrible B-movie, and the words were out of sync with his lips. But he was too late.

An almost exact imitation of the earlier scream briefly filled their ears. Everyone froze in place as the Vietnamese disappeared from view, his death cry devoured by the incessant *whopping* of rotors above. Everyone except Truong Ju-ju.

Leering like a maniac angry with Fletcher's interference, he lunged out at the American, grabbed his wrist, and jerked him off his feet toward the hatch. As if by reflex, Brody's captured AK-47 slid off his shoulder and was suddenly propped in his hands, like a restrained attack dog, muzzled into silence. "Ju-ju, *no!*" But the command was ignored. Dumbfounded, he raised the barrel until the triangle sights were level with Truong's sweat-soaked chest.

But it was too late. Fletcher had vanished into the void without a sound.

Without a sound.

Without a fucking sound! Brody's mind screamed for Snakeman above the downblast as he watched Ju-ju go after the third

NVA prisoner next. Mesmerized by the strange mutiny, Brody was frozen as the air and the craft and his whole world trembled around him. For some reason he could not pull the trigger. Something in the twinkle in Truong's eye as he glanced over a shoulder at him...something about the way Lawless was laughing, his head back, aloof, inviting a good-night kiss from Lady Death. Brody could not will his trigger finger to work. All he could do was lean out the hatch and glance down stupidly, hoping to catch some last sight of his beloved Snakeman or—

"*GOTCHA!*" Fletcher popped up from below, was suddenly face-to-face with him! Using his forefinger, he flicked the Whoremonger on the nose.

Brody screamed like a child who'd finally found the boogie man under his bed. He scampered back on his haunches, away from the hatch. Truong Ju-ju nearly tripped over him as he hurled the third prisoner out after Fletcher.

But then something clicked in Brody's head. Something told him all was not as it seemed. Something his subconscious had spotted beyond Fletcher's shit-eating grin was beckoning him to return to the open hatch and the void's edge, and he crawled back like a nervous spider expecting to be squashed.

When he peered down over the Huey's gleaming skids, there stood Elliot Fletcher and several other GIs, three of whom were attending to the shaken but uninjured prisoners.

The gunship had been hovering less than ten feet above the ground during the final phase of Truong Ju-ju's interrogation.

CHAPTER 5

Treat Brody's gun hand flew up into a crisp salute after Col. Buchanan pinned the Army Commendation Medal on his chest and stepped back. The colonel smiled proudly, returned the salute, and whispered just loud enough for the rest of the formation to hear, "Well done, Specialist. The dedication and downright heroics of *all* you men filling the ranks of the Cav never cease to amaze even me."

"Thank you, sir." Brody couldn't keep the grin off his face. He was not a humble soldier, and the awards ceremony did not embarrass him. In fact, medals were another thing Treat Brody, alias the Whoremonger, ate up with a passion. It was all part of contributing to the smooth running of the Green Machine, and Brody was proud to participate. Heck, he might even make a career of riding gunships into battle, that's how fired-up he was.

"I've put you in for a Silver Star, too, young man, based on your recollection of what happened at that shoot-down, but the recommendation will have to survive the shuffle through Headquarters."

"I understand, sir. No sweat." 'Cause, there's already some deadbeats at Brigade who claim even a Bronze is out of the question since there were no witnesses, in *their* minds. You being the only survivor and all." An SAR team had found the other door gunner's body ripped to pieces an hour or so before the formation was called. "But we'll see about that. I can personally damn well verify I *witnessed* you carry an NVA sergeant over your shoulder as you exchanged gunfire with an overwhelming enemy force...hey, hey!" he added with a little chuckle.

"No sweat, sir. Don't need no medals anyway. Just a mission." He used poor grammar intentionally as memories of the crash flooded through him. Brody felt the bile rising in his throat. A flashback of the tree impaling the copilot bounced about in his head like a low-budget horror movie. The film flickered and broke as Buchanan slapped him on the shoulder and walked down along the front row of the formation toward a makeshift podium.

"Splendid job, son. Simply splendid."

A hundred men wearing jungle fatigues and floppy bush hats stood at the position of parade rest behind Brody, their hands clasped against their lower backs, boots spread apart comfortably. A dozen NCOs kept them in half as many unmoving ranks

42

as the Company CO escorted Battalion Commander Buchanan through the hundred-and-ten-degree heat to the front of the group.

"Splendid job, sumbitch."

Fletcher was standing beside Brody, taunting him with lips that barely moved. "Stupidly splendid." Fletcher was imitating the Nazi colonel he'd seen on an Armed Forces Network TV show called *Hogan's Heroes*. Soldiers in the row behind them broke into scattered laughter, and Brody elbowed his best friend.

"*I* didn't ask for this fiasco, Snakeman," he whispered.

"*Bull* genitals, GI. You bookoo *dinky dau*." Fletcher was imitating their latest housegirl now. "You gung-ho kinda guy. . . always hunting women and heroism like Neil Nazi chase wild dog!"

"Seriously, Fletch. . .but hey!" He glanced around as Buchanan took the podium. "Didn't they invite any goofy reporters over here to make the Whoremonger famous?" Lately, Brody found he was taking to the unsolicited nickname. "Or what the fuck, over?"

"Over a lousy ArCom, Treat? Cut me some slack."

"Not even a slightly prejudiced combat PJ from the Screamin' Chickens?" *PJ* was grunt slang for photojournalist. *Screamin' Chicken* was a derogatory term many Cav troopers used to refer to member of the 101st Airborne Division, whose combat patch boasted a screaming eagle.

"Dream on, *du ma*."

The formation of soldiers stood along one edge of the clearing in the midst of some 10,000 olive drab tents. The shelters dotted barren hills of red dust for as far as the eye could see. Sparse tree lines along the northern and southern stretches of concertina perimeter were the only exception. Helicopters landing and taking off in all directions from every side of the camp lifted the dust, which clung to everything, and an orange haze drifted beneath the afternoon sun.

Crescents of sweat hung along the armpits and lower backs of nearly every man watching Buchanan stride up to his makeshift ammo pallet podium.

"AttenHUT!" One of the many lieutenants present called the men from parade rest to the position of attention, and the land

43

echoed with the crack of a hundred men slamming the insides of their heels together, East German style.

Buchanan frowned but did not say anything about the imitation immediately.

"Just like fucking boot camp." Fletcher stared through the little puffs of dust rising from the lines of boots in front of their rank. "When will it ever end? That's all I wanna know."

Brody was ignoring him. He always ignored the Snakeman's antics when officers of the First Cav got down to business. The Specialist 4th Class ate up these pep rallies almost as much as the chopper rides. He enjoyed watching the Cavalry officers strut their stuff through the dust of the Central Highlands. Someday *he* might go after one of those lieutenant's bars himself. But such an advancement would have to follow quite a combat zone act of heroism. Somehow he'd take out an MG nest single-handedly. Or rescue a wounded soldier during one of Charlie's midnight mortar attacks. *Something* to get the CO's attention. And a battlefield promotion to First Louie. Yes, they'd have to jump a few ranks. The ol' Whoremonger just wouldn't accept a set of butter bars. He'd love to be an officer, a leader of men, but he couldn't suffer the humiliation of being a 2nd lieutenant. Not in The Nam. Being a 2nd lieutenant was worse than being a buck private E-Nothing with no time in grade.

"At ease, gentlemen," Buchanan was saying even before the assistant's words faded beyond the farthest tents. "At ease, at ease. Smoke 'em if you got 'em." Brody listened to the tops on several dozen made-in-Saigon Zippo lighters flip open with a satisfying grate.

"I just want you men to know you're doing a darn fine job here in the valley." Buchanan swatted a mosquito, then tipped his cap back and wiped sweat from his forehead with an o.d. green handkerchief. "Charlie and his NVA stepbrothers are hightailing it into Cambodia as I speak." A huge zebra dragonfly landed on the colorful rows of ribbons over the breast pocket of his khakis, and, surprised and amused, sounding even a bit flattered, he nudged it off and said, "Guess I look like a big loveable bug in these goofy stateside duffs, don't I?" Men in the front row applauded lightly.

"He looks like a bug *dud* to me." Fletcher slipped the words

44

out the corner of his mouth.

"Anyway, we have the enemy on the run. I guess they couldn't hack the sight of all those bee-yootiful helicopters descending on them from the skies like"—he watched the dragonfly hover several feet in front of him for an instant, as if winking approval, before it darted off through the rusty haze—"like steel dragons-on-wing!" Buchanan paused as rowdy cheers and more applause interrupted the ceremony.

Brody felt his own breath quivering as he locked onto the huge First Cavalry Division emblem painted across the podium. Largest of all the Army's unit patches, the insignia was shaped somewhat like a warrior's shield: wide across the top, and tapered along the bottom. A thick, black band crossed the shield from top left to bottom right, and a black horse head filled the top right quadrant of the brilliant gold backdrop. Below the emblem were the words THE FIRST TEAM. It was the Cav's motto.

"We're going to be pursuing those enemy troops as they retreat toward the Cambodian border during the next couple weeks." Buchanan raised his hands for silence as the men resumed applauding, but his fatherly smile—as fatherly as it could get, taking into account the Hitler-style mustache—remained intact. "And I'm sure you men will continue to excel during the coming days as you demonstrated—" A gaggle of Hueys flew over just then, their underbellies and side hatches bristling with weapons, and all eyes went up.

The helicopters were headed southwest across the Tea Plantation, into the heart of the Ia Drang Valley. Every soldier in that formation knew their destination was the Chu Pong Massif.

"As you are all aware"—Buchanan flashed back through history with less than a dozen words—"the Seventh Cav is Custer's old unit." Brody glanced about: Some of the men lost their grins as their minds recreated the slaughter at Little Big Horn. Others became even more excited at the thought of belonging to a unit that was associated with such a famous "Injun'-fightin' general," and the prospect of engaging the indigenous savages and "winning it this time." ". . . And we are going to continue the tradition of the last one hundred . . ." Brody tensed. He couldn't help but fear the colonel was digging his own grave. But Buchanan pulled through admirably. "Nineteen hundred

45

and sixty five is fast drawing to a close, gentlemen. And the enemy knows it. That's why he's beatin' feet in a sorry retreat across the border."

"Fuckin' poet and he don't even know it." Fletcher sneaked a peek at his wristwatch.

"Because Nineteen sixty-six"—the CO leaned over the top of the podium and pounded on the First Cavalry emblem dramatically—"marks the *Year of the Horse!*"

The tremendous applause caused the PA system to squeal with feedback as two Phantom jets swooped past low overhead waving their wings as if on cue. Brody waited for the sonic boom, wondering if they were the same fighter jocks he'd watched over Ju-ju's shoulder the day before, but the F-4Es were cruising too slowly. Buchanan saluted their afterburners, and the men roared even louder, perhaps remembering the countless times Phantoms had charged to their rescue in the past, dishing out generous doses of napalm or 500-pounders to a startled Charlie. Many of the troopers in formation were so caught up in the surge of excitement they slid rifle slings off shoulders and began waving M-16 muzzles in the air.

"Wonderful." Buchanan's chest swelled with pride as a fleet of several dozen gunships rose from the Turkey Farm to the northeast and nearly eclipsed the sun as they flew over. "Fanfucking-*tastic!*" His intentional slip into GI slang brought renewed cheer from the men. Most of them loved this fifty-year-old colonel like a father, and they weren't afraid to show it as many directed sincere thumbs-up gestures at their CO.

"Now the powers that be inform me most of you young bucks will be involved in a little session of. . .kicking ass tonight," Buchanan continued after the gunships were gone. "So let's cut this circle jerk short and mozie on over to your slicks."

"I gotta admit I love it when the ol' bastard talks from the gutter like that." Fletcher winked over at Brody.

"I want you gentlemen to check 'em out good, like you always do," Buchanan quickly corrected his final approach, "'cause something in the air"—he held his hands out, palms up —"tells me the frogs are gonna hit the fan tonight, and I don't see a monsoon ribbon in sight."

A trickle of nervous laughter filtered through the ranks.

"One last thing, before I send you back to your Hog swivels

and rocket pods." Buchanan paused to let two Loachs buzz past overhead, a scant fifty meters off the ground. "The REMFs who censor your outgoing mail have made another request— and I use that word loosely—that you refrain from mentioning our two new Cobras the Division was extremely lucky to get for field testing. I know...I know...." His hands came up defensively as if to shield him from all the groans rising from the formation. "Those sleek-snouted ships are a thrill and a half to behold, but they're not even supposed to be over here, o-FISH-ially"—he cracked a wide smile—"until sixty-seven, if ya catch my drift."

The laughter increased somewhat, but not enough for Buchanan's tastes. "The fine people at Bell Helicopter found it in their hearts to loan us a couple AH-1 prototypes off the record, so to speak. We've scooped the First Aviation Brigade's NETT, gentlemen, but this was supposed to be something you all agreed to keep under your steel pots. No doubt Charlie and Mister NVA are wondering what the hell hit 'em everytime Sharkskinner or Snake Eye makes an appearance, but until Hanoi or the pap-sans at PRG Square clean up their act and forward a snapshot or two to Jane, thou shalt not tell Jody back stateside about Airmobile's newest toy, agreed?"

"AGREED!" a hundred voices responded in unison, casually omitting a "sir" at the end. Brody glanced about as the echo of enthusiasm drifted across the hilltops, and he wondered how many, if any, enemy Lurps were taking down the CO's loudspeaker speech, word for word.

"Very good." Buchanan's body language told his XO it was time to leave.

"Companeeeeee," one of the lieutenants called out authoritatively.

Several NCOs at the end of each row repeated the predrill warning. "Companeeeee."

"AttenHUT!"

The men snapped to attention as Buchanan leaned into his microphone one last time. "Keep up the good work, men. Put a litte extra elbow grease into them mini-gun mounts for the ol' Bull tonight."

He paused to let the entire formation soak up his Kirk Douglas flash of teeth. Then his personality seemed to split abruptly, the voice became as menacing as a prowling gunship hungry for the kill.

"DisMISSED!"

The men waited the traditional moment for Buchanan to step down from the podium, then slowly dispersed.

Brody did not realize he was rubbing the chain of lucky charms around his neck as he walked over to the parked gunship with a majestic *Pegasus* painted across its snout.

The smell of gun oil was heavy in the air. An entire squad of men sat in a semicircle between two silent helicopters, their legs crossed Indian-style. Old bamboo sleeping mats were spread out in front of them. Disassembled machine guns and Hog mounts were strewn about on the oil-slick mats, some freshly cleaned with solvent, others discolored and caked with gunpowder.

Brody loved the smell of gun oil on cold steel. The highlight of his day—when not riding the slicks into a hot LZ—was briskly rubbing lube oil along the working parts of his M-60 with the palm of his hand, until both flesh and metal began to heat up. A soldier came to have an understanding of his weapon that way, came to appreciate it more. But the cleaning solvent that preceded each layer of LSA was a necessary evil, and you couldn't have it both ways. It exuded a stench that the door gunner disliked intensely. His nose wrinkled as he squatted Asian style in front of Fletcher and randomly selected a gleaming firing pin as if to inspect it.

"Going native on us?" Fletcher glanced at Brody's method of relaxing with disgust. There was no hiding the disapproval in his tone.

"It's therapeutic on my tired old haunch muscles, Snakeman." Brody didn't seem offended. "You oughta try it some time. Might help to improve your rotten disposition *tee-tee*. I particularly find it refreshing when I've gotta take a crap." Several of the men looked up from their broken-down MGs and automatic rifles. "Sure beats tryin' to balance my butt across them bamboo poles out at that lousy excuse for a latrine. A man oughta be able to *enjoy* a healthy crap if he's of a mind." Brody felt like he was on a roll and in no mood to stop now. "Yes. . . much more comfortable to just drop the ol' army-issue trous-

48

ers, squat behind a bush somewhere, and—"

"That's a good way to invite some scorpion with a bad attitude to multiply your pecker tenfold." One of the men sounded as if he was about to add even more wisdom to the conversation, but Fletcher cut him off.

"Spare us the particulars, Whoremonger, if you don't mind."

"I second that motion."

A slender private E-deuce, wearing wire-rim glasses and brown over-the-ears hair parted down the middle, slammed the charging handle of an M-16 into place. "If I wanna talk shit, I'll trek on down to the open air market in New Pleiku."

"Sure, Professor." Brody stared at the peace symbol dangling from the nonconformist's dog tags chain. "No sweat."

"Actually"—Lee dropped a tripod into the cleaning tank and splashed half the group—"the food there's not *that* bad. You should try this one soup stall between—"

"Shut the fuck up, Jap."

Shawn Larson had already stripped down to his GI shorts, shower thongs, and green T-shirt. The T-shirt had a silkscreen design across the back that depicted a Huey door gunner throwing mortars out the hatch by hand and read: FLY THE FRIENDLY SKIES OF SOUTH VIETNAM—THRILL CAPITAL OF THE WORLD! He was leaning against a rucksack that should have been full of extra ammo but held a cache of paperback classics instead.

In his mid-twenties, "the Professor" was the only enlisted man in the platoon—probably the battalion, decided Brody—with a master's degree in both philosophy and sociology. He was proud to be a draftee—and not Regular Army, as most gunnies seemed to be, and though he was no anarchist, Larson was far from being a fan of military discipline. The inscription across his web belt buckle read: U.S. ARMY: THE INCOMPETENT LEADING THE UNWILLING TO DO THE IMPOSSIBLE FOR THE UNGRATEFUL.

He still resented the manner in which Uncle Sam outsmarted him during a break between semesters in which the Professor took to the mountains of Montana on a private little field trip in hopes of "discovering himself." The only discovery he made, however, was after he returned to Helena and found his invitation to the Green Machine waiting.

"Pass me some o' that LSA, Jap," Fletcher called across the sleeping mat. Lee slid a stateside can of the self-cleaning lubricant over without looking up. Glancing at Brody, Fletcher searched his pocket flaps before returning his attention to the weapons.

"Where's that shiny new ArCom Neil Nazi pinned on your tit, boy? We was all hopin' to rub our unworthy elbows on it, ya know?" He razzed Treat in the mandatory half-friendly, half-insulting manner. "Kinda help polish it up for the next CA. That way it'd be sparklin' to high heaven and you could just *blind* Charlie without firin' a—"

"Choke on water buffalo balls, Snakeman." Brody caught the gleam in Fletcher's eye, the sign of friendship forged under hostile fire. "You Legs are just jealous." He brought his fingertips to his lips, blew on them for a moment, then proudly scratched the subdued Airborne wings patch over his CIB. "The Colonel's gonna make Yours Truly an Acting Jack bookoo *rikky-tik,* as we all know, and *then* the shit's gonna hit the fan around here," he joked. "No more sluffin' off in this link of the 7th Cav. When you troops aren't out collectin' heads or back here soupin' up the slicks, it's gonna be extended PT at the Tea Plantation, *girls.* And we're talkin' M-16s laid out across the wrists, 'cause this heavily hung buck-sergeant-to-be *gonna* be a no-nonsense NCO." He switched into Abdul Mohammed's brand of jive after glancing around to make sure the black GI was not present at the solvent trough.

Lee laughed without looking up, as did many of the other soldiers there, but Fletcher was silent, his eyes growing big as he stared past Brody.

Anticipating the worst, the Whoremonger slowly turned just enough to confirm his suspicions, then went back to inspecting Fletcher's weapon, rolling his eyeballs skyward in response to the Snakeman's now-you're-shit grin.

"No-nonsense NCO, eh?" Two large black hands clamped down on Brody's shoulders from behind, pushing him down further into the squat until his ankles gave out and he rolled over, taking evasive action.

Lee laughed again, but louder this time.

"Well, how the hell you doin', Sgt. Zack?" Brody somersaulted to safety—instinctively in the direction of Larson, for the platoon dissident would surely take much of the senior NCO's attention from him.

Master Sergeant Leopold Zack's powerful laugh hurt Fletcher's ears when he replied, "Well, I was doin' down right fine 'till I heard one no-account Specialist Echo-four was hot to trot after my job." He glared at Brody with mock anger. "The CO gives him a single atta-boy, and he's suddenly out chasin' a recommendation to AJ." His accent was Southern, not jive. "Well, it won't happen so long as *I'm* Operations NCO, Mister Whorehumper, or whatever they call you nowadays." This business with nicknames in The Nam bothered Zack, for he could never keep them all straight—though he did prefer the men call him "Leo the Lionhearted." But "Leo the Lionhearted" was a lengthy nickname. Few complied. Most referred to him as "Black Bart," because of his ruthless tactics against the enemy. The Vietnamese called him "Black Buddha," because he shaved his head bald every morning and was never without his ear-to-ear smile. To Brody, it was an evil, demonic grin, the kind that warned you its bearer was up to no good.

"No," Zack continued, "so long as *I'm* Operations NCO, ol' Mister Whorebreeder gonna be pumpin' Hogs aboard the meanest, most beeYOOtiful gunships the Seventh of the First can sweet-talk into the skies," he imitated the colonel. "Does this everlovin' E-8 make himself perfectly fucking clear?" He winked down at Brody.

Brody considered making a remark challenging Zack's sexual preference, but the sergeant was a big man. "*Perfectly*, Sarge," Lee answered for him. "Treat was just talkin' about how much he respected your discretion in matters of the rice paddy persuasion and—"

Zack erupted into unrestrained laughter at the crude attempt toward mock flattery. "Better watch your sneaky, Oriental innuendos, Lee." His gaze shifted to the Japanese-American. "I'm hip to your attempts to topple Leo the Lionhearted from power, but I'll never surrender the First Squad throne!" He waved a meaty fist threateningly. "I'll not forsake Second Platoon of Echo Company, Seventh Cav of the First Cavalry Division, Republic of Vietnam, et cetera, et cetera. Jus' better watch your young amber ass, boy, or I'll hand you back over to Charlie."

Zack was the only NCO in the battalion who could get away

51

with a remark like that. Lee forced a slight chuckle but kept his eyes on the flash suppressor he'd been scrubbing away at ever since Brody arrived.

Treat stared up at Zack, returning the wink finally. He held a healthy respect for the stocky sergeant's size. At age thirty-five, he still had the body of a college football player, it seemed. Zack was only five-foot-ten, but at times—usually at night—when they were charging through the jungle after Charlie, he appeared as wide as he was tall. He carried a weight lifter's physique on that barrel-chested frame, yet the men never saw him lifting barbells, or even the makeshift grunt specials, such as cement-filled coffee cans. All he was ever engaged in were army calisthenics. But that was not what Brody really respected about the man.

Zack had brought home one Bronze and two Silver Stars from the Korean War, not to mention five Purple Hearts. He was a dedicated career soldier, with top-sergeant or CSM stripes in his future and the safety of his men foremost in his mind. This was his first tour in Vietnam.

"By the way, what brings you to this unworthy patch of camp, Leo?" Fletcher's tone reminded Brody of some redneck asking a Negro if he was aware he'd wandered into the wrong side of town... if he knew he'd stepped into white-sheet territory, and *would you like to take a tour of our hangin' tree and visit a coupla burnin' crosses up close?* But everyone knew Snakeman enjoyed Zack's company. Really, he sincerely did. At least he enjoyed listening to Mohammed question the NCO's ancestry.

Zack was light complected, and Abdul Mohammed, whose skin shade was black as polished ebony, enjoyed accusing the sergeant of being the tenth generation result of a Southern midnight romp in the haystacks between a plantation owner and one of his slaves.

"The colonel's God, and I'm Moses." Zack unraveled a long strip of C-rat toilet paper that had been rolled up in a thigh pocket. "And now it's time we goin' lay down the law, *boyyys.*"

"Shit."

"Here it comes."

"Rumor Control has it that engagements with Charlie goin' be tricklin' down to zilch as in Zulu," Zack announced. "Mainly because the First Cav has been doin' a fine job o' kickin' butt and has got the NVA on the run outta Ia Drang."

"Three cheers for the Seventh of the First," a soldier down at the far end of the mats muttered with little enthusiasm.

"Word oozin' down the wait-a-minute vine has it Division ain't plannin' no hardcore CAs for a while, 'til we get some word back from Recon and the Lurps, anyway."

"So anyway?" Fletcher pressed him for the bad news. If they were suddenly going to have all this free time on their hands, he could finally slip out of camp and begin his search.

"So anyway, the CO don't want you girls gettin' soft boobs for lack of something to do. He don't want you sluffin' off and kickin' back."

Larson looked up, a frown across his deeply tanned features. Still holding the stripped-down barrel of an M-16, he raised his grimy hands from a solvent tank, letting grease run down his forearms. "You call this sluffin' off, Sarge?" The Professor hated the way Zack and so many of his "lifer buddies" butchered the English language on a continual basis.

"So *anyyy*way"—Zack rested his boot atop a solvent tub and leaned across one thigh, eyeballing Larson—"the colonel came up with this list of do's and don't's."

"Oh, fucking *wonder*ful." Larson could smell a shit detail a mile away. He dropped the rifle barrel into the tank, splashing both Fletcher and Brody.

"Asshole," muttered Snakeman, leaning to the side to cover the tangle of reed snakes slithering about in his upside-down helmet.

"Effective immediately. . ."

Dual discharges in the distance shook the earth, and everyone except Zack and Brody ducked. Two projectiles screamed past a hundred feet overhead, ripping through the thick, humid air on their way to a hilltop three miles away. "Outgoing," Treat observed, and a half dozen newby heads came back up.

Zack continued reading as if interrupted not by danger, but by the noise only. "Effective immediately, you *don't* chase fox-trots of questionable virtue through the outskirts of New Pleiku." *Foxtrot* was military phonetic for *female*. "You *do* inspect your slick with a fine-tooth comb in search of any irreg-ularities that—"

"We already do that, Sarge." Larson slowly shook his head

from side to side and began fishing through the tank of solvent for his rifle barrel—a sure sign he was going to ignore anything else Zack had to say.

"Fine. Now, you *don't* trade greenbacks for war trophies from the Lurps loitering in the company area. Henceforth, the MPs will keep all Sneaky Petes movin' in the direction they're pointed and confiscate all firearms of dubious integrity.

"Dubious integrity?" Larson gave Brody a sarcastic nod.

"And in the event you have already violated this directive"— Zack's smile became an accusing leer as he zeroed-in on Larson—"you *don't* tag same as 'award plaques,' *Professor,* and attempt to ship 'em back to The World through the APO!"

Larson just shrugged and kept wiping down the M-16 barrel without looking up.

"You *do* place your name on the three rosters hanging outside the CP—one for guard duty, one for LPs, and one for KP—and you do check same three times a day to make sure you know what time you're to report for duty where applicable." Zack wadded up an empty cigarette pack on the barrel beside his boot and lobbed it at Lee. "And that *don't* mean spinning around in front of the damn thing three times in one visit, *Lawrrr*ence!"

"Whatever you say, bwana-san."

"So what's the bad news, oh illustrious leader?" Brody experienced a surge of courage and stood up. He tried to knock Zack off balance with a good-natured slug, but the ex-boxer brought his leg up defensively and whirled around. The Whoremonger's feet were kicked out from under him. On the way down, Brody nearly toppled one of the solvent tanks.

No one took sides. No one laughed except Brody and Zack. It was just something traditional between squad vets. The NCO made no attempt to help Treat up.

"The bad news is that a VC agitprop is in the area, gentlemen. Elusive buggers, too. Recon almost had 'em last week, but they slipped past the 'bush, and two tower rats have seen 'em probin' the wire since."

"The bitch?" asked Lee, suddenly interested.

"Right." Zack's chest expanded when he realized he finally had all their attention. "At least twenty-five heavily armed men led by a female Viet Cong in her early twenties. Now what more could you well-hung hot dogs ask for?"

54

"I heard she's a real looker, Sarge." Lee patted his crotch affectionately. "Me an' Little Joe here would sure love to meet her."

"Did you hear that?" Fletcher elbowed Brody. "'Little Joe?'"

"He told *me* he didn't have one," Brody whispered back, "that some geisha up in Tokyo-town gobbled it up!"

Fletcher turned to face Lee. "Gobble gobble. . ."

All the ribbing seemed to go straight over Zack. "Well, you just may get your chance, soldier," he told Lee. "Because beginning tonight, those of you who aren't pullin' guard or LP duty will be humpin' the perimeter and the road to Pleiku in search of little Miss Claymore and her platoon of stick grenadiers."

"After *dark*?" Lee's eyes lit up. He didn't mind riding choppers into the night, even escorting Dustoffs to a blacked-out LZ. But patrolling the boonies on foot after the sun went down was not on his list of extracurricular activities. Lee had become a gunship bum. Bush patrols were something *other* soldiers endured.

"Until reinforcements from Danang and An Khe arrive so we can complete our sweep of the Ia Drang in style, the CO wants you men participating in high-profile roadside patrols at sunup. Seems the cunt Cong and her boys have been ambushin' supply convoys at predawn for the most part. After dusk, you'll also be settin' up counter-ambushes along the Maze in hopes of contacting them."

"Sounds like a twenty-five-hour day to me," the Professor complained.

"Shut up and eat it like a man, Larson." Zack proceeded to light up one of his cigars.

"The Maze" was an intricate tangle of hidden trails meandering through the bush between the Tea Plantation and Plei Me.

"The sooner you band o' outlaws nab this chick"—Zack produced a crude bounty poster the QCs were passing around the area—"the sooner you can catch some Zs before the big operation."

"The big operation?" Lee did not sound as enthusiastic as the NCO towering over him. He took one of the Wanted leaflets and stared at the unsmiling face framed by long, jet-black hair. A

55

Vietnamese mug shot.

"Soon as we get some more cherries in from An Khe"—Zack rubbed his thick hands together—"we gonna hit the Ia Drang in force and pound the NVA flat as their Ho Chi Minh sandals." His knuckles popped, and Lee swallowed so hard that Fletcher heard him and started giggling like a schoolboy who'd slipped a tack on the teacher's chair and was waiting for her to sit down.

At that moment bushes behind one of the helicopters began shaking, and Lee dove for his rifle. Eyes wide, Larson began slamming the parts of his pistol back together.

A large black-and-white magpie rose from the thorns, squawking as its great wings flapped in terror.

Fletcher giggled again, but Larson continued reassembling his sidearm—the bush was still moving.

"Here comes trouble." Zack took his own hand off the exposed butt of a holstered .45 pistol.

Staggering out of the bushes like a four-legged drunk, a large, brown, short-haired mutt with one ear in shreds appeared beneath the parked gunship.

"Choi-oi!" Brody called out the dog's name and, although its tail began wagging slowly, the animal's gaze remained fixed on the escaping bird. *"Choi-oi!"* Brody called again, slapping his thigh threateningly. "Get your AWOL ass over here, you worthless mongrel!"

Choi-oi's head finally came down to earth as he stared at the group of soldiers. It cocked to one side as he attempted to place a face with the voice.

Now that he had the dog's attention, Brody slapped his thigh again. *"Choi-oi, lai-day!"* He switched to Vietnamese. *Get over here!*

Choi-oi started forward, his tail wagging furiously now, then he slid to a halt and began sniffing the air cautiously.

"That's the goofiest dink mutt I ever saw." Zack laughed as he turned and started back to the command post.

"Come on, moron." Brody buried his hand in a thigh pocket as if searching for treats. *"Lai-the fuckin'-day!"*

But *Choi-oi* was having nothing to do with them. He'd caught the scent of cleaning solvent, and this was one dog who hated that smell as much if not more than Brody himself. He sniffed the air again, sneezed, rubbed the earth with his snout and

56

shook his head from side to side, attempting to clear his nostrils. To the men, it looked as if he were refusing Brody's order with a blatant "No!" and they all erupted into laughter at *Choi-oi*'s antics.

The mutt, well aware he was the center of attention now, began wagging nonstop. His front paws danced about uncertainly, shoulder blades dipping, but his hind quarters refused to move.

"Suit yourself, skuzzball." Brody pulled a butterscotch kiss from his thigh pocket, unwrapped it, and plopped it into his mouth. *Choi-oi* began whining, and a satisfied smile crept across Brody's face as he lay back under the sun.

Choi-oi, a mongrel of undetermined origin, had been the camp's mascot since Day One. He'd loitered from tent to tent long before anyone could remember. Some of the old-timers claimed the mutt used to hang around the Special Forces camp at Plei Me until the Green Berets were all out on a mission one night and the 'Yard strikers trapped poor *Choi-oi* in a duffel bag and almost had him for midnight chow. The Viets considered dog a delicacy in that region of the Central Highlands, and *Choi-oi* was enough mongrel to feed a whole longhouse. But *Choi-oi* had escaped somehow.

Legend had it poor *Choi-oi* survived several shootings by both communist and friendly forces, refusing to die. His rib cage contained many large-caliber bullet scars. Sgt. Delgado, the medic, once ran a blood test on the mutt during one of his rare breaks between battles, and the results revealed *Choi-oi*'s original "owners" had fed him hallucinogens sometime in the past, in an obvious attempt to overdose the dog. *Choi-oi* was still prone to weak-kneed, groggy flashbacks when they were least expected. The mutt's courage was well known among First Cav troopers. He seemed to fear nothing (including bombs and bullets), except monsoon downpours and despised Vietnamese prostitutes more than he hated the Viet Cong.

"Choi-oi" was Vietnamese for "outrageous!" or "God-damn!" or "You've got to be kidding!" or, more closely, "holy shit!" In other words, there is no precise translation from the Vietnamese to the English. *Choi-oi*'s personality and his pedigree were similarly unclassifiable.

"Come on, boy." Brody slipped his prized python head off a loop on his web belt and held it out. "Come 'ere!"

Spotting the reptilian appetizer, *Choi-oi* growled and attacked, tail still wagging.

When he was midway across the landing pad tarmac, a shot rang out, the mutt yelped, his front legs collapsed, and he rolled end over end under one of the gunships, blood spraying from the wounded limb.

"What the fu—" Fletcher stood up, and a slug knocked aside the helmet he'd been sitting on. Another round struck a helicopter rotor and ricocheted into the sky with a sharp *twang!*

"Sniper!" Brody finally yelled, diving beside the tank of cleaning solvent. A string of bullets from the tree line beat across the metal container, inches above his head, and the rust-colored liquid began draining down on him.

"Goddamit! I'm gonna get that motherfucker!" Fletcher was grinding his teeth as he jumped over Brody, rifle in hand. ' I'm gonna kill that zip sonofabitch if it's the last thing I do!"

Another burst of AK rounds pounded across the landing pad tarmac like invisible hammers, heading directly for him. After slamming a banana clip into the well of his M-16, Snakeman had a change of heart and rolled to the side and out of the way. He had no idea exactly where the gunman was hiding.

Another bullet flattened a jeep tire behind Lee and then punctured the radiator. With a mournful hiss, the area filled with a silver cloud of steam.

"Anyone got a bead on the bastard?" Fletcher yelled after the sniper popped off the final round before ejecting an empty magazine.

"Somewhere in the trees!" Larson was digging a trench with his bare hands where the tarmac ended and the red clay of the Central Highlands took over. "Somewhere in the treeline between those two choppers!"

"No shit," Brody muttered under his breath as every American there listened to the Soviet-made magazine clatter to the ground in the distance. *"Anybody got a make on that?"*

"Negative!" three soldiers replied as if one. They were all keeping their heads down.

A few more shots ricocheted about the landing pad, keeping the soldiers pinned down. A jeep windshield shattered, then collapsed, sprinkling fragments into Lee's collar, and a bullet passed through dozens of tents, striking the colonel's podium

58

several hundred yards away but failing to hit the First Cavalry horse-head emblem.

"Snakeman!" Brody motioned for Fletcher to coordinate their efforts. He delivered a sequence of hand signals as stray rounds bounced about between them, knocking over a canteen and deflating another tire. "I've had enough of this crap! Cover me, then after I get under that deuce-and-a-half, swing around to your lima!"

"*Count* on it, Treat!" Fletcher rolled from cover and came up beside one of the parked jeeps.

The sudden, deafening silence stopped both soldiers in their tracks.

The shooting had ceased.

Choi-oi began whining again for attention and, high above, the magpie screeched down at him as if with taunting insults.

"Well, fuck me 'till it hurts." Brody lowered his rifle and sat down on an empty gas can, out in the open.

"*Bat con ga xo lon me may!*" Fletcher appeared in the harsh sunlight, waving his fist and rifle at the distant treeline. "Tomorrow you die, *du ma!*"

A few palm fronds seemed to wave back, but most just hung limply in the oppressive, inescapable heat. Brody, watching Snakeman create a scene, just shook his head in resignation.

The sniper was gone.

No one rushed to mount a grand search. They had always proved useless in the past. The VC rifleman managed to elude them every time. He couldn't shoot worth a damn, but he was a veritable escape artist.

Lee stumbled as he was crawling out from under one of the jeeps, and his M-16 discharged, sending a tracer toward the clouds moving in overhead. Every man except one dove behind cover again.

The Whoremonger leaned back against one of the Quad-50s and quietly pounded his fist against an open palm, lost in thought. He listened to the punctured tire hissing and watched bird shit drop from the sky.

CHAPTER 6

Brody hugged the smelly mongrel while Fletcher dabbed his paw with rubbing alcohol as other soldiers climbed out from under jeeps or the tank of cleaning solvent. "You'll be okay, *Choi-oi*." Brody held on tight as Snakeman ran a cotton swab along the bloody injury. "It's only a flesh wound." But if he was expecting the mutt to howl, Treat was pleasantly disappointed. *Choi-oi*'s one good ear stood up, his face rolled to the side, a questioning look across it, then he jumped up and licked the surprised door gunner full across the chops.

"Hold still, Rover!" Fletcher began wrapping the wound with an empty ammo bandolier. "Christ, I never knew canines bled so much." He tightened the cap on the small vial of Iso-propyl and slipped it back in an empty first-aid pouch. "Never hit the ville without it." He winked over at Treat. "Little dab on the ol' whanger after a quickie in Fifty-P Alley, and you're safe. Kills *anything*. Good for crotch rot too, *if* you catch it soon enough."

"Spare me the preventive medicine lecture, Snakeman." Brody set *Choi-oi* down and watched the dog race off into the trees, barking nonstop.

"A little free advice can go a long—"

"Think we oughta follow him?" Lee was beside them now, decked out with ammo belts crisscrossing his chest, bandit style. A heavy Hog-60 lay cradled in his arms. He pointed after the animal.

"*Choi-oi* don't know his ass from an ant hill." Fletcher seemed suddenly disgusted with the mutt.

"Luke the Gook's gone anyway." Larson joined them, a rifle in both hands. "Dropped down into his damn spider hole and beat feet back through the center of the Earth or to his frat house on Berkeley campus."

"If the fucker has a tunnel system, we'd o' found it by now, Professor." Brody locked eyes with him.

Larson looked away. "Then *you* explain it to me, Treat. A rain forest ghost?"

But Brody could provide no explanation. The sniper had been harassing them for weeks now. Random attacks, at different hours of the day or night, often varying in duration. But though the VC had damaged a lot of property, he had yet to kill or even wound anybody. *Choi-oi* was his first victim. At first Buchanan had sent a counter-sniper team after the man, but he proved as elusive as a phantom, and the colonel finally elected to leave him in place, unchallenged. Should the First Cav trap and terminate the guerrilla, the enemy hierarchy might replace him with a marksman who could hit what he was shooting at.

A monstrous shadow fell across Brody's face, and the air was suddenly one continuous chopping vibration, disrupted by a blur of rotors as Warlokk's gunship hovered overhead.

Fletcher rushed up beside Brody and waved the Cobra off as the Whoremonger just shrugged his shoulders. Someone had radioed-in the sniper, and other helicopters could be heard in the distance, rushing to the area.

The warrant officer spotted Treat's indifference, banked slowly to the right, nose dropping, and was gone. He circled the tree line along one edge of the pad several times, then returned to whatever mission Charlie Tango had pulled him from.

The other gunships aborted the assist and never showed up.

"We gotta do something about that asshole Cong sonofabitch." Fletcher wrapped an arm around Brody's shoulder. He seemed to be leading the Spec-4 toward the mess hall, abandoning their disassembled weapons. "Set up some kinda trap or something...work up *some* kinda strategy, you know? The nerd is really startin' to get on my nerves." With a mere chin movement, he motioned Lee to keep an eye on their firearms.

Brody remained pessimistic. 'He doesn't keep any specific pattern, Fletch. We're not even sure he's VC, okay? Might be an NVA pro, direct from Hanoi."

"The way *he* shoots?" Fletcher laughed.

"You never know. Maybe he's psy-ops...just fuckin' with our minds. Did you ever think about that? Lot more goofy things have come outta this alleged war. Remember that time—"

A 2nd lieutenant was running between the tents and around parked vehicles, head twitching back and forth, eyes wide and unblinking. He was decked out in full combat gear: helmet,

61

flak jacket, frag harness, and mask pouch. He wore a pistol and folded poncho-liner on his web belt. The man's ruck bounced about heavily against his haunches and was obviously loaded down with extra ammo magazines. He carried a shiny new M-16 with a 30-round banana clip in one hand.

"Hey, check *this* cat out." Larson joined him. "He's still got traces of *coz* on that flash suppressor."

" Anyone hurt? Everybody okay?" The officer was not even slowing for answers as his eyes darted about, seeking out casualties. "Anyone hurt? Everyone okay?"

"We all seem to be okay, sir." Lee had to sidestep out of the lieutenant's path. "All except *Choi-oi*. But he'll probably be okay *rikky-tik*."

The lieutenant skidded into the tank of cleaning solvent, upsetting it. What remained of the filthy red liquid below the line of bulletholes splashed down onto his spit-shined jungle boots, but he didn't seem to notice. Lee cringed as the corrosives ate down into the carefully pampered layers of black *Kiwi* wax, but the semi-FNG was oblivious of the damage. "Choi-*what?*"

"*Choi-oi*, sir. Our mutt. Well"—Lee sensed a regs violation report brewing—"*Fletcher*'s dog."

"*What?*" Snakeman's chin flew in Lee's direction like a fist. Larson laughed and popped a handful of purple bubble gum into his mouth.

"You know." Lee's features compressed into a hypnotist's as he tried to convey his thoughts. Fletcher could always come up with the best, spur-of-the-moment excuses to jerk them out of a jam. He had a talent for lying without blushing, or breaking eye contact, or allowing a crack into his voice. And now was the time.

"I don't know what the hell you're talking about." Snakeman stomped away, abandoning his plans to share a pot of army brew with Treat.

"*Who* is your squad sergeant?" the lieutenant demanded, fists shaking as he kept them at his sides. *Everyone* in this damned division seemed to delight in keeping him in the dark.

"*Zack!*" Lee spoke more to Brody than anyone, and his tone was one of urgent concern. Sergeant Zack had last been seen bowing out in the direction of the tree line. Perhaps the sniper *had* finally taken out a GI and not just a motor pool full of jeeps.

"*Sgt.* Zack is a *platoon* sergeant," the lieutenant corrected Lee, but the enlisted men were ignoring him now as they raced toward the tree line, following *Choi-oi's* tracks.

But there was no sign of the black NCO. No corpse gathered horseflies under the steaming sun. "And no blood trail anywhere," Larson and Lee announced simultaneously—the men had spread out between the vehicles and parked aircraft.

"What's all the ruckus about over there?" Fletcher pointed in the direction of the Club, a hundred yards away in the middle of the compound.

It sounded like a fight. And it didn't look combat related. Americans were arguing.

The Club had originally been a combination bar and lounge catering exclusively to NCOs, where the sergeants could share free lukewarm beers from companies stateside, most notably Pabst Blue Ribbon and Budweiser. But after the supply sergeant traded a truckload of NVA belts to a rescued Air Force pilot for his portable 'fridge, and Zack "liberated" a generator from the marines during a bogus IG inspection, Col. Buchanan decreed that the enlisted men could also relax there, since there was no EM club to speak of. After all, this *was* a combat zone. It was not uncommon to see officers fraternizing there too. Since it was an unwritten rule that gunship crews did not discriminate because of rank—they all slept in the same chopper while on Alert status or in the boonies, and ate together during field ops—why should their drinking habits be any different? Warrant officers fell into that limbo that knew no rank—you could salute them, but you'd better call them "Mister" and not "Sir" —and were therefore welcome everywhere.

"Somebody better supply me with some answers, gentlemen, and I want them *pronto!*" The lieutenant pushed his·helmet back on his head, obviously bewildered, but he had all but been forgotten. The sniper was old business. Brody and the others were running toward the club. A fight was brewing, and it looked like it was going to be black on black!

When they got closer, all smiles faded. Mohammed was braced in the club's doorway, one arm wrapped around a white nurse's throat, a grenade with no pin clutched in sweat-soaked fingers. His other hand held a straight razor against the wo-

63

man's heart. "Go ahead, Zack!" Abdul was screaming. Spittle collected in a white foam at the edges of his mouth. "*Shoot*, you halfbreed bastard, 'cause it's lights-out, one way or the other! I'm goin' home! My tour's over!"

"You'll go home in a *box*, boy!" Sgt. Zack, feet braced apart firmly, was leaning into his M-16. He was about twenty feet away from Mohammed and aiming for the militant's head. "I can't *miss* at this range, that's for damn sure!"

"Drop the grenade and release Lt. Maddox," Zack demanded in a calm voice, "or me and Mr. Colt gonna catapult your worthless black ass back to Islam, *Clarence*."

"My name is Elijah!" the militant screamed with righteous conviction, dropping his head back for an instant. "But you, Uncle Thomas, and *you!*" He glared at the soldiers gathering around. "You whitebread mo'fuckers can call me Abdul Mohammed!"

"Your name is *shit*, nigger." Zack was slowly advancing, one step at a time.

The insane sparkle left Mohammed's eyes for a moment and he stared across the open space at Zack, unblinking. A grin slowly curled his lips back, and the madness returned as the radical flashed a Death's-head leer. "Then you're the toilet, Leo."

Erupting into a demonic laugh, Mohammed pulled Nurse Maddox down into a squat in front of him then slowly rolled the grenade toward Sgt. Zack.

CHAPTER 7

Zack was the only man there who did not flatten out in the red dust when the frag rolled to a stop in front of his boots. Zack and Brody.

The Whoremonger, true to his reputation for impulsive behavior, was airborne.

He flew through the tension-thick air like a bona fide hero and plopped onto the grenade. Cupping the M-26 against his belly, he curled up into the fetal position, hoping it would be over fast, without too much pain...and wondering why he'd been unable to control the urge to bolt so foolishly into the kill zone. Maximum effective range. Casket City.

Nurse Maddox screamed, but the grenade failed to detonate. She screamed again—longer this time—but it still refused to explode.

The frag was a dud.

"It's the thought that counts, Whoremonoxide," Zack whispered loudly through gritted teeth without looking down. The eye he aimed with still had Abdul Mohammed centered in the M-16's short-range sights.

"That's Whore*monger*." Brody slowly uncoiled and opened his eyes. For some reason he was flushing with embarrassment. The visions of heroism were fading as his ears told him men were gathering around the standoff again.

"Whatever." Zack was no less than ten feet away from the hostage and her captor now.

Brody refused to move below the neck. Perhaps it was his *karma* that was keeping the frag inert. One false move and...

"Put down the blade, Crump." Zack's words were shattering and scattering his thoughts, dissolving the almost spiritual relationship he was forming with the death piece against his gut. "Put down the blade, and we'll get in out of the sun, pop some cans and sip some suds, and talk it over. Lt. Maddox never did anything to hurt you, now did she?"

"I've been shafted for the last time!" Mohammed yelled, pressing the straight razor slightly into Maddox's mint-green blouse. The OR gown was soaked in blood, and the pressure from the shimmering blade stretched the fabric taut, clearly outlining the lieutenant's shapely curves. That Nurse Maddox was wearing no bra quickly became evident, but Brody was not concentrating on the rigid swirl of nipples as he glanced up at her. He was wondering if all the blood was her own, or if she'd just left the aid station. *To mutilate such a jutting set of firm, perky breasts would be a sin against all mankind!* The voice in-

65

side his mind called out to be heard, and Brody slowly shook his head in agreement. He'd have to smuggle this woman to Manila or Cockbang on R&R and enter her in a wet T-shirt contest. *She'd be a knockout on Patpong Road!*

"Drop the razor, Private."

"I been fucked over all my life, Zack!" Mohammed had lost little of his earlier energy. "I been humiliated and cheated on and discriminated against and shafted to the max, ya hear? I been *bookoo* shafted from Boston to Bien Hoa and back. And the crap stops here! Today! *Fini,* you grandson of a honky plantation owner! *This* was the last straw!" He patted his breast pocket without elaborating.

"Just drop the razor blade, and we'll talk about it. You and me and Lt. Maddox and the colonel. It'll be all right."

"No!" Mohammed backed into the doorway, intending to retreat into the Club, but his elbows banged against wood. Someone had quietly locked the entrance behind him. "No more talk. I got mo' damn Article 15's in my two-oh-one than a fag in the monkey house. No mo' talk. Time fo' some action, bro. *Action!*"

"You hurt, Lieutenant?" Blood was now dripping from the nurse's gown, down into the dust around Mohammed's bare feet. It looked fresh to Zack.

"No, not that I know of." Maddox wasn't crying. Her eyes were dry, though she felt soaked with tears inside. She could not get them out. She had screamed earlier because death by shrapnel was shocking—even infuriating—and not on her agenda for today! She was quickly becoming incensed with Abdul Mohammed and his personal problems. He had been a pain in the neck ever since she arrived in-country, always the first soldier in line for the A.M. sickcall. But she was powerless to act. "It's all from the OR," Maddox stammered, glancing down at her chest. "The Blues. . .they brought in an FOB team that got clobbered by a counter-ambush. We just finished sewing them up. I was only slipping into the club for a second. .just a shot to settle my nerves. . . ."

"No excuse necessary, Lieutenant—that wasn't why I was asking." Zack was now less than six feet away. "Vietnam is still a free country. . . last I heard."

"No thanks to deadbeats like me, right?" Mohammed's head

66

leaned forward, eyes bulging. "Is that what you're thinking, *bro*?"

Zack bit his lower lip in disgust and self-control. Soldiers like Crump did disgust him. They had no business being in the military—*his* military. *Damn this draft!* He felt *that* was the cause of all his problems.

"Drop the blade, Soldier."

"You wanna know what my hang-up is, Zack?" The hand that had been controlling the grenade earlier now fumbled for something in Mohammed's thigh pocket. "You really wanna know what all this is about?"

"Just drop the razor, shit-for-brains," Zack muttered, losing his patience.

"You *really* want to know why I'm bringin' all this grief down on Lt. Maddox here? Why I'm draggin' her down into my little ol' world o' hurt?" He moved the blade's edge to her throat.

Zack's lips parted, but Maddox spoke first as the straight razor split flesh. "*I* wanna know, Abdul! *I* want to know the story—the *whole* story! *Tell* me what the problem is!" Blood trickled across the sliver of cold steel, and tears finally welled up in Maddox's eyes.

Brody's eyes dropped from the outline of the lieutenant's full breasts to her belt. She wore the filmy trousers typical to most field hospitals, and as the blood began to seep down along her hips, he found himself wondering if the saturating crimson would reveal whether or not she wore undergarments. Once the crotch became soaked, would they all see her panty lines, or just a simple V like all the shapely bodies they'd drawn in the sand as boys? Would he be able to make out the lips of her vagina from this vantage point?

Brody no longer heard the exchange of words between Zack and Mohammed. He was out of the ball game with an authorized alibi. The trauma from eating the dud put him in another world, free of responsibilities. He could sit this one out, letting older men solve the crisis—no one would care. No one would blame him later, after it was all over. Hell, he was a bona fide hero. He'd recovered Mohammed's fumble and made the danger disappear!

Brody stared up at her, the exchange of words a series of inaudible echoes between his ears that made no sense. He wished the idiot with the straight razor would release the lady in green so she could come over and sit on his face.

Maddox was in her late twenties at the most. She was slender and, despite the unflattering manner in which she kept her long blond hair rolled up in a bun atop her head, extremely beautiful, thought Brody. Never mind the weary face that always had a frown marring it. She was a woman who expected everything to go wrong, a constant pessimism her green, blood shot eyes could not belie.

The lieutenant's father was a high-ranking general officer, stationed in Saigon, who never forgave her for enlisting for Vietnam without discussing the matter with him first. He was forever attempting to get Lisa reassigned to 3rd Field Hospital, a few blocks from MACV, the American Military Assistance Command in Vietnam, but she refused to leave the Central Highlands, preferring to work long shifts in a mobile surgical-aid station camped on the edge of ever-shifting battlefields. When in the mood to tease her father, she'd send him Cambodian crossbows or an NVA pistol the grateful GIs who filtered through her hospital gave her as gifts and joke that she'd captured them herself on "a busy Friday night." All her free time—which was rare indeed—was devoted to the abandoned children at a refugee camp orphanage managed by Catholic nuns outside Pleiku City. There were few romantic interests in her past, and none whatsoever presently.

She was no longer a newby. The day before marked her sixth month in-country. She assumed her lack of promotions was due to a jealous head nurse who resented the radiance Lisa possessed even after a twenty-four-hour shift, but Maddox did not protest. She was doing what she wanted to do. Rank meant little if anything to her; and all her money went to the orphans anyway.

"Drop the blade, Clarence, or you're the lowlife cockroach I always suspected, and I'm the can o' Raid!"

"You wanna know what this is all about, niggah?" Mohammed had fished a Polaroid snapshot from his thigh pocket and threw it, Frisbee fashion, to Zack.

The sergeant was not one to fall for distractions, though, and he let the photo flutter to the ground.

"No sweat, papa-san!" Mohammed came up with another

picture. He held it out for all to see. "'Cause that lily-white fuckwad back in The World send me *three* o' these goddamned things, and a hellacious letter full o' captions, okay? Want me to read 'em to ya? Huh? Want me to?"

Zack refused to look at the photo, but Brody and the others could not avoid the interracial couple tangled up on the cherry-red, satin sheets. A young black woman with flowing, bleached hair covering her shoulders lay on her stomach and elbows, haunches propped up strategically and spread wide for the camera. But a white man was in the way. He had mounted her from behind, and was holding onto ample breasts that swelled out like milk chocolate balloons as he flattened them against her ribcage. Both lovers wore beaming, devilish smiles for the photographer. Everything was in perfect focus exept the man's pale buttocks as he pumped away at his partner.

"That's my *bitch* this honky piece o' dead meat is humpin'!" Mohammed yelled into Zack's face. They were nearly nose-to-nose now. "Wanna hear what that cocksucker had the gall to say to ol' Elijah, Leo*POLLD?* Do you . . . want . . . to . . . hear . . . it?"

"Whatever keeps you mellow, fellah." Someone behind them giggled—it sounded like Fletcher—but Zack was not amused.

Mohammed pulled a piece of paper from his pocket but did not unfold it. He quoted from memory: "White boy say my bitch was the best piece o' beaver he ever had, Leo my man! White boy say he wished he'd switched to dark meat long ago. Can you believe that?"

"*Believe* it," someone whispered in the growing crowd behind Zack. Brody recognized Larson's voice.

"White boy say Abdul's bitch worth at *least* forty greenbacks a lay. Say he gonna shack up with ol' Tanya and send her out on the street nights so he can retire early. Do you believe that jive, *SARG*ent?"

"*Believe* it," the Professor repeated, using a metallic, robot-like tone.

"White boy say he well aware ol' Abdul Elijah Mohammed got five months left on his Tour 365 and that he safe from a fraggin' 'till April showers bring May flowers. White boy say he gonna beat feet by March, say he gonna play it safe, say maybe he take ol' Tanya with him 'cause the black bitch can't do without playin' that ol' ivory skinflute 'least twice a night.

"Well, slamdunk my ding dong, Sergeant, 'cause i's over! This nigger demands an early-out! This nigger demands to be on a flight manifest by tomorrow and on his freedom bird homeward-bound in one notch and a wake-up! This nigger goin' ETS *today*, or Whitey here"—he lifted Nurse Maddox off her feet slightly—"gonna follow Mohammed to the promised land!"

When the blade sliced deeper and Maddox groaned—more from nausea than pain—Zack made his move. The big sergeant jumped forward and pressed Mohammed's nose flat with the muzzle of his M-16. When the militant's eyes merely flared with renewed determination, and not the terror he'd expected, Zack brought the rifle butt up in a blinding swing that connected savagely with Abdul's jaw, knocking him off his feet. But he took Maddox down with him.

"Release the lieutenant!" Zack rammed the rifle's flash suppressor into Mohammed's ear until he drew blood.

"You broke my fuckin' jaw, Leo!" the black radical cried.

"Release Lt. Maddox, or your next home away from home's gonna be a GI-issue casket, Crump!"

"OKAY! Okay, Sergeant." The private hesitated, shaking his head back and forth violently. But then he closed his eyes tightly, released his hold on Maddox, and she rolled to safety. "Okay. . .but you didn't have to go and break my fuckin' jaw." He dropped the straight razor in the dust, and Zack scooped it up and tossed it behind him.

Still using his rifle, he "persuaded" Mohammed over onto his stomach and twisted his arm behind his back. Glancing over his shoulder, he growled, "One o' you men landline the MPs at Holloway to respond over here an' cart this scumbucket off o' my compound."

"With pleasure, Sarge." Zack was no longer looking back at the anxious gunship crewmen, but he recognized Fletcher's voice.

Snakeman stared at the green-and-gold combat patches on the right shoulders of the army cops leading Abdul Mohammed, alias Clarence Crump III, away in handcuffs. He decided the 18th Military Police Brigade emblem, with its green dagger flanked by gold battle axes on a Centurion-like shield, looked strac. Perhaps not as fancy as the First Cav's horse head, but sharp nonetheless. Maybe someday, after he'd put in a tour or two aboard the gunships, really earning his CIB, he'd re-up for the MPs. Yes, that would be quite a change, chasing black-market crooks and PX robbers through the concrete jungles of Saigon instead of VC through the tunnels of Tuy Hoa. It might even be a thrill to trade his rucksack and tent halves for a fancy jeep mounted with red lights and siren.

He briefly envisioned himself parked on a street corner at Tu Do and Le Loi, in starched khakis instead of tattered jungle fatigues, several ladies of the evening pinching his cheeks and running their fingers through the hair on his arms: Super Trooper Elliot Fletcher, Saigon Commando. It actually had a ring to it that wasn't so bad after all, the Snakeman decided.

Maybe he deserved to skate awhile and collect combat pay as a REMF. But then a Huey flew low overhead, its powerful rotors parting the muggy blanket of air that clung to the camp, and dragged him from his daydream. Fletcher watched the slick disappear beyond the treetops, its riders sitting in the open hatch, legs dangling in thin air as they enjoyed the scenery, miles from the mission. And Snakeman forgot about the MPs. He would always be a door-gunner—until the day he retired with the Big-20 under his belt. Or Victor Charlie plucked him from his craft like a feather from some great bird, and he was dragged down into Void Vicious.

"That was real fast thinkin' on your part, Sarge." He was beside Zack now, arms folded across his chest as he watched the huge NCO dust himself off.

"What exactly is it that you want, Fletcher my friend?" Leopold Zack was immediately suspicious of compliments from soldiers and the likes of Snakeman, a Southerner well known to be of the redneck persuasion.

"Nothin', Sarge. Nothin'. . . really. Just wanted you to know me and the guys all think you did a fine job. We was even thinkin' maybe the highest rankin' EM here today oughta write up something for the colonel to see so you could get—"

"*Get* to the point, Snakeoil." Zack's Macon accent matched Fletcher's twang word for word.

Fletcher shrugged his shoulders, did a little dance in the dust, keeping one boot immobile, and fought to keep his smile intact.

71

"Well, actually. . .'"

"I'm listening." Zack's tone did not sound promising. "Spill it."

"I was kinda hopin' you'd find it in your heart of hearts, Sarge, to. . .well. . ."

"I ain't got all day, Snakeperson. Crump really went and cramped my style with this little uprising of his, and I'm goin' to be up to my ying-yang in paperwork, which is what I came to The Nam to avoid, so unless you—"

"It's about my brother, Sarge." Fletcher's face went somber as he draped an arm around the bigger soldier's shoulder, hoping to lead him out of earshot of the others.

"Your brother?" Zack's eyebrows cocked back and he looked down at the PFC, expecting a request for emergency leave. Family was sacred. Family was what serving in the military was all about, as far as Zack was concerned.

"Yessir. He's MIA, and—"

"Oh, that one." Zack's head went up in resignation. He had been expecting this for quite some time, ever since they pulled roots out of An Khe. "I know the whole story, Fletcher. I've read the report."

"Then you know—"

"Missing In Action since 1963. . .shot down over the mouth of the Ia Drang. One o' them air-jockey wingnuts, wasn't he? Not that I'd hold that against the kid. . ." The label was not applied with disrespect.

"Don't know for sure, but I figure he'd about be a major by now," Fletcher calculated.

"He was presumed dead, son," the sergeant interrupted him softly, compassion in the set of his jaw. "You have to accept that and—"

"Bullshit."

"Didn't a Jolly Green check the crash site? I recall readin' something about—"

"The Chinook was shot down too." Fletcher stared at a formation of helicopters rising into the dark cloud formations along the horizon. "But *its* crew was extricated. Nobody actually landed at Richard's crash site. Nobody actually checked the wreckage or sighted any bodies or—"

"Seems I recall the report said something about the SAR

team witnessing several secondary explosions, son. The plane was totally destroyed, wasn't it? Nobody could have survived such a—"

"The report I read said SAR was receiving heavy ground fire, Sarge. I doubt they know their ass from—"

"Are you telling me you want time off to slip out into the sticks and recon a two-year-old crash site for clues or something, Private Fletcher?" Zack's chest expanded with growing impatience.

"Rich coulda bailed out before the Jolly Green got there, Sarge. He coulda parachuted—"

"His flight leader saw no 'chutes deployed in the area. That's what the report said. You knew it as well as I did. I'm sorry, but—"

"All I want is a couple of days off to check out some coordinates, Sarge, forty-eight hours to—"

"Out of the question."

"What if it was your older brother out there somewhere, Sarge?" Fletcher tried for a soft spot.

It didn't work. "Then the colonel would tell me 'out of the question,' sport."

"He might still be hidin' out there somewhere, for Christsake! He might be—"

"No way. Not after two years, son. Be realistic." Zack rubbed at a track of mosquito bites on his forearm.

"They carted half his Phantom off to some commie war museum in Laos, Sarge."

"Meaning what?"

"Meaning Charlie took a special interest in that crash; otherwise they wouldn't have gone to all that trouble to remove the wreckage and—"

"*And* any clues at the site that would assist an SAR in—"

"Richard was sharp! He would have thought of something . . .come up with some sort of signal to. . .left some kind of sign."

Fletcher had exhausted all shades of rationalization. Zack had him by the balls and would twist if he persisted. But how could he give up on his own brother, his own flesh and blood?

"Look"—Zack rested his hand on the door gunner's shoulder gently—"I'll see if I can work something out, but we need everyone we got right now for tonight. Division shoved us up a mission slot. The colonel told 'em we're short grunts and that half the birds are deadlined, but—"

"Fuck it." Snakeman pulled a long, green-and-gold serpent from the helmet hanging on his web belt and began massaging it along the hollow behind flared jaws as he turned to walk away.

"Adequately articulated, I'd say." Zack cocked an eyebrow after revealing he wasn't just another hick lifer with a grade-school education, but Fletcher didn't volunteer a reply or slow his pace.

Choi-oi bounded from the hedgerows at that moment. Eyes locked on the "toy" in Snakeman's caress, his tail wagged energetically.

"*Di di,*" Fletcher muttered, ordering the mutt to go away.

His good ear suddenly erect, *Choi-oi* slid to a stop, obvious anxiety wrinkling his snout. The dog's eyes darted from side to side, and he began howling. (Choi-oi wailed as loudly as an air-raid siren, shifting his canine gaze from soldier to soldier, barking at anyone who would listen.)

"Aw, shit." Sgt. Zack sprinted across the clearing and dove into a bunker moments before the barrage of mortars descended on the Turkey Farm.

After he rolled over a jeep hood and flattened himself beneath its protective engine block, Fletcher cheered as he watched Treat Brody make it out of the kill zone seconds before the first wave of shrapnel swept through.

Then his eyes locked on *Choi-oi.* The loyal mongrel was still in the middle of the clearing, limping about on his bandaged paw, howling his heart out, warning all his two-legged buddies. And the VC were walking their mortars straight for him.

CHAPTER 8

Brody the Whoremonger watched invisible monsters leave giant footprints in the red clay as Charlie walked his mortars practically down on top of the incorrigible mongrel from Plei Me. But Buddha smiled with favor upon *Choi-oi* that afternoon; not a single chunk of shrapnel punctured his hide, as far as Treat could tell. And through it all, the door gunners' mascot howled warning to the men who fed, housed, abused, ignored, taunted, and teased him.

"*Choi-oi,* you idiot!" Brody watched a jeep explode, flip over, and release a billowing orange fireball into the sky as its undercarriage ruptured. "You can *fini* the performance! We hear 'em now too!"

Somewhat shell-shocked, the mutt stopped barking and howling, lowered its head in an attempt to focus on the face rising above the edge of a foxhole, then charged off in Brody's direction, tail wagging furiously. "It's okay! It's okay, boy!" Treat tried to control the excited animal after it leaped on top of him. The dog's weight knocked him off his knees, and they both dropped to the bottom of the trench. *Choi-oi* immediately commenced licking the trooper's soot-covered face.

Brody's smile faded suddenly. "Oh, *Choi-oi.*" Still on his back, he rose to his elbows and smoothed the dog's coat down. "They *did* get you! The bastards *did* get ol' *Choi-oi!*" Blood was trickling from several minute puncture wounds along the mutt's backbone. "You gonna be okay, buddy?"

Choi-oi, sensing trouble by the look of concern on Brody's face, resumed licking the grunt's nose in response. "Sure you are." Treat almost patted him, but *Choi-oi* whimpered in anticipation, aware now he was a hero, WIA, and expected to play the part.

"Smart mutt." He knew the dog would be limping around camp for the next week, mooching handouts even long after his leg wound healed, but who was Brody to burst his bubble? "*Smarrrt* mutt. Yeah...go ahead and soak it up, *Choi-oi,* bask in the limelight while you can. Just sit back and take 'er easy,

75

boy. Let us human heroes handle the Cong from here on out."

He started to climb out of the foxhole, but explosions on both sides sucked the air from his lungs and sent shrapnel crisscrossing the space overhead, and he thought better of it. *Choi-oi* squeezed into a corner, whined once to voice his own concern, then covered sensitive ears with his front paws almost comically.

Lying beside each other, they watched a burst of red tracers—American—sizzle past, but there was no reply in glowing green. Charlie was not mounting a ground attack. Just the routine, zap-em-two-or-three-times-a-week mortar barrage. The enemy was hitting from the safety of jungled hills.

Several Hueys zoomed past in the direction *Choi-oi* had first heard the crump of the sixty mike-mikes being fired, and he barked once with approval.

"That's right, buddy." Brody restrained him as they watched the undersoles of several boots hurtle by. First Team's enroute to bring smoke down on Victor Charlie. First Team's gonna *get some*, pal!" *Choi-oi* barked again in agreement as more sets of boots flew past a couple of feet above their faces. The VC had ceased their mortar attack upon hearing the gunship rotors start up, and now grunts were racing through the tree line to help in the ground search. Brody heard a single burst of automatic weapons fire shortly thereafter, on the far side of the clearing, but he dismissed it as one of the FNGs losing his cool and squeezing off a clip during the ensuing panic.

"Let's you and me just sit back and watch the Hueys raise hell. Whatta ya say, boy?" A chopper banked hard to the right directly over them, and the downblast blew *Choi-oi*'s whiskers back. He lifted his muzzle into the fuel-tainted breeze, and Brody was reminded of his pet back in The World and the nights they'd cruise Hollywood Boulevard in his beat-up old convertible, both of them barking at the whores.

Lisa Maddox had frozen in her tracks when the first mortars fell. She watched in horror, petrified, as the communist projectiles landed right between the two military policemen escorting Mohammed over to their jeep. A sliver of hot, smoking shrapnel the size of her fist slammed through one of the MP's faces, depositing bits of his brain at her feet. Another fragment of fly-i:ig metal—this piece as small as the eye of a needle—struck the dead man's partner in the chest, puncturing his heart. He was dead before his body hit the ground. His trigger finger locked on rock 'n' roll, an entire banana clip chased his soul into the clouds.

Lisa Maddox screamed. She watched both soldiers fall back into the red dust, and she knew what she should be doing... how she should be treating their wounds. But all she could do was scream. Silver smoke was billowing out toward her, a swirling storm of steel was about to roll across the medical school dropout from Alexandria, Virginia—and all she could do was scream.

Her eyes watched Abdul Mohammed—still handcuffed behind the back—drop to his haunches as his escorts perished. The black prisoner was rolling on one side, out of the mortars' path, and slipping his handcuffs under his buttocks and beneath the soles of his feet until his hands were once again in front of him. Now he could at least defend himself. And he was charging toward her!

Still, all Lt. Maddox, leader of men, could do was scream. After all the medevac Dustoffs, all the torn-away limbs and ruined lives that had been wheeled on gurneys into her little world of hurt, the army nurse could only stand there, frozen to the spot, horrified. The results of war, the "fruits" of combat, had always been *brought* to her before. Never had she experienced it firsthand, up close, on such a personal level. Never had she actually participated! And now this madman they called Mohammed was rushing up to her, teeth bared.

"Learned that from the bloods, Lietuenant!" He grabbed her by the wrist and pulled her out of the clearing seconds before a string of shells landed. Broken branches and shredded leaves rained down on them as Mohammed led her deeper into the mangroves, down the hillside away from Charlie's target. "Me and the brothers been practicin' stuff like that coupla months now...." He referred to the handcuffs maneuver, "Ol' Tyrone —you know, from the MAST team—he just spent a stint at the LBJ monkeyhouse on a trumped-up dope charge. Learned all the latest tech*niques:* how to spring back off a wall first to off the Man with his own piece...how to ambush the pigs back on the block with their own—"

"What are you going to do to me?" she demanded, jerking her arm away as she slid to a halt midway down the hill. Her eyes were bulging, and rage was written across her face. Rage and terror. Her OR blouse was ripped down the middle to her waist, revealing the swell between breasts he didn't drool over but could hardly miss. Was he going to tear the rest of her clothes off, fling her into the elephant grass, and rape her? He certainly seemed animal enough, Maddox decided. And sooo black. Black as the pit her grandmother had always threatened her with as a child. Black as the devil's own lair. Lisa Maddox had always been raised to associate dark colors with things evil, objects or persons or situations to be avoided. And Vietnam had become a very dark land indeed. "What are you going to do to me?" she screamed this time, and Mohammed answered with only a bug-eyed, offended look.

He grabbed her by the shoulders, pressing close, and brandished his flaring nostrils inches from her own flawless nose. "I'm going to *save* you, ma'am." Saliva collected in a white foam at the edges of his mouth, but Mohammed's eyes suddenly took on a businesslike glaze, seeking out a mission. "Follow me." He grabbed the edges of her blouse and roughly pulled it together until she clasped the torn zipper and held it in place. Then he started to turn away.

Three guerrillas in black uniforms—sappers barely into their teens toting satchel charges and captured M-14s—stumbled into them before Mohammed had descended between the first few trees. Mouths agape, Maddox wasn't sure if the youths were more taken aback by the black soldier's wild expression or her own blond hair and tattered, revealing clothes. Before they could react, Mohammed flew forward into a karate kick that took both feet off the ground—no great trick if one took into account the hill's steep incline—but he missed nonetheless.

On the way down, he managed to grab the nearest rifle barrel and yanked it from the sapper's grasp without a struggle. Rolling through the trees, he fired off the entire magazine, spraying right to left. He wasted no second thoughts about hitting one of the satchel charges—such were the hazards of gunplay among grunts.

All three Vietnamese suffered stomach wounds.

Two were knocked backward into the trees, but the third stag-

78

gered up the hillside, reaching out for Maddox. In attempting to scramble away from him, the army nurse lost her footing on all the slippery leaves and slid right into the guerrilla's arms.

Perhaps encouraged by Mohammed's display of bravado, the lieutenant brought her fist back, but she hesitated—the youth was crying. He appeared more frightened than she! He was dying, and the horror in his eyes was laced with recognition and haunting relief.

"Lam me!" he cried out as Mohammed grabbed him by the hair from behind. *Mother!*

The black soldier had ripped a machete from one of the dead sappers' belts, and he ran it across the youth's throat with incredible force, severing his neck to the bone. Lisa Maddox closed her eyes tightly as the spray of blood splashed across her face and chest.

"What was it he called me?" she asked later, as they climbed down through the densely wooded hillside, slowly, extremely cautious now, ever-alert for more North Vietnamese as they searched for an access road that would lead them back up to the camp. "What did he say? *'Lam me.'* What does it mean?"

Abdul Mohammed did not answer immediately. He thought it over for a few seconds, as they slid down through a B-52 bomb crater littered with old VC corpses and filled with blood and rain water. "Nothin', Lieutenant." His voice was gentle, his grasp tender as he helped her up out of the pit of floating death. "Don't concern yourself with the last words of a dying gook."

"But surely—" Her model's nose was suddenly wrinkled with disgust and nausea from the stench of their surroundings.

"Forget it, ma'am. Don't mean nothin'," he muttered.

"But—"

"Mother*fucker!*" The black militant whirled around with eyes burning into her when she persisted, refusing to let it go. . .trying to exorcise the teenager's desperate plea from her mind. "The dink called you and your ancestors 'round-eyed *mother*fuckers,' okay!?"

"Oh." Maddox was at a loss for further words as they resumed their trek through the branches and severed limbs. Her eyes fell to the rotting jungle floor and stayed there. Tears streaked down her face, causing days-old eyeliner to slide down against the blood caking on her cheeks.

She would never forget the pleading look in that dying boy's eyes. Never, so long as she lived.

CHAPTER 9

"Saddle up!" Brody called over the heads of men squatting with their disassembled machine guns. "Come on, Professor, don't you hear them rotors winding up? Don't you hear *Pegasus* callin' to you? Time to ride off into Injun' country, boy. Time to *get some!*" But the draftee sitting in a tent on the far side of the Hog-cleaning pad was ignoring him.

One of the soldiers from Delta Company glanced up from the M-60 barrel he was soaking in a tub of solvent and flashed a hungry grin. "Time to go out and kill a commie for mommy!" he began to chant.

And several of the off-duty soldiers around him joined in. "Kill a commie for mommy! Kill a commie for mommy!"

Brody smiled uneasily and flipped the approving thumbs-up in their direction. "Larson!" he called out over the increasing whine of Huey turbines in the background. "Get your goofy ass in gear!"

"Fuck you and the mare you rode in on!" came the unenthusiastic reply from the four-man tent. Its entry flaps were tied back, and with the last shafts of golden dusk, Brody could see the outline of the Professor sitting at his makeshift, ammo-crate desk.

"Hands off your cock and up with your socks!" Treat kicked in the overused boot camp wake-up announcement. "Time for our pre-supper PT, Shawn: We got an FOB mission."

"Get off my case, Whoremonger! I'm busy writing my suicide note."

Shaking his head from side to side like an impatient drill sergeant, Brody placed his hands on his hips, studied a huge, black-and-blue rhino scorpion crawling along the clay at his feet for a moment, then unceremoniously crushed the arachnid under his boot and started toward the tent.

One of the door gunners from Delta glanced up from his smoke-caked swivel mount and muttered, "The CO oughta bust that yellow-lipped pussy back to E-Nothing, and boot his chickenshit ass down to LBJ," as Treat walked by.

Without slowing, Brody merely smiled and said, "The Professor's just havin' a bad month, Nelson. Cut him some slack."

"Well, he's been writin' that damn 'suicide note' of his for months now. And I'm getting tired of hearin' about it, okay?"

"Yah," agreed a stocky weight lifter sitting beside him, who hadn't lifted a barbell since leaving the states but somehow managed to keep his physique firm and bulging while in The Nam. "Wish the damn malingerer would just pull the pin or eat his .45 or jump out a Huey over Void Vicious—whatever he's got planned."

"Malingerer?" Brody watched the giant bend a rifle-cleaning rod between two little fingers. "I'm impressed, Hatchethead. Already up to the *M*s, eh?" His words were soaked with sarcasm.

"My quote is five new words a day, oh mordant one."

Herman "Hatchethead" Monrovia, who got his nickname from the shape of his custom-trimmed butch haircut, had, along with everyone else in Delta Company, received a pocket dictionary from some Webster Company executive in New York City whose son happened to be a First Cav trooper. Everyone, including the executive's son, had dumped the books on the An Khe black market. Everyone except Hatchethead.

He was tired of hearing the "all brawn and no brain" remarks and determined to read the entire dictionary through from A to Z.

"Well, if I was a teacher back at Hollywood High," Brody said, "you'd get an *A* for 'articulate' in my book, Hatchethead."

"'Articulate?'" Monrovia turned to the man seated next to him as Brody walked on. "What the hell does 'articulate' mean?" With thick, greasy fingers, he fumbled for his pocket dictionary and it plopped into the tub of solvent. "You cocksucker, Brody."

"I'm busy." Larson sensed the Whoremonger coming through the flaps, though he had entered silent as a panther on the prowl.

Brody abandoned the theatrics. "Come on, Professor. Zack's on the rag over that incident with Mohammed, and he's out to kill the first grunt that don't play the game. If it ain't the commies, it could just as easily be you and me. He's windin' up a coupla slicks for an FOB romp in the sticks." FOB was complicated infantryman terminology for "Fly Over Border." "Cambodia, here we come!"

Private E-Deuce Shawn Larson paused in his writings to glance up at Brody. He noticed the Spec-4 was, except for his jump boots, wearing sterile clothing, civilian garments with no unit identification or rank insignia. A submachine gun of East-Bloc manufacture, suspended from a sling over his shoulder, hung against the Whoremonger's hip. "Fuck Black Bart with a splintered broomstick," Larson said slowly.

"Gimme a break, sport." Brody frowned. "I already had powdered eggs that were a shade too green. No need to go upsettin' my tummy with gross-out talk, okay? And all we got to look forward to during the mission is a case of ham-and-motherfuckers I saw Lee sliding into *Pegasus*."

"Whatever." The Professor made no move to rise. But his mood suddenly shifted. "Listen-up, *slick*." He smiled proudly and lifted a black-and-white grid notebook until the last shafts of sunset splashed across it.

Brody folded his arms across his chest in resignation as the *whop-whop-whop* of chopper rotors rose to a deafening clamor outside.

"It really pains me to embarrass my family and the schoolgirl I lived in sin with for two years back in the Wonderful World, and all my unborn sons, but I really feel in my heart that the time has come to say good-bye to my miserable existence on this Earth and seek elevation to a higher plain. . . ."

Growing nervous now as he envisioned Sgt. Zack jumping down off their waiting slic to search for the two "idiots who are holding up my mission," Brody silently opened Larson's footlocker and pulled a German-made MP-40 from beneath neatly aligned stacks of translated Yukio Mishima novels.

82

Larson had been penning a suicide note for months now—ever since he arrived in Vietnam. He had yet to carry out the threats of *felo-de-se,* but forced his squad to listen to the daily entries, often soliciting critiques afterward.

"It was never my desire to seek plastic glory against my fellow man on distant, foreign soil. It was never my desire to don the uniform of Imperialist plunderers and journey to a beautiful land of temples and rice paddy panorama to burn down huts and kill women because they wear black pajamas in the night and fight for nationalism and revolution at the sides of their underdog husbands, sons, and fathers. I am no communist sympathizer, but neither do I believe in attempting to change, by force, the traditional customs and political evolution of an entire people, no matter how alien or unpalatable their culture or ideological views are to my own. I will no longer participate in a splendid little war where our 'allies' smile at us in the daytime, produce obscene gestures when we turn our backs, and shoot American-made armament into our bodies after dark. I refuse to kill another man in this hypocritic combat zone of emotions and contradictions. I *will not* carry another weapon in anger against the peoples of Viet Nam, nor will I board another helicopter gunship. And since confinement at hard labor in a stockade filled with deviants, madmen, and other assorted perverts would also be totally unacceptable, I refuse to be incarcerated for my unwillingness to fight further. Since our all-knowing, all-seeing, all-asshole chaplain claims that, because of my past acts of heroism and bravery displayed under fire—I call them simple instincts to survive—I do not qualify for conscientious-objector status, I am left with no other choice but to end this phase of my miserable existence and hope the 'Powers That Be' grant me a more transcendental essence in my next life, though I must admit I would prefer rebirth in my late teens as no one should have to go through another childhood like—"

"Come on, Professor." Brody pulled Larson to his feet and slammed the submachine gun against his chest. "Either *eat* your '40 right now or Zack's gonna have your skull on a platter for midnight chow, and you *know* how he likes fish heads and rice!" Stepping back, the specialist nearly stumbled into a deep trench beside Larson's cot.

The pacifist was becoming "short," or nearing the end of his tour of duty in Vietnam, and, despite the suicidal behavior, had also become obsessed with precautions against rear-echelon disaster. He refused to sleep above ground, in case of a surprise nighttime mortar attack, and when he did eventually retire in the evening, or in the pre-dawn hours after a midnight mission, it was in full combat gear. Larson never slept without his helmet, flak jacket, and boots on as he rapidly approached single-digit midget status.

Pausing to stare into Brody's eyes, Larson realized he could not win a game of mindfuck with the Whoremonger. "Aw, screw it!" He grabbed the weapon and stormed out of the tent, leaving his hundred-page suicide note open, its humidity-soaked pages with their smeared and soggy entries flapping in the rotorwash from outside.

Both gunnies were relieved to see that Zack appeared preoccupied with other matters as they ran toward their slick. Some replacements had arrived just as the mission was about to lift off, and the Black Buddha wanted his newbies aboard for the ride.

PFC Lee had obviously been late for the muster also. He sprinted past Brody and Larson, hoping to sneak aboard one of the gunships before Zack spotted him.

"*Em*-ho!" One of the replacements grabbed Lee as he rushed by, nearly pulling the Japanese-American off his feet. "Long time no see! I thought you snatched a clerk-'n-jerk slot down in Saigon for Christsake. Great to see you, bro!"

"Hey, Beanpole!" The replacement turned to a tall, skinny FNG crouching beneath the whirring rotor blades a few feet away. "It's *Em*-ho! Can you believe our luck?"

"'*Em*-ho?'" Brody pulled Lee aboard their gunship and handed him a ruck stuffed with AK-47 banana clips. "Where the hell'd you get a name like '*Em*-ho?'" He cast a quizzical, accusing smirk.

"Aw, them bicycle seat lickers shared a barracks with me back in Basic. You know how fucked up BCT was. All the DIs' nicknames stuck."

"But '*Em*-ho?' What the hell does '*Em*-ho' mean?"

"E...M...H...O...." Lee frowned, translating. "Early Morning Hard-On."

"What!?" Brody laughed as he strapped himself in beside Larson. "I thought it was something in Japanese! You know, some kinda mysterious ninja stuff, or—"

"My early morning hard-ons were pretty mysterious." Lee sat on the floor in the middle of the cabin and raced to fill his magazines with cartridges before Zack boarded, straight face intact.

"You just gotta elaborate on this line, Big L. I mean, who woulda thought—"

"I used to wake up every morning with this hellacious hard-on poking up through my shorts."

Brody laughed again, louder this time.

"I had a top bunk," Lee explained. "And you know how baggy them army-issue, GI shorts were. My pecker had nowhere else to go but up. Straight out. Shit, they woke you at four in the fuckin' morning, remember? Right in the middle of the greatest wet dreams. It never failed: One minute Nancy Kwan is sittin' on my face...you know Nancy Kwan. That knock-out who played the nymph of the night in *World of Suzie Wong*? Well, one minute she's sittin' on my face, and the next thing I know Drill Sgt. Amsel is bangin' a transcan lid against my bunk and screamin' in my ear to knock him out fifty push-ups for poppin' a boner on army time without Uncle Sammy's permission!

"There I was, four o'clock in the motherfuckin' A.M. and a blinding bare lightbulb is hanging from the ceiling, six inches above my nose, and Amsel's spittin' out nonstop insults about my whanger. The bastard started calling me Em-ho after that. You know, pronouncing it: just the way I did right now, two syllables. And he had this godawful phony accent. Chinese-laundry lisp or something.

"Every morning he'd burst into the barracks yelling, 'Mister Em-ho better not be pullin' on his pud up there! Mister Em-ho, front and center!' All the recruits had quite a perpetual laugh at my expense. Amsel never picked on anybody else!"

"Bummer, bud." Brody leaned closer. With the rotors pulling pitch now, he could barely hear the soldier.

"I damn near overdosed on saltpeter, you know? But nothing worked. If it wasn't Nancy Kwan, then it was France Nuyen in *South Pacific*. Remember her? Sexy little Liat, the island maiden?"

"The musical?" Brody shook his head. He felt obligated to humor the man even though his vision filled with black bulk as Sgt. Zack climbed aboard.

"Yah!"

"I seem to recall it."

"Well, nothin' worked, Whoremonger. Every morning, ol' Peter Pecker poked his head out those o.d. green flaps and went exploring."

Zack gave Lee a sideways, suspicious glance as he moved toward the cockpit but didn't say anything.

"And just like clockwork, Amsel flew through the door with his trashcan lid and came down hard. 'Mista Em-ho! Mista Em-ho!' He was a little white guy who enjoyed imitatin' the black drill sergeants. 'Mista Em-ho! Are you misbehavin,' slick? Are you pullin' on that nasty ol' pud o' yours again?' I tell you, Treat, it was eight weeks of pure, unadulterated hell."

"You and Hatchethead oughta get together."

"Huh?"

"Nothin'. Sounds like that Amsel character was a real ball buster."

"Yah. Always suspected the jerk was a ragin' drag queen between BCT cycles, you know? Otherwise, why would he allot so much time and attention to my em-ho every morning, right?"

"But "Em-ho" *does* you justice, Lee." Brody grinned mischievously. "I never liked 'Jap' much, anyway."

Lee's head flew up and several of the brass cartridges fell with a bounce across *Pegasus*'s floorboards. "You *wouldn't,* Treat! You wouldn't dare."

"'Jap's' out the hatch," Brody announced, extending a hand. "Welcome aboard, Em-ho!"

Irritated, Lee shook his head but not Brody's hand. Concentrating on his ammo clips, he ignored everyone around him. "Goddamned Amsel. Always knew he was a friggin' faggot. Always knew—"

But the cabin seemed to stretch upward in the middle for an instant, the craft's skin began to shudder, and the gunship lifted off the ground. Lee's words were drowned out by the slapping of rotor blades overhead as *Pegasus* ascended into the storm clouds, heading west, toward the Cambodian frontier.

Brody felt suddenly sick in the pit of his gut as he crouched in the reeds with Lee and the others, watching *Pegasus* lift up, away from them. The mythical horse painted across the gunship's snout seemed larger than life, wings almost flapping at the sticky heat, as the helicopter's rotors dragged her up through the trees. Was she really winking down at them, amused at their fear? Brody focused on the legend WIDOW MAKERS, painted in blood-red, Oriental-style script beneath the mural.

Behind him, Fletcher whispered, "Let's boog." And after the craft floated off into the night, he followed the team down through the reeds, beneath a canopy of trees that abruptly, almost frighteningly, blocked out the stars.

Pegasus had been stripped clean before they left the Turkey Farm: huge, removable sheets of tape placed over its ID numbers and U.S. ARMY markings.

But the crew chief told Brody to leave the mural alone. "Don't mess with my horse." He'd been serious as a heart attack. "Ol' *Pegasus* has been with this bird since Day One after delivery, and, in The Nam, you don't fuck with lifer tradition or a crew chief's lucky charms!" The crew chief was Zack.

So *Pegasus* had stayed. Brody felt a sting of sadness in his chest as he jumped from her womb into the dark jungle and watched the great, luminous creature rear up and abandon him. He had always remained aboard before—the ranking gunny— but not tonight.

Tonight Zack was taking his squad across the border for some combat football, and the slick was going back naked. Light and empty.

From her womb. . . He still couldn't decide if the ship was a he or she. Brody loved her like a woman. He could listen to her bitch under pressure, caress her skin and hidden, private parts like a lover. Could flirt or whisper compliments and encouragement and love to her the way he spoke to women down in the Pearl or back in The World. There was always that time of month when she refused to cooperate too, when she protested every descent with shrieks and shudders. Sometimes, even on a quiet, no-contact mission, you were afraid she was just going to fall apart on you. But when they dropped into a hot LZ, and Brody felt the pilot pull pitch the way oldtime cavalrymen had surely jerked back on the reins of their stallions during the great Indian wars, he was positive *Pegasus* was as much man as any warrior riding it. When Brody had his hands on the Hog and was laying down nonstop streams of tracer death upon Cong positions, there was surely nothing feminine about the power he felt.

Take the point!

Zack had actually not spoken at all, but Brody's mind automatically recreated the words as his eyes adjusted to the dark and he read the big sergeant's hand signals.

Watching the small strips of luminous tape positioned between their shoulder blades bob up and down like spirits prowling the rain forest, he melted into the thick brush, concentrating on noise control and booby traps. Now and then lone shafts of moonlight pierced the canopy overhead, revealing they were traversing virgin terrain. Yet the foliage was not difficult to get through. Vast fields of flat ground extended beneath the canopy again and again, and the only obstructions were sparse tree trunks holding up sections of the shroud above. There were no signs of trails. No evidence soldiers had passed this way in ages. Yet Brody *always* felt he was being watched. It was a haunting feeling that always came to him deep in the jungle. He remembered a childhood story: *Hundreds of glowing eyes blinking as one*...

Zack had them inserted a few klicks west of the Sihanouk Trail, just inside the border. The Sihanouk was an offshoot of the Ho Chi Minh Trail, branching away outside O Rang, in Cambodia, and sometimes existing only in the minds of guerrillas who had traveled it months or years before. The jungle often swallowed it up until the maze of footpaths and connected clearings disappeared beneath a blanket of wild, strangling vegetation, especially during the monsoons.

We lay dog here, Zack's fingers spoke again when they came across a stretch of trampled-flat elephant grass.

The seven men checked the ravine for any sign Charlie or the NVA had been there recently and left a surprise or two behind, but the grid was clean. They reconned the area in a circular patrol, checking the high ground to the east and the lowlands to the west, ensuring an enemy regiment wasn't camped over the hill (it had happened before), then they dug in for the night.

Zack deployed two LPs of two men each: one up the far hillside across the ravine, and the other along the trail's northern approach. He kept the remaining two soldiers with him and constructed a shallow trench thirty meters down-scent from the ravine.

They listened to the trickle of runoff rainwater for three days and nights. Without moving. Without making contact.

The mission's objective had been to locate and observe North Vietnamese or Viet Cong supply lines movement without actually engaging the enemy. Get some field intel for MI; that was it. Plot destinations and strength, then beat feet back to the extraction point, rifle barrels cold.

Brody thought of *Choi-oi* as they lay dog in the man-high elephant grass. Laying dog entailed sitting or squatting or lying in the same position, unmoving, watching the world roll past you on all sides. Like a lazy mutt. But the dog's life it wasn't.

Vietnam sired its own battalions of vicious army ants, bloodsucking leeches, yard-long centipedes, and kamikaze mosquitoes. Laying dog in the middle of the jungle subjected the soldier to every form of creepy-crawly thing imaginable, and, though Brody often imagined *Choi-oi* laying dog atop a bunker at the Tea Plantation, his eyes following the movements of every GI in camp, he knew the mongrel would never put up with killer ants.

No, *Choi-oi* would avoid confrontation with nature's surprises at any cost. And so it was with the Whoremonger.

There had been no sign of a single Vietnamese, friend or foe, in two nights, but *something* was out there. Watching them. Brody could *feel* it. And, like *Choi-oi,* he felt the obligation to investigate.

At predawn on Day Three, he woke Fletcher at the bottom of their shallow LP, whispered his intentions, then left the Snakeman with his pet boa.

Treat Brody low-crawled through the tall reeds, foot by slow cautious foot until he was back in the tree line and out of a creeping mist that enveloped the ravine from midnight until noon. Keeping to the shadows, he allowed gut instinct to guide him deeper into the rain forest, closer to the source of that which had been watching him—watching *them*.

As he neared the eerie power, the swirl of emotions and fear pressing down on him grew more and more with each tree he passed, each gulley he descended into. Brody made more noise.

He had abandoned all caution by the time a crimson glow in the east signaled false dawn, yet when he suddenly froze there was no sound of his prey escaping through the trees up ahead, crashing through the bush.

He was alone.

Brody was dropping down into the pit, falling through layers of darkness that became black as a moonless night. He was no one now, worse than dead—insignificant, food for scorpions that could not taste. The Whoremonger was no budding legend; he was nothing. And the branches above were clamping down over his face, one after another, hiding him forever, burying him.

A shaft of golden light, alive with swirling dust particles, lanced down into Brody's dark world of doom, breaking the spell. A gibbon, swinging from tree to tree in the lattice of branches overhead, and a brightly colored parrot, squawking the sleep from ruffled feathers somewhere behind him, assured the soldier he'd escaped never-never land, slipped free of Lady Death's slender, spice-coated fingers.

Abandoning all caution, Brody trampled shrubs and mushrooms and frogs in a frenzy, sprinting at full speed down through the forest's clearings, never looking back.

Not until he was close to where the others were laying dog did the dazed door gunner circle around, catch his breath, and low-crawl back to Fletcher and their LP.

"Has Black Bart been by?" he asked Snakeman, chest heaving.

"Negative," Fletcher's chin lifted in the direction of Zack's position. "Haven't seen any sign of 'im yet. I think them clowns are still sacked out or engagin' in a goddamned circle jer—"

"Mornin', troops." No shadow fell over them, but Leopold Zack's deep voice couldn't have been more accusing or intimidating.

"Que pasa?" Brody managed a confident reply, his eyes still

bulging from the jungle obstacle course.

"Was that your silhouette I spotted emergin' from the tree line coupla eyeball blinks ago, Specialist?" Zack slid in between them and helped himself to a C-ration pack of chocolate Fletcher had just opened.

Brody knew there was no use in lying. "Yah, Sarge. It was me." He glanced away, eyes focusing on two blue-and-green parrots chasing each other about the canopy's lower branches. "No excuses. I've been layin' dog here near eighty hours now, with no sign of Charlie or the NVA. Not even a lost water buffalo. I was beginnin' to feel like a weed with nowhere to go, and—"

"And you were gettin' ants in your pants."

"No shit," Fletcher produced a handful of the large red insects, all painstakingly decapitated.

"But seriously, Sarge." Brody faced Zack for the first time, and the skeptical smirk left the team leader's face—Brody looked like he'd seen worse than a ghost! "There was something out there! I've been feeling it for two nights now—"

"I know," Zack said softly.

"I've been layin' dog here and puttin' up with it, but I just couldn't stand the. . .the *feel* of it creepin' along the hairs of my neck. *We're* supposed to be spyin' on Charlie, but someone. . . something's spyin' on *us!*"

"I know. . ."

"And I had to confront him, her, or *what*ever it is. I had to. I couldn't just lay dog and ignore—"

"I *know*, Brody." Zack reached over and placed his hand on the specialist's shoulder.

"Then you felt it too?" The Whoremonger's eyes lit up again.

"Sure, but don' mean nothin', troop. Forget about it." Zack plopped the last bit of army-issue candy bar in his mouth and began burying the wrapper.

" 'Forget about it?' Whatta ya mean 'forget about it?' "

"Read my lips." Zack broke eye contact as he covered up the shallow hole. "Forget about it."

"But you went out there, too. I know it, now. You went out into the trees to check it out the same as I did." Brody looked hopeful.

"Sure I did." Zack licked his lips, unsmiling. "And?" Brody

leaned forward.

"And what?"

A sharp sigh escaped the door gunner, and he shook his head slowly, as if trying to forget a bad dream. "Didn't you find it?"

"Find *what?*" Zack's eyes rose to meet his. "The. . ." Brody couldn't find the right words when he needed them. "The. . . the *thing.* Didn't you experience the *thing* out there. . .the—"

"The what?" Zack glanced away again. His tone did not tease, but came across uncomfortable and strained.

"The. . ." Brody struggled to remember a phrase from childhood stories someone had read him, but his memory failed him. "Aw, forget it, Leo."

"Ain't nothin' out there, Whoremonger. Nothin' but the jungle." Brody's head whirled around. After all these months, Zack had finally gotten his nickname right. But the platoon sergeant's timing told him more about the man and The Nam and what he had just gone through than Brody wanted to know.

Abandoning all caution, Zack stood up straight and started to leave. He glanced down at Brody and whispered, "Nothin' but the jungle out there, son. Nothin' but the jungle. . .and the magic that makes up the rain forest." Zack winked in a way that told Brody he'd stumbled onto the secret that kept many a soldier behind in the Orient long after less romantic men returned to more routine lives on the other side of this dragon's sea. Zack smiled, and it was a sad, pitying smile, and then he walked away, leaving Brody even more confused than he'd been the first time he had an orgasm.

CHAPTER 10

Col. Buchanan saluted, then bent over and extended his hand. "Congratulations, little guy." He frowned suddenly; where would he pin the ArCom?

"Stay!" Elliot Fletcher pointed down at *Choi-oi* with a stern countenance. "Don't blow it, mutt." Snakeman turned to face Sgt. Zack. "Idiot finally gets to meet Neil Naz, I mean The Bull, one one one, and he can't remember how to shake paws. I spent two weeks teachin' him. Now I don't know why I ever wasted my time."

Choi-oi's tail was wagging furiously. His front paws danced from side to side as he slid his rump about on the hot clay. The colonel had never paid him any attention except to throw empty beer bottles his way; now the giant was trying to stick him with a pin.

"I'm sure PFC Fletcher would be happy to accept the Army Commendation Medal on behalf of *Dinky-dau*, sir," Sgt. Zack volunteered. The dog barked at the black platoon leader, and Snakeman rushed to restrain him.

"It's *Choi-oi*, Colonel," Lee said, unable to restrain a growing smile, "He's real sensitive about how people refer to him."

"Uh, right." Buchanan cleared his throat. "Sure thing." He handed the green ribbon to Fletcher.

"He lets his friends call him Shithead with a capital *S* though, Colonel. Huh, *Choi-oi?*" Corky Cordova dropped into a squat and motioned for the dog to come over to him.

Choi-oi growled and backed away, suspicious, and the platoon of men attending the informal awards ceremony laughed.

On the far side of the landing pad, hidden in the shade of an equipment conex, Lt. Winston shook his head in disgust. "A goddamned dog," he muttered under his breath. "Neil 'the Bull' Buchanan is presenting a U.S. Army Commendation Medal to a goddamned indigenous mutt." He sighed heavily, glanced at his watch, pulled a small notebook from his thigh pocket, scribbled something into it, then turned and walked off in the direction of the club.

"Mind if we join you?"

Brody glanced up from the glowing embers. Even before his eyes adjusted to the dark, he motioned the two shadows outside the triangle of tarmac planks down into the bunker. He recognized Cordova's voice instantly. Sgt. Delgado, the platoon medic, was with him. "Welcome to the Hell Hole." He ex-

93

tended a hand. "You know all the wolves in the Pack, don't you?"

"I think so," Delgado answered tentatively. Fletcher stared over at Cordova coldly but brightened up when Delgado dropped down beside him, legs folding Indian style.

"Evenin', Doc," he said, always happy to see the corpsman in good health. Delgado had proved invaluable on past missions. Even at this late hour, he wore his two ammo bandoliers crisscrossed over his chest, bandito style, but the olive-drab strips of cloth were filled with bandages, morphine, and the precision tools of his trade. To Fletcher, Buck Sgt. Delago was hospital white, not Hispanic. The man could do no wrong. He always carried enough spare tetracycline in his first-aid pouch to keep the Snakeman off sick call after a visit to Pleiku City. And he didn't charge Fletch for the clap shots, the way their old medic, Penicillin-Pete used to. Poor ol' Pete. Won a Silver Star dragging two corpses out of a free-fire zone. Posthumously.

"You're gonna get fleas, or worse." Sgt. Delgado smiled at Brody. "And I ran out o' crab ointment in August." The Whoremonger was stroking the thick coat of fur between *Choi-oi*'s shoulder blades as the dog lay against his shin, eyes closed, absorbing the heat. Larson's bunker was one of the few places on compound where a small campfire could be built without snipers beyond the perimeter shooting at the light. The Professor spent nearly all his spare time reinforcing the Hell Hole, as they called it, increasing his chances of surviving this, his last month in Vietnam.

The Hell Hole was already ten feet deep, with a helipad-tarmac roof. It was topped by a pyramid of sandbags half as high that kept the firelight in and Charlie's mortars out. It was where all the men of Brody's Legion gathered, when they were not working details, sleeping in the slicks, or flying. Admission to the Whoremonger's clique was simple: One had to display that certain shade of insanity mutual to Fletcher's and Larson's; and one had to have survived an unscheduled drop into Void Vicious. "The Pack," as they fancied themselves, rarely entertained newbies, and personalities of "color" usually received a thumbs-down by Fletcher.

Choi-oi's good ear shot up at the mention of his name. "*Choi-oi* don't have no damn fleas, Doc." Brody switched to improper grammar as if the dog would not understand him otherwise. "I pay the housegirls to scrub him down every other day."

Housegirls were Vietnamese women from the nearest ville who were hired to clean some of the permanent structures and wash laundry. Some of the GIs pooled money to pay them to shine boots, too. "The Housegirls?" Cordova laughed. "You're lucky the *housegirls* don't smuggle ol' *Choi-fuckin'-oi* off post to make him top dog in a ten-course Montagenarde meal!"

"Not *our Choi-oi*." Brody covered the animal's ears as he began to whine softly.

"Yep." Cordova leaned forward. "I can picture that ugly mutt's mug atop a platter of steamed rice. . .right between the chicken feet and fishheads."

Choi-oi groaned again and began to struggle, but Brody held him in place. "Knock it off, Corky." He laughed.

"Yep." Cordova reached over and pinched *Choi-oi* on the snout. "Them strikers *lovvvve* mongrel meat!"

Choi-oi barked and slid out backwards from Brody's grasp. He scampered across piles of ammo magazines, paused at the sandbag steps to bark at Cordova some more, then raced out into the night.

"Hey!" *Choi-oi* yelped, and Lawrence Lee tumbled down into the bunker. After rolling against one of the dirt walls, he slowly looked back over a shoulder, out the bunker entrance, then across at the soldiers gathered around the dying embers. *Choi-oi* continued to whine as he raced across the landing pad outside, but Lee still asked, "What the *hell* was that?"

"Em-ho!" Brody replied. " 'Bout time you showed up. Now if I can just talk Doc into hangin' around awhile, we *might* have enough grunts down here to get a card game goin'."

"Did you guys hear about that asshole Abdul?" Lee rolled over into a squat beside Fletcher and began brushing himself off.

"Mohammed?" Brody offered him a C-rations can of peach halves.

"Screw that militant shithead." Fletcher reached out and grabbed the tin. He swallowed the last of the peaches and belched loudly for Lee's benefit.

Delgado watched the juice run down his chin and throat for

a moment, then said, "They got him and Nurse Maddox on the MIA roster, don't they—"

"Not anymore," Lee announced, all smiles. "That goofy Crump turned up a few minutes ago, with the lieutenant praising him as a saint!"

"What?" Larson was tearing up an old copy of the *Stars & Stripes* newspaper and feeding it to the flames.

"Yah, I heard Maddox telling Buchanan he saved her from the mortars. He saved her from a couple kid Cong, too. Disarmed 'em in actual hand-to-hand or somethin' and took 'em both out with their own rifle."

"Oh, no." Fletcher dropped his head in resignation. He'd been hoping the NVA latched onto Mohammed and were even then dragging his anarchist ass north to Hanoi.

"Yah!" Lee withdrew a packet of hot, folded banana leaves from one of the magazine pouches on his web belt. "Maddox says she's droppin' all charges against Abdul. Says she's seen the light! Can you believe that crap?"

"No, I can't believe *that crap!*" Fletcher frowned as he stared down at Lee's snack. He watched, disgust written across his face, as the soldier peeled back two leaves, revealing a combination of sticky rice and *bao:* beef mixed with broccoli, onions, and assorted vegetables. "How can you stomach that shit, anyway?"

"Not shit!" Lee spoke in pidgin-English, squinting over at Elliot. "Snakeman should try! numba one *chop-chop!* Good for your hemorrhoids, GI." Lee's smile flashed ear to ear.

"I no have—I mean I don't have no goddamned hemorrhoids, you fucking—"

"What about Crump?" Delgado interrupted, in no mood for the racial insults he knew were coming. "The colonel's still going to ship his butt down to LBJ, isn't he?"

"Doesn't sound like it. Zack shooed me away before I could get the whole skinny, but from what I managed to pick up, I'd say ol' Elijah is gonna spend a week or two at the psych ward in Nha Trang for evaluation, then he's back on slicks."

"No way!" Fletcher stood up.

"That's the way it sounded, Snakeman." Lee raised both hands defensively.

"Yah, don't go knee-droppin' the messenger." Cordova

laughed.

Fletcher whirled around. "Who the flyin' fuck asked *your* opinion?" He started toward Corky. The stocky machine gunner jumped up, fists raised, but Delgado and Brody rushed between them.

"Save it for Saigon." The medic forced his lips into a tight grin as his eyes scanned both men's frames, counting firearms. Snakeman carried an M-16 slung upside down over one shoulder and a .45 on his hip. Cordova's weapons were back in his tent, but he was ready to rumble nonetheless—he and Lady Death had come to an understanding long ago.

Brody glanced from Cordova to the angry Texan. He was not worried about the Mexican. Corky, who was twenty but looked thirty, was under control. Snakeman's intentions were another matter altogether. In the boonies, Elliot was a good man to have feeding ammo belts into your MG, but back at camp you could never quite be sure where his head was at.

"Come on, Snakeman." Brody pushed Fletcher back to his side of the bunker. "No sense scrapin' your knuckles over somethin' like this. Then Mohammed's pulled off *two* scams at the same time," he said, trying his own brand of reverse psychology, "and without even razzin' ya, pal."

"That coon don't get under *my* skin, Treat." Fletcher started for the steps. "But he positively is *not* gettin' back aboard *Pegasus* again. Ain't no way! not unless it's 'cause he's hitchin' a ride to some LZ with the rest of the Cavalry. Besides, Mohammed made it plain he didn't want to work a gunny slot anymore."

"I know, I know."

"He let everyone *know* he'd break big rocks into little rocks at LBJ before he'd play door gunner again. The spade's a coward, Treat. He don't *deserve* to fly aboard Peg."

"Fancy that." Cordova whispered over to Doc Delgado just loud enough for Fletcher to hear. "A yellow spook."

"I'm warning you!" Snakeman rushed up to the machine gunner again, his forefinger out menacingly. Brody's hand shot up and clamped down on his wrist. Cordova made no aggressive moves as Treat led Fletcher up into the night.

"Jesus." Lee assumed an expression of mock relief after the two were gone. "A coupla tracers and we'd of had a regular Fourth of July fireworks show down here."

Both Doc and Cordova laughed, but they were left uneasy about the confrontation. It was bad enough when you had to worry about which locals were loyal South Vietnamese by day and Viet Cong insurgents by night, but when you couldn't turn your back on the battalion bigot, *everyone* had to start watching over their shoulders. Especially in a combat zone, where thru-and-thru wounds could easily be blamed on either side.

Cordova sat back down on a footlocker, and a shoe box balanced precariously along one edge toppled over onto the ground. "What's all this?" Delgado asked. Several envelopes scattered across the bunker's dirt floor at Lee's feet.

"Oh, those are just Snakeman's compositions back to The World." Lee stooped to gather them up. Eyes opening wide at the mention of Fletcher's nickname, Cordova bent over to help.

"His 'compositions?' "

"Elliot's got bookoo broads back stateside," Lee revealed. "At least claims he does."

Sgt. Delgado permitted himself the liberty to scan addresses. "Each one *is* addressed to a different chick," he admitted.

"And each chick's in a different state," Cordova observed. "Quite a Romeo." Delgado frowned at the army-issue stationery, a door gunner lying in the prone position was depicted in the lower left corner of both envelopes and paper.

"He forces us to listen to him read 'em sometimes." Lee laughed. "The dude's quite a sweet-talker."

"You gotta be kiddin'."

"I shit you not, Sarge. Ask to see his wallet sometime. Crammed full of photos of round-eye foxes. Half are beaver shots, too, and half of *those* got Snakeman in the picture."

"I'm impressed," Delgado replied, only semi-serious.

"So was I when he showed 'em to me. For such an asshole, the guy's got quite a way with women."

"Then why doesn't he ever get any letters at mail call?" Cordova lifted his chin, proud of the observation.

Lee paused a moment, contemplating the remark. "You've got a point," he finally said.

"What are these?" Delgado noticed that something else had dropped out of the shoe box.

"Oh, those are—" Lee started to explain, but the medic cut him off.

"Never mind, *Em-ho*." He recognized the black Ace of Spades playing cards. On the reverse was the First Cavalry Division emblem, with the inscription THE FIRST TEAM above the horsehead patch and WIDOW MAKERS below it. "I was wondering who was placing these on the dead dinks. Hadn't seen any for quite a while, then *BANG!* there's one stickin' out from between every set of VC lips from here to Hoai Nhon."

"Yah. . .well, Fletch *does* like to leave his calling card. Likes the family to know who offed their old man. The Snakeman *do* take his job seriously, Doc."

"Fire in the hole," someone called down into the bunker from above before passing gas. Startled, Lee, Larson and the others turned to face the entryway as the shadow from a crossbow fell across the sandbags.

Doc Delgado was the first to breathe a sigh of relief. "Broken Arrow!" he called out. "Get your red Comanche ass down here!"

Tense silence, then, in a low voice, "Yes, Kimosavi." Two soldiers started down into the bunker. "Permission to escort ace chopper jock Hal Krutch onto the premises." The voice feigned uncertainty.

"Permission granted!"

"Well how the hell are ya all doin' tonight?" The warrant officer behind Corporal Chance "Two-Step" Broken Arrow had to bend low to make it down the final steps into the bunker.

Hal Krutch was probably the tallest pilot in the 7th Cav of the First Cavalry Division. His clean-shaven face appeared long and drooping, but the man was constantly smiling, and the effort stretched the center of his face out so his eyes always looked pained. His light brown hair was kept regulation short and seemed but a small patch of scrub brush on a hilltop. Krutch had big lips, and Lee observed that his chin was a good three inches long. *A stupid look,* Lee decided. *This guy has got the dumbest expression I have ever seen since leaving California.*

"Where's that goddamned Professor Larson?" Krutch ignored the soldier bent over a notebook in the corner of the bunker and glared down at Lee good-naturedly instead.

"Hey, Professor!" Corporal Broken-Arrow brushed past the two and leaned over Larson. "What the hell ya readin', bnored

99

the soldier bent over a notbook in the corner of the bunker and glared down at Lee good-naturedly instead.

"Hey, Professor!" Corporal Broken Arrow brushed past the two and leaned over Larson. "What the hell ya readin', boy?"

"Don't bug me!" Larson growled without looking up. "I'm busy."

"Hey, Professor!" Krutch was soon beside the full-blooded Comanche Indian. "Me and Two-Step are sneakin' down into Plei Nhol for some zipped-up pussy. *Let's go!*"

"I said I'm busy, Stork." Larson still refused to look up. He was penning something across the notebook's narrow, horizontal grids in green ink.

"Somethin' important, eh?" Stork laughed skeptically. Lee laughed too. Anytime Krutch moved his lips it was funny. They called him Stork because almost every time he came out of a burning hut on a combat assault, he was dragging a dead female guerrilla behind him with one hand and holding a crying infant up over his head in the other.

"Yah," Larson mumbled. "Somethin' important." "What could be more important than cheap clit in a war zone, boy?" Krutch persisted.

"*Shit!*" The Professor slammed his pen down on the ammo crate "desk." "I can't think straight with you scrotebags jabberin' away like horny housegirls!"

" 'Scrotebag?' " Broken Arrow turned to face Krutch. "Is that good or bad?"

Krutch just grinned and leaned closer to Larson. "Is that *green* ink you're usin' there, Prof?"

"What about it?" Larson glared.

Broken Arrow waved a finger at him in mock reprimand. "The VC are usin' green ink on their letter bombs this month, bud. Don't you read the memos on the bulletin board over at the CP? And letters or packages addressed in green ink get confiscated." And he snatched up Larson's pen.

"Aw, fuck! Just got a whole pack of 'em from my cousin back in The World. She kipes 'em from the factory where she works. Jesus H.—"

" 'So it is with great reluctance that I say farewell to mother nature and all this lonely planet's creatures, good and bad . . . .' " Broken Arrow was leaning over Larson's shoulder
100

again and reading out of the notebook.

Krutch frowned. "You still writin' that goddamned suicide note?" he asked with accusing eyes, high cheekbones dipping with disapproval.

Two-Step, flipping through the notebook, answered for him. "Looks like the skate is up to over a hundred pages, Stork."

"Can't a guy have some peace around here?" Larson complained, lifting his hands, palms up, in resignation.

"That's just what we're *trying* to get you, Professor!" Krutch and his partner grabbed Larson's wrists and yanked him to his feet. "A *piece* of *ass!*"

Broken Arrow slammed the notebook shut and winked over at Lee as they started to drag Larson up the sandbagged steps.

Lee was in awe of Corporal Chance "Two-Step" Broken Arrow. He'd picked up the nickname after surviving the bite of a deadly krait viper, a snake the GIs called a "two-step" because its victims rarely made it more than a couple of steps after being struck. But Broken Arrow had lived through the ordeal. "By using my faithful medicine man's pouch," he always claimed whenever Brody talked him into retelling the story. Chance wore a small leather pouch on the dog tags chain around his neck "filled with powerful little charms like rattlesnake rattles, gila monster teeth, wolf claws, and eagle feathers," he maintained. "From back on the reservation." The contents were said to be all ground up, and Broken Arrow had kept the pouch flattened over the snake bite, rubbing it into the wound, until they medevaced him down to a field hospital. His leg had swollen to twice its normal size by then, but Two-Step somehow made it without losing a single toe. The texture of the pouch was not unlike a thick teabag. "Powerful medicine in this here pouch," he boasted, but always humbly added, "I owe my life to the spirits of the Earth. No doubt about it. They saved me from the serpent spirit. They could just as easily have turned their backs on me."

Half the troopers of the 7th Cav referred to him as, simply, "that crazy Indian," rather than Two-Step, but there was no mistaking the man, even in a crowd of GIs. Broken Arrow had an extremely muscular torso, yet no one ever saw him working out. The source of his good health and stamina was a mystery.

Most of the troopers had been dragged down, beaten, mind-fucked, then beaten again by The Nam. They often walked about between missions with dark circles under their eyes, sunken cheeks, and that thousand-yard stare, emotionally scarred and physically wrecked.

But not Broken Arrow. The name did not fit, Lee decided. Two-Step was a proud lance rising from the rice paddy mist as he stalked Cong, always volunteering to walk point. His skin seemed to sparkle at times. Two years under the Asian sun, combined with his already dark pigment, made for a smooth, bronze tint. Originally the loner of the squad, he had just extended for a third Tour 365 and was hanging out with Krutch and Larson more and more these last few weeks.

Broken Arrow usually kept a somber, unemotional mask across his features, but the team had laughed for days the time they caught him in An Khe wearing a long black wig that fell to his waistline. The secret out, Two-Step began wearing it during his off duty hours too, and on every R and R. Long hair added power in his movement, he maintained. And it kept the ties to his cultural heritage strong. Zack never said anything so long as the lengthy locks weren't being blown about by rotor-wash and the colonel looked the other way. Lt. Winston avoided the Pack entirely.

"Plei Nhol is off limits this week!" Larson was still protesting as they emerged under a night sky heavy with brilliant, eye-catching stars that seemed to hang almost within reach, all the way to the horizon.

"*That's* why we're goin' there!" Krutch explained patiently, laughing again. "'Cause there won't be any competition!"

"We can help ourselves to the *best* of the boom-boom girls!" Broken Arrow added.

"But it's Off Limits *because* Charlie ambushed the medical convoy last week and the dispensary is low on penicillin!" Larson persisted.

"No sweat!" Krutch pulled a string of multicolored, army-issue prophylactics from his first-aid pouch. With a flip of his wrist, the plastic containers unfolded like a sleeve of credit cards springing open from a wallet. "Now are you a *man*, or a cherry boy?"

Larson shuddered. "Rubbers make me feel like I'm makin'

102

love with a raincoat on," he continued.

"I know this one quickie joint where the chicks are guaran*teed* to be clean as a cube of steamed sugarcane, bud, or half your *piasters* back—nebbah mind!" Two-Step wrapped a comforting arm around the Professor's shoulder.

"Always knew I was gonna lose my pecker over here." Lee listened to Larson complain as artillery rumbled on the horizon and the hills overlooking the Ia Drang crackled like dark clouds alive with heat lightning." One way or the other."

"I'll cover for you clowns," he yelled up out of the bunker. "How long do you plan to be AWOL?"

"We may *never* come back!" threatened Broken Arrow. "Besides," added Krutch, "what can they do if they catch us—send us to Vietnam?"

"They could send your sorry asses to Germany!" someone outside yelled and Lee smiled; he knew several soldiers who had extended their Tour 365 in The Nam another six months to avoid a PCS to that part of "beautiful, exciting Europe."

"Ohhh!" Krutch made a good show of groaning. "Low blow, GI! Low blow, indeed!"

Lee sighed with relief as he listened to the trio break a chainlock off one of the jeeps. At least they weren't stealing a gunship for their joyride over the hill.

CHAPTER 11

The shoeshine boy had been leading them down a maze of back alleys for several minutes now. Silver blankets of smoke clung like a death shroud to the thatched roofs at the village's edge. A leaning structure of adobe and crumbling cinderblocks, complete with French-style red roof tiles, rose from the wisps of evening cooking fires like a floating mirage, but the shoeshine boy was leading them away from it.

The alleys were hard, packed dirt, and not really alleys at all, just narrow trails running down the hillside between rows of bamboo and wood plank dwellings. Most of the homes were constructed entirely of discarded C-rations cases and empty pop bottles. Flattened beer cans were added here and there for decorations.

Now and then, Larson spotted a dark set of mysterious, almond eyes peering out at them from between the slats. He could actually look right into a couple of dilapidated shacks. Old women with black, betal nut-caked teeth squatted beside cooking pots full of rice, infants in their arms—grandchildren, most likely, he decided. Their eyes were downcast, ignoring the passing GIs, though it was obvious they could be heard. Krutch was whistling the theme song from *Goldfinger*.

"Well, will ya look at *that* bookoo *dep* young thing!" Larson pointed through some open blinds to a young woman kneeling in front of a family altar. In her early twenties, she was wearing a long, filmy nightgown. Her right side was to them, and two candles burned on her left. The flickering light revealed her firm, slender curves as if she wore nothing at all, and though the men kept walking, their eyes were locked onto the swirl of upturned nipples. "I think I'm in love," the Professor sighed.

"Good thing Em-ho ain't here." Krutch was laughing again. "He'd reveal our position for sure!"

Larson giggled in response. It was an out-of-character giggle, and Broken Arrow remained unsmiling. "I *told* you," he repeated, "there *are* Victor Charlies up in them there hills, you guys." He motioned to a black shadow of a mountain against the night, rising up to conceal the lower curtain of stars behind them. "It's no laughing matter."

"I think I'd settle for just going back to that little saint prayin' by the candlesticks back there." Larson could still see her outline in the dim glow of candlelight. "You think she'd see anything in a gunship hero like me?" He turned to face Broken Arrow. "You think she'd give up her life in the boonies in exchange for a ticket to the Land of the Big PX?"

"I don't think the local ladies here speak much English, Professor," Two-Step said seriously. "You might have some trouble communicatin' with a real lady. That wasn't no whore back there, you know."

"We could speak the language of love." Larson patted his crotch.

"It's the universal language," Krutch agreed. "But wait 'till you meet Little Oral Anh-hee. She'll clean your rod so you'll start thinkin' straight again, amigo. Right now your balls are draggin' and you'd screw anything that'd bend over. We'll see if you're still in love on the way back to camp."

But Larson could not erase her image from his mind. Maybe Krutch was right. Maybe if he made it back to Hometown, U.S.A., he'd respond to long black hair and dark, exotic eyes differently. But one thing the Professor knew, one thing he was sure about: If he lived to be one hundred and one, Elliot Larson would never forget that beautiful Vietnamese woman's profile. Lines in the night. So simple and graceful. So delicate yet overpowering. If he ever made it out of The Nam, if he ever left this strange land, would he see that defenseless, stunning lady every time he looked in a Chinese restaurant, or saw Asian schoolgirls gathering on campus? Would he see her outline, framed in his mind's wartorn images, each time he passed by an Oriental massage parlor back in The World?

"Like a teacup," the thought escaped him as a harsh whisper.

"Huh?" Krutch wrapped an arm around the Professor, well aware the young soldier was still mesmerized by something he'd seen in a filthy back alley in a war-ravaged village in a forgotten patch of the Central Highlands. In the dead of night.

"Cho Gao. Cho Gao down in the Delta," Krutch said unexpectedly. "Whatever. Just leave it alone, Elliot. Save yourself a load o' grief and a world of hurt. Don't fall in love with any of these heartbreakin' zips, boy."

"Don't let 'em seduce *you*," Broken Arrow added, sounding almost as if he was speaking from experience. "They got a magic all their own."

"Oh?"

"I've read up on it." He glanced away.

"You've *what?*" Larson asked, but he was staring at Krutch, not the Indian. Hal had never addressed him by his first name before.

"Yah. You show these Asian chicks any kindness, and they're hangin' all over you, but let 'em get wind your tour's up and

105

they'll drown you in tears."

"Huh?" Larson bumped into the back of Krutch, who had skidded to a stop in the dark.

"Yah. And everyone knows that if you get a Vee-yet chick's tears on you, you can kiss it good-bye, slick. You're under her spell forever. Takes a *moi* witch doctor to break the curse. But you're never the same, Professor, never."

"Where the hell did you read something like that, *Mad Magazine*?" Larson glanced back at him, eyes narrowed skeptically.

"*Overseas Weekly*, Chump."

"You gotta be shittin' me."

"I wouldn't shit you, Larson-san. You're my favorite turd."

The Professor raised his middle finger in an obscene gesture.

"Seriously. Ask the Stork."

"About the curse, or my status as your favorite shit?"

"Turd."

"Uh, right."

But Warrant Officer Hal Krutch was occupied with other matters. Four heavily armed ARVN military policemen had stepped from the shadows of a doorway, and were blocking their path.

The shoeshine boy was already shaking his fist at them and jabbering away in rapid-fire Vietnamese. Curfew strip meant a loss in profits for their juvenile guide.

One of the QCs lifted his American-made M-16 and pushed the boy's nose flat. None of the four Arvins was smiling.

"Hey! Whoaaa, boys." Krutch lowered his gun out of sight and raised his free hand. "No sweat! No sweat! I'm sure we can come to an understanding here!"

The closest QC motioned toward his wristwatch. "Curfew now! You Pleiku GI?" The question came across as an insult, implying that soldiers attached to units in Pleiku would be the only ones foolish enough to be out on the streets at this hour.

"We're just lookin' for a good time, friend." Krutch slowly slipped the pistol into the waistband along the small of his back. "Just lookin' for a good time."

"Heard you have Numba One after-hours short-time parlor for army *canh-sats*," Two-Step added without prelude.

The shoeshine boy waved a hand in front of his mouth like a

106

lawyer urging his client to remain silent, then launched into a torrent of nonstop chatter. The words came out so quickly all Larson or any of the others could make out was "Firs' Cav!"

One of the QCs pointed at the horse-head patch on Larson's right shoulder, but he spoke to Broken Arrow, "You 9th Cav MPs?" All four rifles came down, and the obvious leader stepped forward, smiling now.

Krutch matched the grin and lifted both hands, extending six fingers and a thumb. "Seventh Cav of the First Division." He winked. "Bookoo better, you *bic?*"

"Ahhh," The QC slowly nodded. "Seventh Cav Numba One!"

"Right." Krutch imitated his nod. "*Fini* bookoo VC!"

The QCs all laughed on cue. "Ahhh." They nodded eagerly. "*Fini* bookoo VC!"

" Well, it's been a real thrill to meet you meatheads," Krutch spoke fast as he shook the nearest soldier's hand. "But we need to be on our way. Go see *boom-boom girl!*"

One of the rifles came back up, and a smile faded, but the leader knocked the barrel aside diplomatically. "Ahhh, boom-boom girl!" He laughed, nodding again. "Okay, you go!" He motioned them past. "Find good time! Boom-boom girl this ville Numba Fuckin' One!"

"Yah!" Larson hurried to catch up with their guide. "Numba Fuckin' One! *Cam on,* gentlemen!"

"Ahhh!" the QC sergeant's smile grew with the formal thanks, however insincere. "You're welcome, Joe. Good you *bic* Vietnamese! Yes, you welcome, my friend."

The QC standing beside him spoke for the first time as Larson was about to round a bend in the alley. "Watch your ass, GI. No sleep with VC business girl or maybe she liberate your loins!"

The ARVN military policemen all laughed. "Maybe you go sleep tonight with boom-boom girl and no wake up," the sergeant added.

"Maybe you bed down VC business girl and *you* go boom-boom!" the QC private clapped his hands so loud Larson ducked and stumbled, but Krutch caught him. He urged him to move along faster—before the real MPs showed up on their rounds. And the shoeshine boy was almost out of sight now, up ahead.

"Did you hear that clown?" Krutch elbowed the Professor.
"'Maybe she liberate your loins?'"

"Could happen."

"But—"

"Yah, I was wondering where he learned to talk like that too."
Krutch watched Larson wipe sweat from his brow with the back
of his hand.

"Probably a Berkeley extension student," Two-Step said
matter-of-factly.

At the northeast edge of the ville, they encountered a high
wall of sandbags, topped with sagging loops of razor-sharp
concertina wire. A break in the middle of the wall was guarded
by two long-haired men in black calico pants. Both carried
American-made carbines with sawed-off barrels and extended
custom-made 40-round magazines.

"VC?" Larson reached out to grab Krutch's pistol. "Mellow
out, Professor." The gunship pilot seemed surprised at Larson's
reaction. "Not all Viets who wear black pajama bottoms are
Cong, my friend, despite what the door gunner's manual might
say." He laughed at what he considered to be a quick-witted
reference to the nonexistent guide to offing Charlie from a gunship. "They're probably just collectin' the cover charge or
something." Krutch laughed.

"Chao ong! Chao ong!" Broken Arrow moved ahead of
them to greet the guards, his long-haired wig in place. "Hello,
hombres! How the hell are ya doin' tonight?" His next sentence
was a slur of pidgin Vietnamese.

The guards, who had been flirting with two women in long,
shoulder-to-ankle sarongs, were so startled by the big Indian's
demeanor they completely forgot about their weapons. Suspicious eyes could not control involuntary smiles. A sort of instant camaraderie was formed because of Two-Step's hair
length. Then they noticed the Americans behind him.

"Who the hell are you guys?" The guard to Krutch's right had
no accent whatsoever.

Probably Filipino, the pilot decided. *A damned Filipino mer-
cenary.* He laughed to himself silently. *What next?*

The shoeshine boy was tugging on one of the guards' belt
buckles now, and both rifles came up defensively. "GI come see

108

boom-boom girls again!" The boy pushed a barrel out of his face, well aware he was now dealing with *two* sets of foreigners.

"You pay me first!" the taller guard demanded, smile gone, hand outstretched.

"Aha!" Krutch reached into his front pocket. "A Filipenis *pimp!"* He produced a Zippo lighter with the First Cav emblem inscribed across it and slapped it into the man's palm. "Enjoy, brothers, courtesy of the notorious and glorious Seventh Cav!"

But the guard did not seem impressed. "You leave guns here!" he ordered.

"What guns?" Krutch asked innocently, raising both hands.

The Filipino scanned their clothing. "What that?" he pointed at Broken Arrow's crossbow accusingly.

Two-Step hesitated, lower jaw dropping. Were these farmers from Mindinao, or *cao bois* from Manila? Krutch thought faster. "Fo' boom-boom girl!" he said, sliding his feet apart and grabbing the weapon. He braced the bow's arms against the insides of his knees, the arrow's tip between the bottoms of his testicles.

"Great gonads, Krutch," Larson whispered as Two-Step swallowed loud enough for all three of them to hear.

"Make boom-boom girl bookoo wet!" the pilot explained, flicking the bowstring with his thumb until it sounded like an out-of-tune cello.

"How make 'wet?'" One of the guards produced a skeptical grin that only curled one side of his face slightly.

"You know"—Krutch rubbed the arrow's shaft sensuously—"business girl no have love inside, same-same GI, right?" He tapped his left breast. "No feeling in heart." Then he brought their attention back down to the arrow's shaft. "No feeling in pussy. You *bic?"*

"Ahhh...." The guards eyes were glued to the ten-inch long stick, its point hidden by the American's trousers. "I *bic.*"

"You know 'dildo?'" Krutch produced his most convincing smile.

"Ahhh... *dildo!"* Both Filipinos shook their heads up and down slowly.

"Good!" Krutch pulled back the curtain of black bamboo beads and ushered Two-Step and the Professor through.

Iron grille stairs led down into an underground bunker larger than any the three Americans had ever seen before. The size of a basketball court, its four walls rose nearly a dozen feet and were paneled with thin teakwood planks. Tin runway tarmac, decorated with dyed and drooping fish net, reinforced the ceiling. Krutch estimated another dozen feet of earth was piled atop the bunker's roof of spliced railroad beams.

Partitions divided the main room into ten smaller cubicles on each side with an unobstructed aisle running down through the middle. The partitions were flimsy shades and shudders, formed from driftwood and thatched elephant grass.

"Quite a setup." Larson whistled as several girls in sarongs rushed toward them, faces aglow with enthusiastic smiles.

"Whooo*EE!*" Broken-Arrow filled his lungs with the stale, smoke-laced air. "I smell *pussy* and the pussy smells *goooood!*"

At the far end of the complex, where the cubicles ended, a tunnel split into two forks. Flashing multicolored lights glowed down one side; flickering candles filled the other.

Krutch was already disappearing into one of the cubicles with two women under his arms. Their sarongs fell away as they glided through the bead drapes, hands already busy with the chopper pilot's belt.

Broken Arrow led Larson down to the end of the underground brothel. Vietnamese and Cambodian men filed in and out of the various cubicles. None of them paid the Americans any attention.

"I haven't seen a single Westerner yet." Larson's head bobbed back and forth as they passed each slot in the wall. The beads hardly concealed the activities going on behind them. Larson's eyes grew as he learned a dozen new positions in as many footsteps. "Are you sure this joint is safe?"

"Don't sweat it, pal." Finally, they had reached the two forking tunnels. "They got a fancy little opium den down that side." Two-Step pointed in the tunnel filled with flickering candles. Naked men and women shared hammocks suspended from the ceiling, or floor mats padded thick with crumpled newspapers which were wrapped in bundles of scented elephant grass. Opium pipes with pots the size of rice cookers were positioned every few feet, with several customers sharing each one—some utilizing long tubes of hose to reach their dream perch below a

110

ceiling decorated with pornographic posters of Chinese and Korean women. "Never really seen you smokin' anything, but I have heard the rumors...."

"Rumors?" Larson could not take his eyes off one couple sharing a far corner in the narrow corridor aglow with dim yellow light: The man sat with his back against a wall, chin against his chest, passed out with the opium pipe still in his mouth. His legs were spread apart, the soles of his feet facing the Professor, and a nude woman lay between them, her haunches propped up, effectively "mooning" the Americans, her face buried in the man's lap, unmoving.

"You know"—Two-Step nudged him with a don't-jive-me elbow to the stomach—"they say you got a contact in An Khe who gets you some *primo* baskets of local high-grade hash. They say you're shippin' a duffel bag full back to someone stateside nearly every week." Broken Arrow laughed. "Don't try and fool ol' Two-Step, pal. Ol' Two-Step's got ESP, didn't ya know?"

"Crock a shit, *pal*," Larson muttered.

"'Bout my ESP?" Broken Arrow leaned back, feigning insult and hurt feelings.

"About the pot."

"Aha!" The Indian slapped him on the back. "No one said anything about Mary-Jane, Professor-san! I thought we were talkin' about hash of the shee-*it!* variety." Chance cleared his throat for effect. "I gotcha!"

Elliot Larson did not reply immedately. His eyes remained on the shapely Vietnamese woman sprawled across her mate's crotch. Moving in drug-induced dreams perhaps, she lifted her haunches a few inches off the ground, slowly and sensuously. He tried to ignore his groin and the irresistible desire to drop his trousers and mount this woman from behind. He tried to ignore the hardness growing against his zipper, straining to burst free, to set out and explore. He wanted to concentrate instead on Larson's reaction. But the Professor was not seeing the same things, was not hearing a slow, romantic tune echo off in the distance somewhere, was not listening to the gentle woman's melodic, singsong voice.

Instead, his mind's eye saw a young girl with red hair and freckles, not yet in her teens, lying in a hospital bed in Seattle, her vital organs wired to a giant machine, her legs disfigured by a disabling childhood disease—a disease the doctors found a cure for two months after she was struck down. "Not a cure, really," he spoke under his breath, then fell back into blurred thoughts. *A vaccine...a vaccine that came too late....*

The ears of his memory were listening to their parents argue about the expensive medical bills—fights that would escalate into beatings and eventual divorce. Mom and Pop split, abandoning his kid sister to social services. Elliot was the only one welfare workers could track down after he dropped out too. And when he came of legal age, all the bills started showing up at his address, which was Kent State University. Then Uncle Sammy came knocking on his door one summer break when the Professor was late returning from a research trip down Mexico way. *But what goes around comes around*, Elliot truly believed, so how could he possibly pass up the opportunity to score so much high-grade hash at government expense?

A cousin in Seattle picked up the duffel bags and footlockers at the airport, sold the hashish to his contacts, or on the street, or whatever he did, and those medical bills the state didn't cover got paid.

Larson felt no guilt at contributing to the growing drug abuse problem in America. America had shafted his sister. America had shafted *him*, sending him to a crazy Asian country to fight a rich man's war while politicians' sons remained in school, driving new convertibles back and forth to the college campus. *If I ever have a kid*, he vowed, *no car! Not unless they get a job and make the payments themselves*. He didn't care if that meant they'd have to work nights.

Until he was caught—*if* he was ever caught—Elliot Larson would play dumb to the plight of the world, turning his back on the voices of his conscience. After all, this was The Nam. A mortar could splash his guilt around the insides of his helmet this very night. A sniper could punch a 5.56mm slug of lead right through the middle of his personality, forever curing a shitty disposition. "Don't mean nothin'," as the gunnies claimed. Nothing meant anything at all. Except that precious short-timer's calendar.

CHAPTER 12

"Her name is Thuy," Lawrence Em-ho Lee told Brody and the others as they leaned out from under the shade of a palm tree to watch a gaggle of slicks fly by. "Thu Thi Thuy. Nineteen years old, same as me." He tugged on one edge of his drooping mustache.

"A real looker, eh?" The Whoremonger pulled a canteen from his web belt, took a short drink, replaced it, and stared at the ten soldiers lounging in the roadside shade. All except Lee and himself were on their backs in the leaves, the top halves of their faces hidden by helmets as they caught up on much deserved sleep.

"Her brother showed me a snapshot, Treat. Old, yellowed and cracked—"

"The photo." Brody smiled.

"Right. The photo. But the girl is. . .well, she's a *woman,* and—"

"Oh, oh, the worst kind."

"Come on, Treat. This is serious shit."

"Ahh, love at first sight."

"The photograph don't do her justice." Lee had been rubbing gun oil along his rifle's trigger assembly for the last five minutes and switched to the bland fiber glass handgrips along the barrel. "She's a fox, I'm tellin' you. A real fox. I can just see it in her eyes."

"You can see *what* in her eyes?" Brody felt it was his obligation to remain skeptical and dispassionate when it came to matters of the heart involving his people, but Lee ignored the question.

"It'd be well worth our time if—"

"Your time, lover-boy." Brody elbowed him.

"*My* time," Lee conceded, ". . .to see if we could try and rescue her."

"Why, Lawrence, I dare say I see shades of Prince Charming —or is it Sir Galahad—in your noble endeavor." Doc Delgado rose from pseudo-slumber beneath the rim of his helmet. "All

113

I can say is she better be a damned good lay. Women aren't worth half the hassles they cause anyway, and if there's one thing I learned in my travels across the globe it's that a hole is a hole is a hole. Now, when it comes to breasts, more than a mouthful is just a waste, and—"

"Thank you, *Sgt. Delgado!*" Brody was not pleased with the interruption or unsolicited words of wisdom.

". . . And you can't live with 'em, or with*out* 'em." The medic was still talking.

Brody turned to Lee. "I'll have a talk with Zack when we get back to the Tea Plantation." He pulled a blade of grass from the earth and ran it between some front teeth. "Always like to keep youz guys happy and content."

Lee had befriended a Vietnamese villager the week before, one of the strike force leader's sons who helped guard the perimeter kiosks at Camp Holloway, and the young man came to him only that morning, complaining South Vietnamese troops swept through their hamlet at predawn, "drafting" several teen-aged males on the spot—which was understandable. But they also arrested his older sister for trying to prevent the roundup— which was not. The villager had no doubts Thu Thi Thuy was being kept for other purposes.

Lee had checked with the local ARVN command at the near-by provincial headquarters before coming to Brody. The Arvins claimed they knew nothing about an overnight raid and maintained no female prisoners had been brought in in over seventy-two hours. To Lee, that meant either the Arvins were lying, or a maverick force of local drug runners, posing as South Vietnamese soldiers, had kidnapped the woman. Such terror after dark was not uncommon in the area. Several such bands of outlaw troops were rumored to be roaming the Central Highlands.

The First Cav door gunners knew many spots around the Ia Drang Valley that were ideal hideouts for AWOLs and dope kingpins, and Lee hoped a soldier as popular among the troops as Brody could talk a few men into helping them search those locations inbetween missions.

"During our off-duty time?" The soldier reclining beside Doc Delgado rose from beneath his helmet. "You just *gots* to be kidding!"

"*What* off-duty time?" another had complained.

114

"Thu Thi Thuy?" Brody was ignoring all the protests. "That's not a 'Yarde name. What's a Lowlander family doing up here near Pleiku?"

"Has something to do with the Saigon regime's integration project," Lee sneered.

"Integration?" Brody had heard about the plan but wasn't sure about the particulars.

"Yah, the fat cats down south want their own people running the strategic-hamlet projects once the SF advisors are phased out."

"The Montagnardes should be left alone." Delgado did not elaborate except to add, "In more ways than one."

All the negative reaction to Lee's "humanitarian" project got him to thinking. Perhaps they could misappropriate a squad or two and rearrange patrol routes in the colonel's war against idleness and that group of insurgents led by a female guerrilla.

"Maybe you wouldn't have to talk with Zack at all," he suggested, sure the NCO would deny the request anyway. "Maybe we could just see about runnin' by those hideouts you guys have spotted from the air before and—"

"*Possible* hideouts." Brody glanced at his wristwatch.

"Right. *Possible* hideouts. Maybe we could just—"

"Let me think it over, Em-ho." He stood up and stretched. "I'm sure we can work something out."

Lee did not look pleased. "I just don't want to wait too long," he hinted. "The longer she's with them, the more they. . ." His voice trailed off.

"The more ways they can dream up to gangbang her eyeballs out, right?" Brody did not pick gentle words. "Christ, Lee. You don't even know the broad. I'll work something out, okay? Just don't go gettin' your pecker all inflamed over this chick. For all you know, she's put on thirty pounds and dropped her tits since that picture was taken."

"Thanks, Whoremonger. Appreciate it." Lee rose to his feet also and slapped the bottom of his M-16 magazine, making sure it was still properly sealed.

"Saddle up!" Brody called out, kicking a couple of rocks down the line of lounging soldiers.

They had spent the last three hours there, reclining beneath the lazy string of palms, waving at one passing convoy, ignoring

115

another. Their job had been to patrol the length of highway between Camp Holloway and the Tea Plantation in an attempt at capturing the beautiful guerrilla leader and her team of vicious bushwackers. "Just patrol back and forth," Zack had advised them. "Back and forth, whether you make contact or not. If a high-profile patrol discourages future ambushes, then that's just dandy too." But the trouble was, all these men were scheduled to ride slicks on escort duty over the Void tonight, so when was a soldier to sleep? Brody opted for this little stretch of trees along a peaceful bend in the road. It was much quieter than back at camp, where helicopters were coming and going twenty-four hours a day, and it provided a vantage point above the surrounding land that discouraged enemy troops from trying to sneak up on them.

He pointed through the sagging line of palms, toward the jungle's edge. "Through the boonies, gentlemen! *Xin loi*, sorry 'bout that and etcetera, okay? Nobody's perfect. Onward through the fog!"

Ten minutes later, Broken Arrow's crossbow came up like a stop sign.

The squad's point man, cautiously slipping through the trees fifty feet to the right and front of the main group of men, signaled for everyone to freeze in place. There was movement up ahead. And noise: a fist striking bone more than flesh. The nauseating kind of sound that comes from one's nose being smashed to a pulp.

M-16 against his hip, its fire selector rock 'n' roll, Brody glided up through the dense trees so much like a panther on the prowl that Lee's lower jaw dropped in awe at the silence with which the soldier worked.

Brody and the Indian located a clearing up ahead, and he paused at its edge just long enough to motion his men up before disappearing between two giant ferns.

Lee sighed in relief as he exchanged nods with the others; such a shift in their manner of gliding through the jungle meant the noise makers were friendly forces.

"Ju-ju!" Brody was yelling when the rest of his squad caught up with him. Lowering his rifle, he hesitated in restraining the Viet scout. "Hey, knock it off, brother, okay? Mellow out!"

Truong Luong Juu, the *Chieu-Hoi* defector who'd thrown

116

Fletcher and half their gunship crew out the hatch after a man-acled prisoner only three or four days before, was beating a skinny man clad in baggy GI shorts dyed black. The suspected Viet Cong was bound hand and foot. The other Arvins held him balanced atop a tree stump. His face was a wax museum post-card of swollen and mutilated flesh.

"What's the story, anyway?" Brody's smile was a nervous one as he sought to learn what was happening. A few Ameri-cans were with Ju-ju, but they seemed content with standing quietly in the background, all eyes and no action yet witnesses to nothing.

"*No* mellow out!" Ju-ju yelled in Brody's face, eyes flaring. He slugged the prisoner again, to accent his anger, and this time Brody made no attempt to restrain him. "This motherfuck'n VC kill good man!" Spittle flew from Ju-ju's lips when he cursed. "Sit in tree," he pointed above them, "and shoot be-tween eye!" Ju-ju pointed at an Arvin's body at the far edge of the clearing, then hit the guerrilla again.

"Okay, okay." Brody raised his hands in defensive resigna-tion. "Fine, fine. We'll just drag his worthless, no-account commie ass back to Battalion, okay? Let the QCs pull his fin-gernails out or something. Get some good intel on his unit, okay?"

"No get intel!" Ju-ju yelled, covering Brody with more sa-liva. The scout waved at a soldier behind him, who was carry-ing a captured automatic rifle. "He have AK! Proof pos'tive! We kill him now! *Here!* Exe-*cute!*"

Brody decided then and there that there was no reasoning with Truong. His eyes were glazed over with bloodlust; the KIA must have been a close friend. Brody had never seen the soldier so enraged after a firefight. Talk of extracting valuable information from the guerilla would not click. Spilled blood was all that mattered to the scout. But Brody kept talking. "No sweat, come on." He smoothly led Ju-ju away from the semi-conscious insurgent. *"Nguc tu,"* he told the other Vietnamese soldiers, which translated roughly into *Take prisoner.*

They stared at a furious Ju-ju, who glanced off into the clouds shaking his head as if he wanted nothing more to do with the war. It had become too *dinky dau.* The Americans with their compassion, and their money and fancy equipment, their long

117

noses and hairy arms, were ruining everything, turning Truong's war upside down.

"You are right," he finally told Brody. "We follow you back to camp."

"Bullshit. . ."

Brody turned as one of the Americans standing behind the group of Arvins broke rank, his face contorted with rage. "What?" The Whoremonger cracked a grin, recognizing Fletcher. He'd been unaware Snakeman was even a part of this combined patrol.

"I said *bullshit!*" The PFC from Texas stormed up to the wobbling, delirious prisoner, placed his .45 automatic against the man's nostrils, and pulled the trigger without further fanfare.

Brody, frozen in shock, watched the communist's thoughts and hopes, fears and memories, dreams and ideology erupt out the bottom of his skull in a spray of warm, sticky, worthless crimson.

CHAPTER 13

"That will be all, Sergeant." Buchanan dismissed the two military policemen with an appreciative smile and casual salute, but the taller MP with three chevrons on each bicep was not leaving.

"You'll have to sign for them right here, sir." He bent over and made an *X* at the bottom of the release forms.

The colonel frowned and glanced at the charges scribbled across the middle of the arrest report. "Supposing I decline to sign?" He glanced over the big MP's shoulder at Krutch and Larson.

"No problem, sir." The sergeant grinned and turned to face

118

the helicopter pilot, ignoring his partner, whose eyeballs had rolled toward the ceiling at the thought of having to transport this idiot they called the Stork one step further. "We'll just cart 'em back to the slammer in Pleiku City, and eventually one of the convoy escorts'll run 'em down to the monkeyhouse at LBJ."

"Hmmm." Buchanan chewed on his ink eraser a moment. "AWOL...resisting apprehension...uniform violations... carrying concealed weapons...patronizing a—" the colonel's eyebrow rose slightly as he double-checked some wording in the handwritten report—"'...a *bunker* of ill-repute....' The list seems to go on and on."

"Aw, come on, Bull," Krutch pleaded. "Don't let 'em take us south. These apes and their goon platoon have contests just to see how many nightsticks they can break over grunts' heads each shift. Why, I've heard that—"

Buchanan winced and waved the Stork silent. Looking up at the military police NCO, he asked, "Want me to add 'disrespect to a noncommissioned officer' to the charges, sergeant?" The colonel sounded serious.

"No sweat, sir." The MP's grin had not wavered. "That kinda talk doesn't bother us any, colonel," his partner added.

Buchanan's eyes shifted to Larson, but the Professor was staring at the tiger cub chained to the CO's desk. It was chewing on a T-bone. Larson was looking at the big cat's stripes, but he was thinking about Broken Arrow. About how the crafty Indian avoided detection when MPs raided the boom-boom bunker. A tight smile escaped Larson now as he reflected on Broken Arrow's innocent expression outside moments ago. The machine gunner had feigned intense surprise when the MPs escorted Larson and Krutch into the colonel's CP, and then he continued toward the mess tent with Zack, shrugging his shoulders at something the black NCO said.

"And what do *you* think I should do, PFC Larson?" Buchanan interrupted.

Shawn Larson hated it when parents or teachers or army sergeants asked him his opinion in their practiced, sarcastic sort of way. Especially when it came to impending discipline. It could only mean trouble worse than he was already in. But he'd never had an actual officer solicit his opinion. The Professor looked up, glanced over at Krutch—who drilled a don't-bury-us look

119

into him—then said, "Cut us some orders for the Delta, sir. I hear they're gettin' hit real hot and heavy down there."

Warrant Officer Krutch looked like he was going to have a heart attack.

"We could get back to smokin' VC and be out of your hair at the same time," Larson reasoned.

There came a twinkle in Buchanan's eyes as he tried to figure out the private's game, then he just shrugged his shoulders, bent over the release papers, and started to sign.

Choi-oi ran into the command post at that moment, barking and wagging his tail. He jumped up onto the colonel's desk, howled in Buchanan's face, then leaped down onto the startled Bengal cub, snatched its bone, and darted back out the door.

Larson and the Stork were already proned-out on the floor. "Oh, no. . . ." Buchanan's head flopped side to side, irritated but helpless as he pushed his chair back. Joints sore and stiff, it took him a few seconds to drop to first one, then both knees as he prepared to crawl under the heavy metal desk. "I suggest you gentlemen take cover," he told the MPs.

A wave of mortars crashed down into camp the blink of an eye later.

Brody did not speak to Fletcher during the rest of the patrol back to the Turkey Farm. They walked through the trees, avoiding trails, and kept to opposite sides of the group. They both were thinking about the incident with the prisoner, where Snakeman canceled the guerrilla's ticket. Neither man's mind was on the jungle. They'd have probably missed the most primitive booby trap or antipersonnel mine, save for the noise ahead and a point man who was not emotionally involved.

Lee motioned the team down and silent with a raised hand.

Up ahead, the sound of cursing reached their ears. Cursing, and another strange noise, not unlike baseball bats against bone.

"It's not Vietnamese." Brody was up beside Em-ho in a flash, the earlier confrontation with Fletcher temporarily on the back burner. Snakeman was a few feet away now, too—not participating in the converstion, but close enough to hear what was going on up ahead, and what the ranking EM planned to do about it.

"And it's definitely not English." Lee flipped the selector
120

lever on his M-16 from SAFE to AUTO. A round was already in the chamber. PFC Lee always went to extremes to keep five tracers riding piggyback on the top of his banana clips. He felt initial trajectories marked by a bright red glow compensated for failing eyesight. But Lee never wore glasses, and every doctor from BCT through Camp Alpha assured him his vision was 20-20, if not better. The last three bullets at the bottom of each magazine were also tracers—to warn him it was time to slam in a fresh clip.

"Hey, GI!" a well-camouflaged machine gunner stood up behind the entire patrol, smiling triumphantly—they'd all walked right over him without spotting his LP!

The soldier's heavy M-60 was held at port arms, tripoded muzzle skyward.

"What the fu—" Brody started.

Lee had spotted the bilingual name tag even from this distance. "Korean," he whispered. "*South* Korean," allies to the joint ARVN-U.S. cause. "Must be their lookout."

"But who the hell are 'they'?" Brody waved the stocky, ROK trooper back down into his position, then turned to face the increasingly violent noise. Rifle still held defensively, he led Lee and the others through the tree line's edge and into a small clearing.

A Korean master sergeant—as tall as any of the Americans present—whirled around, eyes wide at the intrusion. His hands were holding a teakwood plank.

Without glancing back at his target, an arm fell forward, and the plank smashed against the chest of a VC guerrilla sitting on an anthill, hands bound behind his back. The force of the impact knocked him over, out of sight. Two ROK soldiers rushed to pick him back up, and their NCO hurried over to confront Brody.

"What you do here!?" he snapped. Behind the sergeant, two other prisoners were lined up in similar fashion but had yet to be bloodied.

"We *patrol* here!" Brody replied indignantly. He glanced over at the infantrymen beating their captive and displayed the appropriate level of disgust, but the NCO in charge made no attempt to call them off. Planks struck the back of a head, and this time the guerilla fell over forward, semi-conscious but still

121

breathing.

Reading Brody's eyeball language, the NCO said, "We are *South Korean* soldiers!"

"I can see that." He did not want to sound impressed. But inside, deep in his gut, he was. The Koreans had a reputation for being fierce fighters. And he had seen some of them at work, too, on joint operations outside An Khe, before this mission to the Ia Drang. They were fearless, it seemed, and, unlike some Americans who were just fulfilling their Tour 365 and cared little about the politics of Indochina, the Koreans vehemently hated and despised the communists—*any* communists—to a man.

"They are *Viet Cong!*" The sergeant's voice was still raised. He was starting to get defensive.

"No shit."

The Korean moved closer to Brody, shielding his voice. "We have low-profile recon this grid long time now." His voice had become a whisper, his facial expression a friendly, let's-be-buddies smirk. The aroma of *kimchi* on his breath was overpowering, and Brody recoiled. "Charlie *know* we recon this grid." The Korean made the indignant face this time, scrunching up both lips, which in turn made his cheeks rise slightly. "But these fools," he pointed to the prisoners, "try make us lose face: walk right through our AO! You believe that?" His voice rose again and his eyeballs bulged as he lifted himself up slightly on his toes to look down on the American. *A very Oriental style of intimidation,* Brody decided. "You ever see so arro. . .arro—"

"Arrogant," he helped the Korean out. "You ever see so arrogant a communist?" Sgt. ROK did not acknowledge the grammatical assistance but kept right on talking. "We much teach lesson!"

Brody knew exactly what this man was talking about. The VC—even the North Vietnamese—though seldom hesitant in engaging the American soldiers, rarely crossed the Koreans' path. U.S. forces were hampered by the Geneva Convention and pressures of public opinion, not to mention a liberal press corps that was blowing every American bungle or near-atrocity out of proportion. They even went so far as to spend millions of greenbacks building country-club POW camps to house the captured communists in.

The South Koreans, on the other hand, were notorious for refusing to *take* prisoners.

"I am in good mood today." The NCO patted his belly and smiled. "My men catch barking deer in rain forest and we eat good: fresh meat." He rubbed his stomach vigorously now.

"Ahhh, yes: fresh meat." Brody nodded. He was well aware the sergeant was leading up to something. "Is good you eat good." He matched the Korean's smile.

"So today I release these fools." He motioned at the communists. "We slap 'em aroun' little—"

"So they be sure tell *comrades* about lean, mean, fightin' machine Republic o' Korea soldiers." Brody slipped into pidgin-English.

"Yes!" The NCO grasped the Spec-4's upper arm affectionately. "Let 'em go today. They breathe sigh relief at their good fortune and—"

"Their good fortune and their broken jaws," Brody added, wondering now why he even cared one way or the other.

"Must leave longlast impress—...impress—" "Impression." He slapped at a mosquito. "Yes!" The Korean whisked the cloud of marauding insects away. "So they tell their friends: 'Watch out for Rock soldiers! They baddd mo'fuckers!'" Brody thought of Mohammed just then. "'No mess with Rock soldier! You die *rikky-tik*. You die, du ma. You die, fo' sure!'"

"Hey, Sergeant, you guys with the Seventy-seventh rock-hard Lurps out of Cheo Reo?" Lee asked innocently, sudden admiration clouding his eyes. He'd heard all the stories about these near-legendary jungle warriors.

The smile faded from the Korean's face. He glanced over at the prisoners—one had obviously heard Lee's question. The man's eyes darted away, but there was no mistaking the dry swallow.

"Fuck," the Korean muttered, drawing his pistol. The 77th was supposed to be working the hills between Mang Yang Pass and Hong Kong Hill. They'd endeavored long and hard to leave that impression on the local insurgents. That such an innocent, misplaced query might be overheard and misinterpreted was something the master sergeant could not risk.

Before Brody or any of the others could make a move to stop

123

him, or even object verbally, the ROK soldier was standing in front of the guerrilla in the middle.

His gun arm came up and flew to the left. A thunderous discharge took off the end man's ear and half his face with it.

The prisoner in the middle began shrieking nonstop and bouncing up and down on the anthill, with nowhere to go. The .45 automatic shifted to the right and barked again.

This shot was better placed. The hollow-point round entered through the prisoner's gaping mouth, erasing his expression of disbelief. Chunks of fractured lead and bone exploded out the back of his skull. Echoes from the deafening discharge bounced about in the surrounding tree line, appearing to seek out the prisoner in the middle, who had flopped backwards off the antill, desperate in his quest for cover now.

Brody watched the sergeant calmly walk up to the thrashing Vietnamese, lean over and fire a single, carefully placed shot into his forehead without so much as a change in facial expression.

The sound of the discharge quickly faded away, and the clearing was suddenly silent as a tomb.

Brody and the Korean sergeant locked eyes for a moment, and the Korean finally grinned. It was a Death's-head grin. One the American would never be able to match; he was not in the killing spirit today, so he didn't even try. "Let's go." He waved his men out of the clearing, back into the trees.

Fletcher passed close enough to smell the man's lust for Lady Death. Brody only nodded, unable to absorb the *"Now do you understand this game?"* look the Snakeman was giving him.

Elliot Fletcher slowly shook his head from side to side. He was amused at Brody's sudden indifference—to him an obvious sign of weakness. He smiled now, and it was an evil, leering, demon's sort of smile. Brody had no choice but to nod again and flash a nervous grin in reply.

The Korean soldier laughed loudly as blood from three different sources soaked the earth between his jungle boots, and he too produced a satisfied grin to go with his powerful thumbs-up gesture as he stared at the Americans for approval.

All three rain forest warriors locked eyes for a brief instant, but they were not smiling about the same thing.

CHAPTER 14

When he heard the reassuring clamor of gunship rotors shaking his CP's sheet-metal roof overhead, Col. Buchanan climbed out from under his overturned desk.

"You okay, sir?" Krutch and Larson were helping him up. The MPs who'd escorted the two First Cav troopers back to camp from the off-limits ville were already outside. Their patrol jeep had taken a direct hit and was little more than a molten slab of metal now.

Buchanan dropped into a crouch as the vehicle's gas tank exploded and a fireball of swirling black smoke and green flames billowed skyward. "Damned mortar attacks." He wiped the sweat from his brow and struck the HIGH button on the blue-and-white oscillating fan leaning out from the bottom rung of a makeshift bookshelf. The shelves were nearly bare: manuals on counter-sniping and jungle survival, and an out-of-print copy of Nicholas Uhernik's *Saigon Alley: A Study of the People of the Night* were the only tomes in evidence.

Larson had rushed to the doorway and was watching the gunships take turns dropping their rockets on the mortar team's last-known position. *"Get some!"* He raised his fist into the air.

Krutch watched him for a second, surprised that the usually passive Professor was suddenly in such a mood to see blood spilled. Then, when Larson turned back to face him, the reason was evident. Crimson streaks oozed from minor shrapnel wounds across his chest.

"You all right, son?" Buchanan had spotted the injuries too.

Larson almost responded with a "No Sweat," but, glancing over at his accomplice, read Krutch's tic, and feigned discomfort instead. "Well, sir. . .I could—"

"He *could* use a couple days off," Krutch interpreted the convincing grimace. "That's really what we wanted to talk to you about, sir." He moved closer to the CO.

"Come over here, Shawn." Buchanan was ignoring the warrant officer. "Let me take a look at that." He stooped to open

125

a bottom drawer. "I've got a first-aid kit around here some-where. . . ."

Larson was startled; the colonel actually knew his first name. And he *used* it! "I'll be okay, sir." He started to rub the wound but his hand flew back at the contact. It did hurt. "I'm sure it's just—"

"Get your young ass *over* here!" Buchanan wasn't in the mood for unnecessary bravery. Sappers were not storming the wire. KIAs were not piling up or ammo running out. This was practically the rear echelon. The on-call gunships could handle what little threat Charlie posed to the perimeter.

Larson peeled off his sweat-slick fatigues blouse, and all three soldiers were surprised at the size and color of the swelling over his right pectoral.

Though his arms from hands to biceps were tanned a dark brown like most vets in The Nam, his chest was bone white. The area around the wounds was a collage of black and purple shades. "Whooo-EE!" Krutch shook his head. "You really got clobbered, Shawn!"

"Not as bad as it looks, I don't think." Buchanan had the first-aid kit out and was reaching for the tweezers.

"I'll be okay, sir—really!" Larson just wanted to get out of there.

"Maybe it would be better if we just call the medics, sir." Krutch seemed to hold little confidence in Buchanan's abilities as healer.

"I can *walk* over to the dispensary, Colonel." Larson's chest was heaving now. "It's nothing. . .really!"

"Nonsense." Buchanan wiped a trickle of blood away. He motioned for Larson to sit down on the desk top. "I've known men to bleed to death from much more minor injuries, believe it or not," he said. "Now, look here. . .see this?" Once the top layer of thick, dark, coagulating blood was wiped away, a bit of protruding shrapnel became clearly evident. "Looks like bout a quarter-inch chunk of shrapnel, son." He expertly took hold of it with the tweezers' edges. "Have it out in a flash. On the count of three. . ." He watched Larson's chest swell in antici-pation. "Now, are we ready?"

Without awaiting a nod, either in the affirmative or negative, Buchanan suddenly jerked the shrapnel free without counting

126

at all. He slapped a pressure bandage over the puncture wound, but it was not bleeding much. "Hold that in place there," he directed, scraping the smaller bits of splintered metal away without warning.

About to groan, Larson's back stiffened, and he tried to sit up straight, but the colonel's firm hands were on his shoulders, forcing him to lie back against the desk top. "Settle down, settle down," Buchanan said. "Let the bandage do its job. Just rest a couple minutes." He glanced up at Krutch. "Landline the mobile dispensary and have 'em get a couple corpsmen over here. Just to check him out, official-like."

Krutch nodded and headed for a field phone on the other side of the large reinforced tent.

"I appreciate it, sir." Beads of perspiration were rolling down Larson's face.

"You'll be okay, son. I'm not even sure this rates a Purple Heart," he joked, hoping to buoy the private's spirits. "But we'll see. Maybe a three-day pass into Pleiku City is all you really need."

"That's kinda what we were hopin' to talk to you about, Bull." Krutch had made the call for a field ambulance and was back beside his CO.

"'We?'" Buchanan produced a suspicious scowl as he cocked an eyebrow at the chopper jock. "Where, Mister Krutch, do you get this 'we'?"

The warrant officer checked Larson's expression, found the nod of support he was seeking, and proceded with an amended version of their plan. "Well, sir. . .me and the Professor both need a couple more days off from this crazy war."

"What?" Buchanan exploded, the fatherly smile part of the past.

"We need a couple more days down in—"

"'A couple more?'" Buchanan slapped the first-aid kit's lid shut. He pointed out through the doorway at the military policemen trying to retrieve the M-60 from its Hog-support bar in the back seat. "Seems to me two Mike Papas just brought you in from 'a couple' unauthorized days down in that off-limits ville by—"

"Sir," Larson interrupted, pulling a *Choi-oi*. He hoped his wounds would sway Buchanan. "All we're asking for is a

127

couple. . .a *few*"—he changed his mind suddenly—"extra days leave."

"I was prepared to give *you* a day or two off to recover from the punch of shrapnel, Larson." The colonel folded his arms across his chest in a manner that made the biceps bulge to nearly twice their normal size. "But Mister Krutch must remain on the flight line, if you catch my drift." The slightest hint of a grin crept back across his features.

"Sir, we are prepared to. . ." Krutch began, but Buchanan cut him off.

"Prepared to *what?*" he asked suspiciously, eyes narrowing.

The warrant officer pulled a folding made-in-Saigon card from inside his thigh pocket. He handed it to Buchanan.

Inside, a group photo of Krutch, Larson, and two sleazy-looking women of questionable virtue, all arm-in-arm, stared out at the surprised CO. "You don't mean—" he began.

"We are prepared to take this all the way, Colonel," Krutch insised.

"This is blackmail!" Buchanan brought the picture closer to his eyes.

"Unless we get a week off from the war, sir," Larson said, "we plan to initiate the paperwork to make these two. . . ladies—"

"—Of the evening!" Buchanan interjected, eyes blinking rapidly.

"To make them our wives, sir."

"You wouldn't!" Buchanan handed the souvenir card-and-snapshot back to Krutch.

"We *would,* Colonel," Larson threatened. "We *will.*"

"Most certainly," added the helicopter pilot. It was a joke warrant officers in the First Cav subjected their commanders to every once in a while. Oh sure, now and then a naive cherry boy fresh into An Khe with his virginity and two Cong kills under his belt would fall head over heels in love with some forty-year-old Honda Honey who looked twenty and possessed a pelvis lubed like a teenager's. The kid would try to take her back to The World with him, his little souvenir of the Orient. Buchanan or one of his aides usually took the kids aside long enough to explain what life on the outside—life beyond the killing zone and gunship raids—was really like. Maybe show them a young-

128

er set of thighs from Pleiku City or even treat them to an all-nighter with some Danang doom-pussy. Anything to break the spell...pull them through the vulnerable stage years ahead of schedule...with fewer scars on their heart.

But warrant officers—ace chopper jocks—were supposed to be just a bit more seasoned and mature than that.

A marriage application involving one of the locals—and its subsequent CID background investigation—would reach all the way up to division headquarters. And that was the kind of harassment, teasing, and ridicule the CMOH recipient didn't need right now.

"You wouldn't," Buchanan repeated.

"We *would,*" both soldiers affirmed in unison. Frowning, Buchanan took the photo from Krutch again and inspected the women's faces. "Christ, Hal. This one looks like the Moanin' Lisa."

" She *is* the Moanin' Lisa." Larson beamed proudly. "You don't think we'd try and hitch up to some bona fide know-nothing cherry girls, do you, sir? Me and the Stork only go in for real class acts!"

"There *are* no cherry girls left in Vietnam," Krutch reminded him.

"She's a class act, allright." Buchanan was shaking his head in resignation again. "She's probably had every graduate of the Air Force Academy's Class of Sixty-four at one time or another—"

"At least twice." Larson smiled as if he'd just tricked the colonel into a checkmate.

"You two men are disgusting."

"Thank you, sir." Krutch sensed the dismissal coming and brought his hand up in a casual half-salute.

"We work hard at it, sir." Larson imitated the pilot. "I'll have to mull this one over." Buchanan waved them toward the door. He stopped to watch the MPs outside trying to douse their jeep fire with a malfunctioning extinguisher.

"We'd sure appreciate an answer by fourteen hundred hours, sir." Krutch executed a semi-serious about-face.

"So we can start working on the invitations." Larson wanted to see how much it took to detonate a Full Bird.

"Out!" Buchanan threw up his hands. "Get the hell out!"

A thunderclap of an explosion, followed by a succession of rapid secondary blasts, forced the two crewmen back into the CP. The fire in the jeep had reached a box of M-60 ammunition, and tracers were arcing out all over the camp like a Fourth of July fireworks fountain turned atomic.

Larson and Krutch dove over Col. Buchanan's desk in their haste to find cover from the popping rounds. The problem was that their commander was already utilizing the space. Forearms shielding his head from ricochets, the Bull roared as Stork and the Professor piled in on top of him.

Larson bit his lower lip in apprehension as the unmistakable sound of breaking bone reached his ears in between the endless whistle of ricochets and Krutch's insane laughter.

"Which one of you two jerk-offs put Neil Nazi's arm in a cast?" Brody searched expressions across the dying glow of C-4. They had been using the chip of plastic explosive to heat the evening's C-rations earlier, but now everyone was bloated on cans of listless spaghetti and artifical, made-in-Manila meatballs.

Larson laughed. "Hey, it wasn't my fault! The Stork flew to cover and I followed, you know? Blame it on Mr. Krutch." The Professor was wearing every article of protective clothing available: flak jacket, steel pot...even an old chickenplate he'd bought off a single-digit midget from the Headhunters.

"I wasn't looking for someone to blame." Brody reached over to shake Krutch's hand. "I was looking for someone to congratulate."

"Wish we had some potatoes to go with the pasta." Lee rifled through the empty C-ration cans, but the others seemed to be ignoring him.

"Since when don't you get along with the Bull?" Fletcher eyeballed Brody half-accusingly.

"Well, I don't *not* get along with him...I mean—"

"Uh-huh...uh-huh." Fletcher responded with a tell-me-more-lies nod, which didn't seem to anger Brody in the least.

"What I meant was that...well, you know. He's an officer. It's kinda funny to see an officer get his like that."

"But I thought the Bull was your hero," Fletcher baited him. "*Everyone* thought the Bull was your hero."

130

"Fuck you, Snakeman."

Lee leaned forward and flipped the sputtering chip of C-4 over, then placed an empty C-rations can across it. The can had no top or bottom. Holes were punched along its sides for ventilation. Atop the can he placed a small GI coffee pot. "Yah, I like to see them occifers squirm once in a while too."

"So did you guys get your week off?" Fletcher's tone revealed how bored he was getting with the conversation.

"Are you kidding?" Larson rubbed the thick bandage around his chest.

"We were lucky to get two days," Krutch answered. "And that's if Command doesn't hit us with an unannounced CA."

"What's tonight look like?" Lee looked up from his army-issue brew.

"Tonight looks quiet. *Reeeal* quiet. Word from Rumor Control is that the Arvins paid Charlie off so they'll lay low in their tunnels for a couple days."

"Arvin must be movin' some black-market goods around." Brody rubbed his chin.

"Most probably." Krutch reached for the coffee pot. "Regardless, it gives *me* a couple extra hours of Z time to contemplate strategy from here on out."

"'Strategy?'" Brody cast him a suspicious glance. "You guys are gonna go *di-di* boppin' down into one o' them off-limits villes and get your peckers peeled off by some Cong cunt," he predicted.

"At least it'd be a million-dollar wound, sport." "Sure." Brody took the coffee pot from him. "Sure ticket onto a freedom bird back to The World. For what? What would you have waitin' for ya back there? A welfare check from Uncle Sammy to pay the rent on some cramped little skid-row dump where you wouldn't even have a pud to pull on when it got boring? *Ha!* Not me, brother."

Krutch's quick wit had abandoned him. He couldn't come up with a shocking retort or a comical insult to save his life, and the bunker fell silent. The only sound was that of their already overcooked coffee boiling again.

Krutch and Brody were sharing Larson's bunker that night for some small talk before everyone at the Turkey Farm—those who weren't participating in night ops—hit the sack. Fletcher

131

was there too, as was Lee. Truong Ju-ju and one of the QC interpreters, Phung Van Thieu, had been there earlier, but when the two Vietnamese broke out some *nuoc-mam* to go with their rice packets, Snakeman threw them both out, keeping the case of warm '33' beer they had brought along.

"Then what do you think the chances are of us..." Lee's voice trailed off as a jeep rumbled past outside, at ground level, and artillery thundered in the distance.

"Out-going," Fletcher mumbled under his breath.

"Rodg, out-going."

"'Of us' *what*, Em-ho?" Brody tossed a bottle of the *ba-muoi-ba* over to Lee.

"Don't tell me you've still got the hots for that missing villager." Fletcher all but moaned this time.

"I've been checkin' around during my off-hours," he started to explain.

"Then you're *wastin'* your off-hours," Fletcher interrupted. "Anybody who's tellin' you 'whatever' is lying'!"

"I just figured with the little unofficial truce and...well, if they are...if the Arvins are movin' some black market goods, then just maybe they're movin' some—"

"Some sweet 'n' sour cherry-girl cunt?" Fletcher took out his pistol, ejected the magazine, flipped off the safety, and pulled the slide back. A .45-caliber slug flew through the air in a slight arc, end over end. The Snakeman leaned to the side, catching it in his teeth. "Don'...coun'...on...i'." He couldn't pronounce the *T*s with the cartridge in his mouth.

"Well, I was figurin' it wouldn't hurt to check around out in those sectors around her ville. I mean, since we weren't doin' anything anyway—"

"Well, you figured wrong, Em-ho. You figured—"

A lazy shadow watching them from the top of the sandbagged bunker entrance squealed suddenly, and *Choi-oi* came rolling down the steps, barking and growling.

Brody leaned over to grab him, but the mongrel scampered out of his reach, hopping over Lee's and Fletcher's laps too. The Stork tried to clobber him with his empty VC HUNTING CLUB coffee mug, but *Choi-oi* was too fast for all of them. Running a tight circle across the five soldiers and barking non-stop the whole time, he disappeared back up the bunker's olive-

132

drab steps.

"What's *his* major mal*fuck*tion?" Fletcher threw an empty beer can after *Choi-oi*.

"Weirdest goddamned half-breed mutt I ever did see," Krutch added. "Why, I remember the time ol' *Choi-oi* had one of his legendary flashbacks and came stumblin' into the mess hall, eyes crossed, tongue hangin' out and—"

The Stork rolled backwards suddenly, eyes darting about in search of more cover than the sandbags overhead afforded. "Hey!" Fletcher called out, but then he too was diving away from the steps.

"Fire in the hole!" someone else finally yelped.

A grenade was slowly rolling down the steps toward them.

CHAPTER 15

"Hey, hey, *HEY!*" Three sets of boots were stumbling down the sandbagged steps into Larson's bunker. "Greetings and salute*asians!*"

"Yah, you worthless skate motherfuckers!" The voices sounded to Brody like Cordova and Broken Arrow. "Hey, where is everybody?"

But, of course, they knew exactly where everyone was: flattened out against the bunker's elusive corners, each man trying to make his body smaller, less of a target, one with the earth and precious sandbags. Brody and Lee and Fletcher and Larson and Krutch were hoping to survive just one more tempest of shrapnel, secretly praying they would *all* survive, but, failing that, hoping God or Buddha or whoever was in charge Upstairs would take one of the others. Words of guilt, written in the gunsmoke: *"He was my buddy—I loved him, and I'll miss him—but better him than me."* It was one of the reasons soldiers

133

learned a tenth of the way through their Tour 365 that close friendships were better left unformed in The Nam.

Two-Step was down on one knee, picking up the Korean-vintage, pineapple-style grenade. "Hey, mannn, where the *hell* is everybody?" The Indian was as drunk as any of them in the bunker. Brody looked up just long enough to see that the grenade's pin was still intact, but Broken Arrow had his finger looped through it, and he flattened out behind a pile of sandbags again.

Two-Step pulled the pin, the top part of the grenade flipped open, and a two-inch flame leaped up, illuminating the bunker with flickering shards of light.

"A cigarette lighter!" Fletcher was the first one on his feet. "The sonofabitch has only got a cigarette lighter!"

"*KILL* the mother—" Lee was flying across the room feet first, like a martial artist, but Broken Arrow simply knocked him out of the air with a forearm. Em-ho dropped heavily and rolled across the bunker floor, groaning.

"So what's for chow?" Cordova leaned closer to the Indian, a Blue Ruby cigarette in his mouth. Using the flame from Two-Step's grenade, he lit up and the bunker began filling with smoke.

Brody, leaning on an elbow, threw an empty C-rations can at the man. Delgado was with them.

"Sarge, I can't believe you hang out with those two jokers. Shit, we coulda wasted 'em both."

"Yah." The medic sighed with drooping shoulders. "And my mama wishes I'd a been a lawyer. So what else is new?"

"Heyyy, dudes." Two-Step got the corner lantern going again and extinguished his grenade. The Comanche's words were slurred. He sounded as if he'd been chasing some hard liquor with peyote or worse. "Cut us some slacks, okay?"

"Preferably with Sophia Loren gracing the insides of 'em." Delgado winked.

"Ol' Corky and me just got in from a two-day Lurp over the tree line," Broken Arrow continued. "Can ya dig it?"

"Powerful-strange place it was, indeed." Cordova made his eyes grow really big. "Out there in the mist-enshrouded boonies beyond the Chu Pong Massif."

"'Mist-enshrouded?'" Delgado's chest inflated with his

134

smile. His expression was one of pleasant disbelief. "So what you writin'—a book or something'?"

As the light from the lantern grew, injuries both men had sustained in the field became more evident. Both Cordova and Two-Step were covered with cuts. "Jesus." Delgado instantly sobered. "What happened to you guys? I never noticed all the blood topside. I guess it was just so dark and all—"

"Thorns," Broken Arrow said matter-of-factly.

"It was a real bad scene," Cordova explained, lowering his head between his knees as both men sat side-by-side, cross-legged. "Charlie hit the patrol with a monster. Me and goofy here were the only ones to make it out. Charlie—he came out o' the woodwork, man. Spiderholes galore. I even fell in one tryin' to beat feet back to the LZ. Think I cracked some poor fucker's neck with my boot in his face."

"*Fuck* the 'poor fuckers.'" Broken Arrow's mood was souring. He drew a survival knife from the sheath strapped to his calf and began stabbing the sandbags on the floor between his legs. "Take...no...prisoners...." Each word was accented by the sound of the blade slamming down into the bags. "Take ...no...prisoners...."

A *monster* was a cluster of a dozen or more claymore antipersonnel mines jury-rigged to go off at the same time—either by remote control or a trip wire. Claymores threw out over 700 ball bearings in a devastating arc that rarely left anything in the kill zone alive.

"Take...no...prisoners...." Two-Step kept stabbing at the sandbags.

Larson's lips parted, then froze. It looked as though he really wanted to say something about all the work and effort that went into building the bunker, but the Professor wisely decided to remain silent.

"Anyway," Cordova continued, "we had to beat feet through the jungle. LZ was a waste, 'cause our radio man and his Prick-25 was eaten by the monster, you know?"

Lee's eyes were growing bigger than pigeon eggs as he listened to Cordova, all ears. "So we had to hightail it through the thorns, man." Corky allotted a few seconds to stare through each man sitting across the fire from him. "For *milllles*. We ran through thorns for miles...."

135

Lee swallowed hard, and though everyone in the bunker heard him, not one man laughed.

"It was Hades come to haunt me, brothers." Broken Arrow produced his best expression of distress. "Ol' Two-Step thought he was a dead Injun, 'cause he could smell that *nuoc-mam* on Charlie's breath, and at close quarters like that, a soldier's gonna get spooked."

"I never ran so fast in my life," Cordova admitted, running his fingers along the back of his shoulders. He pulled a thorn free without wincing and showed it to them. "See? I didn't even feel that—not even now. That's how charged up I still am, brothers."

The bunker's entryway overhead filled suddenly with a huge, dark shape, and the men below all tensed. Size-thirteen jump boots, reflecting moonlight, slowly started down before Sgt. Zack spoke. "Permission to descend down into the Hell Hole!"

"Enter, Leo!" Krutch called out, moving some gear aside. "Have a fucking seat in front of the soapbox. We're listening to tales of woe." The only way Krutch knew to pluck the men's spirits from the pit was to belittle what they had gone through. "Hope you brought your violin."

"And handkerchief," said Lee. "OD green and government issue." Zack's smile seemed to add light to the dark bunker. "But I won't be staying long. Just trying to track down two polecats who...well, lookie here." He spotted Corky and Two-Step. "Just who I was looking for. Lt. Winston wants you alleged heroes over at the CP for debriefing. MI wants to hear your story. On the double!" He did not sit down. "What?" He glanced around. "No pussy down here?"

"Let's go, Tonto." Cordova grabbed Two-Step's elbow. "Wait 'till the boys in Military Incompetence hear about *this* one." Corky turned to face Zack on the way up the steps.

"Not even an inflatable doll." Lee answered the sergeant's question regarding sexual partners.

"The Chu Pong Massif is one mean motherfucker." Broken Arrow paused in front of the taller NCO and tapped his barrel of a chest with a rigid forefinger. "It's bad news, Leo the Lionhearted. Even for lifers like you...and me.... Some powerful-bad magic floatin' about out there. I don't look forward to returnin' to the Chu Pong anytime soon...."

Zack did not appear intimidated or even offended by the physical contact, but his massive head lifted up and back slightly, like a bloodhound that had located a disagreeable scent.

"Hey, Sarge," Fletcher asked. "What's the word on that goofy Mohammed-Yo'mama. I'll bet he's breakin' big rocks into little rocks down Long Binh-way, right? Deep in the bowels of the LBJ, right? Tell me it's so, Sergeant, sir. I can't get a straight answer outta *any*body."

Pausing a moment for dramatic effect, Zack rubbed his nose as if he couldn't decide whether the subject matter was just distasteful, or of such a personal nature he couldn't discuss it. He stared up the steps and after a loud sigh, he said, "Nurse Maddox elected not to press charges. Seems ol' Clarence the Third saved her young butt from that mortar attack, as well as a couple VC to boot. They got his no-account black ass down in Nha Trang, undergoin' a psychological."

"Christ." Fletcher kicked the coffee pot over, and Lee rushed in to right it.

The display of emotion seemed to amuse Zack. "Wouldn't surprise me if that angel of mercy, bleeding-heart lieutenant put Malcolm Big Mouth in for a medal," the big sergeant added. And then he was gone.

Fletcher glanced over at Brody and smiled. "Fuckin' Leo," he laughed. "Always crackin' us rednecks up. The man *do* have a way with words, don't he?"

"So let's please get back to the business at hand." Lee wrinkled his nose at the smell of spilled brew, but there was something else gnawing at the edges of his nerves. He turned the lantern light up a bit to confirm his suspicions. The odor of fresh blood was heavy in the cramped bunker too. It had collected in two small pools where the Lurp commandos had been squatting. "Are you guys going to slip out through the wire with me tonight or not?"

"Well, all right!" Broken Arrow reached over and clapped Lee on the back. "Plannin' to trot down to the ville for a little midnight quickie, eh Em-ho?"

"Naw," Fletcher answered for him. "Jap wants to recon the cords out at-6868. He's got the hots for one of them village maidens ARVN absconded off into the twilight with—"

"Ain't no such thing as a twilight in The Nam," Cordova
137

maintained. "It's light and then it's dark. Now you see the horror of it...now you don't. Ain't no in-between."

Fletcher ignored him. They could argue about sunsets in the tropics all night. "Jap's got the hots for a village maiden our Arvin buddies absconded off *into the twilight with* coupla days ago," he repeated. "Jap's all hunky-dory with some guy from the ville whose sister was kidnapped—"

"She's a real looker." Lee shook his head, hoping the obvious enthusiasm would sway these vets' decision whether or not to help him.

"Jap wants to play Prince Charming or Sir Galahad or something." Fletcher was critical of the plan, considering it a waste of time and energy. "Five bucks says she can't even speak English—"

"So I'll learn more Vietnamese." Lee was getting angry.

"—And probably wouldn't give us the time of day if we *did* 'rescue' her. Besides"—Snakeman poured himself a refill from what little remained of the murky brew—"them Arvins get pretty damned hostile when you fuck with their women. Remember when they sliced Griff's face from cheek to chin? He wasn't such a pretty boy anymore after that, was he?" His grin disappeared, tone turning serious. "We could actually—"

"Em-ho will *always* be the pretty boy of the Pack," Brody interrupted Fletcher with a laugh, and Lee nodded in agreement.

"We could actually take some casualties on something like this," Fletcher finished his sentence. "Think about it, Jap. Do you really want one of us to lose blood over some Viet bitch. Shit, you don't even know if she's got hair on her pussy."

Delgado erupted into laughter over some image Fletcher's words had conjured up in his mind. Lee was glad Snakeman couldn't tell he was blushing. "If she does, I'll make her shave it off!" he said simply, and Delgado laughed even louder, rolling over onto his side.

"Gimme a break, youz guys," he pleaded.

"And Zack would lop off the heads of anyone lucky enough to survive such an adventure." Brody addressed Fletcher's concerns. He did not look forward to any extracurricular escapades right now but would go along with whatever the others decided.

"Don't waste your time on these local holes, Em-ho," Broken Arrow advised somberly. "If I've said it once, I've said it
138

bookoo billions of times: They're nothin' but a world of hurt, bud. Save your little wee-whanger-woo for some geisha honey back in Tokyo."

" I've never been to Japan." Lee's tone was of someone hurt.

"Oh." The Indian did not sound embarrassed in the least. "In that case, disregard my last."

Cordova avoided the other soldiers' eyes, choosing to stare into the last blue flames of C-4 instead. For weeks now, ever since being transferred to Camp Holloway from An Khe, he'd been heartsick over his separation from Thuan. A refugee from the devastation at Xom Moi to the east, she spoke little English. They had communicated those first days by hand signals and pidgin Vietnamese and with their eyes. Always their eyes.

Cordova had rescued *her* from a squad of Arvins as she walked, barefoot through the dust, from the marketplace back to a hillside abode she shared with her younger brother—their parents were dead. The South Vietnamese soldiers had first confronted her with the intention of searching the pails that hung suspended from a pole across her shoulders, but their interest quickly turned to the modest curves hidden beneath her unflattering peasant's tunic and black pantaloons. Cordova and another GI intervened when Thuan protested their probing fingers and push came to shove. The five Arvins backed down: It was hard to ignore an M-79 leveled at your waist.

Cordova had talked his way past the gate MPs every day for the next two weeks, smuggling food to Thuan and her brother so the girl wouldn't have to endure the dangerous trek to market. Friendship had evolved into trust and companionship, even dependence, and their bond soon matured into love.

Cordova envisioned a day when the war, or at least his tour of duty, would be over, and he could resettle Thuan in one of the bigger cities: Pleiku, or Saigon. Or maybe he could even take her, instead of just down to the beach outside Qui Nhon...*to America*! Yes, wouldn't that blow little Thuan's never-seen-a-city mind!

So it was that Cordova was hurt by his best friend's remarks about Vietnamese girls, and he did not participate in the conversation but just stared into the dying glow of plastic explosive. He listened to Two-Step's irreverent voice somewhere in the dark at his side, but he saw Thuan's innocent smile in the glow of heat beneath the dented GI coffee pot. He loved and needed her so desperately right now.

In his mind, he could see her back in An Khe, in that little cramped bungalow he'd rented for her, sleeping on the hard floor mat, alone and, perhaps, sobbing herself to sleep, waiting for her beloved Corky to return.

Corky. The name made him laugh. *How did that slip into my thoughts?*

"Did you ask for permission to finally say something?" Broken Arrow elbowed him playfully.

"He didn't say anything," Fletcher observed. "He just laughed."

"What you laughin' about, boy?" Doc Delgado stared up at him with an evil grin.

"Screw *you,* hombre!" Cordova pointed down at the medic, his own smile back now.

"Aw, fuck all you clowns and the mules you rode in on!" Lee stomped up the pile of sandbags.

"I'll go with you, Lee!" Cordova called out suddenly, rising back to his feet.

"What?" Broken Arrow rose too, his body language a protest.

"Just let me check a Hog out from the armory. We should take along a little extra insurance in the form of added fire-pow—"

Men were suddenly running past outside, and the bunker entrance became blocked by a looming shadow: Sgt. Zack had returned. Behind the stocky NCO, a European-style *hi-lo* scrambler siren was going off, signaling a rescue operation. "No one's goin' anywhere!" Zack announced. "Unless it's up in one o' my gunships! We got grunts callin' for God, and the only one listenin' tonight is *me*! How many o' you opium warlords are too fucked-up to fly?"

A treetop sniper began peppering the compound with poorly aimed AK shots as soon as the last man, Fletcher, emerged from the Hell Hole. Bent over, free hands holding steel pots atop their heads, the soldiers raced across the steaming tarmac to the waiting gunships.

A crescent moon, glowing faint and orange, hung low over

the horizon. "Ahhh." Brody slammed a banana clip into his M-16, chambered a round, then slung it over his back, upside down. "A good sign . . . *You see that moon, boys?*" he yelled, climbing up into a Huey with winged *Pegasus* across its snout. "It's a damn good sign, *damn* good!"

A green tracer whizzed by his face and disappeared out the opposite hatch without hitting anything, but the Whoremonger didn't seem to notice. He was still staring at the moon. It made him think of an old buddy of his who was flying slicks in I-Corps with the 282nd Attack Helicopter Company. Their gun-ships had large orange moons painted across the snout, with a black Halloween cat, its back arching in anger, standing in front of the moon. The platoon was, of course, known as the Black Cats.

"Where's that cunt-humping coward Larson?" Zack demanded, leaning precariously on a landing skid as flapping rotors above him became invisible, their edges lifting slightly into a silver halo. Starlight filtering through the blades seemed to make his smooth-shaved head gleam.

"He's still down in the bunker!" Fletcher yelled on the run as a five-round burst of bullets ricocheted between his boots, making him dance. "Jesus *H.*!" He dove into *Pegasus* on top of Brody.

"The Professor busy writin' his suicide note, Sarge!" Someone managed to laugh as more tracers floated in and bounced off the metal tarmac planks between lifting ships.

Zack watched a couple arc off into the night gracefully, then climbed into the bird ahead of Brody's. "*Suicide* gonna be his *last* concern when I get through with him!" The sergeant gave his pilot a thumbs-up, and the AC pulled pitch. "Forget him! Let's lift!"

"Everyone up back there?" A strange voice clicked-in to *Pegasus*'s intercom system. A pilot Brody didn't recognize.

"We're up!" He gave the thumbs-up, as Zack had, and the ship tilted tail high and ascended. He could still hear Zack yelling above the clamor of rotors on the ground.

"But Larson's sorry ass is mine when we get back, and—"

"I'm comin'! I'm comin'!" The Professor's head popped up out of the bunker entrance. "Hold on to your trousers, Leo!" Larson glanced around, trying to pinpoint the sniper, but sev-

141

eral rounds struck the sandbag nearest his cheek, and he dropped back out of sight.

"Get your steel pot on!" Zack called to him above the roar of rifle fire off to the right. Gunnies from Delta Company had spotted the sniper's muzzle flash and were pouring red-and-white tracers on full-auto up into a tree line just north of the perimeter.

"I can't find it!" Larson called, trying to dash out of the Hell Hole without his helmet. Another wave of bullets drove him back underground.

Despite all the incoming, there appeared to be only a single rifleman, the same terrible shot who'd been harassing them ever since 7th Cav had accompanied the rest of the division into Ia Drang Valley. "Make a run for my chopper!" Zack directed. He was behind the hatch M-60. "Soon as you hear my Hog start barkin'! I'm gonna lay you down some cover fire!"

He didn't wait for a reply but began firing the heavy machine gun in the direction Delta Company's tracers were all converging. With bullets kicking up dirt and shards of lead and metal on both sides of him, Larson sprinted for Zack's helicopter. He had no rifle but was holding a pistol which he fired blindly into the distant tree line.

Larson flew over a jeep. Its headlight exploded as a round passed between his legs and bits of flying glass sprinkled down his collar.

Larson somersaulted across the last few feet of tarmac. A tracer struck the plank in front of him, exploding in a shower of glowing green sparks, but he rolled through it, uninjured. And then he was clambering aboard the gunship, Zack reaching down to grab his arm and pull him up, and the big metallic predator was lifting off, its rotors screaming protest as they strained against several layers of heat smothering the Turkey Farm.

Zack poured M-60 fire down into the tree line as they passed over it, but when they were several hundred meters away Larson could still clearly see green tracers of East-Bloc manufacture zinging down into the landing pads, one at a time.

The Professor readied the M-60 on his side of the chopper, slid into the monkeystraps, slipped on the headphones, then leaned out the hatch and peered back in the direction of the helipads. None of the other three birds in their rescue formation had banked off to swoop around and finish off the guerrilla; his fate was left to the troops on the ground. And now Larson could see *red* tracers bouncing about, but he knew deep inside, down in the pit of his gut, that they hadn't silenced the gunman. Once again, ol' Luke had eluded them.

"Whew, that was Weird with a capital *W*!" Treat Brody whispered into his mouthpiece as he crouched behind a hatch MG in the gunship following Zack's and Larson's.

"Definitely," the peter pilot replied, eyes glued to his instrument panel. The sniper had managed to hit *Pegasus* in the tail boom, and, though warning alarms were screaming into his headset, the craft was experiencing no loss of power.

Definitely weird, Brody mused as he watched the treetops skim past a couple of yards below in excess of one hundred miles per hour. *Normally you leave a hot LZ like that and it's all over. . .you're home free, but tonight the mission hasn't even begun. It hasn't even started, and already I'm soaked in sweat and ol' Peg took a couple rounds in the rump. Definitely a strange feeling in my one good nut about this. Definitely. . .*

Fletcher was managing the M-60 across the cabin from him, and they exchanged nods as both gunnies readied their weapons, unsure what really lay ahead in the dark. All anyone knew was that it was a rescue of some sort. No word yet on whether they were racing to a hot or cold LZ. "Wasn't that mindfuck to the max back there?" Snakeman had one of his multicolored boas hanging around his neck for good luck.

"Just what I was thinking," Brody clicked into the intercom system again. "One of these nights I'm gonna camp out in that damn tree line and just wait for ol' Luke to pop up outta his spiderhole, then I'm gonna eye-job the sucker so both sockets are of the seven-point-six-two persuasion in regards to diameter! Then I'm gonna—"

"Knock off the chatter, Whoremonger," the pilot overrode him. "LZ in zero-five, and it's supposed to be hot as a whore's hole on Saturday night!"

Brody wanted to ask if that was zero-five minutes or zero-five seconds, but he had his answer soon enough. Green, red, and white tracers were sailing out of the rain forest canopy up ahead like geodes from a volcano. Despite the cover of darkness, the pilot could see a dark blanket of gunsmoke cloaked the landing zone like a death shroud.

There was no one else in the cabin with them, other than the two warrant officers up front. Zack, their regular crew chief, opted to hop aboard one of the other slicks carrying less-experienced soldiers. Brody and the Snakeman were on their own. There were no troopers crowding the harness straps, preparing to charge off upon landing, either. Except for several ammo boxes of 7.62mm latched to the center of the floor, *Pegasus*'s belly was empty, waiting for the squad of grunts down in Void Vicious to clamber aboard.

"What's the skinny, Mister Gabe?" Brody finally figured out who the AC was by the revolver hanging from his web belt. Most pilots carried their sidearms in shoulder holsters. Gabriel was the only chopper jock in the Valley that fancied himself a Wild West gunslinger. "Spill some *nuoc-mam* on us." He risked clicking-in after being told to stay off the system.

Warrant Officer Cliff Gabriel didn't seem perturbed. "Sounds like it's gonna be a Romeo Foxtrot," he replied dryly, hesitation in his tone. "All I know is that we're responding to a Brass Monkey." Romeo Foxtrot was military radio phonetic for *Rat Fuck*, which was how the pilots referred to doomed missions. A *Brass Monkey* was an inter-service radio call for help. It could involve different branches of the armed forces, or even soldiers from the ARVN or ROK services. Regardless, when a Brass Monkey went out over the air, all birds flew balls to the wind. It was an ear-popping code to be used only in cases of extreme emergency.

"Tango Charlie says a squad of Arvins ran into a counter-ambush up ahead," the peter pilot clicked-in. "They've been out in the sticks over a week now, dressed up like NVA, shovelin' in a whole shitload o' intel, but I guess Cong Control got wise to them. Blew a monster on the rice eaters. Heavy casualties, according to Tango Charlie." His ears were glued to the UHF channel. The control tower was feeding them updated information even as they flew to the extraction point. "Should be able to fit 'em all into one chopper—*this one*, unfortunately. Krutch's bird will stay afloat just in case. . . ."

His last few words were drowned out by a series of explosions erupting up ahead. Nonstop exchanges of rifle fire were

144

now competing with the *whop-whop-whop* of rotors beating overhead. Gabriel clicked-in, ". . . And the other two slicks'll circle around, providing cover fir—"

Gabriel was normally a Dustoff pilot; that is, he usually flew unarmed, medical evacuation slicks, or medevacs. But he had played with gunships before, and tonight, with the manner in which they were scrambled from the bunkers and tents, it was every man to the nearest Huey. Gabriel's just happened to be *Pegasus. Boy, will the Stork be pissed when he realizes he hopped into the wrong bird.* Brody leaned into his M-60 and sent a burst of rounds down into a cluster of flashes on the ground. Already they were taking on hostile fire, and *Pegasus* shook and shuddered with the sporadic hits along her underbelly. *I'll bet he doesn't down that much "33" again, even when he's scheduled off.* Krutch *always* piloted *Pegasus.* She was his ship, and he'd babied her through monsoon storms and whirlwinds of VC rounds for going on nine months now. *Boy, is he going to shit a brick when he realies the cyclic and all the other controls are out of whack for a reason!*

Gabriel went by the nickname of "Gunslinger," a title the gunnies had tacked onto him because of the six-inch revolver he wore in a hip holster, the belt drooping cowboy fashion. It was a weapon he'd yet to draw against the enemy, but Gabriel had been shot down over Laos the year before, spending several months as a prisoner of the Pathet Lao before he escaped, and he vowed never to surrender another fingernail. Next time he'd go down shooting.

A hero to the grunts in the field, Gabriel had rescued many of the same wounded soldiers several times over. In his early thirties, with a handlebar moustache across the lower half of his face, Gabe wore his dark black hair in a curly, natural style that drove the brass into tantrums. His short, stocky frame was covered with scars from a dozen crashes he'd managed to walk away from and, though the last shoot-down had been only four weeks earlier, he now walked with a limp.

"I've got purple smoke," the peter pilot muttered over the intercom. His pucker factor was increasing as they neared the LZ.

"I see it." Gabriel's tone changed to alert Brody and the Snakeman. "Goin' down."

The Whoremonger glanced toward the cockpit as if contemplating stealing a candy bar from a drugstore counter, then he slipped on his python's head mask.

It was as if they'd descended into hell.

The jungle was suddenly burning on all sides. Arvins had set off several charges in an attempt to knock trees out of the way, and they'd overdone it. Palms were still falling. One crashed only a few feet from the chopper as they descended in a slow hover down through the double canopy of a crackling and smoking green nightmare. The rotors' edges clipped some fronds, and long sections of the plants were sucked in one hatch and out the other.

"Ten meters and dropping," the AC spoke softly, for the tapes back at Tango Charlie. For the record.

"Where are they?" His peter pilot glanced down through the floor bubbles.

"You tell *me* and we'll both know." The aircraft commander did not sound content. There were no signs of the soldiers they were supposed to extract, the Arvins who'd called for help.

"Hey Snakeman!" Brody called over the whir of rotors and klinking brass, bypassing the intercom. He kicked an empty ammo can across the floor to get Fletcher's attention.

When Elliot turned, it was to find a half-human–half-reptile creature leaning out over the blazing Hog-60. Brody was flicking his tongue through the outstretched jaws of his python mask.

"Well, all RIGHT!" Fletcher called out. "*Get some,* Whoremonger!"

A burst of ground fire beat at the swivel of his own machine gun, knocking the pistol grip out of his fingers and the barrel up. "Whew, close call!" The words escaped him as he slapped the stinging sensation in his right thigh. Fletcher had stopped some small slivers of lead. "Hell, crazy guy!" He flipped Brody the thumbs-up. "Fantastic fuckin' get-up, dude. They're gonna start callin' *you* the Snakeman 'stead o' *me!*"

"There they are!" The AC's words across *Pegasus*'s intercom invaded their noisy world. His chin was the pointer and both door gunners followed it.

Pegasus was hovering less than ten feet off the ground now, and along one edge of the debris-cluttered clearing, several

146

Vietnamese emerged running.

Though they were all wearing North Vietnamese uniforms, bright yellow silk scarves with blood-red stripes running through them—symbolic of the *South* Vietnamese flag—decorated every Arvin's throat. And they carried their AK-47s in their *left* hands.

"Yah, that's gotta be them!" the peter pilot confirmed. "Holy shit!" The AC shielded his face as a Willie Peter grenade exploded in the midst of the fleeing soldiers, and glowing particles of white phosphorous rained down on the clearing.

The explosion's blast rocked *Pegasus,* but Gabriel kept his Huey under control. He even brought it closer to earth as soldiers, screaming with bits of WP sinking down into their flesh like hot coals on wax, clambered up onto the skids. The chopper swung from side to side slightly under their weight.

"Four friendlies on board and counting." Brody glanced over a shoulder then blasted a full belt of MG rounds into the long line of flashes deep in the trees. The flashes were becoming more intense by the second, and one grove was so full of discharging rifles it looked to be on fire. *Fire from the serpent's mouth!* Brody's mind screamed at him. *You finally pissed it off, Treat. Oh, boy. . .the fire-breathin' dragon has come out of its lair to drag you from* Pegasus*'s protection, to drag you back into the heart of Void Vicious.*

A tracer flew past his cheek, and a slug of lead punched him in the flak vest over his right breast. Knocked backward, the monkeystraps kept him on his feet, but he could feel the bandage around his lower back—the one covering holes left by RPG shrapnel during his last crash—split down the middle. Soon his trousers were soaked in fresh blood from an old wound, but the die-hard gunny was stumbling back halfway out the hatch and leaning into his Hog-60 an instant later.

"I got bookoo yellow scarves headed for *Peg*!" Fletcher advised the AC over the intercom. "I count a dozen-plus, Gabe." Snakeman's tone was becoming more excited. "Maybe thirteen now, confirmed. . .with no end in sight!"

He could make out a scarf on every soldier sprinting through the trees, racing for their lives toward the giant metal horse with wings. Many went down under the intense automatic-weapons fire from outside the clearing. Some of the Arvins accidentally shot each other in the mad scramble through knee-high sabers of splintered bamboo. Few were stopping to help up the wounded. Brody had seen the same thing before: It was every man for himself. "Come on! Come on!" he yelled, firing non-stop over their heads. *"Lai-day! Lai-day! Laiday!"*

His eyes scanned the uniforms for that precious ticket to freedom. Some were soaked in crimson, but even on the men covered with blood, he was sure he saw a hint of saffron in there somewhere! He *couldn't* deny anyone access to the slick!

But something was wrong.

"There's not supposed to be this many!" Gabriel was sounding worried as the running mob of wild-eyed infantrymen fought to be the first onto the skids. "Something's wrong here!" he agreed with Fletcher's thoughts as a string of ten more rounds stitched the side of the craft. Fiberglass and narrow strips of metal flew in Brody's face, but he continued firing at the muzzle flashes less than one hundred meters away.

A brilliant explosion on Fletcher's side of the chopper announced the detonation of more white phosphorous cannisters. Burning chunks of the solid chemical rained down on *Pegasus,* damaging her roof, and as small, marble-sized holes appeared, and what remained of the particles burned through in bits here and there, it became evident—a terrifying reality suddenly!—that they might not make it out of this one.

Krutch! Brody's mind screamed over the roar of his M-60. *We flew out of sequence. We left the Stork behind in the wrong gunship. We broke with tradition!*

"We ain't gonna make it out of this one," Brody whispered to himself through gritted teeth without clicking-in. "We ain't gonna make it out of this one 'cause Krutch missed the ride and Gabe ain't part of the karma. He don't belong aboard *Peg*, she won't listen to him. Oh Lordy, we're headed for one helluva world o' hurt. I can taste it in the downblast."

Someone crashed into him from behind, and Brody whirled around, realizing the Arvins who had made it aboard were starting to push and shove as more fought to climb in.

"Just one more time, Buddha-Baby. . ." He ground the edges of his teeth and faced the machine gun again, leaning into it as the barrel began to glow. "Just get me outta one more tight twat. I swear on my mama's grave: I'll burn a joss stick in your

148

memory every morning. . .I'll scrub a hundred temple floors a day. . .I'll—"

"Charlie's a fuckin' lumberjack!" Gabriel's voice cracked slightly as a harsh, tearing sound filled the clearing. One of the tallest trees on Fletcher's side of the ship had split down the middle and was falling straight onto *Pegasus*!

"Take us up! Take us up!" Snakeman yelled at the cockpit, forgetting to click-in in his panic. "*Take us the fuck up!* Or we're here forever!"

Gabriel didn't wait for a second opinion. He *felt* the same thing Fletcher was seeing in his blind spot. He *felt* something monstrous falling toward them. Some giant had emerged from the jungle and was going to stomp them into the mushrooms! It was as if a huge shadow had fallen across his world, and it was the shadow of Death.

Pegasus ascended rapidly despite its new cargo of eight bloodied and mutilated combatants. Brody expected them all to be screaming, but the soldiers just pressed back, away from the hatches, arms outstretched as if to hold each other in, and they were silent as frozen statues now as the ship began to rise, eyes wide in terror, but lips unmoving.

Three Arvins clung to the skids and were swinging back and forth, faces contorted in excruciating pain. One man was missing his foot. Another reached out to Brody, trying to lock eyes with him, too weak to yell for help, but the American refused to look them in the face, refused to pull them out of Void Vicious. He could not take his fingers from the smoking Hog's pistolgrip!

Two of the Arvins clinging to the skids fell away, too exhausted to hold on any longer, and were crushed by the falling tree.

"Meltdown!" Fletcher was yelling over at him. An image of a red-and-brown mushroom cloud flashed in front of Brody's mind's eye, but then he was staring down at his machine gun—the barrel was bright red!

Somehow he willed his fist to stop firing and, though he continued to lean into the butt plate for a crazy instant afterward he finally commanded himself upright, like an apeman emerging from his cave to watch and wonder about lightning, and Treat Brody—First Cavalry door gunner—stumbled backwards away

149

from the hatch. He pulled an oil-slick replacement barrel from behind his pile of Saigon phone books then reached for the Hog's smoking front sights.

"Damn!"

Brody recoiled, his palm and fingers burned to a crisp. The downblast had fanned the red glow black, but the machine gun was still hot.

"Way to go, grace!" Snakeman called over to him, laughing almost hysterically as he leaned into his own MG.

"Fuck you, Fletch," Brody muttered under his breath as he switched barrels. A large-caliber round slammed up through the chopper's floorboards, penetrating several of the thick phone books before stopping an inch from the Whoremonger's last testicle. The impact threw him backwards, out of the crouch, and the fresh barrel tumbled down into the clearing without ever having fired a shot.

None of the Arvins moved to help him up. "Here!" He jumped forward to catch another barrel Fletcher tossed over in his direction. "Now don't distract me anymore, Treat! I got bookoo Cong to kill to fill my quota!"

A dozen men in NVA uniforms squatted in the tracer-streaked clearing below, looks of horror and abandonment etched across their faces, waving rifles over their heads with left hands. *A scene painted in hell.* Brody could not bring himself to look down for long as a million words seemed to fill his mind: words of guilt and sorry and sadness. We gotta go back! *We can't just leave 'em down there to die.*

"I'd say we could lift out a couple more." They'd cleared the treetops now, and the peter pilot's words filled his ears as the warrant officer studied gauges on his instrument panel. "That's if these poor fuckers hangin' from the skids don't drop down into Void Vicious. Scratch a stow, add some mo'."

"I Roger that." Gabriel did not bank away, as Brody was sure he would. "Drop the ladder!" he directed.

"Rodg. . .dropping the ladder!" the copilot relayed the order back to the door gunners.

Sheets of green-and-white tracer were rising on either side of the chopper. Brody couldn't understand why they hadn't already been knocked from the sky. *Don't think that way!* he reprimanded himself, leaning out of the hatch and firing down, at their source, spraying wide swathes of glowing red lead back and forth. *In The Nam, words have power! Talk bad vibes and they just might happen—it's fact. . .don't even THINK it!*

"Brody! Drop the rope ladder!" a metallic voice was hissing at him over the intercom.

Brody glanced over a shoulder, but it wasn't Snakeman. Fletch was also leaning out into the Void. His shoulders and forearms were shaking up and down, and blood trickled from gritted teeth where he bit into his lower lip, but the Hog was no longer barking. No hot lead flowed from Snakeman's M-60 like searing death. His machine gun was jammed on a twisted link, and he didn't even know it.

"Brody! Drop the—"

"Okay! *Okay!*" he yelled, refusing to bother with the mouth-piece. "Hold onto your jockstraps!"

He backed into the hatch, stumbled through the piles of empty brass, and fell backwards over a wounded and groaning Vietnamese. "Sorry, brother!" *Jesus!* He glanced down. The soldier's leg was missing below the knee, but the Arvin did not cry out. There was no anger in his face. He just stared up through Brody with blank eyes—with that thousand-yard stare. "I'm *sorry,* man! Really-I am." He reached down and patted the soldier's shoulder. *"An-ban!"* The American's fingers came away soaked with blood.

Christ! He wanted to throw up. He wanted to throw up all over the man with no leg and then cartwheel out into Void Vicious and be done with it all!

Another tracer tore up through the floor, passed through one of the casualties lying at Brody's feet, and struck the roof beam a half foot above his helmet. The result was a dozen ricochets, and one sliver of lead ripped a gaping hole in the one-legged man's forehead. He flipped back, out of the way, without a sound. His arms remained in the air a few more seconds, life-less fingers twitching, reaching out to Brody for help. . .reach-ing. . .

"Whoremonger!"

"*Right!* I know, I know!" he clicked in. "I'm working on it!"

"Whatta ya mean you're 'working on it?'" Gabriel managed to remain calm somehow.

"I'm up to my armpits in elbows and assholes!"

"Just get the fucking ladder out the hatch!" the peter pilot yelled back.

"Or we're leaving!" AC Gabriel added. The way he said it really meant, *And the deaths of those poor bastards down there will be on your conscience, not mine.*

"Fine!" he exploded. "Bank off, you *jerk-offs!* See if the Whoremonger gives a damn!" But he was already pulling the rescue ladder out of its wall compartment and thrusting it past Fletcher.

The links of rope bounced off the wide-eyed soldier still clinging to the skids outside and slowly unraveled as it dropped toward the ground.

Brody pulled Fletcher back and flipped the Hog latch up. He threw the belt of ammunition to the side, not wasting time with the twisted links, and kicked open a new box.

Slipping the first few rounds in place, he cocked the big gun, slammed its cover home, and leaned out the hatch.

A dozen soldiers with yellow scarves, clutching AKs in their left hands, were fighting over the bottom rungs. The ship lurched to one side as the first man up out of the mob started climbing. *Biggest damn "Lurp team" I've ever seen!* Brody watched one soldier on the ground bayonet another in the back.

"Only two!" Gabriel's voice was laced with stress now as he clicked-in to the door gunner's upside-down world. "Tell 'em only *two* can come up, then we're *outta* here, and the Stork or Holyman can take the rest out!" The helicopter shook as more men jumped onto the ladder. It began to drop slowly, and rolled from side to side. "Tell 'em—"

"I don't think they're in the mood to listen, Gabe!" There were now six Vietnamese hustling up the ladder. A seventh jumped up onto the bottom rung and Peg nearly rolled over onto her side.

"Di-di!" Brody yelled down at the soldiers. "Get off! Too many!" He waved blood-caked hands, his mind scanning seldom-studied pages of his old English-Vietnamese pocket dictionary. *"Nhieu nguoi qua!* Drop, slick! Get the fuck off! *Ra-di!"*

"Overload on your RPGs," Gabriel's copilot announced in a strangely unemotional, businesslike voice. "We're going to sink any second."

152

Sink or swim! Brody's mind screamed. *Sink or swim!* His ears ached, and he didn't know if it was from the voice screaming in his head or the nonstop roar of machine gun fire from the ground. *Sink or swim!*

He knew what he had to do even before Gabriel ordered it.

Aiming down at the last men on the bottom of the ladder, his trigger finger tensed and he yelled for them to drop off again.

They could be REAL North Vietnamese! his mind rationalized as he stared down into the wild eyes of a soldier clinging to the midway point on the ropes. *There's too many of them! The last man up could be holdin' on to a frag. . . he could be Cong to the core, determined to take us all down with him in a spectacular fireball his comrades will talk about around countless monsoon campfires to come!* Brody stared down into the man's eyes and saw his fear and his family and his future. He saw all the enemy soldiers he'd killed since becoming a door gunner, and this man was suddenly no different. There was nothing different in the eyes. . .no secret in their depths of swirling black and white . . .just a plea.

A plea masked with evil intent, he knew. The Whoremonger's gut instinct went to work in that instant Gabriel ordered him to shoot, to fire down into their faces—and it told him this man was Cong to the core. A suicide sapper, sacrificing himself for the cause. A guerilla wrapped in bandoliers of C-4, his dream the destruction of a multi-million-dollar hovering death-trap—a guerrilla with a frag between his nuts: the ultimate orgasm.

He is just a confused country boy! the voice taunted him again. *Just a teenaged draftee, plucked from the bowels of Saigon and clothed in an ARVN uniform and told to follow strangers and do battle with his cousins in the rain forest. He is no different than you, Treat Brody: just doing his job. This war is not worth dying for. . . . What is the world to a man when his wife is a widow? He pleads only for you to save him. Reach out, Treat Brody. Reach out and help this boy, your brother. Pull him from the jaws of death.*

It was a plea Brody could not grant.

Flashbacks of Ju-ju throwing the bound and gagged VC prisoners out the chopper hatch, and Fletcher shooting the prisoner in the jungle clearing, and the Korean sergeant killing three

153

communist POWs at point-blank range passed through Spec4 Brody's head as he centered the Hog-60's front sight on the soldier in the middle, so the tracers would pass down through all of them.

And then he pulled the trigger.

BOOK 2
JUNGLE JUSTICE

CHAPTER 16

They were attaching the wires to her again, and she screamed.

The field-phone wires were the most painful of their torture techniques—something her cadre cell leader had failed to warn her about.

She was naked again, flat on her back across a large table, wrists and ankles strapped to the corners. Saigon policemen in light blue pants and bright white shirts filled the tiny cubicle on Tran Hung Dao street downtown.

A cubby canh-sat with cigar dangling over his lower lip was attaching the inch-long battery clips to her nipples, and the metal teeth scraped her flesh, biting deep, and she screamed again.

"Shut up!" A canh-sat standing behind her head slapped her, and the chubby policeman was pushing her thighs apart, tugging roughly at the lips of her vagina with his clumsy, stublike fingers, snapping the battery clips on there too.

They rattled off another series of questions, but she would not break, she refused to tell them what they wanted to know.

A pudgy hand with short, thick fingers sliced down through the air beside her face: the signal that preceded the pain. Her ears filled with the *whir!* of small, hand-powered generators. Someone was cranking up the field-phone lever.

Jolts of intense pain spider-webbed across her chest, stabbed up into her loins. The same question was yelled in her ear again, over and over—a simple question, really: Where is your unit headquartered? Answers the police already knew. But they needed confirmation, a new source. And she refused to cooperate.

A small cloud of mosquitos floated several feet above her eyes and she stared past the blur of insects, concentrating on the fan blades rotating lazily overhead, slicing through the room's muggy, smoke-choked air.

She concentrated on the blades, and in her mind the blades became a U.S. Army helicopter's rotors passing overhead, and she was with her people, firing nonstop until her ears rang with the discharges and the gunship exploded in a majestic fireball that disappeared deep in the rain forest.

The cheers of her comrades merged with her own screams. The canh-sats were busy with their field-phones again. She must have drifted into a daze, or blacked out. They were slapping her face back and forth, from side to side lightly, bringing her out of it, yelling their questions again.

She turned her face away, trying to shield it but failing miserably. She became aware for the first time that her long, black hair, her entire body, was soaked in perspiration and trembling uncontrollably. She turned to face them, and locked eyes with the nearest policeman, then winked as seductively as she could.

"Ahhh, yes." The captain leaned forward. And she spit in his face.

The oldest canh-sat, the chubby one, was laughing now as her interrogator wiped the spittle away and smashed his fist down across her nose, flattening it.

He removed the small battery clips and flicked her nipples with a rigid forefinger. The purple swirls were no longer hard and erect but had flattened out against the swell of her breasts, and he wanted them taut.

"You will get nothing out of her." The man rubbing his hand glared down at her with hatred and disgust written all over his face.

"Then the interrogation is over?" The cigar smoker rubbed his pudgy hands together in anticipation.

The supervisor turned his back on the canh-sat without answering and hurried out of the room, slamming a door behind him.

The ranking policeman left in the tiny cubicle inhaled on his cigar until the embers glowed a bright red, and then he ground it out in the nipple over her racing heart. She screamed again. This time the pain was more than searing, it sent fire throughout her system, and now she could smell her own flesh burning, see the puffs of smoke rising from her breast. Eyes clenched tightly shut, she screamed until her throat was raw and she feared her lungs might tear, and she never saw or felt the canh-sat roughly removing the field-phone wires and battery clips from between her legs.

The table shook slightly then, but it was not until the outsides

157

of a man's knees were pushing her own farther apart that she looked down and saw a young, muscular canh-sat mounting her. Someone was holding her wrists down—a strange sensation, for she thought she was already strapped to the table—and the last thing she saw before he plunged into her was the long line of police privates, arranged by seniority, trousers piled around ankles, awaiting their turn.

"Kim....Trinh Thi Kim! Wake up...."

The small hand shaking her wrist startled her for a moment, but Trinh Thi Kim did not fall from the tree branch. She immediately recognized the woman's voice a few feet away. "I am sorry," she whispered. "I must have dozed."

"Never mind." The words came in soothing, singsong Vietnamese. "We are all tired. It has been over two nights in the trees. But the Americans come now," the watcher warned. "Beware."

Kim nodded without speaking further. The manner in which she ran long, slender fingers along the stock of her AK-47 assault rifle was answer enough. She was ready.

Kim stared up at the bright, twinkling stars. Somehow, they managed to shine through the tangle of multi-layered canopy above, radiating warmth, yet she felt icy cold inside.

The nightmares always left her feeling that way.

She stared down at the jungle floor, a good fifty meters or more beneath her plank-reinforced perch. The others were getting into position or dropping back behind cover. It would be a devastating ambush, but the Americans were still a klick or so away. Sound traveled far in the rain forest, and though she could not see the luminous tabs at this distance, the racket they were making pinpointed their position almost precisely.

It would be another hour or two before her fighters unleashed the monster on them. Time enough to reflect....

The nightmares were always worse than those three years in Chi Hoa prison had actually been. In the nightmare, the *canh-sats* were always more unfeeling and cruel, more brutal and sadistic than any policemen who had really interrogated her, but fantasy was not that far removed from the plain of reality in the Orient. The scars crisscrossing her nipples were a constant reminder of what she had endured, of the humiliation she had

158

suffered.

And that she had not talked.

Trinh Thi Kim was a female guerrilla cell leader with the Provisional Revolutionary Government of South Vietnam, the PRG. Or the Viet Cong. South-of-the-DMZ, homegrown communists, the Saigon government labeled them. Pawns of Hanoi; brothers-in-arms to the NVA. Nationalist, Kim preferred to be called.

She only wanted to see the country reunited, and the foreigners out. Then all could return to the serene, idyllic life of a thousand years ago, when the emperor was worshiped as a god, and all were provided for. Vietnam could be a beautiful land, when it was at peace.

Born Kha Thi Xinh July 14, 1943, into a life of poverty and abuse outside the Imperial City of Hue, she was twenty-two now. Kim's parents were killed by French friendly fire during a days-long battle with the Viet Minh when she was sixteen. Shortly afterwards, she was recruited into the insurgency by classmates hostile to the French cause, students who had been law-abiding, quiet, and obedient children by day, and hell-raising, night-raiding guerrillas after dark.

Originally trained at a communist tunnel complex along the Viet-Laos border, she was then sent to Saigon with the alias Xuyen Thi Vau, and instructed to seduce American servicemen with the eventual goal blackmail. "You give Vau sensitive info and she promise not to send blow-job snapshots back to *Mrs.* GI Joe stateside."

And she had the looks for it. Barely five-foot-one, she'd never weighed more than a hundred pounds, even when caught off guard and soaked by a monsoon downpour. Long, jet-black, silky strands of hair fell across high cheekbones to her waist, and though she was full-blooded Vietnamese, a Eurasian cast to her features and those exotic cheekbones, which gave her looks an almost Central-Highlands-tribal tint, had hampered her advancement somewhat within the PRG movement.

Firm curves served to accent an unusually well endowed figure for a deprived "country girl."

Kim had no formal education, though an aunt taught her to read and write when she was a child. She could converse in French if need be, and now Pidgin English, a language she spoke with a heavy yet sensuous accent which drove her American boyfriends wild.

And her foreign lovers were many.

But she would never forget the man who betrayed her. After first arriving in Saigon, she botched her original mission and fell in love with a smooth-talking, young consular official at the U.S. embassy. Charmed by the aspiring diplomat, her eyes filled with visions of McDonald's arches and Hollywood Boulevard an ocean away, she confided in him about her shady past. It didn't really matter, he had claimed. After all, she confessed to him long before ever coming close to actually killing anybody. He loved her, and she loved him, and when they made love all through the night—five times in one evening was his record —the heavens exploded. He told her that they were made for each other.

But then one year later his Tour 365 was up, he was gone, and agents from MI, CID, and the VNP were knocking on the door of the bungalow he'd paid three months' future rent on.

She spent three years in prison, both at the Chi Hoa facilities, and in a tiger cage on Con Son Island after she bit a guard's tongue off during an attempted rape, but was released by mistake in all the confusion following the Diem assassination of November 1963.

Xuyen Thi Vau changed her name and disappeared into the jungle for two years, only to reemerge in the Saigon-Cholon resistance movement in early 1965.

And now she was back.

Her comrades call her the Dragonlady—a title admittedly overused and liberally doled out in Indochina these days. The woman's skill with firearms bordered on legendary, and the flames from her weapons were as dangerous as the mythical, fire-breathing creatures. The title was particularly fitting in another way, for when she wore a form-hugging, slit *ao dai* over black satin pantaloons, Trinh Thi Kim looked smashing— the enchanting seductress to watch at any embassy bash.

The GIs had a dozen different names for her, and a ten-thousand dollar bounty on her head. . . .

"There is their point man," the woman at her side whispered.

"They have moved up faster than I anticipated." Kim silently tested the seal of her AK's 30-round magazine. "Tonight perhaps they are not so clumsy." Branches crackled in the distance, and metal scraped against metal. "But they still make more noise than old women at market."

"Yes. We are ready for them," the watcher advised.

The twenty claymores positioned to explode simultaneously were rigged for remote-control detonation. The man with the wires had been anticipating this moment for two nights. They knew this American patrol was somewhere in the vicinity, and now they had them pinpointed.

Kim was the leader of this ragtag band of insurgents, but she didn't mind delegating the choice duties to some of the men. It was a reward. The just deserts for their vigilance and loyalty, for. . .all their suffering under Arc-Light, and the incessant artillery, for. . .all the times they'd been hunted like rats by those monstrous metallic predators, the Cobras.

They always allowed the point man to walk past unmolested before they triggered the ambush. Kim wanted there to be at least one survivor who could return to the camps and tell his buddies and his commander and his news media about her. She kept no scrapbooks, but she loved the publicity her midnight raids were receiving in the American press.

Kim watched the soldier pass by below, twenty or thirty feet off-trail from the main contingent still several dozen meters back. He looked to be an older man, a more mature warrior than the usual assortment of baby-faced teenagers she'd had the pleasure to slaughter lately, but she couldn't tell for sure—not from up in these trees. Not under this cover of darkness.

"Now," she whispered under her breath.

A bright, blinding flash erupted below. Several lightninglike explosions at once, and then the multiple concussions rose, invisible, like a monster's fists, nearly knocking her and the watcher and the others from their tree.

Billowing smoke followed, and with it the cries and moans of the wounded below. Kim and her snipers brought their rifles up and casually picked-off one soldier after another, like sitting ducks in a shooting gallery.

A team stationed along the trail up ahead had already surrounded the point man and disarmed him without firing a shot.

Kim slid down the tree using a rappelling rope stolen from Army Engineers her group had ambushed the month before at a road-building, demo project site east of Pleiku. She reached the ground in seconds and ran through the guerrillas gathering weapons from the dead Americans. Here and there cadre team leaders were quickly slitting the throats of the wounded with bayonets, saving their bullets.

Two teenaged Viet Cong had already tied the uninjured point man to a stout pole of bamboo when she reached him. His wrists were bound behind him but his legs were still free, and when Kim slid up to him, short of breath and excitement in her eyes, he kicked out at her savagely. One boot struck her knee, and she went down hard. The American threw his head back, resigned to certain death, and laughed. "You fuckin' zips!" he yelled, the slaughter of his entire squad motivating him now, fueling the fires of courage, "Go ahead and kill me! I won't cooperate. You'll have to shoot me NOW!"

Trying to fight back the tears of pain appearing along the edges of her dark eyes, Kim struggled back to her feet as the apprentice guerrillas wrapped strong twine around the prisoner's ankles.

"Ha! *GI!*" She jumped to her feet and slapped him hard, the enthusiasm back in her expression. "Why you so eager to die tonight?"

"'Cut the chatter, cunt!" he snapped back. "I'm not even spillin' my name, rank or serial-fucking-number. You better kill me now and get it over with 'cause we put out a call for help and the Cobras'll soon be—"

"Ha!" she slapped him again. "No such call was made. *I* personally put bullet between eyes of your radioman before he even know what happening! You are all 'lone with us, big tough American. No help comes for rescue you!"

"Fuck your mama, bitch!" He spat down at her but missed. A rifle butt slammed into the left side of his face, and one eye swelled shut.

The soldier fought the urge to spit again and composed himself, lips trembling with hate and restrained judgment. He looked her over closely for the first time. Clad entirely in black, he could see even in the dark of the jungle that she had quite a shapely body—not the first female guerrilla he'd ever seen up close like this, not by a long shot, but the first to wear a uniform tailored to show off her thin waist and the sensuous

162

swell of hips and chest. She was really rather pretty, too, he decided. Her long hair actually sparkled under the stars and moonlight when she moved. "Hell." he broke loose of her spell. "Fuck *you*!" His imagination flew into fast-forward, and for an instant he saw her down on her knees, submitting to him, unzipping his trousers, swallowing him up without hesitation.

"Don't you wish!" She slapped him again, punched him in the stomach, and pressed his nose in with her own. "Don't you *wish* you could fuck me!"

Kim grabbed the front of his shirt and ripped it down the middle. "Well . . . maybe I let you!" she taunted, turning to unleash a torrent of Vietnamese at the two teenaged guerrillas. Wide-eyed, and nodding up and down with lower jaws dropping in awe—they'd heard so much about this female Hero of the People, but this was their first patrol with her—the two VC privates unfastened the American's web belt, leaving his trousers vulnerable.

Kim was slowly unbuttoning her blouse. Her eyes darted to the side—both youthful terrorists were really gawking now—and a slight grin appeared on her lips as the black fatigue blouse was forced apart by her jutting breasts.

"What do you think, Patterson?" she read off the name tag on his shirt as she rubbed her chest against his for a tantalizing second. "Do you think you are *man* enough?" Kim grabbed his hair and forced his face down so that his lips brished against her upturned nipples. "Ha!" With the back of her hand she slapped his forehead back. "I really doubt it!"

Shaking the sweat from his eyes, Corporal Patterson glared down at Trinh Thi Kim, but his resolve was softening. He'd never been treated this way before by a woman—not that he'd ever encountered a female guerrilla as her captive before. Patterson was intrigued. Positive he was dead meat any minute now, but intrigued nonetheless.

But she misinterpreted his expression and slapped him again. Harder than before.

Blood trickled from one corner of his mouth.

"No, I no think you have what it take to please, to satisfy Xuyen Thi Vau," she used an old alias. "But we will all know in a minute or two." Kim smiled broadly and glanced over both shoulders as she took hold of his fatigue belt. The guerrillas

163

gathering around laughed on cue. She looked up into the American's unblinking, emotionless eyes. "What are you *staring* at?" She whipped his belt out from its pant loops. "Is the foreign dog trying to mem—...trying to mem'rize Vau's feature?" Dropping her head back, she laughed wickedly.

And just as abruptly she snapped her face forward again, nose to nose with his. Teeth bared, she looked as if she wanted to tear his throat out. "Well, *remember* this face!" She slapped him again, and blood from his lips left fine, crimson points of spray across her own cheek. "Tell your comrades about Xuyen Thi Vau! Tell them she is as beautiful as the rumors claim." Her tone turned somewhat arrogant, but Kim could no longer control her "charm." Her mind was flashing back to the monster's explosion earlier and the exhilaration she felt when bullets punctuated her violent statement about the American presence in Vietnam. "Tell them she is the fiercest jungle fighter you have ever encountered in the rain forest!" Kim waved an arm back at the bodies sprawled along the trail behind them.

Patterson was not sure what this woman's game was—shifting in and out of Pidgin English...speaking fluently when she really got fired up—but he knew he was not going to play along. "Slam it in and break it off, lady," he muttered. Kim responded with a confused tilt of her delicate, deceptive features, then whirled around when one of the others spoke.

"Nhin," a soldier beside her motioned to the American's shiny chromed belt buckle lying on the ground at his feet, and Kim dropped smoothly into a squat. The sinewy movement bringing attention to her firm, flaring thighs, she ignored the appraising looks of every man there and studied the inscription for the first time.

"What have we here?" The customized buckle tilted back and forth in her fingers, reflecting moonlight. Kim glanced up and caught Patterson swallowing hard in anticipation.

Straining to read in the dim glow from above, she suddenly laughed again. Translating the four words into Vietnamese for her followers, Kim repeated the inscription twice, and though many of the guerrillas laughed along with her, it was an uneasy laughter. Cold, narrowed eyes from a dozen VC stared through the American.

"'VIET CONG HUNTING CLUB,' eh?" She dropped the

164

buckle in the dust at her feet. "Well, it seem big brave American GI has become *hunted* tonight." Two women behind her, understanding the English, giggled. Their defiant expressions infuriated the prisoner.

"Suck my cock, commie bitch," he said calmly.

Kim responded with a vicious punch in the throat, and the soldier doubled over as far as the ropes would permit, gagging. One of the women who had giggled rushed up past Kim and struck Patterson in the temple with a karate chop, but the guerilla leader pushed her back.

The blow was delivered with considerable force and could easily have been fatal, but Kim did not even reprimand with her eyes. She glanced down at the groaning American instead. "He wants us to suck on his cock." She turned and translated to the young women standing in shadows, the quiet ones who were not participating in the attitude adjustment session.

Kim reched up and tore the First Cavalry Division patch off Patterson's right shoulder. When he regained enough composure to open his eyes again, she slipped the combat patch under her waistband and dcwn against her crotch, making sure he saw what she was doing.

She stepped to the side, muttered something in gutteral Vietnamese to the female subordinates, and folded her arms across her chest, wrists cupping the bottoms of the breasts provocatively.

The two women rushed up on either side of Patterson, and dropped to their knees.

He smiled uncontrollably for a moment, remembering something that crazy Krutch the Stork had said back at the Tea Plantation. *Taunted and teased in Vietnamese . . . taunted and teased in*—

But then the grin vanished. One of them produced a long dagger from an ankle sheath. Its blade sparkled menacingly in the few shafts of moonlight penetrating the trees and drifting clouds above. The woman expertly sliced through the fabric of his trousers just below the top button, without hitting flesh, then ripped out the zipper with a smooth, sidearmed movement that caused Patterson to gasp involuntarily.

The other woman took hold of his pants along the thigh pockets and pulled them down over his hips.

165

"Ohhh!" Kim feigned astonishment as she stood directly in front of the American again. Her assistants each wrapped their arms around one leg to restrain him as they knelt on either side of their prisoner, but it was an unnecessary precaution, the twine held Patterson securely against the tree trunk. "A *reeeeal* jungle fighter graces our presence tonight!"

Mock surprise in her expression, Kim switched back to Vietnamese as she gently cupped his testicles with the palm of one hand. "He wears no undergarment." She chuckled softly. "Just like VC."

Keeping hold of him, she shifted her stance, not unlike a model exhibiting the latest design from Paris. "He knows undergarment cause *crotch rot*!" Her voice rose but her touch remained tender as her hand lifted his scrotum sack, flattening it out. Patterson's chin rose noticeably with the slight movement, and his swallow could be heard throughout the group as Kim took the knife from the woman kneeling beside him.

"I do not excite you, Patterson?" She took hold of his penis and slowly stretched the limp organ out, massaging its head slightly, her fingers warm to him but the caress cold-blooded and impassive.

"Put a liplock on it, baby." His voice was a rasp now and his eyes closed tightly in silent reprimand. *Why couldn't he just keep his mouth closed?* "We'll see what develops. . . ."

Grimacing, he shook his head at his own behavior, but Patterson harbored no false hopes in his mind. This group planned to kill him. They would have their fun first, torture him a bit, no doubt, but eventually they would tire of the game and pull his prick out by the root, or clamp a set of vise-grips onto his nuts until his personality popped out his ears. But he refused to crack. He would not cower before the enemy. And he wanted her to remember him after he was gone. He wanted Xuyen Thi Vau—or whatever her real name was—to remember the American she could not break down. She talked tough earlier, but he wanted *her* to remember *him*.

"What is 'liplock'?" she teased, running the blade's edge along the base of his penis as it began to swell. Patterson closed his eyes tightly, willing himself soft, insignificant, but he could no longer control it.

"Maybe I was wrong." Kim seemed to be experiencing a

166

change of heart as she stared down at the organ throbbing in her hand. She ran the blade along its base again, but this time she was increasing pressure.

"Hey!" Patterson cried out.

Kim had cut into him, but it was a minor laceration, no deeper than the marks she'd inflicted across both her own wrist when. . .lifetimes ago. . .she contemplated ending it all at the bottom of a pit on Con Son Island.

A trickle of blood dripped down over his testicles, and the heat of it across her hand eased Kim from the memories as she saw herself naked and defenseless, strapped flat on her back to an interrogator's table in downtown Saigon, refusing to give in, to cooperate. . .refusing to talk.

And she found herself comparing that tortured woman in a jail cell on Tran Hung Dao street with the prisoner standing helpless in front of her now.

"*Fini.*" She tossed the dagger, handle first, to its owner and backed away from Patterson. Catching it with one hand, the younger woman wiped the blood across the shallow between her own breasts, and sheathed the blade.

"Off with the rest of his clothing," Kim directed without looking up at Patterson. If he'd wondered about her intentions before, when she yelled the word *Fini!*, the American had no doubts now. He was sure *Fini!* meant death.

When the women had him stripped naked, Kim walked up close and stood there silently for several seconds. Then she pulled the First Cav patch from inside her pants, moist now with her juices. She grabbed Patterson's chin, pulled it down roughly, and rammed the patch into his mouth.

She slapped him again, and still defiant, the American began munching on the gold and black horsehead emblem as if he enjoyed the taste.

His reaction evoked a smile from her, and she flashed back momentarily to a tiny, barren cubicle, bathed in harsh white light, the walls a zebra's skin of disorienting stripes, and the pride she'd felt that night she spat into the *canh-sat's* face. "We have found many of those Airmobile horse patches hanging out of the mouths of our murdered guerrilla fighters." The grin faded as she began cutting the twine from around his biceps, and Patterson thought of Snakeman.

Kim sliced free the rope around his waist and immediately elbowed Patterson in the stomach as hard as she could. As he doubled over, sinking to the ground, she cut through the twine holding his ankles to the bamboo pole and, grabbing the hair on his head, threw him face-first into the mushrooms at her feet. "Well, we too have a tradition, Mister American GI." She dropped down onto one knee and it landed in the small of his back.

Without looking, she raised her hand back, over her head, and one of the Vietnamese placed a patch, two nails, and a hammer in it.

"I grant you your life tonight, *Patterson*!" Kim placed the miniature gold, red, and blue Viet Cong-flag patch over his right shoulder blade. "Go back to wherever you came from and tell your buddies about me." She placed the first nail directly over the small gold star in the center of the patch and held it in place as the flap of distant helicopter rotors reached her ears. Kim slowly raised the hammer over her head as her free hand kept Patterson's face against the earth.

The gunships were rapidly drawing nearer, but the VC woman ignored the almost hypnotic clamor beating at the roof of her rain forest. "Tell your friends about the beauty...and the bravery...and the treachery of Xuyen Thi Vau!"

And then she let the hammer fall.

CHAPTER 17

Queen Cong Kim, as many of her comrades jokingly referred to her, watched in awe as the Cobra gunships swooped in low across the treetops, blasting away at panther shadows with their impressive mini-guns. She watched the two sleek predators glide together down through the openings in the canopy, then dart about unleashing multiple rockets as a smaller Loach scout ship hovered hundreds of feet above them, spotting what appeared to be targets of opportunity but were only monkeys zigzagging through the trees in terror.

"See how he runs." The woman beside Kim pointed down at the American, Patterson. From their safe vantage point high atop a nearby hill, hundreds of meters from the earlier ambush site, the guerrillas could all clearly see the naked corporal running toward the choppers, waving his arms over his head. His pale buttocks were streaked with blood from the VC patch nailed to his back. Try as he might, Patterson could not reach back far enough to pull it off.

Four Huey slicks appeared beyond the Cobras as they dropped down from the night sky suddenly, banking sharply to the right before fanning in for a rough landing. Two of the ships *pranged* across the rain forest floor, obviously set down by the peter pilots. Sparks rose from the skids of one chopper as it slid across discarded equipment on the far side of the ambush site. Soldiers were jumping down from the hatches even as three of the craft were still ten feet or more above the reeds.

Startled by his appearance, one of the troopers fired a burst from the hip as Patterson raced through a patch of tall elephant grass, arms waving over his head like a naked madman, but the rounds passed several inches over his head.

"The bitch wore black!" he was yelling. "It was a whole squad of 'em! They went *that* way!" He pointed at a grove of trees opposite the hilltop where Kim's people squatted in the brush and swamp reeds where she had circled around to after releasing the Americans. "You guys are bringing' smoke down on the wrong place!" He pointed to the flash of rockets dropping from strut pods on the Cobras. "They're long gone!"

"What?" A stocky black sergeant with his head shaved bald rushed up to confront Patterson.

"There was a whole squad o' dinks jumped me back there! Before they blew an animal on us. They beat feet *that* way!" His finger flew to the grove of tamarinds again. "They were led by a woman...a VC girl! She was in charge, and the bitch wore black! Her name was—"

The door gunners aboard the Hueys were firing away unceasingly now at shapes darting through the distant tree line, and gibbons and snakes and lizards the size of tomcats rained down with the leaves and branches. One string of tracers decapitated a huge parrot, and both Viet Cong and Americans watched its colorful feathers fluttering down among the mushrooms.

The guerrilla leader watched, mesmerized by the sleek Cobras with sharks' teeth painted along their snouts.

"You watch the new helicopters, sister." The woman, no relation to Kim, observed. "The ones *My* call Cobras."

"Yes." Kim's eyes appeared dreamy.

"You are impressed."

"Yes, I am. Very impressed."

"Later, I will show you where they camp," the woman said matter-of-factly.

"You know this information?" Kim's face turned to meet the woman's.

"Oh, yes. It is no big secret anymore. Lai is sleeping with one of the northerners. He told her. All the northerners know about it. Later, I will take you there."

"Yes."

"But now we must go. To the tunnels. The Americans will drop napalm soon. They will call down cannon, and Air Force will strafe the jungle." The younger woman sought to tug Kim from her trance.

"Yes, we must retreat to the tunnels." Kim rose, motioning the band of men and women over the hilltop, and east. East toward Mang Yang Pass.

The woman whose survival knife had been used to intimdiate Corporal Patterson glanced back over her shoulder one last time before they ran off down the other side of the hill, into the heart of the dark rain forest.

"What is it, sister?" Kim asked her. "Do you long to watch the Americans some more, to learn more about them? Do you wonder about the rest of them, about the size of their—"

Ignoring her leader's playful jest, the woman slung her SKS over a shoulder and wiped a tear from her eyes.

"I feel sorry for the tree monkeys," she said.

Sgt. Daniel Delgado formed his most reassuring smile before sliding the needle into the infant's arm. The small boy's apprehensive scowl erupted into a shudder and suppressed sobs, but he did not scream. The Vietnamese woman cradling him in her arms had winced as she watched Delgado's thumb force the vaccine through the syringe, and now she guided the child's lips to her breast.

None of the other women gathered around her wore blouses either—only sarongs from the waist down—though few carried children against their hips.

"I'll say one thing for these 'Yarde kids, Lieutenant." Delgado slapped the boy gently on the rump. "I've never seen one cry."

"They have no tears left, Doc." Using a cotton ball, Nurse Maddox rubbed an antiseptic solution over the arm of the next child in line. "Call me Lisa," she said in the same breath. "Please."

"But—"

"I insist." She feigned a businesslike expression, as if the next step involved pulling rank on the corpsman.

"Okay, Lieu—...I mean, Lisa. Sure. I've got no problem with that."

And he shouldn't have. Medic Danny Delgado, known to every soldier in Echo Company as simply "Doc," and Nurse Maddox had been spending nearly all their off-duty time together in this little refugee camp outside Pleiku. Most of the children who lived here were orphans. Their new guardians were young homeless women, themselves barely out of their teens. But even those with parents suffered ailments of every degree and description. The adults were often just too traumatized mentally to properly care for their offspring. Their property and all their possessions, not to mention their sanity, had all become casualties of the war. Many had even watched the graveyards of their ancestors destroyed by the mortars and bombs. And often they didn't even know from which side the projectiles had been launched or the bullets fired.

Maddox and Delgado had set up their first-aid tent in the middle of the sprawling refugee camp with the blessings of the French Catholic nuns who operated it on a bankrupt budget. A camouflage silk parachute was draped over two twelve-foot tent poles and the ropes tied to stakes, lending something of a festive, circuslike atmosphere, for the shelter had no sides below shoulder-height. Dozens of longhouses, Montagnarde dwellings of dried mud, wood walls, and thatched roofs, surrounded the shelter. Heat lightning danced within storm clouds on the horizon, but the American humanitarians did not think they would be bothered by a downpour this day.

"You have the duty tonight, ma'am?" Delgado did not look up as he prepared another yellow fever shot.

"Lisa!" She slugged his arm playfully.

"Hey, watch the sunburn, would ya?" Delgado leaned away, grinning as a little nude girl with hair down to her waist stepped forth to defend him from the woman with hair the color of *pho*.

Maddox ignored the child. "And yes, I have the darn duty tonight. 'Low pussy on the totem pole always gets triage.' Haven't you heard that expression before?" The lieutenant had been in Vietnam over a half year, but she still had less time in-grade than the other nurses working II Corps. She glanced up to gauge his reaction. *"What* sunburn?" She slugged his arm again, and the little nude girl reached out and latched onto her wrist. "Okay. . .okay, honey." She took hold of the child and stared deeply into her eyes with an enough-nonsense expression.

The girl squealed and ran away. She'd never seen anyone with green eyes before. And not only were they *green*, the child would swear to all her young friends later, but *bright* green! At night they must glow, just like the big, black cat-demons that prowled the jungle's edge for orphan girls no one would ever miss.

Delgado hadn't suffered a sunburn in years. Even in Asia. He was a dark-complected Chicano, but Maddox could still tell he was blushing as he lowered his face, pretending to concentrate on the syringe.

"Well?" She pressed him on his knowledge of totem poles.

"Jesus, Lieu—. . .I mean, heck, Lisa. . ."

"What's wrong? Haven't you ever heard a woman over here use language like that before?" she baited him.

"Not. . .well, not 'pussy.'" He glanced up at her but could not stare into her eyes for long. "Only the girls down in. . .I mean. . . ."

Maddox laughed, throwing her head back slightly. Several of the 'Yarde women gathering around frowned at the open display

172

of affection between her and this big witch doctor. Maddox laughed again. She loved to get this man in a corner, and she noticed none of the disapproving looks all the topless women were giving her. Harassing Doc seemed to make the long, hot days go by a lot faster. "You mean the girls down in Fifty-*P* Alley, my friend?"

Delgado shrugged his shoulders. "Something like that."

"Something like that?" she persisted. "Oh, come on, Doc! I really want to know now. You've piqued my curiosity. How *do* those exotic little mysterious Orientals downtown talk? Come on, now, you can level with your Aunt Lisa...."

Delgado grinned but refused to cooperate.

"I'd really like to know, Doc."

He looked up to find the next customer held by a young woman of about eighteen. She was extremely beautiful, with skin as dark and clean as the medic's. Long, black hair with a midnight-blue tint to it framed delicate shoulders. She smiled bashfully down at him from above wide, milk-swollen breasts, and Delgado flushed cherry-red.

"Come on, Doc." Maddox nudged him with her elbow as she reached over to tickle his patient's ear. "How do the girls off-post talk to your warrior-hero types? Do they—"

"Come on Lieu—...er, Lisa. Cut this poor country boy some slack, will you?" He was wondering if the well-endowed mother leaning against his arm spoke any English. And if she filed her teeth down like a lot of the local ladies, believing it made them more beautiful.

Maddox stared at Delgado for a few silent moments, estimating how much she could get away with today. Doc was a mysterious man with two faces, it seemed. He was either bright and cheerful, like today, or he was sitting off to the side somewhere, back at the Tea Plantation or Turkey Farm, alone, staring out into the distance for hours on end.

At first, she thought perhaps he was shooting up some morphine on the side, just trying to get through his tour and the *dau* of spending 365 long ones in The Nam as a medic. But when she inquired with Sgt. Zack about his moods, the tight-lipped NCO would only say he felt the corpsman had just experienced too much grief, seen too many young American boys die in the hundred-degree mud of Pleiku rice paddies.

She decided today was one of those times she could get away with murder. "Come on, Doc. Do *they* use the word 'pussy?' I'll bet they do! How do they put it?" She nudged him again. The 'Yarde woman was taking her child away now, and they both watched the graceful, erotic sway of her hips as she walked to a distant longhouse on stilts. Delgado memorized the dwelling number over the doorway, then glanced up at a green-and-brown Phantom jet swooping past overhead. The exhaust from its dual afterburners settled over the land like a thousand sets of filmy black negligees floating down from the dark storm clouds. "Do they ask 'how much you pay for *pussy*, Joe?'" She stressed the most important word, pretending to bite him with it.

Shrugging his shoulders and choosing a different defense, Delgado allowed his face to bob back and forth slightly as he produced a perplexed frown. "Well, Lisa...actually, they say, 'I souvenir you boom-boom for one *P* Doc. Best pussy in Plei-ku City! And for Doctor Delgado, only *one* piaster." His eyes dropped to inspect the next patient, face remaining expressionless.

Maddox's lower jaw nearly dropped into the dirt. Dumb-founded, she did not speak immediately. "'I souvenir you boom-boom for one P?'" She finally sought to confirm, cring-ing as the Phantom's rolling sonic boom reached them. "They think you're a doctor, Doc?" she asked incredulously.

Delgado looked up at her, mock insult forcing his eyes out of focus. There was obvious pain in the lines below them. "Sure! And why shouldn't they?"

"But—"

But he did not let her interrupt. "Heck, *I'm* the one who plunges that dose of penicillin into their ass Sunday mornings, ain't I? Don't *that* rate a discount?"

"But—"

"And *you've* seen the men I piece back together on the battle-field long before they ever get to the hospital. Don't *that* rate a sheepskin with *MD* across the top of it?"

"But—"

"But *what?*"

Grinning mischievously, Maddox swallowed on purpose, then asked, "And how many clap shots have you administered

174

to your*self* recently?"

Shocked into silence, Delgado was about to say something along the lines, *she* certainly didn't have to worry about the state of his sexual organs, when a backfire beyond the tree line sent the cluster of children scattering in different directions.

A blue jeep, driven by an American in civilian clothing, appeared along the only trail leading into the command.

"Here comes trouble," Delgado muttered in resignation, stuffing small medicine vials in the ammo bandoliers crisscrossing his chest. All his little patients had vanished.

"Trouble with a capital *T*." Maddox agreed. She stood up and brushed off her ER uniform as if preparing for a confrontation.

"Oh, I guess Graves is all right." Delgado relented somewhat. "But there's times I wish he'd just take his spooky tunes games and go blow his horn somewhere else, you know?"

Lisa Maddox rested a hand on her hip. "Yes," she said. "I know." Delgado thought he spotted a twinkle in her eye.

John Graves was the resident CIA agent, their local cloak-and-dagger spook. Carrying a somewhat chunky but powerful frame atop slightly bowed legs, the man appeared to be in his mid-forties but had worked in the Orient so long, Delgado and Maddox both found it hard to tell for sure. Graves wore thick black glasses most of the time but often sauntered out of the woods without them on and still seemed capable of getting around all right. He sported a silver flattop, dark tan, and an ugly scar across one side of his chin but still retained enough prominent features for Maddox and some of the other nurses in Pleiku to consider him handsome in a rugged sort of way.

Delgado often accused the agent of going native long before the United States ever became officially involved with Indochina. Graves squatted instead of sitting, smoked Viet cigarettes, spoke several Asian dialects fluently, and often slipped into 'Yarde slang when conversing with Americans. Delgado was always suspicious the man was up to no good, that his antics out in the boonies could only lead to more suffering and hardship for the hill tribes of Pleiku Province. But Col. Buchanan was forever defending the agent's activities and actions, and Graves himself sincerely felt he topped the regional list of genuine, bona fide patriots.

His Army jeep was painted blue instead of the usual olive-

175

drab shade of green, and that was supposed to distinguish him from the military—let Charlie know he was neutral, an Agriculture consultant to the government of Vietnam. But few were ever fooled. Every villager between Kontum and Saigon knew he was a spy because the real Ag people drove jeepsters and Broncos.

"Greetings, my fellow Americans." He pulled right up to their silken parachute tent and remained behind the steering wheel.

"Well *you* sure look like shit today." Delgado wasn't feeling kind.

"I've missed you too, Doc. And, yes, it's nice to see the two of you also." The agent rubbed at his dark whiskers with the back of his hand. Normally clean-shaven and tidy, not a single hair out of place, he was grubby-looking and ashen colored this morning, as if he'd just been to hell and back.

"You look like a gravedigger clocking a hellacious amount of overtime, John." The lieutenant batted her thin eyelashes politely.

"I've had wet dreams about you, too, Miss Maddox." Graves tipped his shredded *Panama,* avoiding the invitation to fill them in on his current project. He rested his hand on a MAC-10 submachine gun lying across the passenger seat. Children had reappeared from the shadows beneath their longhouses when it became clear the dirty white man was a non hostile and were gathering around the shiny new jeep.

Shiny and new except for one spot.

Delgado slipped his finger through a bullet hole along the fender. "Been gettin' chased by the papa-sans of underaged 'Yarde cherry girls again, Graves? Under eighteen's jailbait even in The Nam." He was not laughing.

"Under fourteen's a noose through the tamarinds," Lt. Maddox added.

The agent was watching the children closely, making sure their hands were empty. "Hell, you know there aren't any cherry girls left in the *Veeyet*-Nam, Doc!"

"Christ!" Maddox shook her head from side to side. "That's all I ever hear from you *men:* 'there's no cherry-girls left! There's no cherry-girls left!' Is that all you can find to complain about?"

176

"Are you claiming to be the exception to the rule, Lisa, honey?" Graves reached into one of the many pockets of his gray safari "TV" suit, pulled out a handful of butterscotch candies wrapped in twists of colorful cellophane, and threw them over his shoulder, high into the air.

The children squealed with delight as they scrambled for the treats, and Lisa smiled at the gesture, as he knew she would. She also ignored his last remark. It was a taunt that always surfaced. One she didn't care to nurture or dignify with a reply. Delgado was wondering how the agent managed to keep the candies from melting in this hundred-and-ten-in-the-shade heat.

"Still in love with that chopper jockey, Warlokk, Lisa?" Graves posed his next question jokingly but leaned back this time, prepared to dodge a swinging fist if need be.

The lieutenant frowned for his benefit, as if both insulted and offended by the remark, and just as she was about to reply with a venomous retort—for Maddox was in love with *no one* right now, especially a pilot who adored himself more than any female on the face of the Earth—Warlokk's Cobra roared over the nearby treetops without warning, buzzed them with a powerful downblast that knocked the bun of hair off her head, and swooped down around the far side of the compound.

Raising dust all along the unguarded perimeter, it returned to hover a few dozen feet over them and slightly off to the side. Warrant Officer Lance "Lawless" Warlokk leaned toward the window of his sleek, sharklike gunship. Blond hair pressed flat against the glass, he produced a thumbs-up for the waving children on the ground and blew a kiss down at the woman in the windswept hairdo.

Eyeballs rolling up into her head, Maddox turned and stalked off, back under the parachute tent. The nose of Warlokk's ship dipped slightly, and he was off like a gigantic metal dragonfly, banking sharply to the left. His rotorwash blew the first-aid tent from its support poles.

"Why that sonofa—" Maddox waved a dainty fist after the ascending Cobra.

The air all around seemed to become one solid chopping vibration as several more helicopters appeared out of nowhere to take its place. A second formation of Hueys—this one more disciplined than the first gaggle—was passing directly overhead.

"Wonder what's going down?" Delgado glanced over at the CIA agent.

"I count over twenty birds, Doc." Graves was still rubbing the stubble on his chin. "And it looks like they're armed for bear."

"They knew where I'd be." The medic sounded disappointed. Or, at the least, as if he were abandoning his boys. . . .ashamed he was missing out on the mission, unable to share the danger . . .to protect them. "They coulda sent a jeep out to get me—"

"Maybe it's a routine fly-by, Doc. Don't get your hemorrhoids into an uproar."

"You know who you sound like?" he started to ask, but *Pegasus* flew over suddenly, and Delgado instantly recognized the winged horse painted across the front as it swooped past, low and heavy with troops yet powerfully throbbing, rotors flapping smooth and rhythmically, fine-tuned by Zack himself.

"Hey, Whoremonger!" The medic waved a fist.

Brody and his pals were hanging out the Huey's side hatches, jungle boots dangling in the air, not yet manning the Hog-60s. Automatic rifles were balanced across their thighs.

And *Choi-oi* was propped on Larson's lap.

"Lieutenant! I mean, uh. . .Lisa." Delgado was waving Nurse Maddox out from under the big pile of collapsing parachute silk as the children gathered close, excited that *he* seemed so excited. "You just gotta come check this sight out!"

As soon as she was by his side, Delgado pointed up at his friends. They were making a second, unauthorized pass over the refugee camp after spotting Doc on the ground: Zack, Larson, Fletcher, Brody and the others—even *Choi-oi*. They were all his team. The best squad on the *First* Team! And they had all been laughing at his luck and directing obscene gestures down at him, until the lieutenant appeared. Now they were all trying to shrink back out of sight, into the hatch, before the nurse recognized any faces.

"That's the goofy doper mutt I was telling you about." Delgado pointed at the barking mongrel on Larson's lap. "You oughta see him when he trips into a flashback."

"You're kidding." Maddox shielded her eyes from the harsh

178

sunlight.

"No shit, ma'am."

Choi-oi seemed to know he was the center of attention. He spotted Delgado's finger and his tail began wagging nonstop. This was his first chopper ride in weeks, and funky dog was eating it up.

But then *Choi-oi* began wailing. He wailed so long and so hard and so loud that Larson's and Fletcher's ears both began to hurt, and a look of near panic creased Delgado's features as he grabbed Lisa Maddox and yelled at the 'Yarde children to lie down flat against the earth.

As soon as *Pegasus* was gone, the first barrage of motors stitched directly through the heart of the refugee camp for orphans and the homeless.

CHAPTER 18

When Gunslinger Gabriel brought his medevac slick down into the devastated refugee camp, banking low against the treetops for a flaring, impressive landing, the Dustoff pilot found he could leave his fancy revolver holstered. No ground attack had followed the barrage of deadly mortars, but there were more than enough bodies littering the red laterite clay to keep him occupied for the next several hours. Most of the casualties were children.

Neither Delgado, the medic, or Nurse Maddox received any injuries. CIA Agent Graves, warmed with his submachine gun and four taped, piggyback magazines of ammo, had disappeared—last seen running in the direction from which the barely audible *crump!*'s signaled the mortars were most likely being launched. Delgado, armed with his M-16 rifle and ten clips of ammunition—the other thirty mag pockets in his crossed bandoliers were stuffed not with bullets but medical supplies—attempted to assist him, but Lt. Maddox, clinging to his arm, dragged the corpsman to a stop.

"We need someone *here*!" she protested. "To protect the children in case there *is* an attack. The children...and me." The pressure of her hands on his arm increased. Delgado nodded, but he couldn't take his eyes from the stretch of trees Graves had disappeared into. Those camp sentries who hadn't fled during the attack now lay in the clay, ripped open and mutilated.

Delgado knew the army nurse was right. The Viet Cong's exact intentions were unclear. Was this just a harassment barrage of twenty mortars with nothing to follow except a deathly silence? They had been known to raid villages in the Central Highlands shortly after American medical teams packed up their aid stations and left. The VC enjoyed making examples of those who cooperated with the "Imperialsts." They hacked off the arm of every child who bore a vaccination scab.

The gaggle of Hueys had flown over the refugee camp just prior to the attack was refused permission to divert from the primary mission and assist the Americans coming under fire. They were answering a call for help ten klicks to the north. Infantrymen were being outflanked and outnumbered by a superior force of NVA Regulars on the outskirts of New Pleiku. And grunts yelling for assistance over bullet-riddled prick-25s was of a higher priority than saving humanitarians from indiscriminate shrapnel.

Warrent Officer Lance "Lawless" Warlokk had violated orders, though, and circled the camp repeatedly during the barrage, laying down mini-gunfire to cover Gabriel's rescue efforts. He darted about the treetops, dodging tracer fire and unleashing whole rocket pods as he played cat and mouse with the elusive VC.

By the time he was running low on fuel and ordnance, CIA Agent Graves managed to locate the main mortar pit and kill all five soldiers manning it with a single ten-round burst from his MAC-10. Flying on fumes, Lawless landed a few feet away from Gabriel's slick, while Graves checked the bullet-riddled bodies of the VC for documents.

"You're welcome!" Lance Warlokk sauntered over to Nurse

Maddox, a cocky grin in place. He bowed before the lieutenant before Delgado could even say anything. "It was my pleasure to deliver you from evil, amen!" Lawless chuckled at his own joke. "Only doing my job."

He stopped very close to Maddox and gently brushed off her uniform, his fingers barely touching the outer edges of her breasts. "Are you all right, Lisa?" It was obvious to everyone that Warlokk felt his demonstration of flying skill and talents would surely overshadow any earlier problems he'd experienced in attempting to court the general's daughter.

"I'm fine, Lance, thank you," she replied curtly, glancing over at a figure emerging from the woods. Safari suit in tatters, CIA Agent Graves looked even worse than before. His face and forearms were black with soot and gunsmoke. His cheeks, chest, and knuckles were streaked with other men's blood. The man looked like a rain-forest ghoul.

"Weren't you supposed to be one of the gunships escorting that gaggle headed for—" Gabriel began, as he strapped the last stretcher onto his slick, but Warlokk cut him off.

"No sweat, Gabe." Lawless walked over and started to wrap an arm around the Dustoff pilot's shoulder, but Gabriel slid out from under the embrace and climbed up into his Huey, its rotors still swishing lazily above them. Warlokk pointed over at one of the fuel cells on his Cobra. "Got a great excuse for Neil Nazi." His grin widened proudly until it was ear-to-ear. "Took a bullet from the ground while passing over an NVA mortar attack at the refugee camp." He folded his arms across his chest smugly. "Had no choice but to set down. Guess I'll just have to wait for one of the jeeps from the Turkey Farm to bring me some fuel. Even my fumes are history." He failed to mention the bullet holes were sustained while engaging hostile ground forces in a contest of sharpshooting skills in support of a Central Intelligence Agency operative's one-man campaign of enemy annihilation through hand-to-hand and rock 'n' roll therapy.

"Guess you'd better get them casualties down to the hospital, Gabe, eh?" Warlokk walked back over to Lisa Maddox's side and draped an arm over her shoulder.

"A little to the left."

Col. Neil Buchanan was a hard man to please when it came

181

to mounting a Bengal tiger head on the wall of his CP most acceptable to the spirits that prowled the Turkey Farm.

"No, no, no. . .to the right now, a little more to the right," he told the three Vietnamese women who had delivered the stuffed head from a so-called "taxidermy expert" in Pleiku whose speciality was preserving Arvin limbs for grim-humored VC agents. Charlie was habitually mounting them along jungle trails in do-not-proceed-from-this-point gestures, palms out and fingers wide. . .Viet Cong flag patches nailed to the open hands. "And a little higher. . .yes, dear, a little higher there. . . ."

The old papa-san who had retired from ARVN the year before and now spent all his free time cleaning the CP, burning latrine refuse, and draining spilled fuel from the helipads, suggested the colonel consult with one of the local 'Yarde holy men to see if any kind of ceremony could remedy the spate of bad luck Buchanan had been experiencing the last few weeks in the form of rocket and mortar attacks. The barrage that landed the day two MPs dragged Krutch and Larson back to camp had inflicted particularly severe damage to the structure, nearly tearing a complete wall out.

The papa-san had surmised evil spirits were most likely behind all the trouble—probably something about the angle Buchanan's CP was positioned in relation to the rest of the camp, or perhaps it might be something as simple as choosing the wrong wall in which to place the entryway. The Montagnarde *mjao* had silently accepted the ten-dollar gift papa-san insisted the colonel pay out, then promptly discovered the problem: a three-thousand-year-old invisible dragon was terrorizing the good spirits roaming the camp, and there was only one way to be rid of the creature and the ill fortune that followed it everywhere.

"You must place tiger in CP," the *mjao* insisted. The dragon, while still in its egg three thousand years ago, had almost been devoured by a tiger, he explained. Tigers were the only animal on earth that it feared. Therefore, a tiger placed strategically inside the CP—preferably directly across from the main entrance so the dragon would see it first thing—would guard the colonel from any further incidents.

"Would a *stuffed* tiger suffice?" Buchanan had asked the old papa-san to translate.

"No sweat," came the quick reply. "And for only one hundred greenbacks, holy man can supply you with one."

"Nebbah mind." The colonel grinned. He just happened to have a couple of dead cats sitting in a freezer over at the mess hall.

"A little lower, honey." Buchanan stood in the CP's doorway, pretending he was a dragon. "There!" He could see the tiger head even while standing a couple of paces outside. "Ooops!" He changed his mind. It just wouldn't do to have these young ladies out of his life so soon. "Back toward the right a little bit, dear...yes, that's it...there you go. No...now, wait a second...."

The housegirls were balanced on the chair behind Buchanan's desk; two held the tiger head in place while a third handled the hammer and nails.

"Up a little bit, *dep* sweetie...there you go...."

Buchanan could not have cared less about the positioning of the tiger head, or dragons, or local superstitions. He just enjoyed gazing up the girls' skirts while they worked. Neil Nazi was a dirty old man.

The girls had just left and he was only seated behind a stack of efficiency reports a minute or two before someone was already knocking on the new tin door of the command post.

"Enter at your own risk." The colonel laughed softly. He was in a good mood today. Two of the three housegirls had worn no undergarments beneath their loose-fitting tribal skirts.

Lt. Winston was leading an enlisted man into the CP. "At ease, at ease." Buchanan returned their salutes without looking up from chopper pilot Warlokk's latest efficiency report and a pile of xeroxed dash-13s his mechanic claimed he was ignoring. "What is it, Winston?"

The lieutenant cleared his throat as if to get *all* the CO's attention. "Corporal Patterson here, sir, recently escaped from the VC."

Buchanan's lowered face did not move, but his eyes flew up.

Patterson's chest and back were so heavily bandaged he could not button his fatigue shirt. The soldier's face was covered with deep thorn gashes. "Do you feel as bad as you look, son?" Buchanan slid the reports aside.

"No, sir." Patterson swallowed noisily, and the sound flashed him back to the night before, when the female guerrilla ran a knife against his family jewels. "They drove a couple nails into my back and split one shoulder blade down the middle. These bandages up front are just for support, and—"

"'They drove a couple *nails* into your back?" Buchanan stood up.

"Yes, sir."

"And you're able to *walk?*"

"No sweat, sir." The soldier beamed. "I'm First Cav, First Team, First and Foremost, the—"

Buchanan waved him silent with a tight grin. "Save the pep talk for the gunnies in the slicks, Corporal."

Lt. Winston handed him the VC-flag patch Xuyen Thi Vau had nailed to Patterson's back. "A woman did this." He was not trying to insult the trooper. "He says a woman was leading the squad of guerrillas. A *woman*, Colonel. I think it's the group we've been looking for."

"Her name was Zoo-yen Tea Vow, Colonel." Patterson pronounced the name from memory. The features of her face were branded across his mind.

"That will be all, Winston."

The lieutenant had been pulling up a seat himself. He froze, crestfallen; he'd been so looking forward to hearing this soldier tell his story again. "Uh. . .yes, sir."

"Oh, and. . .Winston," Buchanan called as the aide was halfway out the door.

"Sir?"

"Make sure Patterson here gets a Purple Heart outta this. I wanna see the paper on it by this afternoon."

"Yes, sir. I'll get right on it." Winston saluted again as he backed out of the CP.

A few moments of silence followed as Buchanan gazed up into the marbled eyes of his tiger head. "Nice Bengal," Patterson said. "I was a member of your uh. . .hunting party that day."

The colonel did not immediately reply but merely nodded his head up and down slowly. A gaggle of choppers flew past outside, and he stared out the door, eyes seeming to cloud over.

"What do you know about dragons, Patterson?"

The corporal was at a loss for words, so he just sat there, running the question over and over in his mind. *Did the colonel just ask "what do you know about dragons?"* He blinked his eyes several times, but that did not help at all. "Sir?"

"Never mind, son." Buchanan smiled suddenly. He shook his head again, but this time as if in self-reprimand, and took his attention off the doorway. He looked back up at the tiger head and remembered the jungle clearing where the Bengal was killed and how Treat Brody showed up there too, wearing a snake head in the midst of all the gunsmoke. "Tell me about this young gal, Xuyen Thi Vau."

Buchanan's field phone rang right after Corporal Patterson left.

It was one of the military policemen up the block, at Camp Holloway. "We got a civilian at the static post here, Colonel. Says he's from some Congressman's office back in The World. Says he has authorization from Division to speak with you. Says you know all about some kind of interview they wanted to conduct." His heavy European accent put the officer on guard.

"Does he have papers?" A look of intense irritation glazed Buchanan's eyes as he stared up into the Bengal's gold flake marbles.

"Yes, sir. Signed by a General Something-or-Other down at Disneyland East. Mad-something, sir. . . Mad-Dog or Mad-Pox or. . . ."

Maddox. Buchanan gnashed his teeth, remembering an old feud he'd had with Gen. Maddox back when they were *both* colonels. Something about corruption in the military entertainment and PX services over in Germany. And now fate had led them both to The Nam. Except that Maddox was suffering a REMF complex down in Sin City, and *he* was commanding a hot-to-trot Air Cavalry battalion up north, where the press corps was claiming in daily news pieces that all the action was. Buchanan scratched his chin. Didn't the aide to Westmoreland have a daughter assigned up here somewhere, a nurse or something? "Anyway. . ."

"Anyway, sir, says here you are to cooper—"

"Can he hear you?" Buchanan scratched at an earlobe.

"No, sir. He's sitting out in his jeep, arguin' with my partner.

185

We got this new directive down from Division that the drivers of all vehicles must open their own trunks and hoods because of those terr bombings last week. We had four men killed—"

"Yes, yes . . . heard all about it. You guys are doing a great job over there."

"Yes, and—"

"Okay, listen." Buchanan cut the MP off but kept his tone cordial. "Tell him I'm not available. Tell him I'm on a C&C over the DMZ somwhere or an ash-n-trash flight into Division —whatever you think he'll buy. I'm not expected back for a couple of days. Got that?"

"Okay, Colonel, whatever you say." The military policeman did not sound very enthusiastic.

"And what was your name, soldier?"

"PFC Bouloi, sir."

"Okay, *Specialist Fourth Class* Bouloi. Thanks for the warning. Carry on, son."

"Yes, sir. Okay, sir! Thank you, sir." In the background, Buchanan could hear the MP yelling at his partner to "get that goddamned jeep outta my checkpoint" before hanging up the field phone.

The colonel wiped sweat from his brow. It was only nine o'clock in the morning, yet his fatigue shirt was already drenched along the lower back and armpits, and it had nothing to do with the Congressional investigation. The Bull ate politicians for breakfast. "Why do I stay here?" he wondered aloud, staring at the framed Medal of Honor hanging beneath flags of the United States, South Vietnam, and Korea on the far wall. The *Congressional* Medal of Honor, he mused with a smile, wondering how the lawmaker's aide was getting along with the recently promoted military policeman.

Why did he put up with the heat and humidity, the bugs and culture shock, and all the letters home to parents of slain teenagers?

And then he remembered. His eyes locked onto the lacquer-wood box sitting atop a *Buffy* elephant statue in the middle of his empty bookcase.

The small brown box that contained the semi-weekly letters from Major Lam Van Minh. Minh of the North Vietnamese Army. Minh the mastermind.

Letters that were both taunting and kind, insulting and complimentary.

The two military officers had been exchanging correspondence through the civilian Vietnamese mail system for nearly a month now. Correspondence that included boasts and threats, suggestions and observations. Buchanan did not take anything Minh said at face value; nor did he allow the communist's letters to influence any of his strategy or battlefield decisions. It was all just a game to the colonel. A contest of wits that was made no less needling by the fact Minh obviously mailed his plain blue envelopes from somewhere below the DMZ... somewhere in *South* Vietnam. And mailed them with relative impunity.

Buchanan walked over to the lacquer-wood box and lifted its finely crafted lid. An envelope with no return address was revealed. It had an Air France airliner stenciled across the bottom lefthand corner. Two colorful stamps decorated the opposite corner, one bright pink, showing a Montagnarde woman standing before several longhouses somewhere in the Central Highlands. The other pictured several ARVN soldiers defending a hamlet—symbolized by a young woman in straw conical hat and wraparound sarong, holding a child to her breast—charging past a flapping South Vietnamese flag, three horizontal, blood-red stripes against a golden saffron field. *So ironic,* Buchanan decided. That kind of stamp from such a soldier.

My Dear Colonel Buchanan of the Illustrious First Air Cavalry Division, *the single paqe inside began. It was the first letter Minh had ever sent him.* Welcome to the Ia Drang Valley. Now go home!

While you still can. Before we box you up, *ship* you home in a teakwood casket. I will personally supervise the body count, my dear counterpart, and rest assured: my comrades will not rest until every foreigner has been driven into the sea.

Yes, I must admit, I'm very impressed by your Airmobile gunship helicopters. But we are the more dedicated soldiers here, don't you agree? Your men are disenchanted and demoralized by this splendid little war for the people of Vietnam. All they want is to go

187

home.

Your politicians will not let you win, so why do you waste your time and mine? Why do you water the earth of this land with the blood of American cherry boys who have yet to even sleep beside a loving woman. And I am not talking about the waifs your president's policy has turned into prostitutes. Who sleeps with your wife back in America at this very moment, my dear Colonel? My people have been fighting outsiders for a thousand years and more. We are motivated. We have a just cause. We will not be defeated. Jungle justice will prevail and—

Buchanan dropped the letter back into the box and slammed its lid shut. "What a crock of shit."

He lit a cigar and blew smoke down into the tiger cub's face, visions of Minh's head on his mantel eliciting the slightest trace of a smile. The cub, nostrils wrinkling inward, sneezed. Its eyes had been following the colonel's every move, and now it lifted its head back and screamed at the ceiling fan. Several soldiers passing by outside craned their necks to peer inside but kept walking. Some broke into a run.

Startled from his daydream by the ear-piercing sound, he mumbled, "Oh, sorry, cat," and stubbed the cigar out in an ashtray.

Buchanan sat down at his desk, reached over to scratch his pet behind the ears, recoiled with claw scratches along his knuckles, and pulled a blank piece of First Cav stationery from the top drawer.

Dear Minhy Mouse, *he wrote*. Soon you die, *du ma*. I have placed a trace on your letters and intend to soon land a thousand of my gunships in the middle of your AO. I plan to ram the skids of my own C&C chopper right up your arse.

Though I must commend you for that recent operation east of Mang Yang Pass. It was brilliant strategy —or did you just stumble onto the convoy? (Or was Queen Cong Xuyen Thi Vau really responsible, and your boot-in-mouth troopers just happened across

the smoking carnage afterwards and decided to leave
an NVA flag lying around?) We rebounded accordingly and shall soon smash your units back across the
border into—

Someone had been knocking at his door for several seconds,
but he only now realized the sound was not the echo of mortar
crumps from memories of the day before.

"Enter at your own risk." He slid the unfinished letter under
his helmet.

Brody and Fletcher appeared, ushering Cordova, Lee, and
Delgado in through the corrugated tin door. "Mornin',
Colonel."

The men were all holding skullcaps from old VC kills. The
cuplike sections of bone were filled with warm beer. "You gentlemen are *no longer* gentlemen in my book." Buchanan
grinned. "In fact, you disgust me."

None of the soldiers believed he was sincere. "Aw, come on,
sir." Fletcher downed his cup in a single gulp, and foam
dripped along his chin. "It's tradition. Cordova made it to
another birthday. And yesterday he chalked up enough Cong
kills to be accepted into Hog Heaven."

"You were a door gunner yesterday, Corky?" Buchanan extended his hand.

"Yes, sir." He accepted it eagerly. "Brody only flew two
missions."

"Only two?" Buchanan's eyes shifted to the Spec-4 in mock
shock. "You're slipping, Whoremonger."

"Had to pay a visit to the dispensary, Colonel." Brody
shrugged. "Nothin' I could do about it. Nurse Maddox *ordered*
me over so she could take the stitches outta my back."

"I see." He glanced at all the other alcohol-dazed faces.
"Where's your buddy Larson?"

"You know the Professor, sir." Lee's eyes refused to meet the
colonel's. "He doesn't like to visit the CP unless he has to."

"He's down in the Hell Hole writin' his suicide note," Fletcher added.

Buchanan laughed, but it was a disgusted chuckle. "Yes, isn't
he always?" The colonel took Cordova's mug and drank from it,
dropping the level to half. "Your birthday, huh?" He decided it

189

was his duty to make the youth feel good. "I'd say you look about twenty-five today. . .maybe twenty-six, tops."

"Twenty, sir." The machine gunner still looked proud as he accepted the skullcap back. At Cordova's age, the older a soldier looked, the happier he was.

"Ahhh yes. . .old enough to earn your way into Hog Heaven and collect combat pay, but not old enough to drink real booze." He playfully took the skullcap back and drank what was left of the beer in it.

"Or old enough to vote," Lee added. He looked unhappy.

"It's only three-point-two, Colonel," Cordova protested lightly.

"We ran out of 'Thirty-three,'" Lee confessed.

"Old enough to kill a hundred gun-totin' Cong but not old enough to vote," Delgado was muttering under his breath, mulling over what Em-ho had said, but Buchanan ignored the medic.

"Any beer drunk from a dead man's cranium is six-percent-plus," he told Corky.

"When you start to get a buzz, it's the Cong's last thoughts you'll see in front of your eyes," Brody claimed, "not pink elephants."

"What the hell is a 'cranium?'" Fletcher whispered over to Lee.

"A skulljob," the Whoremonger replied for him.

Hog Heaven was an elite club of door gunners who'd killed one hundred or more of the enemy. Treat Brody liked to refer to it as the hottest fraternity at the University of South Vietnam. Cav troopers who jumped into Void Vicious and chalked up that many kills were also permitted—one didn't have to be a gunny. But a Tour 365 behind the heavy Hog-60s almost always guaranteed initiation into Hell's elite, if the hazing didn't send you home to Mama in a body bag first. Membership entitled the warriors to wear the plentiful SURE TO GO TO HEAVEN 'CAUSE I'VE SPENT MY TIME IN HELL logo across the backs of their flak jackets, but with a special design in the center: a huge straw conical hat sitting on a pyramidlike pile of one hundred VC skulls, with the words HOG HEAVEN drifting through the gunsmoke from a blazing M-60 above, and ONE HUNDRED CONFIRMED KILLS below.

190

There came a sudden scratching at the door behind Brody's people, and before anyone could inspect the source, *Choi-oi* began barking.

Buchanan's eyes darted from man to man as he grabbed the edges of his desk. "Does that mean what I think it means?" His eyes read *Mortars!* and he was only half joking.

Brody was already through the door and picking up a wet, protesting *Choi-oi*. "Nah," said Fletcher, "the no-good moocher-mongrel's just raisin' Cain 'cause he smells your pussycat there, sir. When he *howls—*"

"*That* means mortars," translated Lee.

"You been chasin' water buffalos through the rice paddies again, boy?" Brody rubbed noses with the dog, who promptly commenced shaking the foul-smelling water from his coat.

"Ohhh!"

"Shit!"

"*Choi*-fucked-up-*oi!*" Everyone complained about getting soaked.

"Take that beast outta here!" Buchanan shielded his face. The CP was cramped at the best of times, and *Choi-oi* was proving that now. "Get 'im out of here!"

Picking up the skullcap drinking mug on his desk, the colonel followed Brody and *Choi-oi* and the others out into the harsh sunlight. "What a party crasher!" He laughed.

A high-powered rifle somewhere in the tree line discharged several hundred feet away. The bullet struck the section of human skull in Buchanan's hand and shattered it as the men all dove for cover.

"You call this chow?" Lance "Lawless" Warlokk stared down at the powdered egg the plump Vietnamese cook's assistant had slopped down on his tray.

"Numba one chop-chop!" she replied, all smiles as she picked her nose, then resumed slapping slices of bread on peanut-butter-and-jelly sandwiches.

"But it's *green*!" He wrinkled his own nostrils, made a face, and headed toward the coffee pot, bypassing the blackened bacon and a huge vat of watery oatmeal. Something was swimming on its back in there.

"*Numba one!*" the cook's aide insisted.

Warlokk hated the way mess hall trays actually *stank* when anything moist was placed in them—something about their composition. He abandoned the eggs between two ice chests filled with cans of soda pop and settled on a cup of black coffee and a banana. Warlokk had once read somewhere that bananas contained certain organic chemicals beneficial to one's mental health. "I'll settle for anything that keeps me from going *dinky-dau* in this insane asylum," he muttered under his breath, grabbing five of them. But these were Vietnamese bananas, small and green with black edges. So did the chemical bit still apply?

He took a stack of toast too. Bread was supposed to help stop the shits, which he got from the malaria pills. "But this crap is green through and through," he complained.

Someone bumped him as he stood in front of the baggies of steamed sugarcane—an indigenous dessert—trying to decide whether the sweet treat would start his cavities to throbbing once more. "Talking to yourself again, Lance Baby?" Dustoff pilot Cliff Gabriel was looking up at him. Elbow resting on the butt of his holstered pistol, Gabe grinned as he twisted one end of a handlebar moustache with his free hand.

Warlokk tried to ignore him as he cut through the fruit juice line, but Gabriel went out of his way to sit across the table from the Cobra jock.

"Got me a date tonight with Lisa," Gabriel lied, testing the other warrant officer.

"Bullshit."

"Would I shit you, Lawless-Kinda-Guy? You're my favorite—"

"I'm your favorite turd." Warlock matched him word for word. "Right."

"But really, my buddy the Cobra Jock," Gabriel persisted, and though he was not sure why, it felt good to rib Loverboy Lance. He just couldn't control himself. "I thumbed a ride back down there last night." Gabe was amazed at how easily he could make up the story as he went along. "After you attempted to leave such an impression on me by hangin' your paws over her shoulder."

"I said it before, and I'll say it again, Gabriel: *bullshit.*"

The men sitting at their table exchanged concerned looks. These warrant officers were not kidding around. Neither one

192

was smiling.

"I showed up...oh, around midnight or so...just before I curfew. We played a round of strip poker and...well, you know how time flies when you're having fun. With the curfew and all, she just had to invite me to stay the night at the refugee camp, and"—Gabriel forced a chuckle—"I just *couldn't* refuse...."

Warlokk slammed his coffee cup down on the table. "Bullshit, asshole! I just happen to know Lt. Maddox had the duty last night for twenty-two hundred to ten hundred this morning." He glanced at his watch. "She's probably still sewin' arms back on, in fact. It's the only way they'll allow her time to help those poor kids at the orphange, if she works graveyards six-and-one."

Gabriel had ignored everything he said. "It was quite a card game, slick. I knew Lisa was stacked in just the right places, but hell, I figured she had one o' those bras with wires in 'em that prop half the boobs in America up. Boy, was *I* wrong! Nurse Maddox can *nurse* this slick driver any day. She needs absolutely *no* support, amigo."

"Now I know why your eyes are brown, Gabe," Warlokk said loudly. "Cause you're so full o' shit!" He took a bowlful of soggy cereal from the soldier's tray next to him and dumped it over the Dustoff pilot's head, then stormed out of the mess hall.

Smile miraculously still intact, Gabriel gave the other men at the table a wonder-what-that-was-all-about shrug. "Thanks, Lawless!" he called after the warrant officer beyond the swinging exit doors. He took a small green cube of cereal out of his hair and plopped it in his mouth. "Just what I needed this week, Lucky Charms!"

Warlokk responded to the Irish accent with an obscene gesture.

The woman behind Kim stumbled in the dark, and several rocks tumbled down the wooded hillside. "Quiet!" the guerrilla leader hissed, "or we will have the whole American Air Cav Division down on our backs. Do you want your body sent back to our hills with a horse head patch wedged between your lips?"

Women in a war zone can be just as raunchy as the men. "Which lips?" The female fighter who had promised to lead Kim to the Airmobile camps laughed lightly.

"Sshhh!" Kim would not take part in the fun. They were only three women tonight. *Heavily armed and clad in black calico* but three women only, nonetheless. "Six tits and a trio of twats," she whispered aloud, thinking back to something a GI had told her in a bar one rainy night the monsoon before.

"What?" The woman behind Kim knew little English.

"Nothing."

"There." The third girl pointed as they reached a bend in the trail and a sea of twinkling lights spread out below, nearly to the horizon. "Is it not as I said?" She sounded proud.

"Yes," Kim spoke as if rewarding her. "It is even more beautiful a sight than I imagined."

Despite the late hour, various groups of helicopters were lifting off or setting down, leaving for and coming in from different directions, unrelated missions. It looked like mass confusion to the female guerrillas, but none of the ships came close to crashing into one another.

It was a sapper's paradise, Kim decided.

"I cannot believe Minh's army has not already struck," the woman beside her mused as they watched the two new Cobra gunships being refueled beneath dim bamboo-green lights.

"I have heard they plan something," the other girl said. "I have heard—"

"Minh's people run for their lives," Kim said. "Ever since First Cav came to Ia Drang."

"Yes, but—"

"Only VC can make any difference now. Believe me, sister, I know."

The three women sat in silence for a few more minutes, watching a Lurp patrol pass through the MP checkpoint on their way into the rain forest for a midnight, moonlit "walk." Having picked up its heavy scent nearly an hour earlier, Kim listened to a panther prowling the hilltop above and behind them while her friends thought about what she'd said and reflected on the stories they'd heard, stories of the Dragonlady from Hue.

"I hear the Americans have love muscles longer than a Bangkok banana." The woman on her right elbowed Kim playfully as her whisper finally broke the tense silence. But the guerrilla leader remained straight-faced.

194

"I can tell you they are *hairy* as monkeys, but I can tell you no more."

"Xinh says she has killed some who have white hair and eyes like the sky."

"Xinh has been known to brag but, yes, of that she speaks the truth." Without saying anything more, Kim pointed to a falling star in the distance, and the others nodded silently.

"I think I would like to sleep with one of them some night." The talkative comrade was rubbing her crotch for their benefit, and Kim giggled for the first time. "Just once, maybe. . .to see what it is like."

"One with the sky-blue eyes," the other girl decided.

"Yes, and white hair."

"None of them have white hair when they are alive," Kim said. "Only when they are scared dead by VC fighters does their hair turn white." But the other girls were pretending not to listen to her.

"His love muscle would have to be very long, though, for me to permit him to live." The outspoken guerilla jabbed her AK at the night. "Yes, I would konk him over the head and hold inspection first. It would have to be very long to please me."

"Six or seven inches."

"At the least. I would refuse to surrender my virginity for anything less." Both girls giggled as another star fell across the flare-laced heavens.

Kim was aghast. She had never heard women talk like this. Even guerrillas. "Be quiet," she said in a reprimanding tone. "The two of you are talking foolishly."

"Xinh says the Americans have special love muscle exercises which are mandatory during their basic training across ocean in States."

"*What?*" Kim's eyes lit up.

"Yes!" The youngest among them sounded serious. "She says the Americans must undergo painful exercises to enlarge their love muscles so they will be prepared when it comes time for them to rape Vietnamese women in the Ia Drang."

"Xinh told you all this?"

"Yes!" The first girl sought out Kim's expression in the darkness. "Xinh and Tuyet."

"You do not believe it?" the other watcher asked.

195

Kim did not respond immediately. Instead, she stared down at the twinkling lights, thinking about the falling star and the GI who once told her there were stars in the night sky made by men and not Buddha.

The soldier had taught her the words to a very special song, a beautiful little tune about what could happen when you wished upon a star.

When she had asked if he thought up the song himself, the soldier had smiled and said, "No, the song was part of the magic of Disneyland." A place he would take her some day. After they married and he rescued her from Vietnam.

He taught her which of the stars were really things he called satellites, and how it was a good thing to wish on stars but a terribly bad thing to wish on satellites and she should know the difference, so he taught her all about this American secret. And though she believed not a word of what he told her, Kim humored the man, promising not to wish on the ones that were a dull gold and did not twinkle but passed quickly through the slower swirl of constellations in a solid arc.

She promised not to wish on stars made in America.

After he left her without warning one night, like a dog with its tail between hind legs, Kim cried for weeks over broken promises. And once she ventured alone and suddenly unafraid to that sprawling MACV complex in Saigon, but the gate MPs threatened to throw her in the monkeyhouse if she ever came back.

She left with lost face and a scar across her heart, both saddened and sorry, convinced the magic was gone forever because she had wished on the wrong star.

"Xinh said *you* have made romance to an American." The girl at Kim's side made the accusation without looking at her.

"But she concedes it was your duty at the time," the second girl spoke seriously and with some pity.

"Tell us, sister. Tell us what it was like. I would not think it any different from—"

"You are right," Kim snapped. "A man is a man is a man. They are all the same. There is no real difference. Especially in their soul. All they care about, all they want—"

"But the Americans are so. . .so big."

"It is not in the size of their. . .love muscle, Lien." She borrowed their choice of words.

"It is in their. . .technique?" The younger woman anticipated the lesson for the evening.

"And just because a man stands taller than the elephant grass does not mean his love muscle—"

"I would fear a man taller than the elephant grass would. . . split my legs apart! I would be afraid he would hurt me." Pain, or the imagination of pain, seeped into her tone with the last words.

"I have liberated the loins from men taller than any you see walking down there," Kim revealed in a cryptic manner, "yet some of their love muscles were no longer than a shriveled-up mango."

"No!"

"Why would I lie about something so ridiculous?"

"Xinh says a GI promised to marry you once. He promised to marry you and take you far away from Vietnam. To America, Kim. She says he promised this and that and when it came time for you to pack he was already gone. Back to his real wife and kids in New'ork City. That is why you fight so fiercely against the Americans. Xinh says—"

"Xinh is full of shit!" Kim spat into the breeze, then fell silent, her anger heavy in the air.

None of them exchanged another word, and after the Lurp patrol passed far out of hearing range, the three VC women started back to their caves.

CHAPTER 19

Major Lam Van Minh stared at the largest map in his command bunker just inside Cambodian territory. It hung on a packed earthen wall across from his folding, made-in-Brooklyn-

U.S.A. desk. The American Special Forces camp at Plei Me was at the center of the map, and Minh studied its defenses, both past and present.

A young NVA private—he appeared seventeen at most and probably did not even own a pair of tweezers with which to remove whiskers yet—entered the spacious room silently, placed a handwritten intelligence report on a growing pile of others, and left without a word.

Minh picked up the note, scanned it, and frowned. More choppers. That bastard Buchanan was bringing more helicopters into his Airmobile camp.

The American colonel was making a blunt statement with this latest show of force. He was taunting Minh. Daring him and his men to leave their tunnels and fight. Out in the open. One on one.

But how could it really be one on one when half the contestants rode the skies on wings of metallic dragons the color of camouflage?

The red star on his map that was Plei Me seemed to sparkle down on Minh. All these weeks he had been planning to surround and decimate the Green Beret advisors there. But now he had to contend with Neil "Bull" Buchanan and his First Air Cavalry Division. "His Echo Company troopers of the Seventh . . ." Minh laughed lightly to himself and picked up a recon photo that showed a gaggle of Hueys taking off from the Turkey Farm. But as he thought about the soldier who had taken the pictures, a proud nineteen-year-old from his own hometown of Son Tay, Minh remembered his son and the smile vanished.

His heart cried at that moment, but the major's eyes remained dry. He had no more tears left. Not for his country. Not for his family. Minh lived only for revenge. For the day he could mount "Bull" Buchanan's severed head on a tall bamboo pole outside his command bunker.

Both teenagers were dead. The nineteen-year-old died only this morning at predawn, after he walked with eight others into a 7th Cav Lurp ambush; his son two years ago, when a South Vietnamese helicopter piloted by American advisors blew the boy out of his sandals and his rice paddy with a 30-caliber machine gun. And all because the youth had been fool enough to carry his AK slung over his back as he tended the water buffalo.

Fool enough, but so proud...

Minh glanced up at the map again, and then he examined the photos. He read and reread the intelligence report, and then he opened the latest message from Col. Buchanan himself—another taunting and insulting note delivered through channels via an address on the DMZ.

Sneering loudly, he crumpled up the single page and tossed it in a trash can. Unlike the American officer, he did not save the correspondence.

Minh opened the top drawer of his desk and took out several darts. An aide brought in another report, but he ignored the intrusion, and after the soldier left whirled around in his swivel chair and began throwing darts at an enlargement of Buchanan's Hanoi Intelligence file photo. Soon he would have to decide whether to attack the Turkey Farm or Plei Me. With the gunships against him on one hand and Green Beret snake-eating madmen on the other, he didn't have enough trustworthy troops to assault both positions simultaneously.

The first dart struck Buchanan's likeness between the eyes, and Minh chuckled, leaning back in his chair. Suddenly, he felt quite at ease. His people had time on their side. They had the tunnels and history and a dedication the draftees from U.S.A. would never know. Many if not all of the soldiers working under Minh believed strongly in family and the reunification of north and south, brother and brother. But if the NVA major did not share their enthusiasm, he was convinced the reasons were valid.

Reared in a village called Son Tay, west of Central Hanoi, the exact day and month of his birth was unknown, though he knew the year to be 1920. Lam Minh always chose to celebrate his birthdays during the Tet Lunar New Year festivities.

Born Tran Luyen, he was also known as Nguyen Van Luc and Ho Chi Phuc. The Vietnamese, borrowing on American humor and Pidgin English called him Hard Luck Lam. The American GIs referred to him as Phuc Head.

Currently in charge of NVA operations between the DMZ and Ia Drang Valley in South Vietnam, Minh received his leadership training and communist indoctrination in East Berlin, Moscow, and Havana after ten years of spearheading guerrilla raids against the French. Earning dual degrees in literature and psychology before being summoned to military service in 1944, he rose rapidly through the ranks with the help of family connections. Fiercely anti-foreigner, Minh has always been realistic about the war. It fuels one of his many weaknesses, black-market activities. He was once accused of maintaining an entire ghost platoon on paper, troops who never existed, but for which he still collected government paychecks, but the allegations went unsubstantiated when the junior officer making them was subsequently "killed in action."

Minh held numerous NVA citations for routine longevity, but only one decoration for valor. It was a medal the major did not deserve; the heroics which he fabricated for himself and the complexity and "literary flow" of the accompanying citation were a masterpiece of fiction he would always be proud of. Yet none in his command were brave enough to doubt Minh's courage under fire. Though his ruthless battlefield tactics were well known among North Vietnamese strategists, the combat officer was probably most notorious for his directives involving suicide sapper assaults, in which waves of doped-up and outgunned human bombs were sent to their deaths against the Americans.

Many of his subordinates joked behind Minh's back that his broad face and flat nose made him the mirror image of China's Mao. At five-foot-six and 150 pounds, he was one of the larger, more intimadating commanders, whose dark brown hair was worn short on the sides and slightly bushy on the top per current NVA style. It was called the Ho Chi Minh Trail cut. Minh carried an ugly bullet hole scar in his right leg below the knee. A second bullet was still imbedded in his shoulder blade. Numerous shrapnel scars decorated his lower back and also attested to his free-fire-zone experience.

Married twice, Minh's first wife was killed in a U.S. bombing raid on Hanoi in 1964. The major moved his second wife from the capital to his hometown of Son Tay after she gave birth to his second son. Fourteen months old, the boy was understandably his pride and joy—and proof Minh could still "produce" at age forty-five.

Planning to bring-up his children as Christians, Minh himself had been raised a Catholic by French nuns, but currently practiced no religion because of his membership in the Communist Party. Other "dirty laundry" Lam Van Minh was constantly trying to hide from his superiors included the fact that his older sister married a French gunrunner shortly before the fall of Dienbienphu eleven years earlier, and now lived in Paris; and his younger sister married an American consular official— both still reside in what romanticists called the Pearl of the Orient but Minh referred to as Sin City: Saigon.

Major Minh glanced up at the converted GI footlocker that held his collection of rare books and memorabilia on Adolf Hitler. Minh was not a fan of the Chief Nazi, but just intrigued by the fascist's speeches. He thought about the strange bits of correspondence the man had exchanged with his mistress before the fall of the Third Reich, and decided perhaps he too, someday, should keep a lady on the side, if only to write to now and then about his frustrations.

Minh was tired of addressing the bulk of his private correspondence to the American named Neil Buchanan.

My Dear Round-Eyed Son of a Plague-Infested Rodent, *he began the latest letter in a vein unkinder than most of the past. Visions of his first son being torn to shreds by a merciless helicopter pilot danced in front of his mind's eye for a moment.* I'm sure you think you have me outguessed, Sir Air Cavalry Colonel. I'm sure you think you know my next move in the Ia Drang, and all my moves to follow. But let me favor you with a tidbit of information that will surely shock and enlighten you. . . .

Minh had no such news up his sleeve. But this Buchanan and all his gunships and all his crazy-eyed door gunners who wore phython masks and left horse-head cards hanging out of the mouths of his dead soldiers were leaving Minh feeling as if he were backed into a corner. And the Ia Drang was supposed to be *his* domain.

It was a time to throw the Airmobile commander a curve.

Brody the Whoremonger had been unable to shake the uneasy feeling in the pit of his gut all night. It was the same belly-flopping nausea that accompanied all jaunts over Void Vicious

201

on bad-luck days, but tonight they were on foot, humping through the heart of the rain forest along the Ia Drang's northern ridge.

Assigned the task of intercepting the midnight marauders led by that semi-legendary female guerrilla, the majority of Brody's squad was, in reality, simply hoping to track down the Arvins responsible for kidnapping the village princess in Em-ho's wet dreams. And it wouldn't hurt to take this latest patrol deeper through Injun Country, Fletcher convinced Brody, right through the canyon where Snakeman's older brother crashed and burned two years earlier.

Let's hustle, gentlemen. Treat wrote the words on a small pad and passed it around for the others to read. Silence in this stretch of the woods was essential, if they were to survive the night. Larson and Krutch, usually the least-disciplined of the clique, were not members of tonight's party—Buchanan finally gave them their weekend in the off-limits ville—and that helped.

Fletcher cautiously picked through the few pieces of aircraft fuselage, shaking his head dejectedly. There was no marking of any sort—nothing to indicate the debris was even left over from an American aircraft. The site had been picked clean by human scavengers long ago.

Richard would have left something. Fletcher's mind raced as he glanced at the shielded luminous hands on his watch, well aware that the rain-forest *presence* was pressing in on them . . . down on them—all around! The swirl of jungle fever was ominous, smothering the patrol not unlike a blanket of apprehension. They were intruders, and trespassers into the Void were not allowed to leave. Not *unchanged,* at least. They were no longer just soldiers on a mission; *that* the rain forest sometimes permitted, Ju-ju would tell you. No, tonight they were mercenaries, trying to steal the jungle's secrets. *Richard would have left me a sign. . . .*

Fletcher ignored the pad, and Brody was tapping him on the shoulder now. Bulging eyes told Snakeman there was movement in the distance, and it wasn't an animal.

Right! Fletcher nodded, the serpents in the hat dangling from his web belt slithering about in an unusual, excited frenzy.

The others, Lee, Delgado, Broken Arrow, Phung, and

Truong Ju-ju, were already moving off through the trunks, parallel with a seldom-used trail, and Fletcher watched the luminous tabs between their shoulder blades bobbing up and down as they slowly became one with the creeping fog. As he rose, something sparkled underfoot, and he dropped back down on one knee, scooped up the sliver of metal, and rushed to join the last man in the team before he disappeared into the swirling green gloom.

Brody led the Cav troopers away from the movement that had seemed to shadow them for the last several hours. Contact was not in the plan tonight. All he wanted to do was satisfy Lee and Snakeman.

The squad dropped into a crouch when they came upon the silhouette of huts at the edge of a vast, mile-wide clearing in the jungle. No lanterns burned in the village. There was only the eerie glow of smoke, gray against the black veil of night, rising ghostlike from the coals of old cooking fires through gaping holes in the thatched roofs.

Brody checked his map as a dog barked on the far side of the hamlet and a flock of magpies took to the darkness. He glanced down at his compass, checked the map again, then stared up at the stars for a moment as if utterly confused.

"This has got to be the place, Em-ho," he whispered for the first time. According to the ARVN troop movements chart he'd studied in the colonel's bunker that afternoon, the South Vietnamese soldiers accused of abducting the sister of Lee's villager friend should be patrolling this stretch of woods and making their camp tonight in the very village the Americans now prepared to enter. "It's your bleeding-heart, humanitarian project, Em-ho." Lee could barely see Brody's smile, and he wondered if the Whoremonger was really as irritated as he tried to sound. "*You* lead the way."

Led by the nervous Asian-American, the team filtered in through the tree line surrounding the village, careful to keep a full twenty meters or more between each man. It wouldn't do to have a nervous sentry take them all out with a single grenade or rock-'n'-roll burst.

Lee's rifle muzzle went up suddenly, and Brody's gun hand imitated it. The team fell silent across the reeds where they were, laying dog. All except Brody.

He was beside Lee in the blink of an eye. "I guess you better start callin' me *Ee*-ho," the pointman whispered so softly Brody practically had to read his lips.

"Huh?"

Lee pointed at a pair of brown buttocks rising up and down behind a patch of bushes. The slender soles of a woman's feet floated in the air on either side of the pumping haunches, sinking slightly with each thrust only to rise again. "Early *Evening* Hard-On."

"Well, what do we have here?" Brody handed Lee his rifle and glided over to the carbine propped up against a palm tree.

Picking up the M-2 without a sound, he waited until the village sentry began to groan out of sync, then gently placed the cool barrel edge against the blur of a crack.

The Vietnamese froze. His hands slid from the woman's breasts below him and clutched dirt, hoping to prove he was unarmed. His back arched in submission, but the woman was in no mood to stop now.

Legs wrapped around his waist, she began pumping herself now, frantically chasing that rare tingle of pleasure that cost nothing in a free-fire zone. Lee and Brody exchanged grins and a wink as they watched her grab the man's haunches, trying to squeeze him deeper into her. An animal-like rasp escaped her lips as she tried to both enjoy herself and control her moans without waking half the village. But Lee's smile quickly faded. The kid at their feet was definitely no Arvin, probably just a lucky teenager who had evaded the draft but not the village chieftan's sense of priorities: The boy would spend his nights guarding his home against thieves and terrorists. And the woman was definitely not being raped, she was *enjoying* this. Which meant she probably wasn't a whore either. A prostitute's movements ceased once her customer collapsed across her chest, or rolled off. *Orgasms were unheard of, right?* Brody's grin remained intact.

When the woman stopped moving, when her long drawn-out sigh took to the night breeze and she uncurled her legs, letting them drop heavily to the ground, Brody tapped her boyfriend again.

The sentry whispered something into the woman's ear, and her whole body tensed. Harshly, she rattled an exclamation in

204

rapid Vietnamese against her mate's ear, then pushed him off and rolled into the reeds, crying out softly as some of the sharp edges sliced into swaying breasts and flaring thighs.

"Not bad." Brody's voice remained hushed. "We shoulda brought along one of them fancy starlight scopes."

Lee forced a laugh, then waved the rest of the team in. Noticing the girl's sarong draped over a bush, he tossed it to her and motioned the man to slide his shorts on. The girl darted off between the huts without pausing to dress.

"What was *that?*" Cordova's rifle came up, but Two-Step already had an M-79 butt plate against his shoulder.

"Want me to waste her amber ass, Whoremonger?" he asked calmly.

"Naw. . . ." Brody did not seem concerned. He told Ju-ju to ask the sentry if there were any Arvins spending the night in the ville.

"He say no," the scout replied after a minute-long conversation in hushed whispers. "He say they pass through two days ago, but only stay hour, and take no women. All the women hide in bunker. Arvin steal one pig and bookoo chickens. Chief, he real mad. Treaten complain Saigon government—"

"What about the Arvins, did they have any women with them?"

"They had three boom-boom girls tagging along, wearing soldier trousers and camou halter tops." Truong had already asked. "But they were some whores this platoon had with them when they passed through last month. I do not think they are same Viets Lee look for, Bro-dee."

"Sorry, Ee-ho." The squad leader shook his head. "But I think Ju-ju's got his shit straight for a change."

Lee frowned. "Let's keep it an "*Em*-ho, okay?"

"Sure." Brody turned back to the sentry.

"Are we gonna recon the ville or not?" Broken Arrow was beside him now.

"Naw, I think Little Luke here has got the perimeter under control, don't you Luke?"

"Yes," the sentry smiled up at him. "I think I do veddy good job, Lieuten'nt." The kid spoke surprisingly good English.

Brody did not bother explaining he wasn't even an NCO yet, much less an officer. He handed the youth his rifle, glanced at

205

his watch, and then the eastern horizon. A faint blanket of silver atop the hills warned of a tropical sunrise within the hour. Brody pointed to an opening in the tree line several meters from where they had left the jungle. It was time to head back to camp.

The last man in the patrol, Broken Arrow, spat into the leaves and glared at the sentry. "You shouldn't mix pussy with perimeter LPs, *punk.* Maybe next time I blow your ass into the night. Now wouldn't *that* be the ultimate orgasm?"

But the young Vietnamese remained undaunted. "Maybe *next time* I bring my sister for you, Indian man."

He laughed and Brody turned back to face the sentry one final time. "Tell me, kid. How was it?"

"How was it?" Confusion drove the guard's smile away.

"The piece of ass." He tilted his head to one side, amused, but the PF still did not understand. "The *girl.* Was she a good fuck?"

The Puff's smile returned, but it was a sad smile. "Oh, veddy good, Joe. Veddy good fuck. Almost."

Ten minutes later, Brody moved up alongside Lee as they walked swiftly through mist that swirled about up to their knees. Movement through mist this heavy granted fast passage. It would be a waste of time to watch for ground-hugging tripwires, they'd be no higher than one's ankles in most cases, so speed became more important than caution.

A vague orange glow along the eastern horizon had replaced the earlier silver. It became visible for the first time since the patrol left the village. Brody spotted it through a break in the trees.

"What is it?" Lee was still upset they'd come up dry again.

"You sure we're headed in the right direction, Em-ho?" Brody kept his voice low.

"Of course I am." Lee produced an insulted look. His eyes grew large and sad as they stared up at the Spec-4 through tired, narrowed lids. "What's the complaint?"

"Let ol' Treat see your compass, bud." Brody remained friendly. "I'll bet the locking arm jammed without you realizing it."

"No way." Lee sounded adamant. "My equipment's in tip-top shape."

"Then I guess the sun screwed up and got outta bed on the wrong side this morning," he replied without emotion, pointing back over the heads of the patrol to a dull glow beyond the trees. "We're heading west."

"Aw, fuck."

"Yah. My sentiments exactly. I'd say we're pretty close to the Cambodian border right about now, slick."

"You're *in* Cambodia, gents," the biggest man Lee had ever seen, clad entirely in black, his face green with camou-paint, dropped from the low branches overhead and landed in a crouch ahead of Brody's squad. "And I wouldn't advise proceedin' any further, less'n you want to meet the monster."

"Meet the monster?" Lee's jaw dropped. This giant in front of them did not appear armed, but he boasted hands that could obviously kill and no doubt had.

Brody was not so intimidated by the Green Beret's size— there was a reason men referred to firearms as equalizers—but he lowered his M-16. He realized they'd nearly walked into an ambush and glanced around, expecting to see eyes in the trees. But there was nothing staring back at him. Nothing. . .no one he could pin down. Brody knew they were out there, though. Waiting for a wrong move, a wrong *look*. "Your people have set up some claymores?" His dry swallow was an apology for their error.

"A *monnster* of a claymore clusterfuck, boy." Bright teeth suddenly flashed back at the specialist as a shaft of sunlight lanced out through the tree line, bathing the SF sergeant's demonic features in warm gold.

"We're Cav." His voice did not crack as another sliver of sunlight caused a trip wire up ahead to sparkle for but an instant. "Seventh Cav of the First Air—"

"I know, I know." The Green Beret waved him silent. Other counterinsurgent commandos were dropping from the trees all around them now. "I spotted the horse head on your shoulder quite aways back, boy. That's why you're still puffin' your pectorals out instead o' gurglin' through a suckin' chest wound."

Brody's dry swallow hurt this time. Creatures with faces streaked green and black had encircled them now, all leering like blood-starved ghouls. He felt he'd just been thrust into the fiery catacombs of hell, and Satan's disciples were closing in for their due.

"We're *xin loi* if we fucked anything up—" Broken Arrow, chest expanding importantly, spoke up as he rested his grenade rifle over a shoulder. It was essential to Two-Step these self-righteous SF-types know he for one wasn't impressed.

"You no screw up nothin', BI." The sergeant, sounding almost Vietnamese now as he spoke with heavy accent, extended a hand and Broken Arrow took it.

The Green Beret groaned loudly, dropped to his knees, then executed a back flip and tumbled through the elephant grass howling like a banshee.

"*Jesus!*" Lee had rushed up and was pointing at Broken Arrow's outstretched fist. The SF sergeant's fingers were still clasped around the Indian's.

"*Aghhhh!*" Broken Arrow stared down at the shreds of bloody flesh along the elbow joint, then threw the severed arm into the trees.

Several of the Green Berets were quietly laughing among themselves. Most of Brody's people had dropped prone against the ground, waiting for a sniper's faraway discharge to reach their ears.

Another NCO was walking up to Broken Arrow. Considerably older than the first, and not as tall, this soldier rubbed at his chin and moustache, trying to hide the smile. "Damned powerful handshake you got there, son." He shook his head in mock awe. "Don't know quite how I'm gonna write this one up or—"

"I barely started to shake—" Two-Step started to protest, and then he noticed Brody and Fletcher fighting grins too, and it hit him—the ol' shake-hands-with-Charlie trick. He'd heard about these *dinky-dau* Special Forces characters borrowing a chopped-off lib from a VC corpse for their rain-forest reunions, but he'd never actually known anyone who had the ruse pulled on him. "Why that sonofa—"

Giggling like a schoolboy who'd just managed to slip a craw-dad down one of his classmate's blouse, the first Green Beret emerged from the reeds. "Guess you Cav clowns aren't so bad after all," he said. "I half expected you to hightail it outta here and—"

208

Like rice stalks shifting in a sea of elephant grass, several shards of light fell across the sergeant's face, and he dropped into a squat. "Can't be too careful about pot shooters." He laughed, making no mention of his yelling scene only moments ago. The sunrise was making targets of them all, and Brody's troops followed suit, moving out of the light.

"We been layin' dog here for three nights now," one of the other jungle experts revealed. "Hope to take out a high-ranker shithead bringin' a payroll in from the airfield at Ba Kev."

"But I think it's gonna be a no-show," the sergeant added. "We're havin' a little unofficial *ba-muoi-ba* contest with an A Team outta Duc Co, and we heard a monster go off couple klicks over those hills there." He pointed toward the west, where the horizon was still dark in spots with fingers of night pushing back the fog.

"I think *they* got Comrade Dung-Breath first." The older NCO frowned.

"We're gonna lay dog awhile longer and see if they break down an' radio in the score," the soldier with three arms told them.

"Well, we were just headin' back to camp ourselves." Brody tried not to sound embarrassed.

"Since when do we have gunship companies stationed *inside* Khmerland?" The older sergeant folded his arms across his chest in a challenge.

"They were just taking the scenic route, right?" The other Green Berets came to Brody's rescue with an out-of-character wink.

"That's a Rodge, Sarge."

"Well, Pleiku City is *that* way." He pointed into the swollen and already sizzling orb of orange heavy across the eastern horizon. Ribbons of last night's storm clouds passed in front of the sun, accenting its power and size.

"Kill a couple commies for us, Sarge," Lee added, and as they turned to leave he whispered over to Brody, "These soggy frogs give me the creeps, Treat."

"Yah, I know what you mean, Em-ho. Kinda like attack dogs lickin' their chops, just darin' you to make a run for it."

A sudden exchange of automatic-weapons fire far away grew into a dull, nonstop crescendo for several moments, and then a helicopter, appearing with a roar from the direction of all the shooting, cruised past across the treetops without any warning and so low every man there dropped back into a crouch again.

The gunship was painted entirely black. Lifeless arms and legs hung out one open hatch. On the other side, a black man in tiger stripes struggled to drag a semiconscious form clinging to the skids up into the chopper.

Kerosene poured from punctured fuel cells, splattering like foul-smelling raindrops across the broken strips of canopy above. Spears dangled from the helicopter's underbelly.

"Spears..," Lee whispered in awe. "Fucking spears."

"Musta been on a spook 'em mission deeper into that nightmare back there than *we* care to go," the Green Beret muttered, and all the men laughed as if it were mandatory. Mandatory and essential for survival this time around.

All the men except Fletcher and Brody. Snakeman and the Whoremonger exchanged Death's-head grins with the Green Beret.

But none of the soldiers was smiling about the same thing.

CHAPTER 20

"Sniper!" Krutch yelled. He'd been lying in a hammock strung beneath *Pegasus*'s belly, watching Brody's people clean their weapons, and now he rolled for the patched-up solvent tank as a string of rounds made splashes, waves, and whistling *twangs* across the Hog-barrel soaking trough.

"No shit!"

Krutch had stepped on Larson's shoulder, and now the Professor was concentrating on finding some cover himself. "Snakeman!" he called out for the nearest registered hero. "Get out there and get that sonofabitch!"

A burst of AK rounds hammered across *Pegasus*'s tail boom, and Krutch groaned in shared pain as his bird was hit. There came a peculiar *zinging* noise, and many of the men looked up to discover the sniper was using the Huey's tail rotor for target practice, knocking it around and around with each shot, until it looked like the propellor on a weathervane at the edge of a tornado.

Larson glanced in the direction he'd last seen Fletcher, expecting a *"Fuck you!"* reply as Snakeman also hid from ricocheting rounds. But the very opposite was the case. Elliot F. was sprinting toward the tree line, firing an M-16 from the hip.

"I'm impressed," Larson whispered under his breath, only the slightest trace of sarcasm still present. "I'm truly fucking impressed." Fletcher's rifle had been broken down for cleaning the last time Larson had looked. The soldier from the Lone Star State had reassembled it in seconds—record time, in the Professor's book! Larson watched the red tracers knock fronds from the high palms on the camp's southern edge. This time the VC rifleman had fired down at them from the opposite end of the Turkey Farm.

And *this* time it became evident the guerilla might not be so blind after all. He had knocked the lighter right from Brody's hand, hadn't he? And what kind of weird game was that, making the tail rotor go around and around. Larson was counting discharges and making comparisons. By his estimates, the gunman had not missed his mark yet.

"*Get some,* Snakeman!" Krutch and Cordova were both shaking their fists as Fletcher charged the tree line, firing four- and five-round bursts, but on the sixth trigger pull, his M-16 locked open on an empty chamber.

Still running a zigzag pattern across the wide-open landing pad, Fletcher ejected the empty banana clip and reached for his mag pouch.

"Aw, fuck me 'till it hurts," he imitated Treat Brody. Because this was not a boonies patrol—this was not a FOB insertion, or a Lurp patrol—he was not wearing his web belt. "Aw, *double* fuck-it!" Fletcher skidded to a halt as the sniper, who he still had not really spotted, dropped a burst of tracers in front of his boots.

Chips of lead and concrete and a sliver of landing-pad tarmac

211

flew up into his face. Fletcher was knocked backward off his feet, and Sgt. Delgado, the medic, appeared out of nowhere. Doc Delgado dove on top of Snakeman, rolling the squad redneck out of the line of fire. Fletcher's forehead was peppered with minute wounds. Blood covered his face, chest, and hands as the corpsman dragged him behind a parked troop lorrie.

"You're red as Two-Step!" Delgado's chest was heaving as they leaned back against the truck tires, watching green tracers float past like smoking Christmas tree ornaments. "Hit bad, or you just in need of some cosmetics?"

Fletcher, still clutching his empty M-16, slammmed the rifle into the ground. *"Damn!"* he growled, ignoring his wounds completely. "I coulda had the sorry sonofa—"

"Who the hell is that?" Delgado was rising to his feet again as Lt. Winston and three raw recruits stumbled into the killing zone, oblivious of the havoc being wrought by the sniper. "Get the hell down, LIEUTENANT!"

Winston, head up in the clouds as he recited the Division's rules and regulations, was escorting the three newbies to Sgt. Zack's tent and never even heard the discharges for all the clamor of helicopters landing and taking off only three hundred yards away. As if from one shot, purple bullet holes appeared in each private's forehead. The teenagers dropped all around Winston like pins in a bowling alley, and Lee tackled the officer, knocking him through the supply sergeant's tent as another burst of rounds left smoke trails in the spot he'd just been occupying.

The Turkey Farm's sniper had finally killed. "Oh my God!" Winston tried to wrestle free of Lee's hold as he realized what was happening. Visions of his hide hanging outside Buchanan's CP filled the lieutenant's head when he peeked through the tent flaps and saw the three puddles of blood gathering under the cherries he'd just been orientating. *"Oh, my God!"*

"The Lord has nothing to do with any of that out there, sir!" Cordova was lying beside him now, crossed forearms shielding his face. "Ol' Luke the Gook has gone rabid on us!"

"Lawless to the rescue! Lawless to the rescue!" A metallic voice boomed across the compound as two Cobras suddenly appeared over the eastern edge of the Turkey Farm. "Lawless to the rescue!" CW2 Warlokk swooped down over the tent flaps

212

and flared out above the tree line in a near-motionless hover. "Bend over, Luke!" The chopper pilot keyed his PA loudspeaker again, and a loud squeal filled ears on the ground. "Spread your knees and kiss your ass good-bye!"

A short burst of bullets from the Cobra's mini-gun system tore the top half of a palm to pieces, and a sputter of green tracers arced up toward him. Lawless was prevented from really unloading on the tree line because of the friendly troops and equipment everywhere below the line of fire.

"Come on, Luke!" From the sporadic burst of green glow, Warlokk sensed he'd at least wounded the sniper. "Give it up, man! Drop your AK and we'll only pull half your molars out with pliers." Brody emitted a restrained laugh. That last bit had been for the GIs proned-out on the ground. "*Chieu*-the-fuck-ing-*Hoi*. Okay, sport?"

Brody and Zack and most of the other men waiting behind cover sensed Warlokk's frustration. A single tracer from his last ten-round burst had ignited a jeep's gas tank and destroyed the packed vehicle. Further shots from such a steep, air-to-ground angle could easily prove cost prohibitive—and we were talking personal paycheck funds here. The U.S. Army was well known for billing soldiers who destroyed government property in a reckless, unauthorized manner.

"I think the sonofabitch is dead," Larson muttered, scraping red clay from an ear.

"Well, I'm gonna find out!" Krutch was already on his feet and racing toward *Pegasus*. "Lawless could use some help up there!"

"Stork—" Larson started to protest, but it was too late. Krutch was already halfway to his ship.

An explosion of multicolored tracers danced between his boots and sent the AC flying over a line of sand-filled oil drums. A single hand rose from behind a drum rim seconds later, middle finger extended in an obscene gesture—Krutch's way of saying he was all right and the sniper's aim wasn't so hot after all.

Lawless, meanwhile, had brought his Cobra down below the treetops and uncomfortabley close to the canopies of several deuce-and-a-half transport trucks.

"What's that crazy-fuck got up his sleeve?" Hal Krutch spat

pebbles from his mouth and scratched the tiny particles of fragmented lead from his scalp. But the pilot his friends knew best as Stork was already well aware of his counterpart's intentions. Warlokk was seeking an angle that would see those mini-gun rounds that missed their target would sail harmlessly out into the surrounding hills.

Sparks flew off the Cobra's rotors as the sniper fired down at it. Less than twenty-five yards from the tree now, Warlokk brought his craft's nose up and unleashed a continual stream of hot, smoking lead that did not stop until the flapping fronds all but disintegrated and an Asian clad in U.S. tiger-stripe fatigues was blown backward into the air, arms and legs flailing.

When the communist sniper's body slammed across a jeep hood, dead as they come in The Nam, *Choi-oi* ran up to the vehicle, growling quite dramatically. His jaws clamped shut on the bloodied hand hanging out over the fender.

"Well awaright, *LAWLESS*!" Lee rolled from the supply sergeant's tent and waved at Warlokk with a shining thumb's-up as Delgado and Winston ran to check on the three privates with head wounds.

"Tear 'im up, *Choi-oi*!" Fletcher clapped as the camp mascot dragged the sniper's body from the deep impact dent molded around its upper torso down onto the ground. The guerilla had died with his eyes open, and, barking in surprise, *Choi-oi* attacked his face, tearing off the man's nose.

With a debonair half-salute and satisfied nod, Warlokk drifted away slowly, beyond the treetops, then banked sharply and was gone.

Men were leaving their places of cover all around the landing pad now. Everywhere except where Treat Brody continued to hug the earth. He listened to Delgado consoling Lt. Winston several feet away: "Forget it, Lieutenant. All three of the poor schmucks were dead before they hit the ground." But Brody could not move. Something was wrong, terribly wrong. That ominous, foreboding he usually only experienced deep in the Void was present. An unspeakable evil was drifting with the gunsmoke across their helipad.

Something was so wrong he could taste it.

And then it happened. Soldiers with shocked and crestfallen faces passed each other as if in a daze, their ears ringing with the thum-thump-thump of Warlokk's rotors. Only the edges of the monstrous blades were visible as they chased each other around in a silver blur of a circle, *like headless ghosts forever roaming the scene of their decapitation,* Brody thought of Vietnamese legend just then as men who were not old enough to drink or vote back in The World watched Delgado zipping up body bags over green newbies who were even younger. Krutch was walking like Frankenstein's monster as he stumbled in the direction of a bullet-riddled *Pegasus,* that glassy, thousand-yard stare intact, and *Choi-oi* was running around in circles, chasing "phantom pain" that throbbed where his tail had once been.

His tail! "My God..." Brody rose slightly from his depression in the red clay. *Choi-oi's* tail was sailing through the air ...And then the thunderous discharge reached his ears.

An empty Pabst can jumped in front of Winston and bounced off into the trees, then two sharp whistles announced richochets and a jeep tire exploded.

Another sniper!

The hissing sound of air escaping from the punctured tire filled Cordova's ears as he sprinted to tackle Winston again. "A different sniper!" he yelled. "They're gunning for the lieutenant!"

Both Winston and Corky tumbled behind cover as a truck headlight shattered and three bullets punctured the heavily patched gun cleaning solvent tank for the fifth time that week.

Several shell-shocked men stood out in the open, too bewildered to move, until finally, one by one, they too dove for cover.

But none of the slugs struck flesh this time. Every soldier on the helipad had ample time to get out of the way.

The bastard's in those palms. A cruel smile lifted the edges of Brody's dust-caked mouth. *On the* north *side of the landing pad—opposite the landing pad—opposite the tree line where Lawless had made his spectacular kill.* It was quickly becoming obvious to Treat Brody and some of the others lying prone across hot tarmac that Warlokk had zapped the wrong zip. Brody gnawed at the edge of his lower lip as he watched more truck tires explode with a hiss. Several windshields shattered, but no bullets were impacting against flesh this time, "Lawless wasted the right rifleman, but it wasn't *our* sniper! It wasn't really *our*

215

half-blind sharpshooter!" Ol' Luke was back in town, and it felt good. It suddenly felt good to get shot at by someone you sort of knew and understood, someone you could identify with . . . who appreciated the finer things about skinning Bengals, and nightlife in the tropics, and The Nam. And couldn't shoot worth a damn.

Fletcher had figured it out too.

He waited for Ol' Luke to fire off his usual thirty-round finale, gave the ricochets ample time to peter out, then dashed for a big tent in the middle of the Turkey Farm.

Death by sniper fire was suddenly highly unlikely now. The mess hall was due to open in five minutes for lunch, and Snakeman wanted to be the first soldier in line.

CHAPTER 21

Twilight had been with them only a few moments when the European-style *hi-lo* siren announced a scramble from its perch atop the CP's highest radio antenna.

Zack, Lee, Cordova, and Fletcher were running toward Pegasus less than a minute later. Larson carried his suicide note with him. "Gotta finish this paragraph in case Charlie cancels my ticket this trip in," he was muttering, but no one was listening. "Wanna make sure I got it all down right 'fore I go."

Krutch had been dozing in the gunship's cabin when the alert frist went off. The turbines had kicked in seconds earlier, and as he spoke into his headset and monitored console dials waiting for his peter pilot to show up, the rotors beqan twirling into a blur.

"Where's Whoremonger?" Zack called up to Fletcher as he scrambled over a plie of body bags and wriggled into his lifeline harness.

216

"Out ridin' with Gunslinger!" Fletcher slapped a belt of bullets into place as he referred to Gabriel. "Wanted to see what Dustoff duty was really all about up close."

"He cleared it with Winston, Sarge!" Cordova yelled above the growing whine of fifty-foot blades slapping the air above them.

Nodding, Zack grabbed Lee's shoulder. Two-Step was running up to *Pegasus* now too, and he told both soldiers to man the M-60s on one of the other birds in the four-ship formation preparing to lift off. "I've only got four crews of five riders each on the rescue roster tonight." He was not apologizing. "You guys grab an MG and stay inside the hatch. I don't know what we've got yet, but we're not taking any grunts in, just *out*!"

"Right, Sarge!"

"Think you can handle it?" Zack produced his best eat-it-like-a-man expression. "Tonight you're gunnies!"

"No sweat, Leo!" Broken Arrow slapped the big NCO on the shoulder as he leaned down from *Pegasus* for an answer. "Hog duty is eight and skate action."

"Some wounded Arvins," Krutch advised Zack with little enthusiasm as the craft began to vibrate wildly. The Stork sounded bored. "Just a couple klicks out. Another FOB farce. Lima Zulu in zero-two. *Everyone* up?"

Zack glanced around quickly. *"We're up!"* he said, but then his head whirled back to take in the front of the craft. Larson was squatting right behind Krutch, nearly in-between the AC and peter pilot positions. "What the hell is *your* problem?"

"The Stork's teachin' me how to fly one of these babies, Sarge." The Professor showed equal apathy.

"What?" Zack placed his hands on his wide hips, managing to stay on his feet even as the gunship rose suddenly to clear a cluster of bamboo poles.

"In case we ever go down or—"

"DON'T talk like that!" Zack moved forward as if to clamp a palm over Larson's mouth. The sergeant was a firm believer in many Vietnamese superstitions, and one was that words had power.

"Two hundred and forty-three Huey's were shot down in Vietnam last month alone, Sarge," the Professor continued. "Being a chopper jock is one of the most short-lived careers in—"

"*Okay,* okay!" Zack's hands flew up, and he turned to check on Fletcher and Cordova. "You two got your shit together? LZ in zero-two or less."

"No sweat." Corky was rubbing gun oil into his M-60's flash suppressor. He'd heard it caused an eerie glow to hang in front of the barrel while the weapon was being fired, a glow the enemy could see from the ground. A frightening, direct-from-your-ancestors'-ghosts glow that sent Charlie running for his spider holes. Stories of phantom gunships cruising over the rain forests were rampant amongst the highlands guerrillas. Oil-soaked flash suppressors only helped lend credence to the myths that ghostships prowled some villages of the jungle, seeking out the Cong that had killed their crews.

Fletcher did not even answer Zack. He already had his head-set on and was leaning into the new swivel-mounted MG, searching the trees up ahead for any sign of the VC.

"What's the word on that mutt o' Brody's?" Zack leaned close to Cordova to make sure his M-60 was in proper working condition.

"Poor mutt's just got a stub left where his tail used to be!" Cordova shouted above the din of flapping rotors as Zack fired a short test burst down into the treetops.

"No shit?" It was the first time he'd shown any concern for the dog.

"Yah! I guess Doc tried to sew it back on, but they couldn't get *Choi-oi* to hold still long enough!"

Zack let out a bellow that revealed his true sentiments after all; and Larson, who'd glanced over his shoulder to see why they were shooting already, shook his head and rolled his eyes toward the roof for Krutch's benefit.

"That musta been quite a sight! But they actually found the tail after *that* clusterfuck?"

"Yah! After they searched the helipad for five minutes, Whoremonger found it in the helmet Fletch keeps looped to his web belt."

"I'll bet—"

"Yep! Elliot thought *Choi-oi's* tail was one o' his pet snakes!"

"Always knew that goofy fuck sucks down drugs." Zack felt

218

free to make such a jest because Fletcher couldn't hear them.

"Naw, Sarge, it was just that everyone got such a case of the mindfuck from that first sniper. The Bull said he was a hard-core NVA Regular with a marksman's badge in his retailored tiger-stripes...33rd Regiment or something. A bona-fide rifleman...a real shooter. Not like—"

"Not like Ol' Luke."

"Right."

Zack fell silent as he stared down at the blur of multi-hued green passing by below. The black career soldier couldn't bring himself to complete the nickname Elliot Fletcher had given their punctually consistent Viet Cong sniper.

A huge red cross against a white background decorated the tail boom protruding up through the trees as Krutch made his first pass over the landing zone.

"Did you catch those fuselage numbers?" Zack clicked-into the intercom and called up to Krutch as he scribbled the ID digits on the palm of his hand.

"Yah, thanks, Leo. I recognized 'em. That's Gabriel's mede-vac down there. We've got movement on his port side. You turds back there, ready or not, down we go!"

"How can you tell which side is port?" the peter pilot muttered into his mike. Except for its tail boom, Gabriel's slick was smashed flat like an accordian.

Fletcher's hands tensed as *Pegasus* banked hard against rock-hard walls of turbulence, flared out over the smoke-laced LZ, and dropped into a hover above Gabriel's Huey. "A helicopter is much harder to keep aloft than a plane," Krutch was telling Larson even as the first rounds from the ground spider-webbed the cockpit glass. "Something goes wrong with a plane, chances are you can bring it down in a glide or something. A chopper, on the other hand—well, a pilot needs two hands and two feet on all the controls to keep a bird like *Pegasus* in check. She's constantly in the mood to dive, kinda like a horse pulling against the reins, you know? If it wasn't for the pressure of hydraulics and one foot against the other, we'd be spinnin' 'round like a top and—"

Zack shook his head as he leaned over Cordova, watching the gunny pick his targets on the jungle floor below. *Krutch is givin' the kid driving lessons with tracers comin' up through* the

219

floorboards. Leo listened to the rattle and shake of *Pegasus* as they descended. A helicopter was never cruising smoothly and quietly, it was always vibrating: a jumble of forces working against one another and kept under control by the pilot's skill. Leo could detect nothing out of sync in the metal bird's magnesium skin. *We're droppin' down into the bowels of Hell and Krutch is givin' gooddamned drivin' lessons to the kid!*

Snakeman's fingers were slick with sweat as he scoured the trees below for targets of opportunity, but he couldn't pinpoint any of the muzzle flashes on the ground. Knuckles bone-white with stress, he gnashed his teeth in frustration. *Brody was down there somewhere!* His best friend—whether Treat acknowledged such a bond or not—was fighting for his life down there, alongside Gabe!

Bullets from the ground hammered *Pegasus*'s rotor ballasts, and sparks showered down from the silver halo above. Fletcher directed a steady stream of tracers down at the single flash he'd spotted out of the corner of his eye. And then he stopped, unsure of himself—Brody might be close to that very spot, he could be engaging Charlie right then and there, in hand-to-hand combat.

Another burst of lead stitched the floor of the helicopter. As shards of fiberglass and magnesium flew about in an OD green whirlwind of of razor-sharp debris, Fletcher fired again, closing his eyes tightly as the refuse was sucked out the hatch past his face by the downblast. He squinted now, but the swirl of particles was still too strong, creating an illusion almost, like fingers rising from the jungle to drag him down into the Void Vicious.

Snatched from Death's claws! A stranger's hideous voice screamed with laughter in the depths of his mind, the swirl of his thoughts, the rock 'n' roll beat of emotions and all-consuming gunsmoke. *Snatched from Death's claws!*

"RPG!" Zack was yelling and firing with his pistol at an angle Cordova could not reach. "You got a black uniform pointin' an RPG at us!"

Krutch ascended swiftly. After clearing the treetops, he banked hard to the right and circled around—so hard, in fact, that Fletcher was slammed back atop a pile of taped-down Saigon phone books. Brody's phone books. Brody didn't like sitting on flak jackets or steel pots. He liked phone books. Said they were more comfortable.

Kept in place by the helicopter's inertia, Fletcher, sitting now, fired more rounds into the trees as Krutch kept the Huey practically on its side for a second tight pass.

"Those flashes!" Corky clicked-in again. "That's where all the bad guys are dug in—those flashes! If we can just—!"

But the chopper was moving swiftly, and the treetops soon obliterated the popping muzzles. They went around and around like a misaligned truck on a never-ending freeway on-ramp loop, and Cordova got dizzy and spilled his oats on Charlie below. Right of the hatch, observed Zack. Without fanfare.

"There you guys go grossin' me out again." The black NCO was not even holding on to anything as *Pegasus* leveled out above a small clearing fifty or so meters from the crash site.

Bits and pieces of bark flew in through the hatch as the slick began to descend and its rotor tips trimmed branches here and there.

"No go!" Zack called out after a couple of tries. The clearing's appearance from the air had been deceptive. "It gets worse the farther down you go! Maybe a Loach could make it, but not—"

"And there's ten-foot-tall-plus bamboo saplings on the jungle floor down there!" Fletcher clicked-in. He was leaning out his own hatch now. "We'll have to use the rope ladder—if there's any survi—"

He started to say survivors. *Words have power! Words have power!* The voices warned. Voices not only in his head, but screaming from the trees, it seemed, the very leaves—*THE JUNGLE WAS ALIVE!*

Brody and Gabriel and Doc Delgado had spotted Krutch's descent all right. Stooped over, with critically wounded Vietnamese soldiers across their soldiers, the Americans hustled through the woods. Two Arvins, also carrying gunshot victims, trotted ahead of them. Delgado, the last man in line, fired an M-16 from the hip back at their pursuers. The ten troopers seemed heavily outnumbered as bark flew from tree trunks all around them.

Brody was in the clearing even before Zack and Fletcher had the rope ladder down to him. The South Vietnamese soldiers had dropped their wounded buddies along the clearing's edge and were taking cover behind fallen, rotting logs, preparing to fire on the Viet Cong as soon as they appeared through the trees, preparing to sacrifice themselves so the Americans and a few wounded Arvins could get out alive.

Gabriel was the first one up onto a rung. The rope swayed back and forth under the combined weight of him and the WIA over his shoulder, and gravity was the victor. Both men dropped backwards into the slick carpet of mushrooms and dead plants.

"Let's go! Let's go! Let's go!" Brody's lips were against the injured Arvin's ear, urging him to attempt a climb under his own power.

Blood suddenly pouring from the hour-old belly wound, the soldier made it up four rungs valiantly, then seemed to collapse in half as a string of bright tracers ripped his back open.

The VC had arrived in force.

"Forget him, Gabe!" Delgado yelled as he fired an entire magazine into the vicious snarls appearing between trees. Some heads popped back in showers of crimson, others forward. "Save yourself!"

"Every man on his own!" Brody agreed as he left the rope. It was snapping to and fro like a lion-trainer's whip now. He rushed to Doc Delgado's side.

Gunslinger Gabriel finally drew his fancy six-inch revolver. His free hand clutching the rope ladder, the Dustoff pilot's gun hand squeezed off a half dozen carefully placed shots at the distant, dark brown faces. And then he was up the ladder like a monkey in a tree.

"Di-di!" Brody yelled out to the Arvins lying prone behind their friends' bodies. The gut shot infantrymen were now both dead. "Get up into the chopper! *Di-di!* Now!"

Whether they were too terrified to move, or simply drunk on adrenaline, Brody was unsure, but the Arvins ignored him and just kept firing widly. Their rifles were propped atop the lifeless remains of their buddies. Brody shook his head in sorrow and sadness, but there was nothing he could do for them. The popular rhyme *When you hear the pitter patter of little feet, it's the Arvin army in full retreat* did not apply here today.

"I'm history!" Delgado switched his rifle to semi-automatic as he slammed the last banana clip home. He pointed up at the other Hueys circling their potential graves. Door gunners aboard all three choppers showered the jungle around them with intense M-60 fire.

Backing toward the dangling rope ladder, Delgado fired short bursts at the shadows shifting about amongst the trees. "Let's fucking *GO!*" He reached down and grabbed one, then the other Arvin and jerked them to their feet. He sent them flying ahead of him toward the ladder.

Both Arvins fired their M-16s into the woods, threw the weapons down as soon as the clips emptied out, then scampered up the rings like gibbons.

Halfway up, a long drawn-out stream of RPD machine gun fire cut both Vietnamese in half, and Brody and Delgado dove into the piles of rotting, spider-infested leaves, holding each other for protection. "You got any frags, Treat?"

"Hell no, Doc! I threw 'em all back at the crash site, you know that!"

"We'll never make it up that ladder—"

"Not as long as that fucking RPD's in action!"

"And I don't have enough ammo left to try and take 'em out!" The roar of gunfire from the metallic predators circling overhead was deafening. Both men were continually slapping red-hot Hog and mini-gun cartridges off each other.

"We could wait and hope the slicks knock out the MB nest." Brody's suggestion came out more like a desperate plea. He'd never forget the expressions of pain and agony on the faces of the Arvins as they were cut down midway up the rope ladder. He didn't want to die in that gruesome fashion. "We could wait for—"

"No such luck." Delgado pressed his body flatter against the ground. *Funny!* his mind laughed in the face of insurmountable danger. *Funny, how, when under fire, you separate the whole entire fucking world into objects that afford cover and those that don't!!* "The machine gun crew found the ravine I tripped through back there. I'd wager they're already pretty well dug in and—"

"Well I'm not going!" Doc Delgado had never heard Brody talk that way before. "I'll stay here and fight to the death with my bare hands if I have to, but I'm not gonna get shot out of thin air like that! I'm not gonna let Charlie pluck me off that ladder

223

like a sittin' duck at a shootin' gal—"

"What the—" Brody suddenly shifted away from Delgado and rolled deeper into the tainted, foul-smelling vegetation. Something had crawled up between the two men—something BIG.

"Aaaarrrhhh!" Brody the Whoremonger sprung up from the rotting jungle floor, an eight-inch bamboo spider clinging to three of the fingers on his gun hand. He slapped the hairy green arachnid against his thigh a dozen times as he sprinted for the rope ladder—he slapped it as hard as he'd slapped the cobra coiled around his leg the week before...harder! But the spider had an affectionate crush on the celebrated gunny and refused to let go.

Front legs poised in the striking position, the three sections of its body began shifting up and down, roller-coaster fashion, *humping* the Whoremonger's knuckles. "Well, fuck me 'till it hurts!" He dove for the bottom rung of the ladder, Doc Delgado hot on his heels.

Pegasus shot up through the treetops the moment she felt their added weight on the rope, long before they could start climbing. Tracers arched up gracefully on both sides of the two men but never really came close to hitting either soldier.

Soon they were safely out of the clearing, but dangling thirty feet below the gunship's belly—a thousand feet over the mesmerizing green hues of Void Vicious.

CHAPTER 22

Zack talked Brody into remaining aboard Pegasus when they landed back at the Turkey Farm. "Got a Jolly Green enroute back to the crash site right now!" he said. Zack did not look eager to return to the Void.

224

A downed-chopper recovery unit, Brody read his mind. *They want me to go back in because I know the site, I know the best way to hook up the doughnut....*

"Only two Chinooks left undamaged in the division right now. The quicker in and out, the better." Zack fixed his do-it-for-ol'-Leo look on the Spec-4. "We can't afford to lose another Jolly Green right now."

Brody wanted to tell him the Huey back in that jungle hell was squashed beyond recognition, much less restoration. That he and Gabriel and the others had survived at all was testimony to an extremely lucky phase his life was in. But he knew arguments involving rationalization would do no good. Leo the Lionhearted had a one-track mind in situations like this.

Brody massaged the new trinket on his dog-tags chain. A chunk of molten RPG lead, plucked from the destroyed Dustoff, was his latest charm. He remained silent, reflections of the napalm run lighting up his eyes.

"The wingnuts pretty much saturated the site with liquid lead," Zack was saying. "And for the most part, Charlie's on the run. But it's still a pretty hot LZ, and they don't wanna take any chance—"

Brody rose from his squat, waving the tall NCO silent. He buckled himself in behind one of the hatch-Hogs. "Up!" his thumb pointed skyward with extreme boredom. "Take it up!"

"You're a good sport, Whoremaniac." Zack slapped him on the back as he signaled Krutch to lift off.

"Take it up and lead me to my maker...."

With one hand, Brody worked the M-60's cocking handle, getting ready for the flight in. With the other, he rubbed the rosary of charms, convinced his good luck could not hold out forever.

They encountered no hostile fire on the way in.

Though several fuel cells had ruptured on impact, and the crash site was heavy with fumes, the downed Huey had never exploded.

The monstrous, double-rotored Chinook was already circling the area when they returned. Every now and then dual machine guns fired long, alternating, and synchronized bursts down into the treetops. From the air, Brody got the feeling that Void Vicious was pressing in on the crash site, almost like an

225

overbearing, green bully, planning to claim its due. "Jungle justice." He laughed softly as they flared into a hover and Zack began lowering the rope ladder. "Seeking jungle justice."

He descended slowly despite Sgt. Zack's proddings to hustle. Brody was positive he was dropping into a green hell to meet the devil himself, that this was surely his last mission, his final hour, that the charms' luck had finally slipped away.

Until he reached the ground.

On solid earth again, things changed. He was no longer viewing the mysterious void from above, from aboard a mythical beast called *Pegasus*. Reality set in quickly, like culture shock. Shots echoing in the distant trees made him wonder if perhaps he hadn't just been hovering a plane above the real world for the last year or so, his perception of combat and the jungle and his future intoxicated by the constant disruption of sharp rotors beating above his head.

Brody touched the crumpled magnesium skin of the downed Huey, and his priorities shifted into their proper sequence. A dark shadow fell over the clearing. Jolly Green, as the grunts called the monstrous CH-47 Chinooks, had moved in as *Pegasus* drifted to the side, out of the way but still in sight, still ever-alert for Charlie.

Brody began working swiftly. First, looping the thick, heavy chains that dropped from the sky under the Huey's mangled fuselage. Having experienced the crash firsthand, he knew exactly where to cross the chains, knew right where the stress fractures were and strong points remained.

In less than five minutes he had a spiderweb of steel around the olive-drab metallic dragonfly. Brody climbed atop the crumpled cabin of the slick and began connecting loose ends to a big, rubberized steel ring the recovery crews called "the doughnut." A large metal hook was already descending on a massive cable winch from the belly of the Jolly Green Giant, so-called because it was probably the biggest helicopter the American Armed Forces fielded. The powerful downblast from its huge dual rotors—one in front and one in back—was so intimidating, enemy troops on the ground often fled rather than confront the behemoth.

As was the common practice, Brody slammed the doughnut down over the Jolly Green's hook with such force, a casual observer might have noticed the big chopper dip ever so slightly. Now the pilot hovering over the hole in the jungle canopy knew for certain his ship was connected to the downed craft, and he began his ascent without further delay.

Brody did not jump down from the Huey. Already prepared, he wrapped his lengthened web belt around one of the support chains, planning to ride the rising payload all the way back to camp.

No one fired up at him, but the Whoremonger could "feel" their presence, could tell they were down there in the trees somewhere watching him steal what the Void had reclaimed. And Brody, rifle hanging from the shoulder sling, horizontal with his hip, fired down at the shadows. He unleashed three-and four-round bursts until his M-16 was empty and the Jolly Green had hoisted him and the dead Huey up over the Dead Man's Zone, out of range of small-arms ground fire.

"It was hell."

"You're supposed to say 'War is hell.' Don't you read Hemingway, or watch shoot-em-ups on TV?"

Brody pondered Krutch's remark for a moment as he stared down into their dying underground campfire. "I never missed an episode of *Combat* back in The World," he finally said. "Vic Morrow was my hero, next to Doc Savage, of course. Still is, I guess, even though knocking Hollyweird is the Numba One pastime around here. But I'm not talking about the *war*, Stork. I'm not talking about all the shooting." He spit into the small piece of sizzling C-4, and its blue flame crackled and popped in protest. "It *was* hell, gentlemen. The jungle."

"What?" Krutch was speaking as a cockpit-confined chopper jockey. But the others knew what Whoremonger was talking about. At least, most of them did.

"There he goes talkin' goofy-gook on us again." Fletcher massaged a sore brow, unable to lock eyes with Treat.

"You buckin' for a psych evaluation, Mr. B.?" Doc Delgado showed his teeth in the growing darkness of Larson's bunker, but it was an unhappy grin. "Is that what you want? Is that how you plan to get out of here alive?"

Brody ignored the medic, shifting his eyes from Lee to Cordova, then finally, Zack. Sgt. Zack had joined them for the first time since they'd skid-hopped and pranged from An Kha into the Ia Drang. "The jungle is alive," Brody whispered, but he was not attempting to be dramatic. "It was trying to get me this time. The jungle was Pissed with a capital *P*, gentlemen. Do you know how many times I crashed into Void Vicious without repercussions? Well, 'enough is enough,' says the jungle."

"The jungle is alive," Fletcher mimicked him sarcastically. "Enough is enough is enough."

"I haven't felt that helpless in a long time," Brody went on. "It was a green hell, you guys. We don't belong out there." Brody shuddered. He felt as if he were betraying a trust. . .*butterflying on his tealok*. He loved her. He loved the jungle. He couldn't face another day unless his nights were spent charging into the Void, machine guns blazing, *Pegasus*'s "wings" flapping protectively overhead. "We don't belong out there," he repeated. "I don't know how the Cong and the NVA survive under that triple canopy without going *dinky-dau*."

"It's definitely mindfuck to the max." Cordova was running a splintered blade of elephant grass between his two front teeth. "Yep, Void Vicious is truly an ever-lovin' trip!"

"We just don't belong in there," Brody repeated.

"Me and Mister Colt here"—Fletcher slapped the stock of his M-16—"we go anywhere we want."

"Brody's right." Two-Step rose to leave.

"Huh?"

"The jungle is an evil place. God, or *the* gods; or Buddha or whatever you fancy to believe in, set it aside for the animals. Men don't belong in there, and those that venture inside *become* animals."

"You're full o' shit, Two-Step." Fletcher did not look up. "As usual."

"The only reason more of us haven't been gobbled up by the void is because we carry our own magic with us, and the spirits who rule the rain forests haven't yet decided how to react—"

"Our own magic?" Fletcher interrupted, showing some interest for the first time, but Broken Arrow was already up the sandbag steps, his outline lost in the darkness outside. "What the fuck was that crazy Indian talking about?" he asked Cordova, as if two brown men could understand each other any better.

"'This.'" Brody lifted the dog-tags chain out of his chest hair. He held a jagged chunk of shrapnel up to the light so that it seemed to glow with its own power, if only for an instant. "And that." He pointed at the helmutful of snakes wiggling against Fletcher's web belt, and the serpent Elliot was at that very moment petting along its snout. Brody forced his eyes from the flickering tongue. "And even *that*!" He singled out Larson's suicide notebook with his chin. "Whatever protects you best is your own personal magic. Even that stupid crossbow Two-Step carries everywhere."

"Hey don't knock it." Cordova was quick to defend the absent Indian. "I've seen him kill Cong with 'that stupid crossbow,' Treat."

"That's just it." Brody laughed innocently. "I'm *not* trying to knock it, Corky. I'm just saying a piece of shrapnel"—he lifted his crash-site necklace higher—"or a sliver of cockpit Plexiglass, or paper in a notebook can't hold a candle to the winds blowin' through the rain forest, gentlemen. I'm talkin' wild winds, too. The very breath of Satan himself, if you ask me. Yes, the very breath of—"

Sgt. Zack erupted into unrestrained laughter. Laughter with a deep Jamaican, voodoo accent to it. Which was quite a trick for, though Leo had been to the dark continent several times before, he had never visited the West Indies. He'd been listening quietly for several minutes, eyes bulging like a little boy's listening to ghost stories about bayou magic beneath a full moon on his grandma's rickety old porch back in Louisiana. But now he exploded. "You clowns are Loon-Tunes! You're all certifiably whacko—do you realize that?" Still laughing, he rose to his feet.

"What about *you*, Leo?" Shawn Larson rose to block the big NCO's exit and thumped his broad chest with an accusing finger. "What about that Gideon you carry in your breast pocket?"

"What Gideon?" He feigned total ignorance.

"What's a 'Gideon'?" Lee asked Cordova.

"Leo here carries a pocket Bible over his heart." Brody jumped up too, suddenly full of renewed energy. "Stopped a bullet in Inchon, didn't it, Zack?" Now the Whoremonger was doing all the laughing.

"Where's Inchon?" Lee asked Cordova.

"Korea, Em-ho. 'Land of the Morning Calm.'" Brody continued his assault. "You've kept the darn thing in that same pocket *religiously*—if you'll pardon the pun—for the last fifteen years, haven't you Zack? For good luck, right? *Admit it!*"

"For good luck," the sergeant confirmed. "Just like Gabriel wears that hip pistol of his, or Lawless changes hairstyles to fit his moods. For good luck, Whorehumper. Read my lips: for . . . good . . . luck! Not because we believe any of it holds any power over our fate. If a bullet's got your name on it, son, then there's not much you can do about it except start lightin' joss sticks and hope you don't come back as a cockroach or—"

"I got you there, Leo," Krutch spoke up, lifting his own dog-tags necklace from beneath a sweat-soaked, olive-drab T-shirt. Between the two dog tags hung a 7.62 machine gun bullet with his name inscribed across the brass cartridge. "And it's my *full* name, chump-san."

Larson seemed somewhat surprised. "I'd a thought you'd have a tracer round 'round your neck, Hal."

Zack was not swayed. "You take Ostrich there." He pointed at the chopper pilot.

Krutch's smile vanished. "It's *Stork,*" he said with zero tonal inflection.

"He's got a tattoo on each arm, right?"

"Got 'em down on Tu Do Street," he said proudly, referring to Saigon's raunchy nightclub district. His new grin was just as raunchy. "Not that any of you boonie rats would know where the big city of sorrows is."

"The *Stork's* got one tattoo of a hawk ripping a dove in half with its talons, in mid-flight," Zack accused.

"Is that true?" Larson sounded hurt and betrayed. He leaned back as if to get a more accurate picture of the warrant officer's true intentions in Indochina.

"I woke up with it there one morning," Krutch admitted, eyes centered on the crackling piece of C-4 melting the bottom of their coffee pot.

"In Saigon?"

"Pleiku City."

"Busted," ribbed Lee.

"Yet on the other bicep he's got a likeness of the Virgin Mary floatin' over old Mexico in some airborne shrine." Zack cocked

230

an eyebrow to gauge Krutch's reaction. "You see, he's just playin' it safe, layin' bets on both sides of the table, just in case."

"Then you should have a pitchfork-totin' devil on that arm, instead of a hawk." Fletcher sounded offended.

"The Virgin Mary?" Larson folded his arms across his chest as he stared straight at Krutch. "Let us see it."

Shoulders dipping with embarrassment, the Stork pulled the short sleeve up. "Woke up with this one in Tijuana."

"Tijuana?"

"Yah. That's in Mexi—"

"I *know* where it's at, Skuzzball."

"Well, I was sixteen. Two weeks after I learned to drive. Woke up with the drips, too."

Zack began laughing again and pushed Larson aside. "What a bunch o' characters."

The men listened in silence as Leo's heavy footsteps faded in the distance, then Krutch lowered his head, scanning faces. Flames from the chip of plastic explosive danced in his eyes dramatically. "Okay," he whispered as if preparing to reveal an important secret, "enough o' this black magic bullshit. Now that Black Bart is gone, let's get down to business." He pulled a plastic-coated map case from a thigh pocket and unfolded it.

Lee's eyes widened, and he glanced up at the bunker entrance, wondering if anyone passing by outside would be able to hear them, and if what they heard could lead to time in the LBJ monkeyhouse, breaking big rocks into little rocks. "What are you dudes up to?" Childhood visions of buried treasure clouded his vision as light from the C-4 dimmed suddenly.

"Here's the plan." Krutch placed the map in front of Larson and spoke almost as if the others were not even there. "Here's Qui Nhon on the coast, and out here, a couple of klicks off the beach in the South China Sea is Hon Trau."

"An *island?*" Lee leaned closer, and Krutch stared up at him, then glanced about, startled, as if he'd been awakened from a dream and wasn't quite sure where he was.

"This is seriously secret shit, Em-ho." He locked eyes with Lee, then slowly made contact with everyone else in the underground bunker. "You guys can't say a word about this—"

"Not to anyone." Larson's expression was one of somber indifference.

231

"What the hell are you two up to?" Brody was afraid he already knew.

"I guess we can tell the Whoremonger." Krutch seemed to search Larson's eyes for approval. "I mean, I know he's notorious for bein' budding lifer material par excellence, but—"

"Yah, no sweat." The Professor nodded.

"If he blabs, we'll just slice his nuts off with a rusty razor blade—"

"And throw him in a vat of rubbing alcohol." "That would do the trick."

"Right."

"What the *hell* is your plan?" Fletcher wasn't in the mood for games.

"We're going AWOL," Krutch said simply.

"Who's 'we'?" Fletcher challenged him.

"Me and the Professor."

"'Me and the Professor,'" Fletcher mimicked him, but in an incredulous tone.

"I've reconned the island by air bookoo times and then some," the warrant officer explained. "It's uninhabited."

"At least we're pretty sure," said Larson.

"And just who do you think is gonna cut you clowns TDY orders for some turd in the ocean called—"

"Hon Trau," Krutch assisted him.

"Like he told you"—Larson yawned—"we're going AWOL."

"Bullshit," Lee, Fletcher, and Brody all chimed in.

"The place is a good six miles offshore"—Krutch kept a straight face—"and a veritable floating market of lip-smackin' veggies: bananas, guava, mango, pineapples. . .coconut trees up the ying-yang. . .some wild boar. . ."

"*This* is becoming boring." Fletcher didn't believe a word they were saying, and he ignored the look of concern etched across Brody's face.

". . .Tangerines and cucumbers. No apples, though—you know Indochina: none anywhere. I really wish the place had some apples, but you can't have everything."

"We'll bring fishing poles and live off the sea." Larson's eyes were blank. "Vitamin A is good for you. Gives you great night vision."

"Why would you need night vision on a fucking uninhabited

island?" Brody was getting angry. Angry and hurt. He was feeling betrayed. Talk of desertion infuriated him, but he said, "You guys didn't even ask me. . .or *any* of us if we wanted to come along."

"You're a fucking lifer, Treat." Larson laughed, but it was a hollow laugh. He had said the word *lifer* with disgust in his tone, and Brody didn't miss the antagonism. "You and Fletch eat this shit up. There won't be no war to feed your adrenaline cravings on Hon Trau. Only pussy. Pussy and pacifism. We're lovers, Big B. Lovers, not fighters."

"Besides"—Krutch reached across the cooling fire pit and shook Brody's shoulder gently—"there won't be any room for you guys."

"Huh?" Lee tilted his head to one side as if tapping water out of his ears after emerging onto the white sand beach from a snorkeling stint off Hon Trau's coral reef.

"We're going to pick up a couple of whores from that ville Neil Nazi put off limits and fly 'em out to Snakeman's Isle, then dump *Pegasus* into the South China Sea and—" Larson started to explain.

"Whatta ya mean 'Snakeman's Isle'?" Krutch frowned.

"I thought we'd name it in honor of Fletch here." The Professor reached over and patted Elliot on the shoulder. "Don't ask me why, it just sticks in my mind."

"Why not the Isle of Stork?" Krutch protested. "Don't the Isle of Stork give it a sort of. . .royal twang?" he asked the others.

"'Royal twang'?" Lee glanced over at Cordova.

"The 'Isle of Stork'?" Larson was unhappy with the way it sounded. The words did not *flow,* and he wanted everything about their sanctuary to. . .flowww. . . ."

"Well, we can't name it '*Snakeman's* Isle,' doofus! Words are power here in the Orient—haven't you learned *any*thing from your Vietnam experience? Words make things happen. I don't wanna wake up with snakes in my shorts some night."

"Hey, brother, we ain't gonna be *sleepin'* in our shorts. We're gonna be nude as newborns, okay? Sandwiched between two of the most beautiful hookers in—"

"Whatta ya mean 'dump *Pegasus* into the South China Sea'?" Brody exploded as Larson's earlier words finally hit him.

233

"Well, we sure won't have any use for her on Hon Trau."

"But she's *our* bird, fuckface! We've all put blood, sweat, and fear into her! *I've* worn my calluses raw massaging her parts and joints and seams and rivets just so she'd carry us through one more mission. And you're talking about *killing*—"

"'Killing' her, Treat?" Krutch did not quite laugh. His Adam's apple bobbed about, then sank loudly. "Come on. She's an *it*. A machine. Just a lousy, fucking green machine that don't work the way it's supposed—"

"Just like the U.S. Army," Larson interrupted him.

"*Pegasus* is like a car you've owned for years. *Years!* She has a...soul—"

"Oh, come on!"

"She has a soul and feelings and guts and drive—just like any horse that—"

"There he goes talkin' that creepy rain-forest crap again." Fletcher exchanged frowns with the Professor.

"Aw, come on, Brody." Krutch stood up. "You've been breathin' chopper downblast for too long, and you think slick farts don't stink. *Pegasus* ain't no different from any other bitch, if you wanna look at it that way."

"Rule Numba One in The Nam." Larson rose too. "Don't get too close to no one. Life is short and cheap in Indochina, pal."

"What the hell is that supposed to do with—" Brody cut him off, but the Professor waved Treat silent.

"Look at all the slicks that have crashed and burned since—"

"*Pegasus* is different." Brody turned his back on them. "*Pegasus* is *part* of us. She's a part of Echo Company, whether you douchebags wanna believe it or not. She'll listen to you if you talk to her in the right tone of voice."

"In a drunken slur." Larson grabbed Krutch's arm and led him toward the sandbagged steps.

"You're not even a pilot, Whoremonger." Krutch slapped him on the back. "Don't take it so hard. Christ, *I'm* the one who's supposed to feel some sort of attachment to my ship, right? But I don't really feel diddley-squat. Just a sort of relief each time we make it outta Void Vicious alive, you know?"

"But—" Brody latched onto the Stork's wrist, preventing him from leaving the Hell Hole.

"Look, if it'll make you feel any better"—Krutch gently re-

234

moved the door gunner's trembling fist — "we'll 'borrow' a different chopper when the big day arrives. Okay sport? Now what more could you fucking ask for from one o' your superhuman superiors?"

"Would ya, Stork? Would you really? Yah! You could take Warlokk's—"

"Genuflect, my son"—the helicopter jockey placed his hand on top of Brody's head reverently and closed his eyes slowly as he nodded—"and your wish is granted."

Lee giggled like a schoolboy amused by the antics of his older brother's friends as they discussed raiding a slumber party down the block in the privacy of their treehouse. But Larson cut the Stork off. "Wouldn't be able to fit our lady friends into it." He referred to Warlokk's gunship. "Cobras only seat two, ya know. But we'll figure somethin' out."

"Maybe we should take one of the Chinooks." Larson smiled at the idea as they emerged into the cool night air outside. "So we can take *four* whores along instead of two."

"Hell, with a Chinook, you could take *forty*! Imagine that: forty fuckin' clits to choke on!"

Brody raced up the steps and grabbed Krutch's arm again. "This is all an act, right? You guys are shittin' us about Hon Bow or Son Chow or whatever the fuck your little island's called, right? *Right?*" Brody grabbed Krutch with both hands and shook him as he posed the question.

A starburst cluster of green-and-gold flares happened to burst behind Brody just then, and as the warrant officer gazed out over his shoulder, artillery rumbled in the distance. The chopper pilot's smile slowly faded.

"Remember when that sound was only thunder, and meant nothing more than a storm approaching?" he asked the Whoremonger.

"What?" Brody searched his eyes for an answer to the fable.

"Now it's usually followed by scramble horns and alert sirens, which are followed by mad dashes across sniper-controlled tarmac into falling-apart slicks, which are followed by seat-of-the-pants rides into Void Vicious, which are followed by Huey cabins full of blood and body bags, which are followed by a harrowing bolder-than-Hollywood escape—if I'm lucky and a tracer don't steal the family jewels, snap the cyclic in half,

235

or light up my life via the fuel cells. My nights end with throbbing migraines, Treat. Did you know that? Midnight mortars and throbbing migraines. And that's if I'm lucky. You clowns...all you have to do is sit back there and bust ammo belts, tryin' to get into Hog Heaven...but *I* gotta bring you back alive, so you can go out and kill Cong the next day. Midnight mortar attacks and throbbing migraines, kid. I got half a Tour 365 left of that to look forward to, and the stats say my chances aren't all that fucking great. You see that?" He pulled out his mint-green military ID card. "It says *US* where yours says *RA*. That means I'm a draftee, friend, here against my will. And the numbers say my chances of makin' it back to The World don't look all that adorable at all."

"What the fuck are you talking about?" Brody felt like laughing in the warrant officer's face.

"But not anymore. That escapade yesterday with the Arvins Gabriel was trying to rescue..."

"Yah?"

"That was the turning point."

"The 'turning point'?"

"Yep. This little police action is getting crazier and crazier. Bookoo *dinky-dau*, pal. It's getting more dangerous by the mission."

"I eat it up, Stork." Brody's heart was pounding and his eyes were wide. A hopeful expression told the helicopter pilot he was waiting for the punch line, a change of heart.

"And it's good there's people like you in the unit, Treat. That's what the First Cav is all about. But me...me and Larson here...we just can't hack all the bullshit anymore. We just don't want to be a part of it—"

"But—"

"People *die* from having your kind of fun."

"Wake me from this dream, Stork!" Brody shook him again. "The squad will dissolve without you as our primary. They'll split us up. I MIGHT HAVE TO RIDE WITH LAWLESS AGAIN!"

"I'm sorry, brother." Krutch steadied him, then gently removed Brody's hands from his wrists a third time. "But Hon Trau is all that matters to me now. I can't stay and fight another month in this war. The mortality rate alone for gunship pilots is

236

enough to depress a doomsayer, you know that. And I can't early-out and go back to the states. I've already tried. There's nothing waitin' for me back there except pressure and a nagging wife anyway, kid."

"Christ, Krutch."

"American women don't know how to fuck, anyway." Larson thrust his chin out.

"Don't generalize," the Stork reprimanded him. "I've had a couple Viet chicks just lay there with their legs spread." He turned to face Brody again. "I used to always keep a revolver on my nightstand back in The World, you know? If I go back there now, I'll end up eating it."

"Bullshit."

"Hon Trau is all that matters to me now, kid. It's all I got left."

Brody expected to see the warrant officer turn and mount a white stallion, then silently ride off into the sunset, but it was already dark, and the only steeds in sight had rotors on them, and everyone was too drunk to work the reins.

"Don't take it too hard." Larson squeezed his upper arm, then turned to follow Hal Krutch into the night mist. "We'll send you a postcard."

Brody's mouth dropped. "Are you guys going *now*?"

Whirling around, Larson placed his forefinger against his lips vertically. Brody sank back, head drooping low between his shoulders in silent apology. "Nah. We're off to Gabe's tent. He's got a couple of nurses over there and a game o' strip poker goin' down."

When they were gone, Brody turned to find that Lee and Fletcher and Cordova were beside him. *Choi-oi* was at his feet, wagging the stump of a tail that Doc Delgado had bandaged up and the housegirls had decorated with shreds of black-and-yellow gift-wrapping paper from the Pleiku PX. They were the First Cav's colors. But Brody dropped into a squat—to the disgust of Snakeman—and began wiping mascara off *Choi-oi's* eyelids. "Fucking housegirls," he muttered. "Trying to make ol' *Choi-oi* look like a transvestite or something."

A snake dropped from Fletcher's helmet and slithered off toward the tree line like a nervous sidewinder, and *Choi-oi* gave silent, cautious, one-footstep-at-a-time chase.

Brody stood and gazed off in the direction he'd last seen Krutch and the Professor. *Choi-oi's* appearance had brought a strange semblance of reality back to his outlook. "You think those guys were serious?"

Fletcher started to say something but caught himself and turned away from the dim tower lights so Brody wouldn't see the preamble of a laugh.

"Nah," Lee finally revealed. "Before you came down in the bunker this evening, Stork told Larson, 'Let's fuck with the Whoremonger tonight.'"

CHAPTER 23

Specialist 4th-Class Brody was positive his eyes were playing tricks on him.

He had never spent a night on perimeter LP where the shifting shadows moved about so radically out there. Out there in the dark. Out there beyond the wire, where Charlie was in charge. Maybe his purple vision was going out on him. Maybe a thousand hours aboard a gunship floating along the edge of Void Vicious really did alter one's senses, as Larson the Professor claimed. Maybe his eyes *were* playing tricks on him. But this was The Nam and you couldn't be too careful about—

There it was again!

Brody flipped his rifle's selector from SAFE to AUTO. After nightfall, one didn't worry about ammo conservation. It was hard enough to hit targets in the dark as it was. Switch to rock-'n'-roll and saturate the free fire zone with tracer glow!

Heat lightning crackled in the distance, and Brody saw it again: someone darting through the reeds down at the bottom of the hill . . . about a hundred meters away now. But then the scent hit him, and he hustled to untie the poncho liner from his web

238

belt.

The downpour of rain hit Brody's foxhole before he could cover himself. He was drenched within a minute but methodically continued unfolding the green plastic poncho.

He did not wear it like a rain jacket but draped the edges over yard-long stakes protruding at an angle along the front of his position. *Should have already had the damn thing off my belt and on the berm,* he reprimanded himself mentally. Brody made no excuses, even though he'd been watching the stars and one satellite in particular only ten minutes before. There had been no clouds.

Lightning clashed overhead without warning, and thunder that seemed only a score of yards above the LP pressed him flat against the earth. *Jesus!* he cupped his ears. *Only in the tropics...*

She stumbled in on top of him just as the American decided it would be safer to keep his head up—the storm be damned! She had apparently been running up the hillside when she slipped in the mud or jumped down into the foxhole for shelter, mistaking his poncho liner for a natural outcropping in the dark.

Brody came up swinging. His fist struck flesh—a chin—and the intruder was knocked back, but Brody couldn't get to his rifle. *Christ!* his mind fast-forwarded on him as a woman's voice spoke in rapid, pleading Vietnamese. Lightning flashed overhead again, bathing her rain-soaked features in brilliant silver for but an instant.

"You're a girl!"

She switched to English upon hearing his voice. "No hurt. Please! No...hurt."

"No! No hurt." He grabbed her arms, restricting her movements, taking charge. Taking control as he assessed the situation.

Lightning crackled above them again, and for the first time he realized how beautiful she was. The rain had soaked her white peasant's blouse through and through, revealing every curve and point in her figure. Long black hair was pasted against high cheekbones. Even in the foxhole—by the bolts of lightning—he could see in her dark, terrified eyes—those slow, exotic orbs, narrowed with fear—that his visitor was no sapper

239

attempting to breach the concertina. She wore a wraparound sarong below the waist, which had come loose, and Brody grasped the edges and held it together for her. "Who *are* you?" he asked.

"English..." she stammered as thunder pressed them closer together. "My...English...not...good...."

"Oh, no sweat, baby." He whipped his fatigue shirt off and draped it over her trembling shoulders, which was a futile gesture for everything he wore was soaked too.

"I...I lost." She hugged him as the storm's attempts to rip the sky apart over that small stretch of Vietnam shrank their world to the walls of a flooded foxhole.

"Nebbah mind...nebbah mind." Brody stroked her hair, unable to shake the nagging notion that this was all unreal, she was just a fantasy. That had to be it! He'd fallen asleep on guard duty, and was dreaming all this up. But water was up to their knees now, and none of his wet dreams had ever been this cold. She was trembling against him. He could smell the sweet scent of her hair; and her nipples, taut and contracted from the rainfall and the breeze and the horror of the storm, were quivering against his own chest, protruding through tears in her blouse and rubbing on his own flesh.

Her hand dropped, and it brushed against his crotch, and the lightning illuminated the surprise in her eyes. He hoped she couldn't see him blushing, and then it was dark again, and he was running his own hand down along the outer swell of her breasts...*large breasts for a Montagnarde.* His mind raced. *Large and warm.* He tried to ignore the warning signs flashing in the back of his head, the voices, female voices that mocked at him and laughed at his luck and screamed. *Why would she take to you like this, Treat Brody—you, a rain-soaked soldier in need of a shave!* But his hand ignored his better judgment as it slid down along a flat stomach, resting atop the firm bridge of her hip. "My name is—"

A harsh, clicking noise behind her prompted the woman to cry out, and Brody pulled her close again. "It's okay...okay." His lips brushed against hers in the dark as he reached down for the field phone. Lightning exploded like fireworks overhead—a spiderweb of glowing silver lingered against the black sky for several seconds, and he stared into the depths of her eyes, tasting her breath, wanting her, *craving* this gift the night had dropped nearly in his lap, but Brody fought the urge to kiss her. He resisted the instincts that demanded he lay her down in the mud and rip the flowered skirt away.

"I'll bet you're the village girl, aren't you?" He lifted the field phone and cupped the receiver against an ear. "The village girl Lee has been looking for. . ."

" I . . . lost . . . ." Tears mingled with the rain on her cheeks, and her eyes dropped to stare at Brody's crotch.

"Whoremonger!" A worried voice was screaming into his ear through the field phone. "You all right out there? We heard screamin' or something weird comin' from your end of the wire."

"Yah . . . *yah*! Hey, no sweat, Sarge."

It was Doc Delgado. "Well, okay. But keep your eyes open. Snakeman reported seein' something funky dancin' through the lightning beyond your LP, whatever *that* means. Just keep your head up. Charlie Tango says this storm'll be with us 'til dawn, then its fogsoup 'til noon, over."

"Roger, Doc. Say, Doc! What time do you plan to make your next rounds? I got somethin' to show ya, over."

"Forget it, goofus. Yours truly ain't gettin' wet just to baby sit a bunch o' grown-up gunnies. Winston crapped out in the CP, and Neil Nazi's up in Pleiku, getting his cast replaced. I'm stayin' right where I'm at. If you need somethin', ring me on the field phone, out."

"But, Sarge . . . *hey, Sarge!*" "What?" Delgado was still on the line.

"I need you out here now! I gotta *show* you something. You just gotta relieve me for a few minutes. You'll never believe what just walked in outa the rain."

CHAPTER 24

Elliot "the Snakeman" Fletcher waited for the last echo of discharges to roll off down the hillside before he slowly looked up from his prone position beneath the gun-cleaning trough. Two of the sniper's bullets had punctured the solvent tank again, and a rusty-colored liquid was soaking the American's back. Two helicopters were buzzing the tree line, but, once again, it seemed the half-blind rifleman had eluded them.

"Corpsman up!" someone was yelling on the other side of Col. Buchanan's command post. "I need a medic over here—*NOW!*"

Fletcher slowly slid his rifle out from beneath his chest and tested the magazine's seal tight. He rose into a push-ups position, struck his head on the bottom of the trough, and sank back into the red clay dust, sighing in pain and defeat. "Hopeless," he muttered, thinking about the sniper. "Totally fucking hopeless."

Doc Delgado ran past, and a renewed strength surged through Fletcher's system. He gave chase, knocking the solvent tank aside before jumping to his feet, ignoring the throbbing in his head.

Lt. Winston's intestines were hanging out his mouth when they found him.

The officer had dived under one of the V-100 assault tanks when all the shooting started, and a newby from Delta Company—over two hundred yards away—dropped his carbine during the mad scramble for cover. The weapon discharged a three-round burst, striking the heavily armored vehicle's two front balloonlike tractor tires, and the results were not unlike a giant rogue elephant dropping to its knees on top of a hyena.

"Can't say I ever much cared for the guy," Brody whispered over to Fletcher as they watched Delgado and Krutch scrape Winston into a body bag while a skycrane hovered overhead, hoisting the front end of the tank off the ground. "But what a way to go."

"Yah," Fletcher agreed. "I rarely lose sleep over the welfare of officers myself, but we got to put a stop to this kinda crap. Somebody's gotta get a message to Charlie; he can't go around wastin' First Cav—"

"Charlie didn't kill Winston," Brody reminded him. "One o' the FNG's from Delta accidentally—"

"Charlie caused the whole abortion." Fletcher held up a hand, "Which makes him as guilty as the man who fired—or dropped—the weapon, in my book."

"Well, whatever."

"Whatever, my ass! Charlie as good as smoked Lt. Winston as that newby across the way! And I'm not going to rest until—"

Choi-oi was standing in front of the tent Brody shared with Larson, and he was wailing. Wailing long and hard, his stub of a tail wagging furiously as front paws scraped the earth. The dog sounded as if he'd cornered a rattlesnake. Men were diving for cover, convinced a mortar attack was imminent.

"Well, what the heck do we have here!?" Sgt. Zack, who'd been walking past the tent on his way from the scene of Winston's death, chose to rush down into Larson's bunker the moment *Choi-oi* sounded the "alarm."

But this time the mongrel was not warning the men of a mortar attack. This time he'd located an undesirable female on the premises. Undesirable, that was, in *his* opinion.

Zack was marching a beautiful Vietnamese woman out of the Hell Hole at gunpoint. Her hands were on top of her head, slender fingers interlaced. Her wide eyes scanned the faces of soldiers running up for a look, and a relieved smile softened her features when she finally spotted Brody in the hostile-looking mob.

"Oh...uh, about her, Sarge...."

"About *her*, eh?" Zack holstered his pistol once he saw the two were acquainted. "Just what the flying fuck—if you'll pardon my French, miss"—he tipped his helmet to the long-haired woman wearing one of Treat Brody's oversized fatigue shirts and nothing else—"is this...*lady* doing in your hooch?"

"Uh...well, Sarge...it's a long story." Brody was at least man enough to stand beside the woman and drape an arm around her shoulder protectively, but another man was standing in the midst of the two dozen GIs, an Arvin military policeman.

243

And he didn't like what he was seeing.

"No need story." Phung Van Thieu stepped forth, pulling a rolled-up bounty poster from inside his flak vest. "She VC. I take. Make answers. You see."

"Sounds okay to me, Fungus Breath," Zack replied. The men called the QC Fungus Breath because of a particularly foul-smelling brand of *nuoc-nam* he favored dousing on everything he ate. *Nuoc-nam* was a fermented fish sauce many Americans likened to a visit to the latrine on a hot day without wind.

Brody snatched up the bounty poster. It was similar to the bulletin distributed a few weeks earlier in that both drawings showed a Vietnamese woman in her twenties with long black hair. But the similarities ended there, and the posters were poor photocopies. "This don't prove shit," he told Phung Van Thieu."

"Nebbah mind." The QC was still smiling. "She VC. I take."

"Let 'im have 'er, Whoremaniac." Zack dismissed the entire affair with a wave of his hand. "We got work to do."

But Zack did not immediately walk away. He froze in his tracks, in fact: Phung was removing the fatigue shirt and throwing it to Brody. "She no wear American or Arvin clothes," he snapped, grin gone. "She VC. No deserve."

Zack and the others stared at her jutting breasts, speechless. The woman stared at the ground, unmoving, as Phung hand-cuffed her hands behind her back.

Zack glanced at Brody as the Spec-4 started over toward Phung. The look in the tall NCO's eyes said *You've been balling THAT?* But he did not actually speak.

"You can't take her away, Fungus Breath." Brody tried his buddy-buddy approach. "She's just a village girl. I brought her here 'cause I thought she was the one Lee was searching for, but I was wrong. Now I'm just trying to get her to some shelter—"

"Nebbah mind, Bro-dee." The QC's smile returned. "I give her bookoo shelter—at monkeyhouse."

Rain clouds were passing overhead swiftly, and several large drops began falling across the camp as the door gunner pleaded her case. "You've got the wrong woman, Phung. Her village was accidentally bombed by South Vietnamese planes last night during the storm. You know, that lightning show last night! The SVN Air Force hit the wrong target."

244

"I no believe." Phung Van Thieu was adamant. "She tell you this crap?"

"Well...yes. She was shell shocked." Brody shielded his head from the increasing rain but made no attempt to cover the woman. Many of the men had tired of the show and were seeking shelter from the downpour. Others, like Fletcher and Ju-ju stayed to watch. "You should have seen her. She was all singed by powder and her clothes were shredded and everything," he exaggerated somewhat. "She was wearing peasant garb when she stumbled into my LP, Phung. No weapons. Not even black pajamas—she had on a goddamned wraparound sarong. Now have you ever heard of a sapper tryin' to breach the wire in a sarong?"

"What she tell you her name is, Bro-dee?"

"Ask her yourself." Brody folded his arms across his chest, only half convinced of her innocence. What *had* she been doing out in the boonies in the middle of the night? He'd checked with the FACs only that morning—after a landline to Pleiku revealed no official knowledge of any air strikes on the area—and the Forward Air Controllers claimed they'd called in not a single artillery barrage all night.

"I ask you, Bro-dee?"

He stared at the woman for a moment. She was soaked with rainwater but did not move other than to tremble. The water was warm. She was shaking with fear. Brody watched the drops run down the firm slopes of her breasts and fall from her upturned nipples, and he found himself wishing he could take her back down into Larson's bunker and dry her beneath his own body ...cuddle her...hold her, flesh against flesh...until the rain and the war and everyone around them was blocked out by a wall of passion.

"Her name is Von," he answered finally. "Vu Y-Von."

Phung produced a satisfied smirk. Brody was unsure if the QC just didn't believe that was really her name, or if he'd recognized it. "I take. *Fini* talk." He turned to escort her away.

"Wait!" Brody pleaded with his eyes as the sky thundered above.

Phung recognized the look as one a desperately lonely soldier would manifest should he be awakened from a much-needed romantic dream in the midst of a combat zone. "She Viet

Cong, Bro-dee. Top Ten cadre."

"You recognize her?" He did not hide his skepticism.

"No, but . . . ." Phung held out the bounty poster.

"You recognize her from *that*?"

"She VC. I . . .*feel* it inside, you *bic*?"

"You 'feel' it? You gotta be shittin' me, Thieu."

"You lucky today, Bro-dee. She maybe booby-trap your hooch. You should thank dog." He pointed at *Choi-oi*.

"Booby trap!? With *what*?"

Choi-oi began wailing as Phung Thieu pointed at him. Thunder boomed overhead, and lightning crackled all around, and *Choi-oi* howled all the louder as the QC ignored Brody now and started to lead the prisoner away.

"It's okay, *Choi-fuckin'-oi*." Fletcher grinned despite the increasing downpour. "That smelly ol' whore is leavin' your turf."

Then they heard the whistle falling between thunderclaps, and Krutch the Stork yelled, *"Incoming!"* as he dove down into Larson's bunker. A wave of mortars splashed in, right on cue.

Phung Van Thieu was not paid enough by the Army of the Republic of Viet Nam to be a dead hero, in his opinion. He hustled down into the Hell Hole after the sprinting Snakeman, nearly cart-wheeling over *Choi-oi*. The dog was running circles around the soldiers, still howling out the warning.

From his position beneath a parked jeep's engine block, Treat Brody glanced up through the barrage of smoking shrapnel and raindrops to see the woman of his dreams escaping in all the confusion. He watched her run down the hillside through the exploding mortars, naked into the jungle, hands still manacled behind her back.

CHAPTER 25

Lance Warlokk knew he was risking his career by violating the curfew regulation, but the GIs didn't call him "Lawless" for nothing, and one *had* to keep his reputation polished if he was going to make a legend of himself in The Nam, right? So it was that the warrant officer cast all caution aside, determined to enjoy the ride, as he held on to the waist of one very lovely Honda Honey from Pleiku City.

An unexpected ash-and-trash mission down south had seen him back to the Turkey Farm well after twenty-three hundred hours, which had totally ruined his plans to thumb a ride with the MPs out to the refugee camp. Lisa Maddox was rumored to be spending her seven-day R and R at the orphanage, and chopper jock Warlokk decided it was time he volunteered some of his skill and charisma to the cause. Charity had always been the pilot's weak point, but if his favorite army nurse was involved, he'd surely allot a couple of hours here or there to help out the kiddies. And court the uppity bitch.

One of the crew chiefs, Sgt. Zack, had listened to his sob story with the required amount of mock compassion and had suggested Lance hire one of the motor-scooter girls who could be found loitering outside the MP's meat market at all hours of the day and night to drive him out to the camp on her Honda-50. The trip only took a half hour at most, cost less P than a short-time, and he could probably make it through the QC checkpoints unscathed if he wore his First Cav baseball cap with the SAT CONG patch across the front of it.

He gave the woman a generous tip, hoping to search her dark eyes for some hint of the impression he'd made on her, but she merely nodded her thanks silently as she slipped the *piasters* under her blouse, all her attention focused on the ground shyly as she backed the Honda up and turned it around.

Warlokk followed her outline in the dark as she disappeared down a bend in the road—the motor-scooter's taillight had been disconnected—stood in the swirl of her scent for a moment, until exhaust fumes invaded it, then walked past the sleeping guard at the refugee camp's main entrance.

"Shit," he muttered under his breath as he spotted a blacked-out Huey sitting alone on one of the helipads, its rotor blades still swishing lazily through the humid night air. "That fucking Gabe don't know when to quit." An American was reaching up to catch the rotor as it came around, and Warlokk watched him tie it down. The AC jumped to the ground, said something to the peter pilot stringing a hammock in the cabin, then started for the administration building. Warlokk could tell by his gait the man was Gabriel. There were no stretchers aboard the slick, and no other troops. "Paying a little, off-the-record visit, eh, Gunslinger?" He posed the question to himself, never thinking of comparing their reasons for coming to the camp after dark. The Dustoff pilot had violated his ethics by using a helicopter in his romantic pursuits. Worlokk had hired a Honda Honey. That set them apart, in Lawless's book.

"What the fu—" A blue jeep was parked in front of the long-house where all the orphanage and refugee records were kept. One man and four Vietnamese women were inside.

Warlokk and Gabriel reached the vehicle at the same time.

"Graves!" the Cobra pilot shouted upon recognizing the CIA agent. "What the hell are *you* doing here?"

Obviously intoxicated, with four young women sharing his bottle of vodka, Graves leaned back, an ear-to-ear smile across his whiskers, and offered a drink to the two pilots. "Hey, fella!"

"Maybe I move in with you." The woman seated beside the CIA agent was still talking as if no intruders were interrupting their conversation. "But you make promise, Hoa, okay? You promise Hoa you never butterfly, you *bic*? Hoa no like joke. You butterfly, you die, sure? Hoa catch you butterfly, Johnny, Hoa wait 'till you sleep, then *cut off your DICK!*" She obviously spoke as if ignoring the other three women present also. *"Em cat chim anh!"*

Feigning total innocence, Graves glanced over at Warlokk, down at the woman fondling his groin, then back at the helicopter pilot. "Blow jobs don't count." He laughed. But Lance was no longer listening to Graves.

Instead, he was hearing Lisa's words from the month before. They had been sitting at one of the cable-spool tables on the longhouse veranda, watching a herd of elephants make its way

248

through the tangle of trees and man-high reeds at the edge of the compound. Drinking iced coffee—yes, he could remember it very clearly now. He had been teasing her about the pretty young administration-building secretary who brought them small baggies of the strong refreshment. "So many 'Yarde girls running around the Central Highlands," he had said, "And soooo little time."

"Oh, I am sure you can *make* time," Lisa had replied with an accusing wink.

"But I would much better like to get to know *you* better, my dear," Lance had countered.

"I'm sure." He would never forget how she broke eye contact and remarked, "At least *I* would not slice off your nectar-prober when I caught you butterflying on me with one of your mistresses."

"Butterfly!?" he had pointed at himself with both hands. *"Me?"*

To "butterfly" was the local lingo for cheating on one's *manoi*. Graves's drunken laughter coaxed him back from the memory.

Gabriel rushed around for a better vantage point. He wanted to make sure the head bobbing up and down over the spook's lap didn't have blond hair. "You've no fucking shame, Graves!" He smiled in relief, shaking his head from side to side as the woman sensed his approach and paused to gauge his intention with alcohol-glazed eyes.

"Hey, it's my goddamned birthday, mates! One o' the boys from Air America brought these lovely ladies up from Dalat to help me celebrate."

"Air America?" Warlokk scanned the compound for other helicopters or small fixed-wing craft.

"They had to go." He waved the pilot's concern away and finished off the bottle. "Some kind o' FOB rat fuck. You know how it goes."

"Yah, we know how it goes." Lance and the Gunslinger exchanged shrugs.

"Now I got to figure out some way to smuggle these beauty queens down south before their politician papa-san misses 'em."

"Messin' with jailbait, eh, Graves?" Warlokk laughed. The

woman hovering over his lap had gone back to work.

"Nah." His hands went out to encompass the girls. "Meet wives Number four, five, six, and...uh, nine, I believe." He frowned at the arithmetic.

"Ten." The woman slobbering over his zipper rose from her chore briefly. "Me Numba Ten wife." She smiled over at Gabriel.

"Well, you're doin' Numba *One* job, honey." Graves gently forced her head back down.

Warlokk glanced up at the darkened windows of the administration longhouse. "Everybody take the night off or something?"

"They probably shut down operations out of respect for this pervert's privacy." Gabriel spoke with sarcasm as he tried to focus on the blur of hair over the agent's crotch.

"It's Saturday night, gents," Graves reminded them. "The head man always closes the doors early on Saturday night."

"Well, I'll be seein' you two later." Gabriel turned to leave. He knew exactly where Lisa Maddox stayed when she spent her nights at the camp.

"Hey, Gunslinger." Warlokk pointed at the parked medevac in the opposite direction. "Your ride home is waitin' for you over *there!*"

Gabriel slowed to a stop and allowed his head to drop with fatigue. He was tired of competing with Lance for Lisa's affections, ever-elusive as they might be. He turned to face the other pilot. "What?"

"I think you'd better get that Dustoff back to the Turkey Farm before Neil Nazi finds out you're using government property in your quest for the ultimate in army-issue pussy."

"What?" Gabriel rested his hands on his hips in a stance that dared Warlokk to continue through dangerous territory.

"You're wasting your time with Lisa, Gabe." He stepped a few paces closer but paused with several meters still between them. "You two have different personalities. Nurses like Maddox are attracted to dudes outside their profession. Dudes like me. You fly medevacs, bud. I fly Cobra gunships. Lisa needs a real warrior between her legs, not a do-gooder with red crosses painted across the sides of his bird."

Gabriel had glided up nose to nose with Warlokk now, but

Lance's confident smile did not waver. "Why don't we let Lisa decide that?"

"Because *I'm* deciding it." Warlokk tapped the rank insignia on his collar.

"You wouldn't pull ran—"

"Oh yes I would." Warlokk laughed as Gabriel backed away in shock and insult. "In fact, I'm ordering you to *di-di* right now, pal. Get that slick back to the Turkey Farm, or—"

Gabriel motioned to the portable radio on his web belt. "I'm on call," he said.

"Then go spend it in your cockpit." Warlokk pointed to the peter pilot's cigarette glowing in the distance. "While *this* chopper jock gets *his* cock lubed by a *real*—"

Gabriel didn't let him finish. "Why you sonofa—" Gabriel swung hard. He swung as hard as he'd ever thrown a fist before, but Lawless was a born fighter, and he easily sidestepped the move.

The Dustoff pilot's legs flew out from under him, and Gabriel found himself flat on his back. Warlokk was upon him in a flash, pressing him into the dusty red clay with a knee across his sternum. "I oughta kick your fucking ass for that." He brought the edge of his hand back in a martial-arts move but hesitated.

"I saved *your* worthless ass more than a couple times, you sonofabitch!" Gabriel was not pleading for mercy. He was reminding Warlokk how disloyal it was for two chopper pilots to fight over a woman. And a woman neither of them was even married to.

Something passed before Lance Warlokk's eyes. A memory, or a flashback, or the momentary blur of vision-revealing guilt, and he lowered his fist. "Fuck you, Gabe."

"Yo' mama," Gabriel shot back with his best jive accent. Warlokk laughed. He leaned back and rolled off the Gunslinger. "Christ." He shook his head in resignation. "Okay, let's go talk to Lisa about it."

Gabriel checked his wristwatch. "It's getting pretty late," he said. "Why don't we forget about it and call it a night."

"No, Lisa sure don't need no beauty sleep, that's for sure. And I wanna get this over with. Once and for all." He helped Gabriel up off the ground.

251

They both knew the way over to her small bungalow-on-stilts, though neither soldier had ever been inside. A small candle was flickering in the window, behind bug screen shutters. "Looks like she's still awake."

"Good." Both men pictured her poring over medical journals until the predawn hours found her exhausted. Lance held a finger to his lips for silence.

"What's *that?*" As they drew closer, it appeared the tiny dwelling was shaking slightly.

Gabriel started to grab Warlokk's arm in hopes of restraining him, but Lawless had caught the scent of romance on the hot, sticky breeze, and was already racing up the rickety planklike steps. Gabe was right behind him.

The Cobra pilot could not restrain himself when he reached the top. He tried to kick the door in, but it held, and both warrant officers put their shoulders to the teakwood. In an explosion of splinters, it crashed inward.

"Well, fuck me 'till it hurts." Warlokk imitated one of his favorite door gunners as they recognized the brown man lying between Lisa Maddox's soft, creamy legs.

Lisa's ankles were locked together over her lover's thrusting hips. Panic in her eyes, she unwrapped her legs and slapped his biceps to get the attention of the American totally absorbed in devouring her breasts. The dimly lit room fell silent as the medic from Echo Company slid off the bed, onto the floor, and Nurse Maddox pulled the hospital-issue sheets back up to her chin.

"Well if it ain't Danny Delgado." Gabe the Gunslinger scratched the stubble on his chin. "Playin' Doctor before his time."

CHAPTER 26

"Phung Van Thieu bookoo stupid." Truong Ju-ju was still trying to console Brody, although the Whoremonger had gotten over the escape of his rain lady the day before. "All Viets are Mister Lucas or Miss Lucas to Phung unless they wear ARVN uniform. He see VC in *every*one. So sorry he fuck you over like this, but—"

"Nebbah mind, nebbah mind." Treat glanced over at Fletcher and grinned as he continued running the barrel-cleaning rod in and out of the Chinese-made revolver he'd taken off the captured NVA sergeant. "I was mesmerized by her beauty and the lightning and thunder, but I've gotten over it." Brody truly felt he was talking fact, but there came a nagging pang of hurt in his chest, and he wondered if he still really cared that much about her. The pain was where he decided his heart had to be, and it became worse the more he thought about Vu Y-Von, or whatever her name really was. Could it really be the heartache poets wrote about? He laughed the thought off.

"What is. . .mez—. . .mez—"

But Larson interrupted their conversation again for the third time that evening. "Okay," he said, replacing the coffee pot over a chip of C-4. "What about this: 'I've come to the ultimate conclusion that the best contribution I could make to the war effort would be to eat a grenade in the middle of the ammunition depot down in Long Binh, therefore. . .'"

Brody stared at Fletcher as the Professor read the latest entry from his ongoing suicide note. Snakeman was flipping a piece of metal over and over in his fingers. A shiny sliver of magnesium that seemed to catch dim shards of light in the Hell Hole and reflect them accusingly directly in Brody's eyes. "What ya got there, Elliot?"

Fletcher glanced over at Larson, who kept reading without looking up at them. "From that crash site," he told the gunny. "It just happened to sparkle that night."

"That valley near where your brother crashed?"

"Yah. When we were leaving, it sparkled like. . .well, almost

253

as if from its own power. There wasn't enough moonlight out that night, Treat, not enough to cast that srong a reflection, you know? So I figured it just had to be a sign of some sort, but—"

"Let me check it out." Brody reached out.

"Nah." Fletcher slipped the crash site souvenir down into a pocket. "It's nothing. Just a strip of metal that don't mean nothin' at all. No sign. Nothing scribbled on it. Nothing cryptic. Just a piece out of a plane."

"Well, just hang in there."

"It's hopeless. Richard didn't leave anything for me to find." Larson was still reading his suicide note to the half dozen men in the underground bunker, but his voice was lower now as Fletcher continued to speak. "Even if he did, how could I be sure we were searching the right crash site? I might as well just give it the fuck up."

"No true-blue gunny-buddy o' mine would talk that way." Brody reached across the pit and slapped him on the shoulder. "Just keep the faith, Snakeman. The Pack will come through for you in the end. If we all gotta extend another six months to help you find Rich, we'll do it! Right, Professor?"

Larson just kept reading his suicide note. Louder now. Shaking his head at the obvious answer, Fletcher pulled one of the baby boas from his upside-down helmet and began feeding it small bits of chicken.

"Come on, Doc!" Krutch had been ribbing Delgado all night. "Is it true, or isn't it? Is she really a natural blond or not?"

Eyes growing large, Lee stared at the helicopter pilots, listening to their conversation closely for the first time. Delgado was flushing but determined to remain silent about the incident.

"I overheard Gabe and Warlokk talking all about it. Confess! Was it a good piece of snatch?"

Frowning, Delgado turned to face Krutch for the first time. "Nurse Maddox is a real lady," he said. "I wouldn't know if she is a natural blond or not."

"Come on, come on! I know all the fuck about it, Casanova! You were ballin' the bitch in the middle of the orphanage or something, and those two chopper jockeys walked right in on the two of you—"

"They kicked the goddamned door in!" Delgado slipped.

254

"Ah-HA!" The Stork flapped his arms in victory. "You *did* get into Lt. Maddox's pants! Well ALL-fucking-RIGHT!" He raised his VC skullcap and toasted the medic, splashed beer on *Choi-oi,* then leaned closer to Delgado. "Tell me, brother, how did it taste?"

"How did *what* taste?" The corpsman dropped back away from him.

"Come on." Cordova was sitting between them, and Krutch pushed him aside, trying to grasp Delgado's upper lip and chin. "Lemme see your front teeth. I wanna see if you got any blond pubic hairs caught in—"

Larson elbowed the Stork hard.

"And since I find it reprehensible that the United States Government actually pays me to oppress and—"

"Shut the fuck up, Professor." Brody poured lukewarm coffee over Larson's head.

"Whatta you guys think about this?" Fletcher had put his snake away and produced his correspondence packet.

My Dearest Melodie,

Yes, dear. . .Vietnam is a very stressful place to be. Any more keepsakes you could send me would be greatly appreciated. We spend long hours in elephant grass a dozen feet high, patrolling for Charlie—that's GI jargon for Viet Cong—and encountering hostile fire on a daily basis. But with photos such as the ones you've sent me kept constantly close to my heart, I've no doubt yours truly will survive his Tour 365. . . .

"How come you don't talk like that in real life?" Brody laughed.

Before Fletcher could respond, Delgado, seeking to avoid dueling with Krutch, asked, "Is that the chick in Colorado Springs who keeps sendin' you the snatch shots, Snakeman?"

"Cheyenne," Fletcher corrected him. "Cheyenne, Wyoming, but yah, same-same, GI. Great tits. Nipples the size of silver-dollar pancakes." From inside his T-shirt, he pulled a pair of pink panties she'd sent and stuffed them in his mouth.

"That's the way I like 'em." Doc smiled.

"So Lisa Maddox has silver-dollar–sized nipples, eh?" Krutch slid beside the corpsman. "Bet they go good with her blond hair!"

"Cut me some slack, Stork," Delgado pleaded.

"Yah, lay off the guy," Brody said. Krutch ignored them both. "I just gotta know, Danny Boy: Why didn't Gabe and Lawless pound your sorry ass into the ground? It's no secret they were both hot to trot after Lisa's tight little ass, then who comes along but some quiet Mexican medic and POW-*eeeeeh!* Ol' Doc scores a home-run!"

Delgado thought about that for a second, and a smile stretched his normally somber features. "Warlokk and Gabriel got class, Hal," he said softly, "unlike *some* helicopter pilots we know."

"Shafted!" Lee called out, and everyone except Larson laughed—the Professor was still trying to wipe the spilled coffee off his suicide note.

"What could they do?" Delgado continued. "Bruise their knuckles over a woman?"

"It's been known to happen before." Cordova winked.

"And Lieutenant Lisa's not a bad piece of ass, for an angel of mercy," added Lee.

"Well, Warlokk and Gabriel have been through too much together to let a cunt come between them. You know the phrase...'"

"Women," Lee recited it. "Can't live with 'em....'"

"...And can't live without 'em," Brody finished it.

"A cunt?" Krutch feigned shock. "You get in Maddox's pants...now your nose smells like trout in the tropics, and you have the gall to call that round-eyed princess a cunt? A minute ago she was a LAAAdy."

"It slipped out."

"No shit."

"Look"—Delgado held his hands up—"she is, was, and forever will be a real lady in my book, okay? I'm tired, and the word slipped out, and I fucking TAKE IT BACK, okay?" He punched the Stork lightly, spilling more beer on *Choi-oi*. The dog moved to the other side of the bunker.

"Okay, okay...'" Krutch gave him a casual, half salute. "Now tell me a little more about her tits. Does she—"

Several shadows were moving about near the mouth of the bunker entrance, and everyone around Delgado tensed. Brody and Fletcher grabbed their rifles: It was too late at night, and much too quiet.

256

"Permission to descend into Hell," a hearty voice boomed forth from above.

Instant relief: Everyone recognized Zack. "Enter at your own risk," Krutch replied loudly.

"Why, Patterson!" Brody called out upon recognizing one of the soldiers following the NCO down into the cramped bunker. "Good to see you, Slick! We heard some Queen Cong had put you in a C-130 on your way to Japan. Them Lurp patrols getting *that* dangerous?"

"Aw, she only split my shoulder-blade down the middle." He shrugged off all the attention. But he didn't mention the hammer and nails.

They'd all heard the story already. About the VC guerrilla nailing a Cong-flag patch to Patterson's back, then releasing him naked in the middle of Void Vicious. But they wouldn't bring up particulars unless he did first.

Brody noticed Fletcher was bristling. Abdul Mohammed was also with Zack. "What's *he* doing back?"

Frowning, Zack anticipated trouble but had no other squad slots in which to fit the dissident troublemaker. "Crump the Third is hereby assigned to you girls," he decreed. "Keep him honest."

"Well, we don't want him." Fletcher went back to feeding his snakes.

"The feeling is mutual." Mohammed thrust his chin out, always the militant.

"He passed his psychological," Zack revealed, sounding apologetic.

"What a scam," Fletcher replied.

"More like the regulation snafu." Mohammed stared down at Elliot. "But I'll get out of here yet. You geeks just wait and see."

"We'd just as soon not put up with your antics in the meantime." Snakeman was blunt. "And we don't want you flyin' aboard *Pegasus*." He looked up and locked eyes with the radical. "Never again. Is that clear, Clarence?"

Mohammed hated it when people like Zack and this Texan redneck called him by his old first name. His lips curled up with disgust, but he didn't say anything.

"Crump's got ground duties 'till he rotates," Zack revealed.

"He won't be goin' into the Void unless Charlie whips somethin' big up on us."

"So anyway. . ." Patterson hoped a big smile would lift everyone's spirits. He set down his duffel bag and opened it almost ceremoniously. "Ol' Saint Pat's got some presents for the boys in the Pack!"

First, he took a hammer and some nails out of the GI luggage, set them to one side, and carefully produced two eight-by-ten framed plaques.

One had a large photo of him posing with four bathing-suit–clad nurses at a beach on Nha Trang, his chest covered with bandages. A customized card taped to the lower corner of the glass read:

> THERE IS NO HUNTING
> LIKE THE HUNTING OF MAN
> AND THOSE WHO HAVE HUNTED
> ARMED MEN LONG ENOUGH
> AND LIKED IT
> NEVER CARE FOR ANYTHING ELSE
> THEREAFTER

"Ahhh," Brody recognized the passage. "And this one could go on the other wall." He began pounding on the packed earth.

Brody wasn't sure if the plaque was made of polished teak or laquer wood, but it was even more beautiful: four gorgeous Asian women wearing South Vietnamese tiger-stripe trousers posed with one boot each atop the body of a dead Viet Cong guerrilla. The women were all topless, except for ammo belts criss-crossing their well-endowed chests. They carried weapons of American and Israeli manufacture. Inscribed above the inlaid picture were the words:

> HOG HEAVEN: IT ISN'T THE PRICE YOU
> PAID TO BE A MEMBER. . . . IT'S THE
> PRICE YOU SACRIFICED TO BECOME
> ELIGIBLE!

And below the erotic photograph was the passage from some unknown warrior:

> YOU HAVE NEVER LIVED
> UNTIL YOU HAVE ALMOST DIED. . . .
> FOR THOSE WHO FIGHT FOR IT
> LIFE HAS A FLAVOR

THE PROTECTED WILL NEVER KNOW.

"A fitting and welcome addition to any home." Brody supervised the interior decorating, while the others looked on with a renewed sense of pride and self-esteem—esteem that had often suffered greatly because of things war made men do. . .things they often would fail to confront until years later, when they were back in The World, alone and bored. . .bored beyond description with the cancerous routine of everyday civilian life. Things that came back to haunt them as they stood at their window, staring at the cold skyscrapers of New York or Chicago or Los Angeles, or the barren prairies of Midwest America. Things they remembered only when the rain poured down, or the heat brought out the mosquitoes.

"And I've got something else for my blood brothers in the Pack." Patterson reached into his duffel bag.

"Didn't know you could fit an LBFM in luggage that small," Cordova acted as if he was about to take his belt and trousers off.

"Ain't no little brown fucking machines in *this* duffel." Patterson laughed. "Sorry 'bout that, Corky! But, hey, you clowns remember when I got all your ring sizes before they switched me to Lurps? And I promised to get you some far-out mementos on my well-deserved vacation?"

"Aw, ya didn't have to go an' do nothin' for us like—" Zack started to roll his shoulders back and forth, but Fletcher cut him off.

"He didn't, Sarge. He didn't get *you* something. Did he ever take *your* ring size? Get the wax outta your ears, honcho-san. Saint Pat said 'blood brothers in the Pack.' Now, true, you is a blood, and true, you is a brother, but you ain't a *blood* brother, and you ain't no member of the Pack, so—"

Patterson caught the reflection of embarrassment in Zack's eyes and the tone of blatant bigotry in Fletcher's voice. "Actually," he interrupted Snakeman, "I also asked Leo for his ring size. I mean, he's always been the best crew chief a gunship could ask for, right?"

"What about me?" Mohammed asked. "Did you get ol' Elijah a present from Honolouie-Louie, Saint Pat?"

"Fuck you, Crump." Patterson, like the others, didn't much care for the militant's antics.

"So where *did* you go for R and R?" Brody sought to head off any confrontations.

"Saigon." Patterson grinned. "Picked these little gems up in the Pearl of the—"

"*Saigon!?*" Fletcher exploded. "You spent your goddamned R and R in-country?"

"Well, I didn't have much scrip saved up to do bookoo traveling, Fletch. It all went to buyin' you guys these."

Patterson pulled a neatly folded, velvet cloth from the duffel bag and laid it out on Lee's Ouija board. "Enjoy!" he drew back the top flap, revealing several rings cast from silver. "They've all got your initials inside," he explained, and Doc Delgado started handing them out.

"You're an all-right dude, Saint Pat." Larson nodded slowly as he examined the jewelry. The Professor didn't much care for their design, but it was the thought that counted. Across the base of each ring was an intricately carved gunship with VC skulls caught on the front skids. All the rings had red stones with brilliant facets that threw shards of eerie crimson across the words VC HUNTING CLUB on the bottom and HH-100 across the top.

"Outstanding!" Brody modeled his ring for the others, moving his fist about in front of the crackling C-4 to get the best sparkles. The rings would become their bond, the symbol that held the Pack together. The camaraderie already developing in Larson's bunker, the atmosphere of brotherhood forged under hostile fire, was becoming almost overwhelming, and Zack, the hint of a tear fighting to mar his rough, weatherbeaten features, started for the steps. He needed some fresh air. He desperately needed to get outside.

"Where the fuck *you* goin', Leo?" Larson stood up and motioned the big NCO over. "Lemme check out your rock. I've never seen a size-fifty ring before."

His smile lighting up his face, Zack complied and, a few minutes later, said, "Oh, by the way, Snakeoil...the colonel—"

"*I'm* Snakeoil." Fletcher stood up. "I mean, Snake*man!* He's the Professor."

"Uh...right." Zack struggled to remain friendly. After all, they'd just presented him with a ring that had *The Pack* inscribed above his initials on the inside. "Anyway, *Larson.* The
260

colonel wanted me to tell you your Congressional complaint or investigation or whatever it was—"

"*Is,*" Shawn interrupted him.

"Well, it's on hold and probably permanently shit-canned, so I guess that makes it a 'was.' Anyway, he just wanted me to tell you the politician's aide went back to The World, so. . ."

"Fuck it," Larson grumbled. "Don't mean shit. I'm gettin' shorter by the day anyway."

"Just wanted to let you know."

"Thanks for nothin'."

Zack started for the steps again, then turned and faced Cordova instead. "Oh, and Cork-it. . ." he said.

"Corky, Sarge, if you don't mind—that's if you *have* a—"

"Yah, right. Anyway, the CO also wanted me to advise you your request for R and R couldn't be approved at this moment. Too much shit driftin' toward the fan bookoo *rikky-tik,* and—"

"Don't sweat it, Sarge. I expected as much when I filled out the forms." But Cordova was not so calm on the inside. He had received no letters from Thuan in An Khe for some weeks now and had hoped to check on her. Corky had no leave saved up, but he did have an R and R due him. "Maybe when we get back to An Khe."

"There you go," Zack nodded. "I'll be sure and check on—" But the big squad sergeant fell silent. Everyone in the bunker stopped talking, and the only sound was the piece of C-4 crackling under Lee's coffee pot. The C-4 and rotors. Chopper blades beating at hot, sticky air in the distance.

"Slicks on the horizon." A towering shadow had fallen across the bunker's entrance. They all recognized Herman "Hatchet-head" Monrovia's voice. "A foretoken gaggle if I ever saw one!" The body-builder announced, then was off to the next bunker.

" 'Foretoken?' " Fletcher glanced over at the Professor.

"I think he means unscheduled." Larson started for the sand-bagged steps, and the others followed.

"Somebody oughta take that gorilla's dictionary away from him."

Four helicopters set down with little fanfare in the middle of Echo Company's landing pad, and though it became quickly evident there were no stretchers or wounded aboard, none of

261

Brody's people went back to the Hell Hole. The troops climbing down from the Hueys and stumbling over chopper skids were obviously newbies, their jungle fatigues were still shiny and gleamed under the setting sun. Half the soldiers were without weapons, and Zack, shaking his head from side to side in irritation, immediately directed them toward the underground armory. This wasn't *that* much of a rear-echelon compound!

Two privates, following Zack's gesture, started over toward Brody, dragging their rucks and M-16s and tense, newby expressions. "Two FNGs coming up." Fletcher made the required scowl. It was an unwritten rule that new men in the unit—unless they were already wearing a combat patch or CIB—were given the cold shoulder and virtually ignored their first three months in-country. The next three they were finally recognized as existing on Planet Earth. One hundred and eighty days after their arrival, they were considered vets. Unless a claymore or hollow-point sent them home early, in which case they became posthumous veterans. Newbies often brought favorable attention upon themselves long before that first six months was up—usually in a firefight—but there would always be old-timers in every platoon who refused to acknowledge their presence until they'd paid longevity dues.

"That must be Winston's replacement." Brody spotted a first lieutenant stepping down from the Huey's hatch.

"At least he's not another second louie." Fletcher spat into the dust, and little red puffs rose in silent reply.

"Looks like he *might* have his shit together," Lee observed.

The officer's name-tag read VANCE. Five feet ten inches tall on his better days, he had a slim but physically fit build and a baby face below a neatly trimmed black crewcut.

Looks like an innocent little kid who got off at the wrong bus stop, Brody mused as he noticed the red dots lining the lieutenant's forearms. Mosquito bites. He remembered how, his own first night at the Camp Alpha in-processing center, exhausted after so many days at sea, he fell asleep on his assigned cot without bothering to set up his mosquito net. "The dude's got a hawk's nose."

"That's a good sign," decided Lee.

"But it looks out of place," Fletcher argued mildly. Snakeman didn't like the officer's piercing blue eyes—visible from even this distance. "Twenty, you think?" he asked Brody as they sized up the new lieutenant.

"Twenty-one tops."

Vance had been born on Valentine's Day in 1944. That made him twenty-two. A recent graduate of West Point, where he majored in Asian history and politics, the lieutenant was a master of foreign languages and hoped to spend this tour of duty polishing his Vietnamese.

Vance seemed to home in on Brody and his people and strode over to their cluster. "Evenin', sir." Fletcher saluted for the group. It was a casual, half salute, and the lieutenant responded with a frown as his hand flew crisply to his right eyebrow. He gave the door gunners a quick once-over, paying particular attention to the way they were clad: dirty, blood-caked flak vests with no fatigue blouses underneath. Only Lee wore an olive-drab T-shirt, and it had FTA stenciled across the front in bold letters.

" 'Fuck the Army,' eh?" Vance grinned at Em-ho, but it was a conniving twist of the lips that worried every soldier standing there. "Me, I've been fucking the army for the last four years, gentlemen. I consider myself married to it!"

Fletcher noticed he wore no wedding band on his ring finger. A small gold crucifix caught a ray of setting sun and sparkled for an instant. It was hanging from his dog-tags chain, over a white T-shirt. "The supply shack's that way." Snakeman pointed to a ramshackle structure *Choi-oi* was urinating against. "They can get you some green T-shirts."

"We only wear green T-shirts in The Nam," Lee added. "GIs back in The World can't wear 'em. . .only here in—"

"I'm quite familiar with the RVN dress code, soldier," Vance snapped.

Then why the fuck aren't you wearing one? Fletcher thought to himself. The lieutenant wasn't really arrogant. He wasn't really behaving like a lifer, either. But he was definitely overdoing the I'm-an-officer-and-you're-an-enlisted-man routine. Fletcher smiled as other thoughts flitted through his mind. They were going to have fun breaking this dude in.

Vance didn't miss the change in expression. He stared down at Fletcher's scuffed boots. "I suggest you put a shine on 'em, Private." He moved closer to focus on the name tag. "Fletcher,

263

is it?"

"A *what*, sir?" Snakeman's lower jaw dropped.

"A shine. You've heard of a shine, haven't you, soldier? A *spit* shine."

"Uh...this is The Nam, sir." He glanced over at Brody for support. "We don't normally—"

"What he means, sir—" Brody began, but the lieutenant cut him off.

"This is Echo Company, isn't it?" He pulled a perspiration-soaked set of military orders from his stateside utilities.

"Uh...yes, sir." Fletcher nodded. *Vance knew damn well it was!*

"Then you troopers better *all* have your boots looking sharp before sun-up, hadn't you?" He turned to leave, and the cross against his throat sparkled again.

"Uh...right, Lieutenant...wilco."

After Vance was gone, Fletcher, referring to the crucifix, added, "I wonder if he walks on water too."

"Aw, eat it like a man, Snakeoil." Zack, passing by with a bundle of body bags under one arm had heard it all. "A coat o' *Kiwi* wouldn't hurt none o' you skates. Helps preserve the boot, too. Prevents cracking."

"But I don't think we *got* a can of shoe polish anywhere around," Fletcher replied. But Leo the Lionhearted was gone.

"Hi!" one of the newbies stepped in front of Elliot, hand extended.

Without saying anything, the gunny stared down through the shorter soldier until he withdrew it and dropped the enthusiastic smile. His name tag read CHAPPELL, and he was a buck private, the lowest rank in the army.

Soldiers usually made PV-2 or Private First Class before they arrived in Vietnam. "What did you fuck up to keep slick-sleeves?" was Fletcher's greeting.

"Aw, the drill sergeant in basic found a girly magazine under the mattress of my bunk and put a flag on my two-oh-one file. It wasn't really *my* skin magazine. The bay bully was always—"

"Hey, I don't wanna hear your whole fuckin' life history, cherry boy."

"Oh...sorry..."

E-1 Aaron Chappell was barely eighteen, maybe less, Brody

decided. An obvious virgin both physically and mentally, he was short and thin—everyone's kid brother. He seemed almost a clone of Treat's younger brother, in fact: black-frame glasses that made his dark eyes appear larger than they really were, a pencil-thin mustache that would take years to amount to anything the housegirls would even notice, and a nervous tic in one eye. Chappell's hair was as black as any of the locals', but also receding. He'd be bald before he was twenty-five, Brody predicted.

The recruit standing beside Chappell was bigger, but no older, it seemed. Shaggy blond hair was creeping over his ears, in violation of army regulations. *Him and Vance are gonna get along great,* Brody decided. Determined to make new friends and an impression on the vets, the private grabbed Fletcher's hand. "Name's Nelson," he said. "My friends call me Nasty Nel!" His teeth flashed almost menacingly.

Fletcher looked like he was going to punch the kid out at first. But Brody could see he was intrigued by the nickname. "And why, pray tell, do they call you Nasty Nel, newby?"

A smile growing at Snakeman's reaction, Nelson dropped his pack, slid the straps apart, and opened the top flap. " 'Cause o' my collection o' pussy hair." He pulled out an egg carton containing not produce but small plastic vials, sealed with wax of different colors.

"Your collection of *what?*" Fletcher dropped to one knee beside the FNG.

"Fucking pubic hair!" Lee was right beside him. "Are they from *girls?*"

"'Course they're from—" Fletcher started ro rebuke Em-ho.

"They're from *women,*" Nelson proclaimed proudly. He pulled out the first vial and read the information taped to the side as the men all inspected the strands of red hair. "Cynthia. Collinsville, Connecitcut, September nineteen sixty-four... three stars...."

"Three stars?" Fletcher's eyes lit up. "What's 'three stars' mean?"

Nelson held the vial up against the fading sunlight. "Well, in Cynthia's case, she had big boobs, but just laid there, Miss Moaner but couldn't pump up a flat bicycle tire."

Brody picked a vial with blond strands in it. "Martha.

265

Altoona, Pennsylvania," he read the label, chuckling between words.

"Dit it *taste* like tuna?" Fletcher asked Nelson.

"October nineteen sixty-four," Treat contined. "Four stars."

"I used to call her Magic Lips," Nelson frowned. "Threw herself in front of a freight train when we moved."

"You must move around a lot." Lee had a vial out now. "Albany, New York...two stars..."

"What's the name?" Nelson glanced up, preoccupation in his eyes.

"Christina."

"Oh, yah...Topheavy Tina. She was really into kinky stuff. I was glad to get outta her apartment with my life!"

"Your life?"

"Thought she was snorin' pretty good when I brought out the trusty ol' scissors, but she woke up, disarmed me, so to speak, and chased me twenty blocks in the buff before some transit cop decked her."

"Wow."

"Yah, *two* wow-wow's."

Out of the corner of his eye, Brody noticed Lt. Vance leaving the supply tent. Still without any OD green T-shirts, he was heading back over to where they encircled Nelson's collection. "Here comes trouble."

"With a capital *T*." Fletcher spotted the officer too and also decided they'd never be able to disperse quickly enough. But *Choi-oi* came to their rescue.

"Darn mutt!" Vance was trying to kick the mongrel loose, but Echo Company's mascot had its jaw locked on the lieutenant's pants leg. "Beat it!"

"What about *this* one?" Cordova was holding up a vialful of gold-brown samples. "It's got five stars on it, but nothing else."

Choi-oi had trotted off after a daring magpie, and Vance stood behind him now.

"Oh, that one's from my mother." Nelson beamed proudly.

"Your MOTHER?" every head in the group turned to face him.

Avoiding their eyes, Nelson shrugged his shoulders. "Well, not my real mother. I never knew *her*. But my play mother."

"What the flying fuck is a play mother?" Fletcher's chest expanded.

266

"His *step* mother, right?" Lee had heard the term before.

"Yep. Now this one"—Nelson held up two more vials—"is from a former cherry girl in Oklahoma. And this one's from a whore in Frankfurt. The cherry girl had big tits, though . . . ."

"Wait a minute! Wait a minute!" said Fletcher. "I wanna know more about your 'play mother.'"

"Not much to tell." Nelson was good at shrugging his shoulders.

"We got all night," replied Larson.

"Well, she popped my cherry when I was thirteen."

"Thirteen?" Lee sounded envious.

"Yah. We moved around a lot. My old man was career military, and after he retired at 38, went into sales. Traveled all the time. My play mother was only five years older than me when I came home from school one afternoon, and she was lying on the couch with nothin' but a see-through nightie on, pretending to be asleep. I went over for a closer look, and next thing I knew she was sittin' on my face and puttin' a liplock on the ol' ding-dong."

"Holy moly." Lee hadn't been this impressed in quite a while.

"Yah. I wasn't quite sure what was goin' down at first," Nelson giggled, confident he had the entire squad in the palm of his hand now. "If you get my drift."

Fletcher led them in another round of laughter. "Do you still see her?" Cordova asked.

"Nah, not since I enlisted. Dad doesn't like her to get near military camps."

"I can't understand why," Brody said sarcastically. "You fucking *enlisted*?" Larson's smile disappeared.

"Sure. Didn't every—"

"Jesus." The Professor walked away, shaking his head. "Another RA lifer in the making. Why don't they send 'em all to Delta?"

"I have to give my play mother credit," Nelson was saying. "She had one hell of a bag o' tricks up her pantyhose."

"Do you have a pic—" Fletcher started to ask for a photograph when Lt. Vance's shadow fell across Nelson's face.

"Don't you men have something better do do?" the officer asked. "I thought for sure I'd be smellin' some boot polish on

267

the air by now. . . ."

"We were just about to break out the Kiwi, sir." Brody motioned the soldiers in the direction of the tent halves covering Larson's bunker. It was time to discuss strategy.

When they were safely concealed beneath the Hell Hole's reinforced planks, Larson said, "I can see that bastard is going to be a real pain in the ass."

"Some one better help the good lieutenant see the light real soon," Fletcher said, "or person or persons unknown with less of a sense of humor than myself might elect to introduce the sonofabitch to the business end of a frag and—"

Brody's hand came up, demanding silence. Nelson and Chappell might still be lingering outside. "Cool it, Snakeman," he said. "We get your drift, brother."

"It's only a matter of time." Lee offered his own bit of wisdom.

A woman's voice outside reached their ears. "Sounds like one of the housegirls," Cordova offered. She was arguing loudly with one of the perimeter MPs.

Brody's people all climbed back up to the bunker entrance in time to see two military policemen leading an angry-looking mama-san off the compound to a waiting *canh-sat* Land Rover. "Was she trickin' without a VD card?" The Whoremonger laughed as one of the MPs flipped him the thumbs-up.

"Misappropriating government property for resale on the Pleiku black market." The MP grinned, holding up a roll of toilet paper. "Had a balloon full o' Thai heroin stuffed up her ying-yang, too." He nodded triumphantly. "At least that's what we suspect it is. We'll have to wait for the lab results from CID and—"

Brody didn't want to hear all that. "Bet you dirty old bicycle-seat lickers really got off on the strip search, eh?"

Frowning in mock revulsion, the MP held his nose but did not make any further comment. Brody thought he saw something furry protruding from the bundle the old woman was carrying—a tail wagging, or something—but *Choi-oi* didn't even have one anymore, so he didn't pay it much attention.

"Hey, Treat!" Larson was calling up to him. "Did you notice this?"

"Why don't you two newbies come on down into our. . .

268

parlor?" Brody wrapped an arm around Chappell's shoulder, feeling as if his kid brother had come to visit him. "I think Lee's got a fresh pot o' brew perking."

"You might as well join us too," Fletcher told Nelson, who, with the help of his pubic hair collection, had been the first newby ever to win Snakeman's friendship so quickly.

Back down in the bunker, Larson handed Brody a piece of paper that had been taped to the You Have Never Lived Until You've Almost Died plaque. "I don't know if it's a joke, or what."

Brody suddenly swallowed hard as he read by the light of the glowing C-4:

Spec-4 Brody,
I take dog. You want back, you leave
$100 at big tamarind tree on road to
Pleiku. You no want, okay, we eat!

The hand-scribbled note was unsigned. "That fucking mama-san!" He charged up the sandbags. "That bitch stole *Choi-oi!*"

By the time he reached the ground, the Land Rover's tail-lights were but a dim red glow a half mile down the access road from the compound's main gate. Brody sprinted over to one of the MP jeeps, but the sentries were unsympathetic.

"We can't send a unit out to chase down the VNPs over a dog," one of them told him.

"Besides"—a buck sergeant sat down behind one of the vehicle's steering wheels and began filling out a clipboard—"we just got a directive down from Division. They got another rabies epidemic gettin' out of hand in Pleiku City. The general says no more mutt mascots. He says all indigenous mongrels are to be shot on the spot as a precautionary measure and—"

"What?" Brody couldn't believe what he was hearing. He glanced down the roadway again; maybe he could catch up with the Land Rover on foot if he chucked the jungle boots.

"Hey, I don't make the bullshit rules around here, Whore-monger. I just enforce 'em."

"I got twenty bucks on me." Broday rifled through his pockets. "It's yours if you loan me your jeep for just—"

The alert scrambler high atop Col. Buchanan's command post began wailing suddenly.

"Oh, shit." The MPs all began putting on their flak jackets and replacing helmet liners with steel pots. The *hi-lo* siren could mean anything from a rescue mission going out to incoming ordnance.

"Let's go!" Zack had emerged from the CP with three rifles in his hands. "Into the choppers!" His eyes were searching for Chappell and Nelson, the only newbies who hadn't checked out weapons yet. "The Green Berets at Plei Me are calling for help!"

BOOK 3
ISLAND MAGIC

CHAPTER 27

An unusually merciless sun had been beating down on the Central Highlands for nine hours when the gaggle of Hueys limped back into camp. Riddled with bullets, many of the gunships pranged across the landing pad tarmac, their pilots exhausted. Door gunners leaning against their swivel mounts and infantrymen sitting on the edge of the open hatch of each bird all displayed that thousand-yard stare common to battle-weary troops. Faces were blackened with gunpowder and soot. Blood leaked from shrapnel holes in the floorboards.

After *Pegasus* set down, Spec-4 Brody was the first to drop to the ground. The entire flight back, he had been planning to kiss the earth if they weren't shot from the sky by a final, farewell burst of tracers, but when his jungle boots finally touched solid laterite, he merely pulled his ruck and rifle from the cabin and started for his tent, dragging them through the red dust behind him. He spoke to no one.

Brody glanced at his watch as he started down the sandbagged steps into the Hell Hole. The cracked crystal had stopped on October 19th. They had been out in the boonies three days, yet it had seemed three years.

The Special Forces camp at Plei Me had been saved, but none of Brody's people would ever be the same.

He glanced up. Fletcher and Larson started down the steps, bringing that warm feeling back into the bunker, but something was still missing. He stared over at the thick wood plank jutting out from the packed earth wall halfway up the steps. The plank where *Choi-oi* always used to lie with his chops resting on his front paws as he watched their every move, guarding his buddies from the VC and the lifers and the Vietnamese women. The crazy dog hated Vietnamese women—especially housegirls and prostitutes. Yes, poor old *Choi-oi* was what was missing.

No one else in the squad seemed to care enough about the mutt's fate at the hands of his dognappers to chip in any scrip for the ransom. Not even after Brody reminded them about all the times *Choi-oi's* howling fits had warned them about mortars whistling through the air and descending in their direction. On the hairy chopper ride over to Plei Me he'd even gone so far as to ask Zack for the hundred-dollar loan. But the money sat folded up in his pocket now. Three days had passed. It would be a waste of time to leave the MPCs beside the big tamarind now. *Choi-oi* was surely the source of indigestion in a score of Montagnarde bellies already. He'd just have to return the money to Leo. *Life's a bitch and then you die,* he repeated the phrase to himself. *Choi-oi* and Plei Me and his desire to kill a mama-san was behind him. It was time to start living that day to day, miserable GI existence again.

"I'm sure gonna miss that goofy doper mutt, *Choi-oi.*" Fletcher said as Brody pulled a block of C-4 from his ruck and whittled a sliver into the pit. He needed some army brew right now even more than a can of lukewarm beer.

"Yah, me too," said Larson. They were obviously trying to make him feel better. But Brody felt *Choi-oi* had been betrayed by the others in the Pack, and he felt they deserved the silent treatment for a while.

Stripping off his shirt and trousers, Brody walked over to the outdoor showers wearing only his jungle boots and a flak jacket. He ignored the cluster of housegirls giggling at him as he soaped himself down. They always seemed to gather within view of the poorly screened shower stalls to wash laundry and perform their seamstress duties and watch the soldiers bathe. Zack maintained the Vietnamese employees did not view nudity in the same light Westerners did, and that showering naked in front of them was something they were used to, but Brody could never quite get over the feeling a trick had been played on him. If they were ignoring him, then why were they always giggling like that?

Tonight Brody didn't pay any attention to the housegirls. He soaped himself down and concentrated on the good times he'd had with *Choi-oi*, but Lt. Vance's face kept popping into his thoughts as he listened to one of the seamstresses humming a traditional, sad war ballad in her singsong voice.

Vance. He had not really done that bad at Plei Me, for a newby officer. But he made it plain he had no combat experience and was too proud to take the suggestions of his enlisted men and put them to good use. That would come with time, Brody

273

knew. He just hoped they all survived the lieutenant's transitional period.

Second Platoon had been lucky at Plei Me. It had suffered no physical casualties, though, he recalled, Chappell and Nelson had weathered quite an initiation into Hell's elite. The two newbies, along with Cordova, Broken Arrow, Lee, and Mohammed, were part of a contingent of reinforcements assigned to stay behind at the Special Forces camp in the face of anticipated secondary assaults by the NVA, but Brody didn't think the compound would see any more action any time soon.

"Attention, all personnel in the company area...." the loudspeaker atop the CP's array of antennae was blaring suddenly, intruding into his thoughts. "Report in zero-five for a muster along landing pad Echo. Colonel Buchanan has a few words for you gentlemen who just got in from Plei Me."

Brody did not rush to rinse himself off. Instead, he applied more soap. There was no hot water in the huge tank suspended over the shower stalls, but hours beneath the steaming sun had made it luke warm, and he leaned hard into the chain handle that released a fine spray above.

He closed his eyes and immediately saw the fighting at Plei Me reenacted over and over again. Trees were burning in the jungle, flares were floating on the night mist, tracers were arcing back and forth on both sides, guerrillas were hanging from bangalore torpedoes across the wire, and a husky North Vietnamese soldier was suddenly standing in full view on the other side of the clearing from Brody's position. Holding a LAW, a Light Anti-Tank Weapon and pointing it directly at his squad, the communist hesitated for only a moment as he adjusted his sights, and that was all the time Treat needed. Unleashing an entire banana clip on full-automatic, he watched the tracers cut the man in half. As he crumpled backward, the shoulder-launched rocket soared skyward in a wild climb, out of control.

It passed up between two South Vietnamese Air Force jets that were swooping in low to drop napalm on the NVA positions, disappeared into the belly of some heavy storm clouds drifting over the battlefield, and exploded with a ferocity that seemed to create a sudden if brief downpour.

"The LAW is the law," he remembered Fletcher saying as they watched the smoking chunks of fiery shrapnel arc back

274

down to earth.

Brody knew there were mortar shells that were so sensitive they sometimes detonated within clouds dense with rainwater on their way to the target, but he had never heard of a LAW doing that.

Brody took his time rinsing the soap from his face and hair as Buchanan's voice came over the loudspeaker system.

"You gentlemen are to be commended for a job well done," he was saying. "You may not have seen me at Plei Me, but I was there, flying over the battle in a Charlie-Charlie, helping the officers on the ground direct strategy, and it has been some time, I must admit, since I've seen such courage and ingenuity displayed on the battlefield. But we will have plenty of time later to hand out medals. I feel you all deserve a brief explanation and synopsis about what you've participated in these last few days, and what we feel the North Vietnamese have planned for Ia Drang and the Central Highlands."

After the soap rinsed away, Brody peeked out through sore lids and noticed four housegirls were standing along the wire mesh wall twenty yards away, their fingers in the loops like baseball fans leaning against a backstop, watching him shower. Without changing facial expression, he turned around, bent over, and began soaping down his legs again, giving them a full moon at dusk to ponder.

"The arrival of the First Cavalry Division in the Pleiku area has coincided with an NVA plan to cut South Vietnam in half," Buchanan was saying. "Their initial strategy was to attack the Special Forces camp at Plei Me in hopes the area ARVN commander would commit his troops in a relief attempt. The communists would then ambush and destroy said relief column. Such a large number of reinforcements moving toward Plei Me would weaken the remaining regional defense positions, the NVA felt, and they could then attack these camps also. Once the region was under North Vietnamese control, their units could then regroup and drive eastward to the coast, effectively severing South Vietnam.

"But our crafty allies got wise to the plan"—Buchanan laughed over the PA—"and had our people from the First Team supplement their relief column. In fact, *we* airlifted the Arvins in by chopper, which kind of threw a Chi-Com into old Minh's spokes." Scattered cheers rose from different parts of the camp, but it was not the bravado that normally would have been heard following a successful mission. "Artillery and air support also helped ARVN repel the attacks, as you men all well know.

"It took three days of vicious fighting, but we. . .*you* reached the SF camp and were able to reinforce the defenders. We've left some men behind at Plei Me to make sure the NVA don't try some kind of last-ditch suicidal bullshit, but our intel tells us the vast majority of the North Vietnamese are retreating toward the Cambodian border. The Thirty-third NVA Regiment, which provided the bulk of the attackers against the Green Berets, has been ordered by Hanoi to withdraw across the border along with the Thirty-second and Sixty-sixth regiments, which have also been in the area."

Brody, still bent over at the waist, glanced up between his knees at the housegirls. He motioned for the youngest, prettiest one to come into the shower stall and join him, but they all giggled and ran away, holding their hands over smiles and a torrent of birdlike chatter.

"And now for the good news." Buchanan's tone turned sarcastic. "You all get four hours of sleep and then it's back on the slicks for a high-speed jaunt out into the sticks. General Westmoreland was extremely pleased with our performance at Plei Me. But he is convinced more can be done. He is ordering the 1st Brigade of the First Air Cav into the jungle west of Plei Me."

"Why the fuck would we wanna do that!?" Several groans rose in unison across the Turkey Farm.

Buchanan clearly heard them. "Our gunships are to seek out and engage the North Vietnamese soldiers before they can successfully retreat across the border into Cambodia. We are now the exterminators, gentlemen, and the NVA have become bigger cockroaches than they've ever been before. We are to seek out and destroy the NVA before they can reach sanctuary. Westy doesn't want to see a red-and-gold flag flying beneath any rainforest canopy of the Central Highlands."

276

CHAPTER 28

Brody was getting high just breathing in all the gunsmoke. It was an adrenaline high—not narcotic—and he leaned into the M-60's handles as he fired down at the treetops, sucking it in and loving every second of it.

"Gonna be a hot LZ," Krutch advised over the intercom as they descended in a tight circle down toward the clearing. Tracers glowing hot-green tore up through the floorboards, and some type of projectile Brody could not identify roared in one hatch and out the other without exploding. Whatever it was, the thing left a billowing trail of smoke in the chopper's cabin.

"Bookoo muzzle flashes on the whiskey side," Brody wanted to yell into his headset mike, but he forced himself to remain calm as one belt ran out and he dragged another can under the machine gun. "Got bookoo hostiles on—"

"They're on *all* sides!" the Stork advised him as the Huey flared into a hover below the treetops and began its landing. "But got no choice now. Settin' it down." He clicked-off and glanced back over a shoulder. "Hold on to your asses!" he yelled at the six infantrymen preparing to jump out both side hatches.

Larson was among them. Brody looked up at the Professor as he slapped a fresh ammo belt in place and flipped him a thumbs-up. All of the grunts *except* Larson were jumping up and down, growling and screaming war cries as they psyched eaach other up.

"My address book!" Larson yelled above the constant thumping of rotors beating overhead as Brody fired off long, sustained bursts at figures darting through the tree line on the banks of the Tae River.

"What!?" Brody sounded irritated. He didn't have time for conversation. They were only ten feet off the ground now, and soldiers were already jumping down into the tall elephant grass.

"My address book!" Larson repeated. "It's back in the bunker! It's got my kid sister's address in it! It's got a safety-deposit-box key, and some cash inside it! If anything happens to me—"

"Ain't nothin' gonna happen to ya!" Zack clamped a hand over his shoulder and propelled him out the hatch.

Krutch watched him roll through the reeds, missing by only a few inches a man who'd been impaled on a ten-foot-high bamboo stake.

"Do you see that guy, Zack?" Krutch clicked in. He was referring to the soldier who jumped down onto the green pole. The stake had ripped straight up through his stomach and was protruding a couple of feet above his shoulder blades. The man's feet were a yard off the earth. His body appeared lifeless.

"Yah! Take 'er down a little more, and I'll see if I can grab hold o' him!"

The bamboo stakes were hidden throughout likely landing areas by the VC and NVA, in hopes of destroying helicopters by snapping their rotors, but this time an unlucky trooper had discovered the poles the hard way. He had died so that *Pegasus* could live.

Krutch, who had been firing his mini-guns at running targets of opportunity, concentrated now on bringing the craft's skids closer to the soldier suspended from the stake. With Brody and Fletcher firing constantly, Zack managed to grab the dead man by the back of his flak jacket collar and hoist him up into the cabin. The floorboards quickly became soaked and sticky with his blood. "He's gone." Zack's fingers were against the corporal's throat, and he spoke through the intercom for the record.

The craft was lighter now that all of its passengers except one had dismounted, and Krutch, using an evasive maneuver, ascended above the treetops quickly, then banked sharply out of the clearing to monitor the action on the ground.

It was November first, and an Air Cavalry squadron had spotted enemy troops moving along the Tae River. Ten helicopters brought over seventy-five soldiers in to saturate the area with Cavalry troopers, and five of the slicks had dropped men off ahead of Krutch. Birds had landed in front and behind of *Pegasus,* and now two more were touching down.

"Gimme a better angle, Stork!" Fletcher was calling over the intercom. "I can see a whole *mess* o' pith helmets bobbin' about down there, but I need a better—"

Krutch had seen them too, and he was banking high on purpose: He planned to take the North Vietnamese out himself, using the XM-21 mounted in the Huey's nose. "Hold on to your ass, Snakeman, while a real hero shows you how it's done!"

But Krutch pulled back at the last moment. The Americans and Vietnamese were clashing on the ground now. They were too close together for him to risk a shot at this range.

"Damnit," the Stork cussed.

Brody was slipping his python head on. He could feel it, they were going to get close today. Close to the enemy. Close enough for him to cause some cardiacs if his shooting skills weren't good enough.

"Got a squad retreating to the Sierra-Echo over there," the peter pilot clicked-in and pointed.

"Bad guys?" Krutch's neck stretched.

"Roger. Ten-plus."

"Rog. Hey, Whoremonger. I owe you one chump. You can have these guys."

Krutch brought the gunship into a dive, swooped past the running NVA only a few feet over their heads, then circled around on the right, and flared out so that Brody's MG was pointing at them.

The Whoremonger had been firing even before he had anything in his sights. They'd done it this way before. He knew Krutch would have him blocking the retreating soldiers' path with the helicopter itself, and playing those kinds of games could get hairy.

All twelve Vietnamese were catapulted backwards by the long burst even before he could steady the M-60 on any one soldier.

"Not bad for an enlisted man." Krutch had dropped down between several trees until he was only a few feet off the ground and now, nose down, he ascended again.

A shoulder-fired rocket impacted against one of the palms, and the rolling concussion shook *Pegasus* violently, but she remained in the air.

"Anyone see where the hell *that* came from?" Zack asked, but it didn't matter, the helicopter was already several hundred yards on the other side of the river and circling around again. Two Cobras swooped past below them, converging on the puff of smoke where the black-pajama-clad man holding the LAW had been standing.

"Was that who I think it was?" Krutch had been concentrating on the terrain and hadn't gotten as good a look at the Cobras as his door gunners had.

"Yah!" Fletcher answered as he fired small bursts at a sampan negotiating some outcroppings of rocks in the middle of the river. "Sharkskinner and Snake Eye."

"That cocksucking Warlokk!" Krutch laughed. "Never happy unless he's in the middle of the shit!"

The sampan had been flying a red North Vietnamese flag with a yellow star in the center, and Fletcher's first burst ripped the middle of the small boat in half. Zack cheered as it split apart and sank. Those passengers that hadn't been hit—there were five communists in uniform aboard—dove into the water, and Snakeman raked the waves with additional bursts.

"Way to go, Lawless!" The peter pilot watched rocket pods on the Cobra unload, and an entire hillside disappeared beneath a blanket of black smoke as several trees began to fall.

"I don't think he got the bastard," Brody muttered.

"Sure he did," the peter pilot responded. "Wanna put some scrip down on it?"

"Ain't got the time." Krutch was switching frequencies. "The Bull wants us over on the November-Whiskey to search for stragglers." They watched a Huey with a large red cross on a white background swerve in and out of the smoke left by Warlokk's rocket attack and disappear beyond a clump of trees.

"There goes Gunslinger Gabriel." Fletcher identified the tail-boom numbers.

"You guys and your nicknames." Zack shook his head.

"We could get a real party goin' here." Brody was firing at suspicious bushes now. There were no more NVA to be found.

The initial firefight that Shawn Larson participated in on the ground lasted less than an hour. When their follow-up sweep was completed, over one hundred North Vietnamese Regulars were accounted for. Their bodies were buried in a mass grave on the south side of the Tae River. Blood trails in the elephant grass revealed twice as many wounded were dragged off into the jungle.

Five Americans died in the riverside shoot-out. One was the soldier who jumped down onto the giant bamboo stake.

"We have a tunnel complex over here." Brody listened to radio traffic on the ground. "An entire field hospital and boo-koo documents."

Krutch and the other slick pilots set their Hueys down on high ground while the Cobras remained in the air, prowling for more enemy guerrillas. A black Loach C&C chopper swirled down from just below the clouds as all the gunsmoke began drifting away, and it landed in the middle of the most secured clearing.

Colonel Neil Buchanan was on the ground only five minutes when he radioed Division, asking for several dozen more slicks filled with First Cav troopers. "Something's wrong here," he told his aides as they rounded up the captured weapons and documents. "Something's terribly wrong." The Bull had a bad feeling about those hills rising beside the Tae River.

And it was a good thing he called for reinforcements.

NVA officers quickly regrouped, massing their men on the jungled hilltops surrounding the initial battlefield. Emerging from a heavily camouflaged cave entrance on a distant cliff overlooking the valley, Major Lam Van Minh scanned his defenses for several minutes with a pair of high-powered binoculars, gauged the amount of American firepower at his doorstep, then ordered his men—who outnumbered the First Cav troopers eight to one—to attack.

A few moments after the first shots were fired, additional helicopter gunships swept over the hilltops in a dramatic arrival, and, though the communists still outnumbered the Americans, managed to drive the converging NVA companies back, deep into the rain forest.

"Our interpreters have advised me the documents your men captured provided MI with much needed intelligence about North Vietnamese activities in the region," Buchanan told his officers. "We have definitely been doing battle with the Thirty-third NVA Regiment, and remnants of the Thirty-second and Sixty-sixth. Their reasons for it are beyond me, but the commies have detailed on the captured maps their intended escape routes should they happen to engage us and come out on the losing end.

"I want the boys in Echo Company," he told Lt. Vance and

281

two captains, "to plant some black boxes in these areas and lay some counter-ambushes." He rolled out the acetate and began scribbling lines, X's and L's across certain sectors of the area.

"Counter-ambushes, sir?" Vance stared across the makeshift table fashioned from four C-ration cases nailed together.

"I guarantee you the bad bad NVA aren't cowering in their dark tunnels, young man. We had one Lurp team fired upon two hours ago at these cords." The Colonel ran his forefinger along some ridges signifying rises in elevation. "If the Viets hadn't stumbled off-sides and pissed off the five machine gunners who happened to be leading the squad, I'd be writing letters home to loved ones right about now."

"Uh, right."

"Now take that group of misfits led by the hot dog with the python mask, and bring me back a body count," he told Vance.

"Python mask, sir?"

"Never mind," one of the captains said. "We know who he's talking about."

"We'll introduce you to Snakeman and the Whore-monger. . ."

". . . And the whole goofy group."

"I think I've already met them."

"This sucks the big one, Treat. You know that, don't ya.? This really sucks the big one." Fletcher was complaining about the black box mission. He didn't like playing foot soldier. His place was aboard the gunships, though he seldom pulled actual door gunner duty. "This stretch o' woods really gives me the creeps, I'm tellin' you. It makes the hairs on the back of my neck stand up."

"I know what you mean, Fletch. Believe me, I know what you mean."

Ten to twenty of the detection relay devices were to be plant-ed, Zack advised them. They were a good two miles away from the heavily fortified camp beside the Tae River and had buried half the boxes when Snakeman voiced his concern.

With men sent out several dozen meters in all four directions to provide security, Brody went to work again. Two holes were dug a few feet apart from each other behind foliage near trails or disturbed areas showing recent use.

282

"Perfect." He nodded, examining the monovial windows, which verified the black boxes were implanted level with the earth's surface. He arranged plants, broken ferns, and logs around the devices, careful not to use material that might attract larger animals. "Now life gets tricky." He removed the self-destruct safety wires. Enemy troops could not remove the boxes now without triggering a lethal blast.

The devices sent radio messages back to a receiver, signaling observers when there were ground vibrations—such as those made by passing troops or vehicles—in the area, as well as human sweat or uric acid. Unfortunately the mechanisms could not differentiate among North Vietnamese soldiers and elephants or leopards.

Five minutes later, they were digging again. "Well, what do we have here?" Fletcher and Larson's entrenching tools had struck something solid.

"Time to bring out the bolo beans." Snakeman dropped his ruck to the ground, basked for a few moments in the exhilaration of the carefree, lightness he felt when not carrying the heavy pack, then pulled a cigar box out.

Every man there knew what the Whoremonger had discovered: an enemy ammunition cache.

Fletcher picked ten cartridges from the box. "How many?" he asked Brody, who had slipped the blade of his commando knife into the buried footlocker's hasps and pried the lid open.

"Looks like four AK-47s and 'bout a dozen magazines. Can you handle that?"

"No sweat, GI." Fletcher selected two more bullets to fit the Kalashnikovs.

Larson frowned and turned away as he watched what they were about to do. He'd heard of this type of procedure—booby-trapping weapons the enemy had hidden for future use—but had never actually seen someone do it.

The *bolo beans* were ammunition tampered with in a way that caused them to explode on discharge. Rather than powder within the crimped brass expanding to force a lead bullet down a barrel toward its target, the rifle's firing pin detonated either a plastic explosives charge implanted within the cartridge, or the ammo blew up because the neck of the cartridge around the bullet had been over-crimped, preventing the lead from escaping.

283

With nowhere to go, the explosive gases disintegrated the seams around the primer, in effect, forcing the weapon to explode in the soldier's face. Bolts slammed back through a sharpshooter's eyes were not uncommon.

"Okay." Brody had replaced the cartridges at the top of each magazine with a bolo bean. "Let's get it all put back exactly the way we found it and bury the sonofabitch before—"

Sporadic shooting erupted over a hilltop in the distance, and all the men except two proned-out against the earth. "Wish I could see the suckers fire their first and last shots using this crap." Fletcher laughed grimly as he and Brody worked to rebury the footlocker.

"Could be months before they make it back to this spot," Brody replied. "Or, could be minutes." He motioned toward the exchange of gunfire up ahead. It was reaching a dull crescendo, and lightninglike flashes lit up the night as several gunships swooped past overhead and unleashed their rocket pods beyond the string of hilltops.

"Those chopper jocks know we're down here, don't they?" Larson was getting worried as bits and pieces of shrapnel whizzed through the branches several yards above their boonie hats. Brody and Snakeman loved it when the mission allowed them to don the floppy covers, but Larson felt insecure without his steel pot.

"I hope so." Brody glanced at his maps and compass. A tingling sensation raced down his spine for a second as he worried a mistake in his topographical skills might have caused a repeat of the earlier incident with Lee, but they were right on course.

"Maybe we better call in," Larson suggested.

"No way." Fletcher shook his head. "Zack wants us maintaining radio silence, you know that. Radio fucking silence on all black box larks. It's SOP, Professor.

"Yah, fuck SOP and this whole excuse for a picnic." Several additional gunships had swooped into the area and seemed to be ringing the valley on the other side of the hills. Nose cannons pointed toward the center of the clearing that Brody was sure must lie beyond the treetops, they were unloading with everything they had.

"What the heck." Fletcher reflected the concerns felt by every man there. The Hueys were dispersing. Rapidly. Though

284

secondary explosions were now sending shrapnel and fireballs up into the clouds drifting low across the jungle, the helicopters were pulling back. All of them.

"I'm gettin' bad vibes about this, Snakeman," Brody told Fletcher. "Bookoo bad vibes, brother."

The thump of multiple rotors was growing more distant with each passing second as green tracers continued to arc up into the night in random bursts. *Desperate bursts,* feared Elliot. "It's not vibes you're feeling," he told Treat as the hair began to stand up on the back of his own neck. The air currents pressed down on them as he spoke. Big blades were chopping at the hot, muggy night, something huge was passing overhead.

"A Chinook?" Larson's eyes locked onto Brody.

The Whoremonger hesitated only a moment longer. "Dig in!" he yelled, abandoning all caution now. "It's a goddamned skycrane!"

The men all broke out their folding shovels and tore into the rainforest floor. It was soft, and accommodating, they didn't need foxholes. Just enough of a depression to squeeze their bodies down below the surface of the—

A blinding flash ripped away the darkness with a grinding screech that turned night into day and threatened to melt the eardrums of every man on Brody's team. "Prepare for the blast!" he was yelling as he flattened himself into the mud and clay and dirt, hoping he wouldn't become part of the dust of death. *Just get me outta one more, Buddha, ol' buddy. . .just one more and I'll—* "Prepare for the—" he was yelling over his thoughts when the wall of trees flew past over them with a rumbling, almost quiet delicacy. And then the roar swept over the hillsides after them, and the air was sucked from Brody's lungs. He felt sure the hair on his scalp and the skin along his back and buttocks and all his clothing were being peeled away, and then the pressure against his skull and his thoughts and his very ability to continue breathing became so intense he cried for his mother. One time, and without any words leaving his throat.

And then he blacked out.

The CH-54 Tarhe "flying crane" had dropped a 10,000-pound bomb on a North Vietnamese position only eighteen hundred meters from where Brody's people had been planting the bolo beans.

Shaking the daze from his head, Brody glanced up from his trench in time to see the bottom of a nukelike mushroom cloud rising up through the luminous glow of rippling heat blanketing the earth.

The Hueys were back. They criss-crossed the area, flying dangerously close to one another as they bathed the kill zone with powerful spotlights.

"Mother*fuckers*!" Brody pushed hinself up out of the dust. His uniform had been ripped from his body. Lacerations covered his flesh from heat to toe. But the M-16 he had cradled beneath his frame inside the shallow trench was still intact.

Fletcher, just as naked, laughed at Brody's appearance as the Whoremonger stood up slowly, rifle in hand but wearing not a stitch. "Fuck you, Snakeman!" Treat was in no mood to humor anyone. It had been a miracle they all were not killed! He glanced around at the other soldiers crawling out from under layers of bark, shredded mushrooms and monkey fur. "You guys okay?"

Larson's trousers were in shreds below the belt. His flak jacket was still intact. He started counting heads. "I think everyone made it," he told Brody.

One soldier wavered on his knees from side to side. His clothes, too, had been ripped from his body. His limbs were streaked with blood, but the wounds appeared superficial, mostly splinters from the trees. "I think I 'enjoyed' getting a VC flag nailed to my back a bit more than *that* firecrackers display," Patterson moaned.

"The motherfuckers used a ten-thousand-pounder on us," Brody decided. "Look at the damn cloud, if you don't believe me."

"That shit-for-brains Vance must have overlooked calling our position in." Fletcher's tone was sarcastic. "Wait 'till I get my hands on the little prick."

"If there's anything left of him." Brody searched around for something to clothe himself with, but without success.

Lt. Vance had been with the other black box team, a half klick to the west. Sgt. Zack was showing him the ropes. "Leo shoulda took over if he knew the lieutenant was humpin' through the woods with his head up his ass," Larson said.

"If I know the Black Buddha," responded Brody, "he'll let a West Pointer dig his own grave before opening his mouth. He probably figured it wouldn't hurt to let Vance have the reins for a while. Who'd have guessed Division would send a skycrane down?" He stared at the flames dancing from treetop to treetop in the distance. "Come on. We better go look for the bodies."

The enormous blast had not left a crater. Ten-thousand-pound bombs were equipped with six-foot-long poles attached to their nose cones, so a level explosion at "ground zero" was guaranteed virtually every time. Every human and animal within a one-mile radius was killed by the devastating concussion. A circle the size of a football field was completely cleared of all flora and fauna, and the earth was baked hard and flat. There was absolutely no dust left on the ground.

Shawn Larson had never seen a "Daisy Cutter"—as the huge bombs were called by the GIs—used before. He was convinced President Johnson had finally decided to use tactical nuclear weapons aqainst the North Vietnamese and was hesitant in entering what he was sure to be the danger zone, until Fletcher explained the dynamics of the ordnance to him.

"This is insane," he mumbled when they reached the first hilltop. On the other side, they could see the area leveled by the bomb. It was as if a giant pizza pan had been dropped in the middle of the jungle, pressing one huge section of trees flat. A ring of fire marked the edges of the pan, and outside the ring, trees that hadn't been uprooted by the enormous explosion were pushed outward in odd, diagonal positions, as if planted to keep giant intruders out. But Brody's team just walked between them.

"Over there!" Fletcher ran toward a group of NVA clustered around a tree trunk, firing his rifle from the hip, but the men were already dead. When Brody and the others caught up to him, they realized the Vietnamese had been killed by the blast. Blood ran from their eyes, ears, and noses. And from the gaping tears Snakeman had stitched across their bellies.

"Holy Mother of God." Larson just shook his head from side to side slowly, mesmerized by the sight.

"Better you than me, Luke!" Fletcher was making a show of shaking the dead soldiers' hands, then placing his First Cav, Ace of Spades playing cards between their lips.

"You're goin' straight to hell, Snakeman." Larson spat at the baked earth, and steam rose from the spittle. "Do you fucking realize that?"

"Better to rule in Hell than serve in Heaven, Professor. Didn't none o' your books ever teach ya that?" Fletcher flashed a Death's-head grin as he forced a dead NVA's cheeks into a smile.

Larson closed his eyes tightly as the Texan carefully placed a cigarette in the dead man's mouth and lit it with his Zippo. "Takes nuts to do what you do," Larson sneered. "Takes big fuckin' nuts, Elliot. Brass balls, in fact. How the heck do you live with yourself? How do you sleep at night?"

Fletcher stopped what he was doing and stared over at the Professor for a moment. "Okay." He shook his own head this time. "I get it. You don't want me hoggin' all the fun. Fine." He walked up to Larson and handed him some cards. "Here, you can help spread the word."

Treat Brody turned away from the team when Larson spoke about "nuts," realizing for the first time how naked and vulnerable and...visible he was to the rest of the men in his squad. He flushed as one of the newbies walked past him to see what Fletcher was doing, but the troop didn't seem to notice.

The Whoremonger had lost his left testicle during a mishap as a child. The accident had involved a firearm. His seventeen-year-old cousin brought a magnum revolver over one afternoon when all the adults were off to a party somewhere in the Hollywood Hills. Treat was only thirteen when they broke out the beer and began toying with the weapon. Sitting in expensive rattan chairs across from each other, the older cousin was showing Treat all the safety features on the long-barreled pistol when it suddenly discharged, blowing half his balls off.

It had taken the ambulance only a few minutes to reach the house. Though the pain was creeping up on him, Treat managed to laugh at the shocked expressions on the attendants' faces. His cousin spent the next half hour crying and apologizing...and also laughing along: The blood alcohol in both young Brodys turned out to be point-two-zero—twice the legal limit for motor-vehicle drivers. His mother yelled at him for getting blood on the rattan chairs.

When he finally came down from the beer-induced high, the

pain had been unendurable, but somehow he made it through that month. The doctors sewed him up—what was left of his scrotum—and he was just thankful the slug had not severed his penis. At least he still had something to handle. . .something to entertain the ladies with in years to come. The injury did not seem to affect his sex drive or performance, and was barely noticeable in a room with the lights turned down low.

It was no longer dark in the Ia Drang Valley. Flares were drifting down through the pall of smoke in all directions. "Ain't this a trip?" Patterson was walking by now, too, but he didn't seem to notice either.

Can't walk around with my hand over my balls, he decided. *That would only get their attention.* He stared down at Fletcher and Larson. *They shouldn't be staring at my whanger anyway . . .Real men avoid staring at other guys below the belt, right?*

"Let's move it!" he directed, and the soot-covered, nude warriors followed him down through the broken bamboo, avoiding the clearing.

Vance's squad was engaging a superior enemy force when Brody's people finally located them. "Get your asses down!" Zack was yelling as the automatic-weapons fire from a distant tree line increased. "The bastards got an MG!"

"What the hell happened to you men?" Lt. Vance was keeping a radio receiver to his ear. He had just finished calling for a Cobra.

"The Daisy Cutter got 'em." Zack realized immediately. "We happened onto a cave back there," he told Brody and the others, "right before we saw the flash. Straight out of a nuclear nightmare, wasn't it?" His bright teeth flashed against the darkness as flares dropped behind the newcomers. "We were comin' down through this gulley to check on ground zero—the lieutenant here wanted to pick up a couple souvenirs." Zack spoke without assigning blame—he was not accusing the lieutenant of anything they all hadn't done a time or two in the past. "When that group of dug-in NVA over there unloaded on us."

"I figure there's about a dozen of 'em." An enlisted man holding binoculars to his eyes was estimating the size of the enemy force.

"Holy shi—" The lieutenant rose slightly from where they

were all lying prone behind several logs to get a better look at the shadows suddenly darting about beneath flickering flares: At least a hundred North Vietnamese, bayonets sparkling on the ends of their rifle barrels, were charging toward the Americans.

CHAPTER 29

Warm rotorwash from a gunship hovering fifty feet above his face woke Brody. He instinctively reached for his weapon only to realize it was still clutched in his hand—the pistol grip anyway—the rest of the weapon had been destroyed by shrapnel. He rolled over slowly, tasting the dirt and bits of lead in his mouth, overjoyed to find he still had all his limbs.

A medical-evacuation helicopter was on the ground beside him, rotors swishing lazily—almost in slow motion, his mind told him. He could still hear deafening explosions in his ears, but there were no shells bursting as before, no smoke swirling about, obscuring everything. "You're okay, Whorehealer!" Zack was calling down to him as he helped lift a stretcher onto Gabriel's Dustoff slick. "Knocked you on your ass, but you're okay, son! Snakeoil, too! I checked him myself!"

Brody couldn't imitate the NCO's smile. He couldn't summon the enthusiasm from deep in his gut as he recalled now what had just happened five, maybe ten minutes ago.

Lt. Vance had called mortars down on their own position.

It was coming back to him quickly now: Wave upon wave of North Vietnamese sappers had rushed their position, but the M-60s being manned by Sgt. Zack himself and a trooper Brody didn't recognize whittled the communists down to manageable numbers. Until the Americans began running low on ammunition.

The NVA seemed to have no shortage of soldiers to field, and the gunships Vance had ordered had yet to arrive. The lieutenant panicked when Zack suggested—no, *ordered* him—to radio for artillery support. The officer had called in the wrong coordinates, and good men had died because of his mistake.

As the first wave of mortars slammed down among them, Zack took the radio and guided the projectiles off, until they were falling in the midst of the charging Vietnamese, and soon after, Warlokk and his gunships swooped in to finish off the survivors.

Vance had not sustained a scratch.

"This is it!" Larson was walking around in circles, kicking over discarded equipment and licking his wounds. "This is fucking *it!* I can't take any more crap! If Charlie don't kill me, our own leaders will! We're screwed if we do, and motherfuckin' screwed if we don't."

"I'm sorry!" Vance was still on his knees, bandaging a dead man. A boy, really. A teenager with no head.

"FUCK YOU, Lieutenant!" Larson whirled around, only to stalk off, away from the officer. "Nobody's *talkin'* to you!"

"I'm sorry!" Vance locked eyes with Brody. "Anybody coulda made the same mistake. We were under fire. We were bein' attacked, for Christsake! Just a number. . . Just one lousy number!"

"Is that it?" Dustoff pilot Gabriel was shouting down to Zack as they loaded the last casualty aboard.

The tall black NCO responded with a thumbs-up, and Gunslinger pulled pitch, his craft ascending.

There was no dust to shield their faces against, the Daisy Cutter had taken care of that. "I was only off by one lousy number," the lieutenant was mumbling to himself and anyone who would listen.

As soon as the green Huey with red crosses on its sides was gone, Krutch's gunship dropped down from the night sky to take its place. A jealous pang shot through Brody's gut, but the door gunners he'd expected to see aboard *Pegasus* were not leaning out her hatches. Only Stork and his copilot were in the helicopter.

"Hop aboard!" the warrant officer called to Zack and his squad. "I'll take ya outta Hell's Kitchen myself! Man, what the *hell* happened back there?" He flipped a thumb over his shoulder, referring to the clearing created by the 10,000-pound bomb. "It looks like the end of the world."

Larson started to climb aboard, but Zack said, "We won't be going!"

"What?" The Professor fixed a cold, hate-filled stare on Leo.

"We have to sweep the tree line and link up with two platoons from Delta Company." Zack was now holding the PR-25 radio.

Larson's hands remained on the chopper's handholds. He glanced over at Brody and Fletcher and Patterson and Vance, the only soldiers there who were still breathing. "I'm dirty and I'm hungry and I'm half-deaf and half-blind and one hundred fucking percent naked, Zack. I ain't going anywhere except back to the Turkey Farm."

"He's bleedin' too," Brody, who was helping Patterson load body bags in through the hatch, observed.

"Yah!" Larson had not noticed the shrapnel wound near his right underarm. It was a minor flesh wound but seemed to be bleeding more than a scalp injury, which usually looked worse than it was. "I'm fuckin' bleedin' too!"

"Fine!" Zack sounded as if he was glad to be rid of him. "Escort those KIAs back to the officer in charge of the dead, then report to the dispensary!"

"You got it." Larson climbed aboard without anyone's help, though Fletcher had rushed up beside him.

"That's the last of them." Patterson was wiping back tears.

"See you dudes back at the Hell Hole." The Professor produced the thumbs-up. "And...hey! Watch your asses down there, okay?"

Krutch guided *Pegasus* into a slow, vertical ascent. "Hell Hole, my ass!" he yelled back at Larson. "I've had enough o' this bullshit!"

"What the hell you talking about, Stork!?" Brody had noticed the new black-brown-and-green camouflage paint scheme for the first time. He could even smell it now.

"Hon Trau, here we come!" The chopper pilot's head dropped back as he let out an almost insane little laugh.

"Krutch, you promised!" the Whoremonger yelled. He was waving his rifle now as the craft rose above hearing range. "You promised you wouldn't take *Pegasus*!"

292

But the men aboard the Huey—both alive and dead—were ignoring the soldiers on the ground. Treat Brody aimed what was left of his M-16 at the belly of the bird, knowing full well he could never pull the trigger. And then he remembered the black fiberglass handgrips and barrel had been destroyed in the mortar attack—melted down until they resembled a Mattel toy the garbage truck had run over.

Pegasus had not been off the ground thirty seconds when automatic-weapons fire raked the ground on either side of Zack and his men. An entire 30-round banana clip of white tracers arced up out of the distant tree line, chasing after the Huey, and Brody's breath stopped as he watched sparks bounce off the bottoms of the skids in a silver shower.

"Mamma Mia Farrow!" Krutch nearly soiled his pants as two of the tracers punched up through the floorboards. Both struck his copilot, and tore his lower jaw off.

"My God! *My God!*" Larson had been crouching between the two stations. He wrapped his arm around the man's throat, trying to stop the bleeding, but it flowed forth like water from a faucet turned up all the way. "Hal! What do I do?" The warrant officer on Krutch's left was moaning loudly as blood gurgled out the terrible exit wound.

Krutch knew the high-caliber rounds had probably ripped up through the seat of his pants. His internal organs had most likely been scrambled. Krutch glanced at the floor, and his suspicions were confirmed: it was already soaked with blood dripping from the lower tip of his chickenplate. "Pull him out, back with the rest of the KIAs and—"

"But he's still breathing!" Larson protested.

"He's dead, Shawn." And no sooner had the words left Krutch's lips than the sickening noises coming from the peter pilot ended.

"Whatta we do now?" Larson's eyes were as big as golf balls. He'd just finished dragging the dead warrant officer back out of his splintered chair and had laid him in between the other KIAs. "What the *hell* do we do now?"

Krutch pointed up at the craft's trembling ceiling. "Well, the Jesus nut hasn't flown off. I guess we're still airmobile, okay? So knock off the panic and lower your pucker factor, dude."

Krutch didn't seem the least bit phased by what had just transpired. "First thing we do is head for Pleiku and drop off our passengers." He motioned with his chin over a shoulder toward the body bags enduring the bumpy ride without complaint. "Have a seat." His chin dropped to the copilot position on his left.

"But. . ."

"Hey, bud, didn't I spend bookoo hours trainin' you to fly this conglomeration of opposing forces and aerodynamic lickbacks?"

"But. . ."

"Didn't I teach ya how to fly ol' *Pegasus* with a blindfold on, 'cause I wanted to take a snooze back in the cabin on them ash-and-trash jokes?"

"But. . ."

"Didn't I—"

"But the blood, Stork. What about all the—"

"Grab a rag from the X-box and have at it, Prof. I'm kinda fuckin' busy right now."

"And after Pleiku?" Larson swallowed hard and went to work.

"After Pleiku, my man, we drop this crate o' bent rotors in Plei Nhol or the outskirts of same, pick up some cherry girls of questionable virtue, then beat feet out to Hon Trau."

"The Island, Stork?" Larson eased into the peter pilot's station and felt the seat of his pants growing sticky already with the blood he'd missed.

"The island, my man." Krutch licked his lips. "Early retirement and a plentiful supply of free pussy."

"We gonna make babies, Stork?" Shawn Larson smiled for the first time since he'd boarded the gunship.

"We gonna make bookoo babies." He grinned. "A couple hundred, at least. This war's gonna end someday, but. . .but we'll still be on our tropical island, and I'm gonna be the *Emperor* of the Isle of Stork." Krutch nodded proudly at the thought. "You can be my prime minister."

"Fuck you, *bud.*"

"Okay." The AC kept his eyes on the treetops passing a few feet below the nose bubble in a green blur. "You can be the emperor. I'll be in charge of the whorehouse."

CHAPTER 30

Brody watched *Pegasus* limp off into the haze beyond the tree-tops after Krutch overcame the sudden burst of ground fire, maintaining control of the craft. He watched his beautiful gunship disappear into the blanket of smoke engulfing Ia Drang Valley, and then his attention returned to the matter at hand—rout and terminate the lone gunman left behind by the retreating NVA, the sniper who'd fired a burst up at the ascending Huey.

Zack and Patterson were already directing long streams of tracer up at a certain treetop, and Brody, loading an M-16 he had taken off a dead soldier, joined them.

Brody missed it when the sniper was knocked from his perch and dropped in a long, graceful fall to the earth, arms and legs barely flailing. As if he'd been resigned to death long ago. As if he were contented...the last holdout in a suicide squad. Brody missed it because all the cordite lining his throat and nostrils finally got the best of the Whoremonger and sent him into a sneezing fit.

"It's all over, Sneezy!" Zack called to him when he finally lifted his face from the baked-solid dirt. The sergeant and Vance and the others were already on their feet, cautiously walking over to check on the body.

"Maintain your position in the event we're fired upon," Lt. Vance told him.

"Eat the big one, asshole," Brody muttered under his breath, not bothering to raise his voice. Who was *this* bastard to tell him what to do, anyway? And after what *he'd* done, after the boner *he'd* pulled?

"Did you say something, Specialist?" Vance was not even watching the trees now.

"I said, GO FUCK YOURSELF, *sir*!" But two Cobras had flown low overhead just then, drowning out his words, and, though Zack and Vance both read his lips, neither the NCO nor officer paused in their haste to reach the tree line.

Patterson was suddenly proned-out beside him. "Better watch your ass, Treat."

"Hey, *fuck* him, man. The dude's got his head up his rectal cavity, and it's gonna be the death of us all sooner or later. Somebody oughta lose a grenade on the next Lurp and frag his butter-bar ass."

"He's a First Louie, pal."

"Well, he *acts* like a goddamned butter bar." Brody was going through an abandoned ruck, seeing with his fingers. He was probing for extra ammo magazines while his eyes scanned the tree line.

"Yah, I've seen his kind before, Treat. He means well."

"Bullshit!" Brody locked eyes with the taller man. "How can you say that, Saint Pat? The fucker almost got us killed?"

"Well, he wasn't the first one to screw up some cords under stress, guy. Shit, I seem to recall an incident when a certain Whoremonger first arrived in-country. He was clearin' his pistol in front of the mess hall or somethin', tryin' to act cool. But the dumbfuck forgot to eject the magazine before lettin' the hammer drop."

The slightest trace of a grin cracked the Spec-4's grim mask. "And fuck you too, *pal*."

Patterson smiled along as he scratched the wound over his shoulder blade. "Yah, I seen his kind before. They come from military families or something. Started young, probably a GI kindergarten, know what I mean? Their papa-sans raised 'em to believe there ain't no life outside the U.S. Army, my friend. And the only honor on Earth can be found in the amount of scrambled eggs on an officer's hat. Christ, to guys like that, enlisted men are idiots from Bumfuck Egypt, and NCOs are a necessary evil. He can't help it, the arrogance is bred into him from birth. He's brought up to act a certain way, a totally shitty way, granted, but it's a mortal sin for these clowns to listen to lowlifes like us and really be *listening*, you know? To them, we don't even exist."

"Except as cannon fodder." Brody frowned.

"Right."

They both watched Vance making a point of staying to the right of Zack—and not following him—as they rushed the tree line. "I kinda had a feeling, a *gut* twitch or something, that the scrote would be different after. . .that the mistake—calling the arty down on top of us like that—would have humbled him."

"No chance."

"But it hasn't changed him a friggin' bit."

"You're readin' him like a book, Brody." Zack was waving them up to his position now—the North Vietnamese soldier was a confirmed addition to the body count—and he followed Patterson up from their prone position behind the logs.

"Yah, well I just wonder how the final chapter's gonna read and whether or not Yours Truly is going to join the KIA list."

"I read back issues of the *Stars & Stripes,* Amigo," Saint Pat said. "I'll keep you posted."

Brody directed a bewildered scowl in his direction, then raced the infantryman into the tamarinds.

They linked up with another platoon thirty minutes later, and Brody's people were on the first extraction chopper soon after, headed back to the Tea Plantation for C-rations and a shower.

They never made it.

It happened five minutes after their Huey ascended up out of the Void and passed over the circle of death left by the 10,000-pound Daisy Cutter. "You grunts part o' Hal Krutch's crew?" The peter pilot glanced over a shoulder.

"Yah!" Brody watched him turn a volume-control dial up and switch on an exterior radio speaker.

"Sounds like the Stork broke a wing," the AC added.

". . .Been hit by intense ground fire over. . ." Heavy static laced the radio transmission, but there was no mistaking Krutch's voice. ". . .Going down over. . ." And the garbled message faded.

"Did you get the cords?" Brody yelled, trying to move forward through all the crouching soldiers packed into the cabin.

"Naw. . .he's too far out, but I'm sure Charlie Tango picked them up. They probably got a team headed out right now to—"

"He's flyin' *Pegasus*!" Brody pounded his fist against the wall and stumbled over to the speaker beside the peter pilot's station. "*Pegasus* is goin' down, Leo!" He stared at Zack as he planted his ear against it.

The black sergeant's hands both rose, palms up, in a whatya-gonna-do? expression, and at that very moment, an earsplitting squeal rose from the area above their heads, near the swash plate assembly.

"Sounds like the trani." The aircraft commander remained

calm, despite the alarms ringing along the front console.

"Oil flow's readin' zero!" The peter pilot's voice cracked with excitement.

"How long's it been—"

"It just dropped!"

"Fuck."

"*I swear!* It just went straight to zero!"

The grinding, whirring sound near the rotor's main shaft was quickly growing louder. "Then we're fucked." The AC's voice remained emotionless. "Truly fucked."

"We still got fifteen minutes to land somewhere." The co-pilot scanned treetops for a nonexistent break in the canopy. "The manual says we got fifteen minutes after a transmission begins seizing to—"

"Screw the book, kid. We're Fucked with a capital—"

More alarms were screaming now. "Chips in the turbine." The peter pilot scanned his console frantically. "I got chips in the—"

"Yep!" the AC glanced back over a shoulder at the men all staring breathlessly toward the cockpit. "Hold on to your helmets, ladies. Pleiku International Whirlylines will be making an unscheduled stop at Void Vicious in approximately. . ."

Tree branches scraped at the bottom of the helicopter's skids as he spoke.

They'd brought along eight whores with them instead of four.

On his final approach over Hon Trau, Krutch spotted an old, broken-down barrackslike facility he'd not noticed on previous recons of the island and opted for a different, more secluded slice of paradise, a few klicks farther out to sea.

At the moment, he was busy exploring the patch of mile-wide land with the eight scantily clad Vietnamese women, while Larson worked at camouflaging *Pegasus*. He laughed aloud as he thought about their escape plan. A phony Mayday message that had gone off without a hitch. *And Krutch's idea to paint the bird with camouflage tones the day before their desertion.* Yes, the Stork was a genius, a bona fide, friggin' genius. Nobody would ever find them here!

"Ah, yes." Krutch had escorted the ladies of questionable virtue down several hundred yards of white sand beach before finding the lagoon and giant oak leaning out over it. "Behold, my dears. That's where we can built our treehouse."

"Treehouse?" One of the women frowned as she watched something dark and furry swing from branch to branch high overhead. "You mean live like monkey?"

"No, no, no." Krutch laughed as he draped his arms around two of the prostitutes. "Live like royalty. High and mighty. You wanna stay safely off the ground, you know, in case of lions and tigers and bears. Or whatever. . ."

"Royalty?" a girl who couldn't have been over seventeen narrowed her eyes skeptically.

"Sure, honey. King and queen."

"Oh!" Her eyes lit up. "Like *Thailand!*"

"Right! Jus' like Thailand, babe." Krutch worked fast to keep their spirits up. He'd had to lie to them just to get them into the chopper: promise them a pot of gold. And the rainbow was supposed to end in Bangkok, where there was no more war. They'd managed to fake engine trouble after passing over Qui Nhon and insisted it was either land on the island, or perish at sea. Only temporary, he had told them. Only temporary until the Jolly Greens already on their way to the Kingdom of Siam detour down here to pick us up.

"I hungry." One of the older women—she looked perhaps twenty-five at most—stopped walking, refusing to go any further. Dainty arms crossed over the bottoms of her breasts, she forced them to swell up over her halter-top's brim provocatively as she stood her ground in the sand, the tide licking at her toes.

"No sweat, beautiful." Where had he seen her before? "Just let me scale that palm over there, and we'll all partake in some sweet-and-sour coconuts, if you get my meaning. . . ." He scratched at his crotch and winked at her.

"You promise steak." One of the other women summoned her courage.

"Steak and *lobster!*" two more chimed in, also refusing to continue the stroll.

"Okay, okay. No sweat!" Krutch was losing his cool. "Just gimme a minute. Sometimes you gotta work at it a little bit to achieve genuine paradise, okay?" He turned his back on the collection of swaying chests and yelled in the direction of the vine-covered helicopter, "*Professor!*"

North Vietnamese soldiers were waiting for them when the AC auto-gyroed down into a one-in-a-million clearing. "It wasn't on my map!" the peter pilot was shaking his head as they pranged across huge roots and the windshield spider-webbed with bullet holes.

"And visiting the Void wasn't on my fuckin' agenda for today!" Aircraft Commander Lance Warlokk was unstrapping and preparing to jump over equipment when a burst of tracers tore the copilot's arm off above the elbow.

Brody had already jumped from the Huey, and he and the rest of the soldiers dove into prone positions forming a semicircle out from the craft as bullets by the hundreds kicked up clods all around them. "Wasn't that Lawless back there?" Patterson yelled into his ear. "I thought he only flew Cobras!"

Who gives a flyin' fuck at a time like this? the Whoremonger's expression replied as he emptied half a banana clip at muzzle flashes fifty feet away, in the misty tree line. *I hope he gets a call out!* Brody's mind raced as his lungs sucked in the gunsmoke, *That fuckin' Warlokk better get a call for help out before he abandons ship!*

"Jesus!" The warrant officer was the only one left inside the cabin as he grabbed onto his copilot, trying to keep him from falling directly on the wound. "Oh my sweet *Jesus!*" The blood was gushing out at him like water from a hose back on the farm.

"Help me, Lance! My God! Pleeeeeasssse help me!" The man's name tag flashed in front of him, big as a billboard: NIMM. "Please, Lance!" Big as a billboard, but Warlokk was seeing something else as he held on to his copilot.

"Don't let me bleed to death."

Blood still gushed from the cavity where the copilot's arm had been torn away, and Warlokk tried to wrap an ammo bandolier around the gaping hole, but the thick shreds of flesh were bringing the bile up his throat, and all the magazines were in the way, the damn bandolier wouldn't cooperate, and he was slipping in the blood.

A single bullet entered through the hatch and struck the peter pilot in the forehead, snapping his neck back with an insulting, punching sound. The man was already dead, but Warlokk, eyes tightly closed, dropped against an M-60 mount and vomited onto a body bag.

300

"Come on, Lawless!" A big black man was dragging him down out of the hatch, toward cover. A big black man with his head shaved bald.

"Zack, you crazy old fart!" Warlokk's words were slurred.

"Yah, I love you too, Mister W! You're drunk on adrenaline, boy! But Leo the Lionhearted'll walk the kinks outta ya! Let's go! Sober up, son!"

Bullets were zinging in all around them, but Zack managed to drag the chopper jock through the bouncing dirt clods over to a huge log. Brody and Lt. Vance were already behind it. Every couple of seconds, the Whoremonger would pop up above the bark and fire off a five-or-ten round burst without really taking aim; he was just shooting at the sound. Several NVA soldiers trying to rush their position went down anyway, dead as they dropped.

"I can't seem to raise the Turkey Farm!" Vance was still hugging his radio. "I was hopin' to get some choppers to—"

"Jesus *H.*, Lieutenant!" Brody snapped at him. "We're outta range. Drop that prick-25 and pick up your weapon and start shooting at the bad guys! I'm down to my last couple mags!"

"I suggest you watch your tone, Specialist, or—" The officer was throwing his chin out.

"Or *what*?" Brody cut him off. "What the fuck do you think you're going to do after we all run out of ammo and the NVA saunter down here and fight over who gets to mount your head on a bamboo pole in front of Ho Chi Minh's hooch back in Hanoi? *Huh?* What the flyin' fuck do you think—"

Vance threw the radio down and grabbed Brody. The Spec-4 had donned one of the dead men's blood-caked flak vests, and the lieutenant grabbed him by the front zipper flaps. In a rage, eyes bulging, he lifted the Whoremonger up slightly off the ground. *"What?"*

"Lemme go, you sonofabitch!" Brody's own eyes flew wide, but his terror was a reflection of the muzzle flashes on the other side of the fallen log.

"I've *had it* with your disrespectful—"

Vance shrank back slightly as Brody brought up his fist, but hot lead threw the first punch.

The round struck the Whoremonger directly over the heart, knocking him free of the lieutenant's grasp.

CHAPTER 31

Hal Krutch stretched, yawned, and stretched again. He rolled over, sighed at the pristine beauty of the sun rising over the calm, South China Sea, then pulled the poncho up over his head again. Some wild parrots had flocked to the branches above their camp, attracted, no doubt, to the colorful lean-to the Americans had built, and he listened to the birds sing for a few minutes. Waves crashing against the sand sent a fine mist drifting over the beach, and he faced the woman beside him again. Proud of himself, he sighed again as he quietly lifted the poncho liner a bit to permit more light inside. She was truly beautiful—a goddess. He allowed himself the privilege of running his tongue between the firm slope of her breasts.

She was still asleep, and he smiled, stretching her head back as he licked one nipple, then the other, counting to himself, *one thousand one...one thousand two...* to see how long it took for them to tighten and pop erect.

She seemed to sleep like many Asian women he had spent nights with: sloe eyes half closed—or were they half open? And then his lips were parting to engulf the swell of flesh over her racing heart and she was giggling and rolling from her side onto her back, opening her legs, taking him in.

They made love again, as they had all through the predawn hours, rough and savagely. She growled in his ear, nibbled at the tip of his nose and, just when he was confident she was finished, his pelvis began pounding harder, driving her eyes tightly shut as the uncontrollable sensations wracked her exhausted body.

His arms came back, the wrists sliding under her ankles, and then he was forcing her thighs up, the soles of her feet against the clouds, she thought. Her fingers dug into his haunches, taking him in deeper, pulling him from his world and into hers.

When he finally exploded, legs trembling and chest heaving, she eased him off his elbows, onto his side and finally, his back —so gentle was she in spite of his desire to hurt her. But she was not through with him.

302

Playful revenge sparkling in her dark eyes, the woman stayed atop Krutch, riding him into the earth as he squirmed against the all-consuming surge of passion sending jolts tingling through his body—it was supposed to be over. *Over!*

But her business with the American was far from concluded. His midnight lover was not yet a satisfied customer. When she finally began groaning out of sync and her elbows locked, the woman threw her jutting breasts out and her proud head back— the edge of her long hair tickling his testicles—and Krutch found himself thinking back to that time he spent an afternoon with the men of the Pack, drinking lukewarm beer from VC skullcaps. "Make romance to me!" The words left her as a deep rasp as the skin along her throat grew taut.

Make love to her? he thought to himself. What the hell had they been doing for the last seven hours?

When the tiny shriek of bliss finally left her lips and the woman collapsed across his chest, Krutch had recovered somewhat.

Rolling onto his side, he withdrew from her without warning, laughed as she reacted by curling up into the fetal position, then lifted her up in his arms, waded out onto the sand, and threw her into the ocean.

Laughing again, the Stork brushed his hands clean and started off in the direction he'd last seen Larson strolling with two talented maidens the evening before. *Definitely seen this chick's face somewhere before,* he decided. *But I guess it don't really matter—so long as she remembers who's king and who's the head princess!*

"No can swim!" the woman was floundering ten yards off shore, splashing her hands and arms frantically. "I . . . no . . . can . . . swim . . . ."

She went under once, but Krutch just laughed again, soon enough she'd learn the water was only knee-deep. A coral reef ran out for more than a hundred yards from the beach before dropping off into deeper waters. It was a smooth, colorful coral that gave the ocean a turquoise tint, and the ex-chopper pilot loved it! "You'll be okay, Miss Y-Von, or whatever your name is! Just drop your toes and enjoy the feeling!"

The woman stopped screaming as he walked down the beach away from her, following footsteps. He disappeared in the hedgerows clumped where the tide had washed away hollows in the sand overnight. She still slapped at the water, angry he would abandon her, but she no longer sounded frightened.

And it appeared she might never have been.

Still chuckling to himself, Hal Krutch began whistling as he wandered down through the palms and flowers, following the footprints of Shawn and his two girl friends. It was a carefree time, and he resisted the urge to forget about the Professor and go exploring on his own, even though he was curious how the other five women had spent the night—and such a jaunt might provide interesting clues. Laughter reached his ears, and the smile returned. He *loved* the sound of whores frolicking in the surf. The little trail he was foraging down through the reeds was never very far from the beach, and Krutch scurried halfway up a leaning palm until he spotted the women about a hundred yards away, naked above the waist, laughing and throwing handfuls of water at each other as they built a giant sand castle.

Hhmmm. He rubbed his chin thoughtfully after dropping back to the ground. Krutch counted only four women. Perhaps Shawn had taken *three* pairs of boobs to fashion his pillow for that first historic night with no mortars beneath the tropical stars. "You little rascal." He chuckled under his breath as he spotted Larson's sleeping bag beneath a cluster of palms. "Still suffocating under a pile o' pussy, eh?"

Larson had picked a good spot. Nestled at the farthest point where a quiet lagoon intruded upon the jungle, his temporary shelter was perpetually shaded—if not by swaying palms, then by the edge of the jungle's canopy that hung out over the lagoon like a ledge, though the closest trees supporting it were several hundred feet away.

Truly paradise. Krutch was smiling as he shook his head from side to side, still impressed with the beauty and serenity of the island. It would have been nice to sleep-in until dusk, then dance like savages, naked beneath the moon, and make love all night, choosing a different woman with each hour's passing. But he had heard a panther scream along about midnight, and they had better not press their luck: The quicker a treehouse was built, the safer they would all be. "Come on, Peter-Pecker." He kicked at the sleeping bag. "We got work to do, and time is tight."

The sleeping bag was empty.

Frowning—he didn't have time to play hide and seek—Krutch searched about for footprints, but there was too much vegetation in the camp. His eyes scanned the lagoon's banks in both directions and spotted a curl of blue smoke rising from a campfire in the distance.

"Fuckin' skate." Krutch laughed, refusing to allow Larson's antics to irritate him, determined to keep the spirit of freedom in each breath. He started toward the smoke, whistling again. "Come out, come out, wherever you are!" he called.

But something was wrong.

The smile left his face as he got closer to the campfire and noticed the object in the sand at the lagoon's edge.

Krutch started running as fast as he could, until he realized he was all alone, and he skidded to a stop in the sand. All alone, just he and the dead woman.

She was one of the eight girls they had picked up in Plei Nhol. Now she was buried up to her neck in the sand. Her hair was tangled with seaweed. Something had ripped her nose and ears off during the night. Footprints told him it was probably a wild boar. But who had buried her here in the first place, and had she been buried alive? Tiny sand crabs climbed in and out of the sockets where her eyes had once been.

Fletcher pulled Brody's flak vest apart and brought his fist down over the soldier's heart as hard as he could. The Whoremonger's rigid body trembled slightly under the assault, but Treat did not regain consciousness.

"I...I d-didn't mean to...I mean," Lt. Vance stammered as rounds kicked bark from the log he was leaning against. "I'm s-sorry!"

"It seems that's all you're goddamned good at, isn't it?" Fletcher glared at him as he dropped his head sideways an inch above Brody's face, right ear over his lips. "Apologizing!"

"Is he breathing?" Zack did not look down at them, he was too busy firing at the figures darting through the trees in the distance.

"Heart attack!" Snakeman confirmed, tilting Brody's head back to open his airway. He pinched the Spec-4's nostrils shut, then placed his mouth over Brody's, forcing air down into his

305

lungs.

"But how—" the lieutenant began.

Fletcher's interlaced thumbs added pressure to the edges of both hands as he placed them at the tip of Brody's sternum and pushed against the dying man's ribcage several brisk times. "Blunt trauma," he told Vance before repeating the mouth-to-mouth. "The bullet was stopped by his body armor—"

"Thank God!" Vance was wiping the sweat from his eyes.

"But the force of the impact shocked the heart. Musta smacked him between beats or some such weird shit. Stopped the ol' thumper cold."

"You don't seem particularly worried about—" Vance watched Fletcher resume breathing life into the specialist.

"Why don't you shut up and watch," Zack snarled as he switched ammo clips. "You might learn something."

Brody groaned. He groaned and threw up in Snakeman's face, then pushed him out of sight, rolled over onto his side and groaned some more.

"Treat! You're alive!" Fletcher slapped his palms together as if he'd just surprised himself.

"No shit, Sherlock." Brody held his head as Zack unleashed long, sustained bursts at the dwindling number of Vietnamese. "I feel like a bucketful of decapitated toads. Man, is my head a-throbbin', brother!"

"Your chest!" Fletcher resisted the urge to shake him. "How's your chest?"

And he remembered.

Brody remembered, and he wanted to bolt to his feet and tear Vance's head off, but he was too weak. Too weak, and in too much pain. His whole body ached, and it was getting worse.

He threw up again.

"Leo! Can you knock it off with the fuckin' M-16?" Brody was holding his ears as the discharges bounced back off the trees all around, searching him out.

Coincidentally, Zack stopped firing at that moment. He was down to his last magazine, but he had also run out of targets. "I think the bastards pulled back," he said.

"Maybe you zapped 'em all, Zack," Fletcher was no longer watching his best friend suffer the dry heaves, but he peeked over the top of the log.

306

"No such luck, Snakeoil. They're out there. Just waiting...."

"Waiting for what?" Lt. Vance was in between them both now. Brody seemed lost in the shuffle for survival.

"For the right time to charge in and cancel our tickets."

A strange disturbance in the air reached Fletcher's ears, and he held up his hand for silence, but the sound was gone that quickly.

Brody rolled over, onto his back. "Did you guys hear that?" he asked.

The dull thumping noise cracked along on the atmosphere again, but instead of fading out, it changed pitch and grew louder.

"Choppers!" a jubilant Fletcher called out.

"And what's *that?*" Zack cupped a hand to his ear. A dog was wailing and howling in the distance. A mutt somewhere high in the sky.

"*Choi-oi!*" Brody pointed up at the excited mongrel wagging his stub of a tail in the open hatch of a Huey that burst forth across the treetops and flared into a hover directly over their position. Broken Arrow, Lee, and Mohammed were crowded around behind him, bristling with automatic rifles. Corky Cordova was leaning out the opposite hatch, blasting away at the tree line with his Hog-60, but he wasn't receiving any hostile fire in return, and the gunship pilot brought his craft down for a bumpy landing less than a dozen feet away from the dead log that had saved Zack and Brody and the others.

"*Choi-oi!* Where the hell did you guys ever find ol' *Choi-oi*?" Brody staggered over to the chopper and hugged the excited animal. *Choi-oi* jumped up and down as he slobbered all over the Whoremonger's face, unaware that Treat had just cheated Lady Death at a game of eat-your-heart-out eight ball.

"You know that old mama-san that kidnapped his worthless no-account ass?" Lee petted the dog's head and scratched its ears as Brody hugged him.

"How could I forget?"

"Well, best we can figure it, some Arvin QCs blew her shit away on a comm-symp sweep of those villages south of the Turkey Farm. Fungus-Breath said he saw a brown doper-mutt running from the scene. Ol' *Choi-oi*...hey!"

307

Choi-oi barked upon hearing his name spoken by Lee, jumped from Brody's arms, and ran off into the jungle.

"Aw, shit!" Brody hung his head in despair. "Don't tell me he saw a fuckin' panther prowlin' the trees or something." He was in no shape to chase after the dog, and definitely not in the mood. "*Choi-oi!* Get your brown butt back here!"

"Ready to lift?" The peter pilot glanced over his shoulder, back at the group of misfits huddled around Brody.

"Hold on jus' a minute, pal!" Mohammed's sign language won over the warrant officers up front.

"*Choi-oi* musta beat feet back to the Turkey Farm," Lee continued his story, "only to find the town deserted, so to speak. So he did the next best thing and followed instinct, he trotted on over to Plei Me, his old home."

"All the way to Plei Me?" Brody forced his eyes apart.

"Yah! And who do you think was waitin' there to receive his undeserving tailless ass but us, the handsome but ragtag remnants of the Pack!"

"You're kidding."

"Nope. It was great timing on *Choi-oi's* part. We were just getting ready to leave the Green Berets. Those 'Yardes woulda made *Choi-oi* into mutt soup!"

"I take it the siege of Plei Me is over?" Brody was starting to see amoebalike ghosts float across his field of vision. He knew immediately they were taking shape within his eyes, but he ignored the danger signs.

"More or less." Broken Arrow's smile faded. "It's a long story, Whoremonger. We'll fill you in later."

"It looks like you could use a couple days sleep," observed Lee. "What the hell happened out here?"

Brody glanced at Warlokk who, for the first time Treat could remember, wore the thousand-yard stare. He looked at a dejected, withdrawn Vance, who had climbed into the helicopter and was seated cross-legged, staring at his lap; tried to will him to raise his head and lock eyes, but the lieutenant was in another world altogether. "How did you luck-out and find us?" Brody did not answer Lee's question. They could talk about that later, too.

Mohammed pointed up at the sky. "The Man's up there somewhere."

"The Man?"

"Buchanan, boy! The colonel saved your unworthy wretched asses. He's been flyin' circles around everybody all day in his Charlie-Charlie copter. When he spotted you, he called us off our relay back to the Turkey Farm to pick you up."

"No shit." Brody was starting to waver back and forth on his feet, and Broken Arrow reached down, grabbed him under the arms and hoisted him up into the slick.

Mohammed flipped the pilot a thumbs-up, and the rotors immediately increased their pitch as the security team climbed back into the craft. "W-wait a minute." Brody forced his eyes back open. "W-what about. . .what about my d-dog? You bastards better not leave *Choi—*"

A barking dog, pursued by several wild boars, emerged from the jungle. He trotted across the clearing and bounded over the fallen log, running casually really, teasing the hogs and wagging his stub of a tail as the men began cheering him on. "Speak of the devil." Mohammed helped Treat Brody to sit up just as *Choi-oi* jumped up the skids of the rising gunship, into the cabin on top of them.

Blood seemed to be rushing to the Whoremonger's head, but he smiled as his vision faded again. The last thing he saw before blacking out was the mongrel mutt from Plei Me standing on his chest, doing a little doggie dance with his one good ear standing up. Was the excited animal actually winking down at him as he slobbered all over the dazed soldier? *Choi-oi* had retrieved Brody's python-head mask.

As the first week of November drew to a close, the First Air Cavalry Division's lst Brigade had scored an impressive victory over the NVA's 33rd Regiment. Thirty brave American soldiers were killed in action. But when the body count came in, it was learned some fourteen hundred North Vietnamese troops died in the fierce fighting for the Ia Drang Valley. It was the first real test of the U.S. Army's airmobile concept, and it was rapidly proving to be an unqualified success.

CHAPTER 32

"Have you seen Shawn?" Ex-chopper jock Hal Krutch raced up to the half-naked girls building a sand castle on the beach.

"Storky!" The closest one rushed forward and draped her arms around his neck. Her sarong fell away and, pushing her weight against him, she managed to trip him backwards, into the surf. "Where you be *all* night, Storky!" She smothered him with kisses and rubbed her breasts against his chest. "You no want share you'self with rest girls on i'land?"

"Shawn!" He grabbed her by the hair and pulled her face away. "My buddy, Larson! Where is he?"

"Hey, Stork! Mellow out!" The Professor rose from beneath a portion of the sand castle. His head had been hidden by the watchtower on one end. "What's the problem, bud?" The two women he had disappeared with the night before were hugging him from both sides. Larson was the pickle inside a sandwich of voluptuous flesh. "Ain't this Heaven, brother?"

Krutch counted heads quickly. "We're missing one chick," he said, testing the Professor.

Larson glanced about, unconcerned. "So? More than a mouthful is a waste, right? Hell, I can only fill one hole at a time and—"

"She didn't spend the night with you?"

"Fuck no. I thought she was with you. Well, that's not true, actually. I didn't even *realize* one o' the cunts was missing, okay? And why would I care?" He bent over and kissed a breast passionately, making the woman giggle and slap at him playfully, "I already had my hands full."

"Get up."

"Huh?" Larson tilted his head to one side, shielding the sun from his eyes.

"Come on. I want to show you something."

"Can't it wait? I was trying to break my old record for number of orgasms on a white sand beach." Larson smiled crookedly, but he did not laugh.

Krutch grabbed his hand and pulled him up out of the crumbling castle as waves began reclaiming the sand. "This way," he motioned toward the lagoon.

"Okay, okay. . .Jesus! First time I ever seen you with such a hair up your feathered ass, Storky." He imitated the slender, top-heavy girl who'd pushed Krutch down into the water.

The girls exploded into tears and sobs of horror when he showed them what he had found. Krutch thought they might have reacted with cold indifference, born of lifetimes in a war zone, but they all broke down. These whores were close, it seemed.

"What was her name?" he asked the girl who had slept with him all night.

"Kit," came the soft, almost accusing reply. More than a couple of the girls were staring at Krutch suspiciously.

"Kit?" he asked. "You mean like 'Kitten'?"

"No," came the businesslike reply. "Just Kit. She country girl. Father sell her to whorehouse when she still have cherry. Long time 'go."

"What?"

"Daughters worth nothing to Vietnamese man. Daughters are not sons. Cannot farm good. Cannot fight. Good only for fucking, and there is never enough money to feed more children, so sell to the whorehouse. Buy new water buffalo."

"Oh." Krutch forced a chuckle, but it was not from hearing the woes of being a female in the Orient. "Heck, woman, I don't even know *your* name."

"Call me Kim." She did not look into his eyes.

"Kim. It is a very common name in Vietnam. In all of Asia, in fact. In Korea, I think every other woman is named Kim." He could not take his eyes from the sand crabs crawling over the dead woman's jet-black hair. It still looked radiant and silky, even with the seaweed braided through it.

"That is why I like it." She glanced away. If their eyes met, he might remember her.

Kim did not think this man Krutch was even around that day the Vietnamese military policeman strip-searched her in the rain. Larson might have been, but she couldn't remember his face. He was certainly not one of the half dozen soldiers who had stood around gawking at her as the QC put on the handcuffs. She probably looked different anyway. Kim dismissed

311

the concern, the raindrops had plastered her long hair against her face, and the GIs were doubtlessly staring at nothing above her breasts or below her crotch. Didn't all Vietnamese women look alike to the Americans anyway?

"*Why* you do this to Kit!?" One of the women rushed up and struck Krutch on the chest with her tiny fist.

"Me?" He drew back defensively. "I spent the whole fucking night with Miss 36-24-34 here, okay?" Krutch wrapped an arm around Kim for support, as if she were more than an alibi.

The woman whirled around and punched Larson in the chin. "*Why* you do this?" she screamed.

"I was with you!" The Professor yelled back. He quickly unzipped his trousers and drew back the flaps. "Remember *this.*"

"Oh." Her lips wrinkled into a perplexed expression, and she chose to stare at her feet rather than at the other girls standing around the dead and buried prostitute.

"Maybe one of *you* did it?" Krutch folded his arms across his chest. "An old grudge, perhaps?"

"Yah!" Larson was quick to support the former warrant officer. "No white mice around here to throw you into the monkeyhouse." He referred to the Vietnamese policemen, who often wore white shirts in the bigger cities. "Maybe one o' you ladies of questionable virtue decided to even out an old score, eh?"

The women obviously were confused by half the words Krutch and Larson were using, but there was no mistaking what they were getting at.

"No way." Kim walked over to a pile of driftwood and found a round, flat piece. "We friends." She waited for the others to nod their agreement. "Never hurt each other."

"Nebbah happen." The woman who'd struck the Professor in the chin lifted her own defiantly. "We *friends.*"

"Good for you." Larson shook his head in resignation. It was beginning to look like paradise lost on the Isle of Stork.

"What are you going to do with that?" Krutch pointed at the chunk of driftwood.

"We must dig up and bury her." Kim handed the improvised shovel to the closest woman, who accepted it with mixed emotions.

"Well, don't be gone from home too long." Krutch dismissed the incident as just another Vietnam vendetta between women of the Far East. Nothing could phase him, after what he'd seen in The Nam so far.

"Don't stay out past dark." Larson allowed himself an uncharacteristic chuckle, but the circumstances, he felt, warranted a bit of insanity. He'd probably made love to the murderer last night, but then, how many innocents had *he* himself killed since riding the gunships into that green hell back there? He glanced across the strip of blue sea in the direction of the South Vietnamese mainland.

Arm in arm, the two Americans strode back toward Krutch's lean-to. "Tell me the truth, Stork." Larson locked eyes with him after they were out of hearing range of the women. "You plugged the bitch last night, didn't you?"

Krutch reacted with a look of utter horror across his features, but the Professor felt it was feigned. "What the fuck are you saying, Shawn?"

"I've heard the stories."

"*What* stories?" He stopped walking, and Larson stooped to pick up a seashell.

"The ones about all you chopper jocks bein' double vets and all."

"Double vets? Gimme a break, dude. Not this chopper jock. Uh, make that ex-chopper jock."

"Right. Sure."

"Really. Who was feeding you that kinda crap, anyway?"

"They say to become a double vet one has to seduce a Viet Cong chick, then snap her neck when you're makin' love to her."

"You call that 'making love'?" Krutch glanced out to sea.

"They say once you screw a woman that way you become addicted to the position." Larson produced a nervous little laugh, and Krutch shifted gears on him.

"What if I think *you* did it, Mister Innocent?"

Larson laughed louder this time. "Look, Stork. I really think the war has finally driven me bonkers. I just don't care anymore. Not like I used to."

"What does that have to do with—"

"I just don't care if you offed the bitch, okay?" He grabbed Krutch's wrist and searched his eyes. "But can I ask you one favor?"

"I didn't fucking kill any—"

"Okay, okay. . .fine." Larson released him. "But just in case you did, do me a favor, buddy, all right?"

"Screw you, Shawn."

"Warm, but no cigar, Hal. Just do me a favor, okay? You can knock off as many of 'em as you want—whatever gets your rocks off, pal. Just leave me the one with the big boobs, okay?"

Krutch turned his back on Larson and stalked off through the ankle-deep sand, in the direction of the shelter. He left the Professor with an obscene gesture to contemplate.

North Vietnamese Major Lam Van Minh was consulting his man-high map of the Ia Drang Valley when the messenger rushed into the fortified bunker. Minh turned to find the soldier's eyes bulging with eagerness to deliver obviously urgent news.

"What is it?" The major was losing his appreciation for military courtesy and discipline of late. He was obsessed with only one thing: mounting the head of Bull Buchanan on a bamboo pole in front of his command post.

"The Americans, sir." Sweat was rolling in layers down the young private's chocolate-brown forehead.

Minh had been busy planning a second surprise assault on the Green Beret camp at Plei Me from his jungle headquarters nestled in caves and tunnels within the shadow of Chu Pong's highest mountain. Despite the setbacks involving the first attack on the SF camp and his retreat from the west banks of the meandering Ia Drang River, the NVA major had managed to regroup some 4,000 rain forest fighters from the 66th and 33rd regiments. Even now, they were readying weapons and equipment all around the hillside fortifications below, awaiting his directions.

"I haven't got all day," he told the private.

"The Americans, sir. They have. . .they are landing now at the bottom of the mountain."

"Now?" Minh dropped his swagger stick, eyes growing wide. *"Here?"*

"Yes, Major. In areas seven and eight of the valley. The watchers say an entire battalion has landed by helicopter."

"Well, well. . ." Minh wrung his hands as he rushed over to

314

the bunker entrance and scanned in a southerly direction with his field binoculars. He could not see the gunships, but he could certainly hear them now. "I would dare to say the green beanies at Plei Me can wait another day or two." Only a battalion, he licked his lips hungrily. Only a battalion, against his four thousand combat-hardened NVA Regulars.

Minh called for his aides to assemble and dismissed the runner with a hearty pat on the back. Two small, black Loach choppers were circling above the gunships on the ground, the private told him before leaving. That had to mean one was a C&C ship, Minh decided.

Yes, he would personally inspect this unexpected landing-in-force of the Air Cavalry Americans, then expedite the plotting of strategy guaranteeing their slaughter. Minh had not consulted his chart today, but if luck were in his stars, he just might have Col. Neil Buchanan's head mounted on that pole by sundown.

CHAPTER 33

Corky Cordova was thinking of Thuan as the strange, new gunship rumbling beneath his boots carried the Pack into battle. He held on to the canvas netting that served as his seat and listened to the men growling and screaming war cries, trying to outpsyche one another, but he was hearing the unfamiliar rotor spin of a ship he had never ridden in before, feeling the skin of the bird rattle and vibrate and lurch beneath his fingers. . .and seeing Thuan. She was as beautiful as ever as she stood before his mind's eye, a filmy nightgown he had ordered from the PX hanging loosely from her shoulders and from the tips of her breasts. *Man, I'm gonna cream my trousers if I don't stop seeing her that way.* Corky glanced around. The thump and pop of

315

giant blades slicing through the air overhead created a sort of numbing silence within the Hueys, but no one had read his thoughts. No one knew how badly he missed Thuan. He had not received a letter in weeks now. He'd even written to her brother after getting back from Plei Me, but the boy never responded. Corky stared at Brody, then glanced away when Treat looked up. Even the Whoremonger had no idea how much he lusted for just one night beside Thuan. One more night.

"She sure the fuck ain't *Peg,* is she?" Fletcher was elbowing him, and Cordova locked eyes with the combat-hardened private.

"Thuan?" he replied like a complete fool, but Snakeman had not heard him because of the intense downblast. The pitch had changed, they were descending down below the Dead Man's zone.

"Huh?"

"What!?"

Fletcher patted the wall of the chopper and shook his head in the negative. "I said she sure ain't the smooth-runnin' bitch *Pegasus* was. You know what I mean?"

"Yah." Cordova lowered his face. "I miss her too."

The gunship Brody and Zack and the others had babied for the last year had yet to be located by the rescue teams. They found nothing whatsoever in the vicinity of the coordinates her pilot, Warrant Officer Hal Krutch, had given after he dropped a load of body bags off at the Pleiku military morgue. Not even scattered wreckage or a squawker signal. Krutch, his peter pilot, and Shawn Larson were officially on the MIA roster.

Someday I'm gonna request a much-deserved R and R to a place far, far away from Ia Drang. Spec-4 Brody rubbed at the bruise over his heart. He had no doubt the two jesters were very much alive and sucking in all the paradise they could on the little deserted island Brody had dreamed about for three nights running. Before the division pulled up tent stakes and returned to An Khe, he would definitely have to make one last visit to the boom-boom bunker at Plei Nhol to ascertain just how many ladies of the evening had waved good-bye to Madame X and never come back.

Nurse Maddox had checked Brody out personally. The equipment at the field hospital could find no evidence the specialist had suffered cardiac arrest from the contest with an AK-47 bullet, but she also didn't doubt Fletcher's and Patterson's account of the incident; Zack was also backing them up. So the lieutenant wrote a report suggesting the Spec-4 take a couple of weeks off. "Not in Saigon." She had laughed. "I don't want you coming back to the highlands with something worse than a heart attack. Heart attacks we can sometimes cure." She had suggested some rest and relaxation in Japan. She could place him on the next medevac manifest, in fact. But Brody refused. He could walk and talk, and his hearing was back. He was pretty sure he could still shoot straight, too. And the Whoremonger smelled trouble brewing in the valley. The division was headed for some kind of action in Ia Drang, and he *would* die if he missed out on all the excitement.

So Brody was back with the Pack. And, though he suffered from what seemed to be a permanent case of heartburn, loving every minute of it.

ing with little respite since the middle of October, but the commanding general told Buchanan to request volunteers from his battalion for a massive sweep of the valley. Echo Company had captured several important documents in a vast maze of subterranean tunnels hidden beneath the NVA field hospital—organizational papers that supplemented evacuation orders located earlier—and Westmoreland was eager to land as many gunships full of troops west of the North Vietnamese retreat, heading them off at the pass, so to speak.

The Chu Pong Massif Pass.

The seemingly endless fleet of Hueys that landed at LZ X-Ray the morning of November fourteenth met little resistance initially. As Brody's chopper circled the landing zone, descending swiftly, the fighting spirit seized him too, and he began stomping his boots with Cordova and Patterson and the others as the blanket of green below their gunship's skids became treetops rising above them.

He ignored the lieutenant, preparing to be the first man off. Vance and he had an unspoken understanding: They would stay out of each other's way.

A single discharge greeted their bird's landing. The round ripped at the muggy veil of mist cloaking the clearing, passed

317

between Vance and the specialist, and struck Zack in the thigh as he was jumping to the ground.

The Black Buddha was big, but he was no match for a twirling slug of hot lead. The bullet was deflected by bone and tore down along his leg until being stopped by the bridge of his kneecap. Blood sprayed everywhere.

"*God*dammnit!" Leo fired a long, thirty-round burst at the nearest clump of trees, well aware it was the only action he would see in the near future.

"Grab his '16!" Patterson and Broken Arrow were already lifting him back up into the helicopter as the nearest door gunner took over, saturating the LZ's edge with streams of red-and-white tracer.

"You watch my boys, ya hear?" Zack grabbed Brody's arm as he started down through the hatch past the wounded NCO. "Don't let nothin' happen to my boys. Ya listenin' to me, Brody?" He was speaking of "his boys" but he was talking about Lt. Vance.

Zack didn't care much for the officer's leadership abilities, either. He had reacted to Zack being shot as if a judge had just sentenced him to die, and he didn't quite understand jungle justice yet.

"What's my name?"

Zack's eyes narrowed suspiciously as the tremors began wracking his body and a corpsman tied a tourniquet below the tear to his femoral artery. "Wha—?"

"What's my name?" The Spec-4 glanced over at the busy door gunner. He was wishing that this was *Peg,* and that *he* was behind the blazing Hog-60.

Zack reached out and grasped the gunny's lucky-charms necklace, and the trace of a sparkle danced in the depths of his eyes. "Brody! Your name's Brody!" Zack shook his head as if waking in darkness to a dream he fought to remember. Why was this white boy fucking with him?

"What's my *real* name, Leo?"

"Your real name. . .your real name. . ." The corpsman was slamming thorazine into the trembling sergeant. "Whoresomething. . .yah, that's it! *Whoresomething!*"

"Think again, dude!" Brody broke away, shattering the spell that was so important to Sgt. Zack, and made for the hatch.

"Whoremonger! Take care of our men, *Whoremonger*!" He remembered, and Brody turned and scraped his silver VC HUNTING CLUB ring against Zack's. It may only have been static electricity, but a spark danced between the two warriors —not unlike the sign he thought he saw in the big NCO's pitch-black eyes—and the Whoremonger gave Zack the thumbs-up as he dropped down onto the skids.

"You can bank on it, Leo the Lionhearted!" Brody flashed an eerie Death's-head grin as he suddenly came to understand about the jungle rain-forest and the evil that attracts men to it. "I'll bring 'em all back to you safe and fucking sound, chump! You just line up the VC skullcaps, and keep the beer on tap lukewarm!"

Krutch had been prepared for their escape from combat for several days before he and the Professor actually went AWOL. He had stashed a whole footlocker of Budweiser onboard *Pegasus,* but here it was only their seventh day in paradise, and they were already down to six cans.

Progress on the treehouse was slower than either of them had expected—several hostile gibbons had been protesting their plans to build the elaborate, multi-storied dwelling from the start—and the women had taken up residence several hundred yards down the beach at another lagoon. Kim had reinforced nagging suspicions in them with her stories of American atrocities, and the prostitutes decided there might be safety in numbers.

Krutch had repeatedly propositioned them in the last few days, but Kim—she seemed in charge of the invisible chastity belts now—adamantly proclaimed, *No tea, no talk...no money, no honey!* An obvious reversal of her earlier attitude.

"Ain't no different than the mainland anymore," Larson protested vigorously. "I mean, how much is a short time worth over here? One coconut? Two?"

"Maybe we oughta start pullin' shifts on guard." Krutch brought the subject up during one lonely sunset. "Just in case they decide to bury one of *us* up to our necks in the sand."

"Oh, come on!" Larson threw his hands up. "Why waste the time? I fucking *know* you wasted that cunt, Stork. I just *know* it!"

Krutch just shook his head, tired of defending himself. "Well, then"—he prepared his bedroll beneath the stars—"since *I'm* your prime suspect, I guess *you're* the one who should lose sleep over this. You can have the first watch."

Later, as they watched falling stars disappear along the horizon and satellites traverse the heavens, the big cat roaming the rain forest screamed at the crescent moon again. "Maybe it was that damn panther, Hal."

"Leopard," Krutch corrected him. One thing the Stork prided himself on was his knowledge of pussy.

"Whatever. What if that leopard tore the girl's nose and ears off?"

"Leopards don't bury women up to their necks, boy."

"Oh, right. I forgot about that." Larson swallowed with a dry throat, wondering how he could ever fail to remember something so horrible.

"Have you ever seen what members of the cat family do to people in the wild, Professor?" Krutch picked up a huge conch shell and blew into it without warning.

Larson nearly bailed out of his beachcombers. "You asshole, Krutch."

Stork threw the shell into the sea. "Well, have you? Panthers love female cadavers best. I saw it in Rhodesia, once. They especially crave the groin area—it's so soft there, you know. Well, they get ahold of them ol' vaginal lips with their fangs and jerk up."

"Cut me some slack, dude."

"They clamp down on that ol' juicy pussy and rip upward, boy, and they don't stop until they've torn the ribcage open and her tits are flappin' in the dust! Now whatta ya think about that?"

"You oughta write a horror novel, Stork. You could title it 'The Horrible Demented Whore,' or something like that." Larson knocked a sand crab off his leg, and a shudder ran through him as he thought about the dead girl's polished eye sockets.

"Already have, Professor, already have. It's back in my locker down An Khe-way, collectin' dust just like the forty-four rejection slips sittin' on top of it."

The next morning they found the arms and legs of another bargirl, washed-up on their private, picture-post-card, white

320

sand beach.

"He says there's ten thousand-plus NVA in the hills sur-rounding us, Colonel." Vance radioed up to Buchanan in his Command & Control helicopter.

Brody's people had just captured a North Vietnamese strag-gler after sweeping the gullies near where Sgt. Zack had been fired upon from. The lone soldier might have been exaggerating a bit in hopes his words instilled enough caution in the Ameri-cans to guarantee his safe transfer to a POW camp in lieu of exe-cution on the spot. But Buchanan was taking no chances.

"Have Bravo Company sweep eastward from LZ X-RAY." He listened to the Man in charge, circling in the Loach above his, give the directive, and ordered the soldiers in Vance's team to swing around and supplement their efforts. "And secure a defensive position until we can mass a contingent on the Whiskey."

The terse acknowledgment was followed a few minutes later by one of the fiercest and most disorganized firefights Brody ever participated in, as the Americans ran headlong into two North Vietnamese companies.

Brody and Cordova and Fletcher watched men they hardly knew in the human wave ahead drop face-first into the reeds, cut to pieces by an intense crossfire of several machine gun nests. Before he knew it, Vance was beside him.

They were operating almost as a separate unit from the other platoons sweeping the area, and the lieutenant's face was against his. Vance spoke so low none of the others lying behind logs and dead bodies could hear him. "I'm going to pull our people back!"

It almost came out as a question, a request, really, as rico-chets bounced in all around them and gunships swooped in low overhead, unleashing their rocket pods but having little effect against the well-dug-in NVA positions. Three of the MG nests were set up in cavelike rock overhangs, and difficult for the Cobras to get at.

For once, Brody agreed with him. "We're clearly out-fucking-numbered, Lieutenant!" he said. "I do believe I would readily concur with your decision!"

Firing magazine after magazine from the hip on rock-'n'-

roll, most of Echo Company got out before a squad containing the newbies, Chappell and Nelson and the others, was hit by an L-ambush and decimated.

"Forget it." Brody caught the look of concern and anguish in Vance's eyes. "There's nothing we can do for them right now. We'd get slaughtered trying to cross that clearing. You've got us pulling back, and that's the right thing to do. Let the Cobra jocks get some!"

The team soon found itself on the other side of LZ X-Ray. Slicks were still bringing men in from the First Battalion of the Seventh Cavalry, and Brody began to wonder for the first time if this might turn out to be Little Big Horn all over again. *Those who ignore history are destined to repeat it* . . .The words rang in his head for some reason, but Custer's situation couldn't apply here! There were absolutely no similarities present except that they were heavily outnumbered and members of the famous general's old unit.

"Jesus!" Fletcher and he shared the same log as several RPGs ripped into their defenses with brain-jarring blasts that knocked Snakeman's collection of reptiles off his web belt.

Something more important, more spellbinding had captured his attention. Another crossfire opened up after four Hueys landed in the middle of the already hot LZ. Soldiers jumping down out of the hatches were cut to pieces despite the streams of cover fire sent out by troopers in Brody's squad.

One of the choppers, its human cargo disgorged, managed to ascend through the hail of lead converging on the landing zone, but two ships remained on the ground, just sitting there, the windshields shattered by bullet holes and the pilots dead.

As he was switching magazines, Brody watched the rotors swishing through the gunsmoke. The jet turbines were screaming, but the birds just sat there, fat and helpless, as the warriors who had jumped from them scrambled through the reeds and elephant grass of LZ X-Ray, fighting for their lives.

The fourth ship lifted off the ground finally, and the violent downblast from its rotors swept some of the gunsmoke aside magically, breaking the spell. But it was still a cursed clearing, and grunts continued to die.

There were absolutely no similarities present except that they were heavily outnumbered and members of the famous gener-

al's old unit.... Brody repeatedly tried to shake the words from his head, but there was no delaying it, they were headed for a world of hurt.

His uniform was drenched in sweat, as if he'd just stepped from the shower into a monsoon downpour.

CHAPTER 34

Krutch was glad they hadn't chucked the firearms into the middle of the ocean upon landing, as they had originally planned.

He sat in front of the campfire, cradling the M-16 in his arms, and it felt good. "I'm not sure what the hell is going on on this goofy, crazy island, but the motherfuckin' boogie-man ain't gonna get the Stork, that's for sure."

"Do you mind?" Larson turned over in the white pebbles, and one side of the sand castle they'd built that afternoon came crashing down on his face. He shook the grit out of his hair, and Krutch thought of *Choi-oi* just then. "I was trying to get some sleep."

"How can you sleep on the beach?" Krutch rubbed the barrel of his rifle. "Nobody could fall asleep on the beach. Not at night. Not with the tide rising. You're weird, Shawn. Yah... Larson, the weird professor."

The woman's limbs had not been severed from her torso. They'd been pulled out by the roots.

The day after her toes scraped against Larson's snorkeling mask—giving the deserter quite a scare—they found the head of still another girl, bobbing in the surf.

The sharks had found her first.

"Yep, wish we'd brought along ol' *Choi-oi*." Krutch threw a twig into the flames as he scanned the eerie glow on the horizon. As a child, he'd collected comic books called *Tales from*

323

the Crypt, but now he was actually *living* a mystery more bizarre and frightening than anything he'd ever found in the pages of that series. In the last week, he'd helped Kim bury two women, and the hair had yet to settle along the back of his neck again. "Ol' *Choi-oi* could sure enough protect us from whichever one of those deranged wenches is killin' off all the cunt on this island. Do you realize we're facing a crisis here, Shawn?"

"What?" Larson pulled half his sleeping bag over his face.

"The Isle of Stork is actually on the verge of suffering a pussy shortage, my friend. Why, it could wreck the whole economy and—"

"I don't even remember what it looks like. Now put a cork in it, so I can chase some *Z*'s. Okay, pelican-breath?"

Five minutes later, the Professor was snoring. To Krutch, he sounded like a sea gull in heat.

The woman waited until the two Americans beside their campfire were sleeping before she rose from her own mat of palm fronds and thatched reeds. The others in her dwindling group had stayed up with her until well after four o'clock, making small talk about Pleiku in an attempt to remain awake. It was the only way they could think of to maintain some sort of guard after dark.

But the four others had dozed off now, and the woman picked the prostitute laying farthest from the others.

Silent as a panther on the prowl, she dropped to one knee beside the girl and slammed the empty machine gun barrel from *Pegasus* against her temple with a dull thud, crushing one side of her skull.

She paused a few moments, listening to movement somewhere beyond the tree line, deep in the island's dense patch of woods. And she smiled slowly.

It was the panther. She wanted to laugh, to throw her head back in defiance, challenging the big cat. It would be stupid for the black beast to attack, for she would tear its throat out, and smother the bitches at her feet in its blood. The woman was angry. Angry at the world. And everything that dared move in the night.

When the crackling of branches ceased, she contemplated killing the rest of the girls, but decided it would be better to
324

wait. Wait a day, or a week. The terror that grew in their eyes as each new sunset approached was well worth the delay. She had never enjoyed her work so much before.

The woman was beginning to feel guilty. Biting her lower lip brought her back to reality, and she dragged the dead girl's body through the sand, to the far side of the lagoon.

There was a waterfall back beyond the trees somewhere, and as she reached the trickle of a stream that emptied out into the lagoon, the din of water crashing down nearly caused her to miss the mild groan.

The girl whose face she'd just disfigured was still alive. "How nice!" the woman whispered to herself at the unexpected bonus as she took the twine looped around her shoulder and threw it over a sturdy branch.

After the noose was fashioned, she tightened it around the girl's ankles and quickly hoisted her up off the ground, upside-down, until her head was a few inches above the pebbles.

Taking the razor-sharp blade from her waistband, she made incisions across the girl's knees and stomach. And then she began peeling her skin off.

Brody's people found the bodies of everyone in the squad of newbies except Chappell and Nelson when they mounted a rescue raid that afternoon. The two privates were promptly placed on the MIA roster and presumed prisoners of war. *Missing, but in NVA "custody," presumed prisoners, but probably dead.* It was all a play on words to Brody, and he hated it.

He and Vance both wanted to pursue the North Vietnamese all the way to Hanoi, if necessary, but the officers circling the battlefield in Loach choppers denied the requests throughout a heated radio-net argument. Brody wasn't that angry about the recruits getting dragged off into the jungle—he didn't even know them . . . not really—but he was furious the NVA had had the gall to go after prisoners at all. The communists had snatched a couple newbies right out from under him during the biggest combat assault the First Cav had ever mounted. And someone was gonna pay!

Vance advised Brody he was going to make his way down through the staggered lines of cover to one of the captains leading three platoons from Delta Company. "I'll feed *him* a cock-

'n'-bull story that'll authorize a Cav pursuit after that squad that captured Chappell and Nelson," he said. "Then we'll be free and clear to do as we see fit, and maybe get a Cobra or two at our disposal...."

Two Cobras is all we got! thought Brody. He didn't know what the lieutenant was up to, but he definitely had *this* Spec-4's cooperation.

"Fucking forget it!" Fletcher blocked his departure from the pile of rotting logs.

"What?" Vance couldn't believe his ears. And neither could Brody.

"We don't stand a chance out there." He turned to face Treat, ignoring the officer. "And you know it!"

"It may be the only chance Chappell and the others have."

"Bullshit. We're no help to anybody if we're dead!" Fletcher seemed to have a point, machine guns were raking their position again from two different points.

"Wouldn't you want some of us to volunteer to take some risks if it were your life at stake?" Vance asked him.

"There's no risk involved!" Snakeman thrust his nose against the lieutenant's. "It's certain death out there."

"Well—"

"Choppers are still floatin' in, for Christsake! Wait 'till we get the upper hand on this fucking abortion, and then you can play hero as much as you—"

"Well, I'm still in charge around here and—"

"Are you sure?" Fletcher cut him off.

"Annnnnd, what I say *goes,* Private Fletcher." Vance didn't have to look down at his name tag.

"Fucking fine." Fletcher watched him run an impressive, textbook, zigzag sprint down through the gully and dive in over the heads of two Delta Company machine gunners. "Stupid college boy," he added.

"Ol' college boy is right." Mohammed spoke up for the first time that day. Most of the time he'd been busy keeping his head and rifle muzzle down low.

"Fuck you and your opinion, Crump." Fletcher did not look at the black soldier. "I shoulda fragged the sonofabitch while I had the chance."

"Snakeman!" Brody glanced around, but no one else had

heard him.

"All I know is that *I* wouldn't want to be abandoned by my brothers." Mohammed rushed off after the lieutenant. "*I* wouldn't chicken out when the big test came. And *this,* Snake-oil"—the militant's words were barely audible over the sluggish pounding of M-60 chambers—"look like it gonna be da FI-nal exxxammmmm!"

His jaw tightening, Fletcher turned to face Abdul Mohammed, only to find him trotting down through the ricochets like a bored gazelle. "You're lookin' at one dead nigger," he bragged to Brody as he lifted his M-16 and lined the sights up between Mohammed's shoulder blades.

As he squeezed gently on the trigger and the rifle butt kicked back against his shoulder, a chunk of lead slammed into his left arm, knocking the weapon from his hands. And then a second bullet struck his side. And a third, and a fourth.

Snakeman was knocked out of his balled-up crouch by the succession of smoking lead. The seventh round that hit him was a glowing white tracer, and it knocked him all the way down into the sea of elephant grass, a cartwheeling shower of crimson.

CHAPTER 35

Larson could not sleep.

Try as he would, he could not shake the memory of the woman they'd found hanging upside-down from the tree. The panther was leaning against her when they made the gruesome discovery. Leaning with its front paws gouged into her thighs. The big cat stood on muscular hind legs, arching its back, but the sight they came upon was not of a friendly feline stretching in preparation for scratching up the furniture. The panther's face was smeared with blood as it tore out the girl's entrails with its teeth. Larson would never forget what he had seen that evening as the dusk passed and twilight approached. *Crimson on black velvet.* That's how he would remember the panther's surprised face when they rushed into the clearing beside the lagoon. And steam. *Steam rising from the wet entrails.* Even in the oppressive heat of Vietnam. Steam.

Krutch had shot the panther with a frantic ten-round burst from his M-16. The girls were all standing behind him when he did it, and they screamed, most of them. Two of the bullets struck the girl's body. It had sounded like someone hitting a punching bag with two sharp jabs. *Thump thump!*

Larson could not forget that sound. Whenever he closed his eyes, he saw the bullets sending a shudder through her delicate frame, even though she was already dead. He saw the puncture wound deflate her stomach, and the other soft-nosed slug rip one breast open, scattering cartilage across the pebbles.

He heard the sound even now, it seem, between the crashing of the waves. *Thump thump!*

Larson glanced at his watch and slapped an ankle. The ants had found him in his treetop perch again.

He and Krutch had abandoned plans to build a treehouse. There was just too much trouble involved, and they were not even sure anymore if it was worth staying on the island. "Thank God we didn't dump *Pegasus* into the sea," the Stork had said just that morning.

Larson was spending his nights in a hammock he'd strung between two of the highest branches in the tallest tree he could find. He changed locations every evening and took great pains to ensure no one saw which way he walked after the sun went down. Things were getting a little too much out of hand...just a little too strange for his tastes.

He slapped at another ant. They were soldier ants, big black ones; and the word was apparently out, a caravan of six-legged warriors was headed his way.

Larson climbed to the ground and decided to hike over to the waterfall. The rocks there glowed with a faint luminescence at night, and sometimes the girls spent their evenings skinnydipping.

"Professor!" Krutch's voice reached his ears as he was half-

way across the lagoon, and Larson swam back to shore after wading a hundred feet, careful to keep his rifle above the surface. He had never heard Krutch yell like that. It sounded as if the Stork had broken a wing!

Hal Krutch seemed determined to defy not only the odds but also common sense, refusing to move his camp off the vulnerable beach up to a more defensible position in the trees. Since Day One at the island, he'd slept on the white sand, often forgetting just where he'd left his weapon, determined to keep the Isle of Stork the paradise he'd been searching for all his life.

Not that Larson was that impressed with the alleged display of courage. It *had* to be Hal who was killing the women, Shawn was convinced. Why else would he be so carefree about security and his own safety after dark?

But maybe the girls, surmising the same thing, had finally ganged up on the ex-chopper pilot. Larson's feet carried him faster through the reeds and elephant grass as visions of Krutch being hacked to death by several machetes filled his head.

The girls were running toward Krutch's shelterhalf too when Larson rounded a bend in the beach. All of them.

Kim drew his unzipped sleeping-bag cover back, but it was empty.

One of the women standing behind Larson screamed, and he whirled around, rifle leveled, to find her pointing at the tree line...something swaying back and forth beneath a branch, over a campfire.

Hal Krutch's hair and shoulders were burning by the time Larson reached the body. He fired an entire burst at the knots of twine holding the pilot's ankles to the branch, and Krutch's body dropped into the campfire, face first.

Larson dragged him out, but the American war hero was dead. His face was a pulpy slab of red meat: someone had hacked all his identifiable features away with a knife or razor blade or something. *Maybe a machete.* Larson's vision returned to haunt him.

But the women had all been accounted for. Or so it seemed. Kim rolled his body over and dropped into a squat beside the mutilated face. She brushed soot and ashes away until a jagged crevice below the swollen nasal cavity revealed something hanging from the tears where his lips had been.

"What's this?" she slowly drew a long piece of shredded flesh out and laid it across the pilot's chest.

"Oh, sweet Jesus!" Larson turned and threw up on the woman standing behind him, and then he ran. Tears filling his eyes, he ran as hard and as far and as long as he could.

The object Kim had withdrawn was a severed penis.

"Is he gonna make it?"

"Yah, I think the honky motherfucker'll pull through."

The air overhead was disturbed by several sets of rotors slicing through the muggy heat, but no one glanced up.

"I don't know. . . . Seven bullets is an awful lot for any trooper to take."

"He'll make it."

"White boy *better* make it. I wanna see the look on his face when he opens his eyes and sees *this!*"

PFC Elliot Fletcher, alias Snakeman, struggled to open his eyes. It was as if he'd been tripped up at the edge of Void Vicious and had fallen over that unchallengeable line. . .was tumbling down, head over bootheels, into the pit. . .that deep, dark, bottomless pit. . . .

But then there was a ray of light below him. A spark and a flash and a roomful of mirrors, and his whole world was turned upside-down. Men were crouching all around him. . .*warriors*. Faces he knew; some he didn't. Some wearing shirts; many bare-chested. "Come onnnnn, Snakeman." One of them was squeezing his hand, wiping his brow. Another jabbed needles in his arm. He thought he recognized Doc Delgado. Good ol' Doc Delgado. *Hospital white, not Hispanic. . .hospital white, not Hispanic.* . . "You can make it, bro. . . ."

He tried to force the lids apart, but they would not cooperate. Pain surged through his body now. . .*all* through it. . .in and out every limb, swirling around in his gut, twisting his testicles —like little elves on the rampage, chasing each other through his system with jackhammers and Frisbees. Frisbees studded with razor blades.

"Yah, Snakeman's gonna pull through," he heard one of them say. An accent. But not an ethnic accent. Hollywood. No, cigar store simple. An Indian accent. Broken Arrow! His favorite cigar-store Indian.

But he couldn't open his eyelids, and the pain became all-consuming. The light in the pit began to flicker. And then it went out.

Someone was pumping on his chest.

"White boy *better* make it!" A faint voice reached him through tons and tons of storm clouds pressing down on his heart. "Abdul better *not* be wastin' his time!"

"I can't understand it!" That damned lieutenant was talking now. "Sure, seven holes in 'im, but that sniper didn't hit nothin' vital, did he? He should pull through, shouldn't he?"

"Shock's settin' in, Lou." It was Brody's voice. Good old Brody, his buddy. Treat the Whoremonger. "The shock of stoppin' all that lead is doin' a job on his attitude."

Fletcher could *feel* Brody's lips beside his ear now. He could *feel* the gunny whispering to him. "Come on, Fletch, you can hang on, dude. Do ya hear me? We got things to do, Snakeman, places to go. . .women to fuck and pussy to suck. Come on, bud. . .open your eyes for ol' Treat. Just hang in there. We got a slick circlin' above us now! Can ya hear them beautiful rotor blades choppin' up the Veeyet at-mo-sphere, pal? Can ya feel that downblast in your face? Just a couple more minutes, Elliot . . .just a couple more. . . ."

"White boy Snakeoil never *could* get it right, Treat. He don't even know how to *die* right!"

"God damn it." Reddish foam bubbled up at the edges of Fletcher's lips and he willed his eyes to open. He would rip that no-account troublemaker's heart out even it it killed him. Despite the pain, despite the drunk and dazed sluggishness controlling his movements, the loss of power, he would rise up and kill the sonofabitch if it was the last thing he ever—

The sight greeting Fletcher's eyes caused him to sit up as if he'd been struck in the belly with a sledgehammer.

"What the *fuuuuuuck*!" His eyes darted about, searching for friendly faces, seeking someone to reassure him, to pat him on the head and confirm that what he was seeing was a nightmare.

He was receiving a transfusion. AND ABDUL MOHAM-MED WAS GIVING THE BLOOD!

"Settle down, Snakeman!"

Brody was in front of his face now, both hands against his

upper arms, gently pushing him back down, accidentally pinching one of the wounds, hurting him. But the pain meant nothing now.

"Get that nigger's blood OUTTA me, do you hear? GET IT OUT OF ME!"

"Settle down, Snakeman!" Brody's fingers were soaked in his blood now. "Just settle down, and you're gonna be all right."

"I'm gonna turn BLACK! I'm gonna turn fucking *BLACK*! And my hair's going to curl up like a Brillo pad. BRODY! Pull them tubes outta me, brother. PULL 'EM OUT!"

"Screw this bullshit," Mohammed was muttering as he shifted about on the ground, preparing to get up and leave, but Brody used facial expressions and hand movements in an effort to keep him beside the Snakeman.

"Come on, Fletch, mellow out!" Brody coaxed his best friend. "We checked everywhere, and Mohammed's the only guy this side of Cambodia who's got your blood type. You just got too many holes in you, brother! You'd never last until the slick got you back to the hospital." Gabriel's Dustoff chopper was landing several feet away as he spoke, and Nurse Maddox was one of the medics who jumped off even before the skids touched earth. She exchanged smiles with Delgado, but there was no real display of emotion of affection in front of the soldiers.

"Am I gonna die, Treat?" Fletcher's hand rose and clamped down on Brody's collar. "Just level with me, am I at the staircase to Hell?"

Brody broke eye contact, shaking his head from side to side, but he felt he was telling the truth. "No, you're not buyin' no farms today, Snakeman. You're gonna make it! You might even be able to stay in the Green Machine—"

"If you're as stupid as I think you are," Mohammed cut in, and Brody silenced him with an angry glare.

"Doc here says he don't think ol' Luke hit nothin' vital, dude. Doc says you ain't gonna lose your pecker or your pancreas or any o' that crap! Now what more could you possibly ask for?" He moved aside as Lt. Maddox and two corpsmen from the slick flopped down a stretcher and began sliding Snakeman onto it.

"I'm not askin', Treat, I'M BEGGIN' you. Rip these damn tubes out of my arm!"

"The tubes stay." Maddox took over with a cold, businesslike tone.

"But—" Fletcher started to protest.

"That's an *order*, soldier," she snapped, without looking into his eyes. Maddox was too busy wrapping bandages as her assistants strapped Snakeman to the stretcher.

"But—"

"The tubes stay in, Elliot. I'm levelin' with you, the tubes stay in, or you're a goner, okay? You don't listen to me now, and you'll be takin' orders from the Devil himself."

Fletcher was shocked into a pleasant silence. *She knew my first name!* He laid his head back on the stretcher and nodded. "Yah...." He hesitated. "Okay, ma'am, whatever you say." *The foxy lady who dropped her drawers for Delgado knows my first name!*

As they were carrying him over to the slick, Fletcher turned to Mohammed and said, "You're fucked, boy. I'm gonna kill you for this."

The black militant glanced over at Brody, who was helping with the stretcher, and produced the brightest, most satisfied smile the Whoremonger had ever seen.

CHAPTER 36

Shawn Larson, Private Investigator. That's what he fancied himself tonight. *Just the facts, mama-san.*

The Professor was sitting in a tree over Kim's new camp, watching the crescent moon set beyond the mists along the horizon. And watching Kim.

Kim had surfaced as the leader of the females on their private

333

little island, but now there was only one girl left besides her. They'd found the dismembered bodies of the others floating in the surf during the past week. And Kim was Larson's primary suspect.

At first, it had seemed unlikely. Hadn't she been in the midst of the others as they all ran up to Krutch's mutilated body? But it had taken Larson a good five minutes to cross the lagoon, and she could have swum to Vung Tau for brunch and back for all he knew. It only took seconds to hack up someone's face if your knife was sharp enough.

The only other survivor of the mysterious murders was also forming her own conclusions, it appeared, she had built her solitary camp upstream from the lagoon, beside the waterfall. A foolish tactical decision, Larson felt. It would be hard to hear intruders entering the area at night, with that hypnotic roar of falling water in your ears. But maybe that was how she wanted it. Perhaps the girl didn't want to hear her attacker creeping up through the sticks and pebbles. She was probably resigned to her fate, Larson decided. Her destiny was to die in her sleep.

Movement.

Larson rubbed his eyes, but they were not deceiving him. Kim was getting up.

He glanced at his watch: four o'clock. More than three hours before sunrise. He hoped he would have no problem following her in the dark. But then, he felt he knew exactly where she was going.

He waited until she was out of sight past the bend in the beach before he dropped from his perch. She was heading for the girl camped beside the waterfall.

Kim was saving Shawn Larson for last.

She paused within the tall sea of elephant grass, watching the girl bathing beneath the waterfall. The girl was a woman, really. They had all been women. But she had saved the prettiest for last. This one, with her flawless body and cover girl face and hair the texture of silk that sparkled even under the stars on a night with no moon...this one with smooth hands that had never worked a plow, would meet a special fate. One could not get calluses from giving hand jobs—just calloused, perhaps. And because the soles of her feet were soft as silk and not sand-

334

paper harsh, like Kim's, she would die a cruel, merciless death.

The rocks around this waterfall gave off a luminous glow, and the girl look almost like a spirit as she stood in the middle of it, one arm raised above the other as she soaped herself down with the slice of PX soap Hal had rationed to them all before his execution.

Yes, sweet Hal had made love to this one too, Kim decided. He had corrupted them all, and on the night he invited himself to return to Kim's arms, she had challenged him to a bout of kinky lovemaking. *With bookoo twine.* And then she killed him. Poor Krutch had never planned on so much pain.

She giggled at the thought but quickly placed a hand over her mouth, in the timeless Oriental fashion. *Hide the mouth, always hide the mouth,* she thought as she gazed up at the waterfall, following it to the clifftops, several hundred feet into the night sky. She could not really see the top, though, and she was glad of that. It was better not to be able to see everything. Some things had to remain clouded in mystery. *Hide all things sensuous.*

Kim watched the woman wipe soap from her breasts with slender fingers adorned with rings the GIs in her life had given her. They were all the proof the prosecution needed. And the sentence was death.

Kim was communist to the core now. Not that she really understood what communism was. But she had attended all the indoctrination sessions and listened to the political cadre on the long marches through treacherous jungle, and she believed. She hated the foreigners and the way the country remained divided because of them. And she believed the communists held the answer to reuniting north and south.

Those who cooperated with the Imperialists needed to be shown the correct path. Those who continued to stray had to be taught a lesson. And people who blatantly ignored, even scoffed at the teachings, like the women she had spent the last couple of weeks with, received a one-way ticket to nowhere. And Kim was the executioner.

She had no weapons with her tonight. Only her hands.

She would surely need one to finish off the one they called Professor, but tonight was a recreational encounter. Another chance to practice the skills the hand-to-hand instructors had

335

taught her during those long treks down the Sihanouk Trail, when the days were spent hiding from the Arc-Light, and the nights were a multi-wrestling contest. Unsure why, Kim unbuttoned her blouse and let her sarong drop to a fluffy pile around her feet. She stepped from the reeds, smooth as polished amber, her breasts heavy as she climbed up over the rocks, swaying slightly, as the adrenaline rushed through her veins and her chest tightened.

She wanted to laugh. To giggle and rush into the waterfall as she had in Hue twenty years earlier—a naked child, joining her girl friends. But her hands were raised in front of her eyes, and the fingers were out in a death stance as she approached the woman inside the waterfall, silent as a leopard stalking its prey.

Startled, Kim wanted to scream as the man clothed in rags charged from the edge of the rain forest toward her, but she could only open her mouth. Nothing. She was frozen to the spot.

The man was doing enough yelling for both of them. Matted hair down to his shoulders, the Asian was swinging a machete over his head. He slid to a stop ten feet away from her, eyes bulging. Small, winged bugs were crawling about in his scraggly beard. It was a Ho Chi Minh beard, Kim decided. She smiled, and the tension in her fingers slackened. Slowly, she brought her palms up to show she was unarmed.

The wild man charged, the long blade over his head gleaming for an instant, and a single shot rang out. It was a tracer. A hot, green tracer that sizzled past Kim's face, leaving a phantom glow in front of her eyes. The bullet struck the Vietnamese in the chest, knocking him backwards, out of sight.

Larson rushed up out of the reeds and planted the flash suppressor of his M-16 against the wild man's forehead, but he was dead, lifeless eyes staring up at the stars that seemed to weep for him and the satellites that couldn't have cared less.

Larson rubbed the bullet casing for good luck. It was the bullet with Hal Krutch's name on it. The bullet on the dog tags necklace Shawn had removed from the Stork's body before he buried him beside the lagoon on their splendid little island.

Jet jockeys ain't shit. Krutch's words rang in his mind as he stared down at the six-pack. *Them fancy fighter planes take*

*some twelve-point-seven or A-A flak and chances are they'll
live to coast into an emergency landing somewhere. Jet jockeys
would have you think chopper pilots are washed-up wanna-
be's, but I'm here to tell ya it just ain't so, Shawn-buddy.*

The six-pack was the term Krutch attached to the main
gauges on the instrument panel, which included the amp meter,
and fuel, oil and transmission temperatures and pressure. He
stared at the CHIP LIGHT warning light a moment, then his
eyes strayed to all the other bulbs that would probably start
flashing the instant he tried this stunt: FIRE, high and low
RPM indicators, and on and on.

*Anyone can fly a fighter. . .but it takes a special breed of sad-
ist to wanna pilot a gunship.* Ol' Pegasus just wouldn't stay in
the air if the Stork wasn't breathin' fire with both hands and feet
on all four vital controls. All the countless dials staring back at
him were making Larson dizzy. He flipped a switch, and they
began to glow a soft red.

"Just like lantern outside boom-boom bunker." The girl sitting beside Kim behind him giggled, and the Professor just
shook his head silently. If only she knew how slim their
chances of getting off the ground really were. Typical female,
he decided. Placing all her trust in the big, brave American.

*A jet. . .well, a jet is designed to glide back to earth if worse
comes to worse, but a whirlybird—well, they would rather just
rip apart down the middle, throwing pieces out in all directions.
You see, a chopper is an odd collection of opposing forces
brought together against its will, just waiting to bust loose on
you. Yep, it takes a real pro to keep it all together, running
smoothly.*

A sobering thought, Larson mused as he contemplated the
MASTER switch leering down at him. Krutch had always
talked about how the master switch was often used by pilots to
start all the necessary accessory switches when emergencies
demanded the gunships jump within a minute after the scramble sirens were tripped.

He stretched his shoulders before strapping in. Larson was
wearing Krutch's old shoulder holster and his .38 revolver. It
felt both good and restricting at the same time. He adjusted it,
wondering why his thoughts had shifted to Gunslinger Gabriel
instead of the Stork. Gabe wore his sidearm on his hip. Could

337

it be because Gabriel was a Dustoff pilot, who often flew to gunship crashes?

Larson wondered how much fuel was left inside *Pegasus*. She normally carried 800 pounds of jet kerosene, aside from the 600 pounds of ammo and rockets, and the weight of the crew and "pack," or human cargo. The term made him laugh aloud. For months, Krutch and Warlokk and the other pilots had chuckled whenever they mentioned the Pack was *UP*! and ready to lift off. To chopper jocks, the "pack" was any live freight seated behind the cockpit stations. To Larson and the rest of Brody's people, The Pack was named for killers of the *Cainis Lupus* persuasion: They considered themselves a pack of wolves.

There were no more rockets aboard the ship; he remembered watching Krutch fire them all off as they attempted to escape that green hell back on the mainland. He ignored the red button on the cyclic switch that fired the two-point-five's and pulled a yellow lever up through the safety wire beside the peter pilot's seat, jettisoning the empty rocket pods. They struck the sand noiselessly.

Glancing over a shoulder, he asked, "You up in back?' with a tight grin across his lips.

"What?" Kim narrowed her worried eyes. The girl seated beside her clutched Kim's wrist and said, "Huh?"

Chuckling to himself, Larson settled back in the uncomfortable seat and shook his head. He'd never be able to do it. Nevertheless, he placed the balls of his feet on the tail rotor pedals and made a growling sound, flashing back briefly to a time when his childhood had been more than family fights and a sick sister. He was seated behind the steering wheel of a go-cart on a large asphalt racetrack in a town called Durango, Colorado. Sipping on an icy bottle of Pepsi-Cola, revving up the engine— a thirteen-year-old Mario Andretti. Tomorrow was supposed to be the big day: a visit to Mesa Verde's cliff dwellings. But today he was King of the Road.

He shook the memory from his head, angry with himself. He should be frightened out of his mind now, not daydreaming, and he concentrated on the controls.

Larson placed his right hand on the directional cyclic rising up between his knees. His left hand took hold of the motorcycle-style throttle on the collective stick rising up from the floor on the left side of his seat. It controlled the power and pitch of the main overhead rotor.

It was now or never, he decided. Their island paradise was becoming more dangerous than the war zone itself. He and Krutch had never in their wildest dreams predicted stragglers might be hiding out on the island—Vietnamese who had also gone AWOL from the insanity of war only to go mad on the lonely atoll. There was no telling how many more machete-waving maniacs inhabited the dense stretch of jungle in the island's center. Larson only hoped that the man he had killed— they found Chinese Communist markings on the machete's handle and an NVA star belt buckle on the body—was the same deserter who murdered his best friend.

He glanced down at the flex mounts outside. Most gunships carried six-barreled MGs on them, but *Pegasus* had always relied on her two hatch gunnies, usually Brody and Fletcher. They were added weight, but he didn't have the tools to take them off.

"Here goes nothing, ladies." He went down the checklist, hit, flipped, and flicked what Krutch had showed him, tripped the master switch, and listened to the turbines whine.

A loud sigh left the Professor, and the girl sitting beside Kim began clapping as the drooping blades above her began moving slowly with a powerful swish.

"Next stop, homeland or Hell." He winked back at Kim, but her face remained motionless. He remembered now that she had not enjoyed the chopper ride *out* to the island either. "Neb-bah mind, honey. Just close your eyes, enjoy the trip, and leave the driving to Big L." *I just hope Void Vicious don't take notice of us today, that's all.* Larson planned on setting down in the vicinity of their final Mayday call, but he had never been very good with navigational equipment and was just hoping to reach the mainland somewhere between Pleiku and Qui Nhon.

First, he had to get *Peg* off the ground.

Larson twisted the throttle to bring rotor and engine speed up to operating levels, then increased power and pitch with pressure on the governor. He pulled up on the collective stick and applied pressure to the left foot pedal, increasing the tail rotor's spin so as to neutralize the torque. Without both smooth, simultaneous actions, the ship would spin like a top and rip apart upon lifting off the ground.

He glanced at the N_1 tachometer, which told him how much of his maximum power was being used, and then his N_2, the dual needles of which displayed engine and rotor speed. Krutch had told him the normal reading for blade speed and motor output should be somewhere around 6600 RPMs.

Larson slipped the cyclic stick forward. While pulling up on the collective—the whole time increasing weight on his left foot—the craft lurched forward without pausing to rise into a hover.

He kept the nose low, praying for altitude, pulled back on the collective some more, and released the friction lock, and *Pegasus* shot up through a break in the trees before he even realized quite what was happening.

The crossed sabers painted across the snouts of twelve Hueys floating below the clouds up ahead was confirmation Larson was off course. The mural on the lead ship belonged to a bird operating out of Kontum, north of Pleiku. The 9th Cav had been fighting pitched battles with the communists at the time he and Krutch had deserted. Battles along the tri-border with Cambodia and Laos. And that was no gaggle up ahead, they were flying tight, hardly ten feet separating the rotor tips of each gunship.

It was twilight over Vietnam—a condition many vets claim does not exist in Southeast Asia but one Larson just knew would greet him on his solo flight—and the optical illusions that accompany twilight over Vietnam started playing their tricks on his eyes. The Professor, keeping his distance, followed the twelve ships west, guiding on the last Huey's red Grimes light as the glow on the horizon quickly faded.

Until his fuel alarm began screaming. "Hold onto your tits, ladies," he called over a shoulder. If there was one thing Krutch had taught him, it was that you didn't argue with fuel indicators. Ignoring them completely, as Larson had been doing, was an open invitation to disaster.

They were setting down right *here*!

It was a miracle he found the clearing in the dark. The crescent moon riding the horizon had helped, but he would never know how *Pegasus* managed to land in the sea of elephant grass without clipping the tree line.

Larson pushed the collective stick down while pulling back on the cyclic as the downblast uprooted swamp reeds and whipped them up into a swirling funnel. When the ten-foot-high bamboo stake shot up a few inches in front of his windshield, he rammed the collective to the floor and pranged over it. Several more booby traps—designed especially to crash helicopters landing for the first time in a strange LZ—splintered under the ship's belly, but no explosions followed.

"Let's go! Let's go! Let's go!" Larson could already smell the kerosene fumes. He unassed and climbed into the cabin to find the more innocent of his two passengers with her feet off the floor and her back flattened against the ceiling. Her breasts hung down through a ripped-open blouse on either side of a long bamboo pole that had burst up through the floorboards, impaling her. She would never giggle at his poor flying habits again.

"Oh, *babes*!" Blood dripping from her open mouth splattered onto his face, and he wiped it away frantically, as if it were acid. Her startled eyes were still open, but she was staring straight through him, bits and pieces of her heart hanging from the jagged bamboo point protruding above the roof.

Larson searched the cabin for Kim as he prepared to bail out the hatch, but she had already jumped from the opposite opening and was running through the clearing away from the helicopter.

"Kim!" he yelled at the top of his lungs, but she never looked back once and quickly disappeared into the jungle, clothes hanging from her delicate frame in bloody shreds.

CHAPTER 37

Forty-eight hours after Elliot *Snakeman* Fletcher was wounded in action and airlifted out of the Ia Drang Valley, Major Minh ran out of soldiers. The North Vietnamese officer had no more volunteers to man the suicide squads Hanoi had hoped to field against and eventually slaughter the First Air Cavalry Division. After three days and nights of constant fighting—much of it hand-to-hand combat—the communist ranks were so mutilated they could no longer contain the Americans within LZ X-Ray or any of its adjoining clearings. And additional waves of First Team gunships swept into the valley to reinforce the First and Third Brigades. The surviving North Vietnamese Regulars trickled back from the front lines, shocked by the power and might of the helicopter assault.

The first battle for the Ia Drang's LZ X-Ray ended officially on November 16, 1965. Crippled beyond Minh's imagination, three NVA Regiments would be out of action for several months to come. The major would not be able to mount Bull Buchanan's head outside his command post *this* day.

"The final body count is eighteen hundred-plus NVA Regulars." The colonel tapped his new swagger stick against the podium ten days later, after the month-long campaign for the region ended November 26th. Few of the men applauded this, his latest pep rally. Some 240 Americans had perished defending the Ia Drang Valley. And now they were preparing to pull out. "I just want you gentlemen to know you did a fine job out there." He pointed in the direction of the setting sun. "I appreciate what you went through. And your brothers who were not able to return with us appreciate it."

Brody raised the mental wall that blocked the colonel's words out. He was still stunned by the three-day shoot-out leading to Snakeman's injuries. They'd counted over 600 bodies on that one and sustained 79 American KIAs. He was burnt-out, beat-up, chewed-apart, and felt like a puddle of spit. The Whoremonger was ready for a rest.

When the final tally was made, however, they'd only lost a

total of four helicopters, and three of those had been recovered. Buchanan already had his cast off and was itching for more C&C action. And Zack, Brody observed, was loitering around the company area *in* a leg cast, refusing to be medevaced to the rear echelon.

Buchanan was making a joke about a North Vietnamese major who had slipped through his fingers during the final sweep of the Chu Pong Massif when two lieutenants ran up to the podium and interrupted him with hushed whispers.

A captain was called over to assume charge of the company muster, and Buchanan rushed off to his CP without so much as a fancy tongue-twisting farewell.

PFC Shawn Larson rose from his chair and saluted him as he rushed through the door.

"Where's Mister Krutch?" Buchanan demanded. Larson explained about the hostile fire they had taken shortly after leaving the free fire zone two weeks earlier. He synopsized the crash landing, the death of the peter pilot, and the ten days Larson had spent eluding guerrillas in the jungle after Hal Krutch fell into a tiger pit booby-trap and was impaled by a dozen bamboo stakes. It had been impossible to recover the body, Larson alleged. He did not mention Kim, or the unauthorized landing in Plei Nhol, or the ladies of questionable virtue they had relocated on the Isle of Stork.

Then he told Buchanan about the prisoner-of-war camp. "You say you recognized two of the soldiers being escorted through the jungle?" Buchanan asked after he was through repeating his story for the fifth time since being rescued by a Special Forces FOB patrol. The colonel didn't want to know why *Pegasus* went down thirty miles from the cords Krutch had radioed to the Pleiku tower before vanishing over Void Vicious.

"Yes, sir! Chappell and Nelson, the two newbies." The NVA weren't "escorting" them through the jungle trails at all, they were kicking, punching, and dragging the men toward the border. Chappell and Nelson were fresh out of boot camp and recalled, perhaps a bit better than many jungle vets, how they were supposed to counteract with the enemy if captured.

Totally lost beneath the triple canopy of the rain forest, Larson had followed the small patrol of communists, deciding he might at least be able to provide some sort of valuable reconnaissance if their trek led them to a camp or major trail. Then it would be only a matter of time before he could retrace his path, head southeast, and hope for the best.

He was well aware he might end up lost for life. "And you saw a third Caucasian in the cluster of huts?" Buchanan was already preparing his gear.

Larson shook his head in the affirmative. Chappell and Nelson had been the only U.S. soldiers plucked from the Ia Drang. The NVA had taken them to a striking plateau overlooking a trianglelike network of hamlets. Crystalline caves dotted the limestone hill at the plateau's edge, but the Vietnamese all seemed to be living in small straw huts in the clearing. The structures in the middle were reinforced with anti-personnel mines and encircled by a sagging wall of rusty concertina. Arvins appeared to make up the bulk of the prisoners, but there was one white man in their midst, and he appeared to be an American.

Larson feared he was probably wrong, but the POW's facial features seemed a close match to the description Elliot Fletcher had given him of his missing brother, Richard. It was just a long shot, and the odds were against such a stroke of luck, but it was a chance they would have to take.

"We've pretty much narrowed it down to an area immediately east of Polei Noh Yo, sir." One of the lieutenants pointed to the large map on the CP wall.

"Advise the men to saddle up," Buchanan told his aides. "I want volunteers for an off-the-record scramble. I want seven ships filled." He turned to Larson. "Would seven gunships do the job?"

"I think seven would be just fine, Colonel." Larson did not look enthusiastic, and he knew the CO would let him sit this one out without retribution, but things were changing within the pacifist. He knew he had to go along, if only for the ride.

"Okay!" Buchanan pounded a fist against the palm of his hand. "I want seven birds pregnant and off the nest in zero-five!" He motioned the lieutenant out. "Chappell and Nelson and whoever's behind door numba three have been waiting for us long enough as it is."

All seven gunships began taking on fire the moment they fell in range of the jutting plateau rising up above the cooking fires of Polei Noh Yo. Fifty-one-caliber shells, fired by 12.7-mm heavy machine-guns-on-wheels, punched fist-sized holes in more than one Huey, but the ships stayed aloft.

Bringing his Cobra in from the west, blacked-out, Lance Warlokk pounced on the dual MG batteries long before Buchanan even had his squadron dropping from the I.P. stage of convergence, and the deadly guns were silenced before they could do any real damage.

Flares popped on all sides of the plateau as the crafts flared-in for simultaneous landings—and none of them was fired by the Americans.

Eerie shadows played against the tree line as soldiers jumped from the choppers even before they touched down and charged toward the nearby huts and muzzle flashes.

His nose cannon burping grenade after grenade down into the ring of thatched straw, Warlokk had set the plateau's structures on fire all by himself, driving the North Vietnamese out into the open, where Brody's people engaged them in hand-to-hand and close quarters bayonet drill.

"Just like boot camp. Right, Em-ho?" The Whoremonger slashed at two Vietnamese with little effort, and both men collapsed, disemboweled. They were fighting like girls here; it had to be a support company manning the stockade facility.

"You die, *Du Ma,* Amsel!" Lee's rifle butt flew up and broke another jaw as they charged toward the bamboo cages in the center of the compound. He was pretending each enemy soldier he encountered was his old drill sergeant from Basic Training.

"Over here!" Lt. Vance was yelling. "I've got a spiderhole over here!" Cordova rushed past him toward the tunnel entrance as the officer was waving Brody's people toward a pile of smoldering bricks.

"Fire in the hole!" Corky lobbed a frag underground. A muffled blast shook the earth, and he was rushing down into the hole even as the smoke began billowing up to the surface.

Brody nodded to Vance as he slid up in front of him. The lieutenant had proven himself over and over again since that first day he'd asked Treat for permission to pull back from insurmountable odds. Throughout the latter half of the Ia Drang campaign, he had distinguished himself by rushing one enemy position after another and coordinating several fire missions when artillery and manpower were not the answer. Brody even took him aside privately one morning—and it was a time when neither soldier was in the mood for conversation due to lack of sleep—in an attempt to reassure the officer the troops were no longer grading him.

"You don't have to prove anything to any of these grunts, Lou," he had told Vance. Locking eyes and nodding as if they'd just shared a valuable secret, the officer did not seem as hyper as before. But he was still gun happy when the situation called for a little more caution, and Brody wondered if, after the incident with the lethal friendly fire, Vance didn't have a death wish. Maybe the man didn't want to survive this campaign. There was most likely an investigation waiting for him back in An Khe. Perhaps he was after a posthumous medal rather than bad paper in his back pocket. He already had the blood of his troops on his hands.

Chest heaving from the lack of oxygen in the tunnel—the grenade had sucked most of it up—Cordova rushed down through the winding maze in a crouch, .45 automatic extended at arm's length. Sooner or later he would hit a fresh pocket of air. He hoped he would meet some Cong before that.

Viet Cong. They had encountered several VC sappers integrated into the ranks of the North Vietnamese topside. Cordova surmised the area had been a Cong-controlled hamlet before the NVA retreat from the Ia Drang, and that North Vietnamese presence at this facility was only temporary.

Cordova wanted Cong.

Charlie had killed all his best friends. Oh sure, he'd watched a lot of good men die by NVA bullets, but that was long after those first bloody engagements with the VC of Binh Dinh Province, where Corky had learned you don't make close friends in The Nam. Unless you want to be another recipient of the big hurt.

"Let's call it quits!" Lt. Vance was right behind him. He'd dropped down into the spiderhole too after instructing Brody to secure the area and check for ventilation shafts or secret exits.

"What?" Cordova could not believe his ears. "This thing could go on for miles. There's more action above ground, Corky. We can fill this fucker with gasoline later and burn the mothers out!"

346

Cordova hesitated. He was getting a gut feeling about this tunnel. He was getting a feeling. The lieutenant could back out if he wanted to. Cordova would go it alone.

"Did you hear me, Corky?"

Vance's gun hand was shaking. He'd been chasing glory for so long these past two weeks, he wasn't sure where reality began and Void Vicious ended anymore. But he knew he sure didn't want to die underground, in a VC tunnel.

Buchanan had been noncommittal about a court martial, but there would certainly be follow-up investigations as to why GIs had died at the hands of an American mortar team. When friendly fire claimed U.S. casualties on such a scale, it was SOP that a general officer chair the committee looking into the incident. It was also SOP that heads roll.

So Vance was unsure about his future. Did he have a career with the military he loved? or was he finished? The week following the tragedy, he had gone so far as to contemplate suicide. But, as firefights escalated in the area and he was thrown into repeated leadership roles at the forefront of a battle-weary combat unit, the lieutenant's attitude slowly changed. He began to think more and more like his men. "Don't mean nothin'," had become a favorite phrase of his, and following the infantryman's bible was replaced with a "fuck-it" strategy that placed survival above commendations and the lust for enemy blood above the Geneva Convention. Eventually, he no longer cared what happened to him after the Ia Drang. He lived not even day to day, but for the moment. He was a warrior drunk on adrenaline. A legend in his own mind. Indestructable.

As night Lurps turned into day ambushes and back into after-dark ops, Vance's men thought less and less about the mistake involving the mortars. The lieutenant was just the man who told them what to do, the one who kept them together, the guy who made the tough decisions and took the heat. They were content to follow him through the boonies, for the most part. So long as the Whoremonger was there to give his nod of approval.

"Let's go, friend." Vance's voice took on a sterner tone as they reach a fork in the tunnel. "We don't have time to... LOOK OUT!"

Two Vietnamese men wearing black shorts suddenly appeared in the sloping tunnel on their left. One was carrying an

347

old French-made MAT-49 submachine gun, and though both Americans heard something slam forward as the gunman raised his weapon, there was no discharge.

Until Cordova fired four rounds off. He jerked the trigger in each time, flinching as the flames lit up the narrow corridor—not really even taking aim. But the Vieg Cong tumbled backwards, both felled by body hits.

Vance started to reach forward to snatch the submachine gun away from them, but someone was faster. A woman.

A slender Vietnamese girl with waist-length hair, black calico pantaloons, and a khaki long-sleeve shirt rolled up to her elbows, scooped up the weapon. She raised it threateningly, but Cordova hesitated.

"Shoot 'er!" Vance shouted, but even before giving Corky a chance to react, the lieutenant was brushing past him, unloading all eight rounds in his own automatic.

Like a rag doll, the girl flopped back, her face erased by hot lead, her fragile features but a reflection in Cordova's tear-filled eyes. A reflection that was shattered, and collapsing.

Collapsing under its own weight. Burdened by memories that were flooding back now to haunt the American.

Cordova sank to his knees, trying to control the sobbing. He started to reach forward, then abruptly fell back against the tunnel wall. Dropping his pistol in the dust, he folded his arms over bent knees, rested his forehead against them, and hid his eyes from Lt. Vance. Hid his eyes and cried his heart out.

The woman wearing the VC bag was Thuan, the lover from Xom Moi he had left in An Khe.

Col. Buchanan was the kind of commanding officer that liked to get involved with his men. With his help—he had been leaning out the open door of his C&C Loach and firing his hunting rifle down at the enemy—the plateau was secured less than one hour after the seven gunships landed. Chappell and Nelson were rescued unharmed.

Echo Company did not lose a single man. A pile of 54 communist bodies quickly grew in the hamlet's public square.

Brody and Broken Arrow led the charge through the bamboo cages, liberating prisoners. Thirty-two South Vietnamese soldiers were freed, and in an underground pit they found three women who appeared dirty and hungry, but had not been molested.

"Well Treat, do you see what *I* see?" Two-Step shone a powerful flashlight down on the apprehensive faces.

"Looks like the Cong been dressin' up as Arvins again when they go out on their pussy patrols." Delgado was not smiling.

"Hey, Professor!" Brody called over to Larson, who was still aboard one of the gunships, covering the grunts on the ground with a hatch-60. "Plug into the PA and make an announcement. Get Em-ho Lee-Lee the fuck over here! We got a surprise for him!"

Standing at the bottom of the pit was a woman bearing an uncanny likeness to the missing village maiden in the faded photograph Lee had shown them weeks earlier.

Patterson was disappointed at whom he found in the last bamboo cage.

It was an American, all right. But it wasn't Snakeman's brother. It wasn't Richard Fletcher, Air Force pilot, MIA for two years running. "Aw, fuck . . . ." He reached into the cage to give the bruised and battered prisoner of war a hand. "You're the last friendly face I expected to see in . . .well, actually—I take that back. You're—"

"Greetings and salute*asians,* my fellow American!" The squatting man wore a tattered TV suit, a silver flattop, and thick black glasses with one lens shattered.

CIA Agent John Graves rose to his feet and dusted himself off.

"Well, you don't look much the worse for wear. Did the bastards pull any of your fingernails out?"

"My MAC-10 jammed on me." Graves's eyes darted about at all the drifting flares and helicopter activity. He seemed relieved the shooting had died down to solitary discharges here and there. "And the pricks got my jeep. Probably on the black market in Phnom Penh by now. Gonna come outta my paycheck, don't you know?"

Patterson just shook his head from side to side as he scratched the scab forming along one shoulder blade.

He was almost glad Snakeman was recovering at a hospital in Japan. Now he wouldn't have to tell him the POW Larson had spotted and mistaken for his brother was really Agent Graves.

349

They found no other American prisoners at Polei Noh Yo. There was no evidence Richard Fletcher had ever been there.

CHAPTER 38

"Brody!" Lawrence "Em-ho" Lee was running around the main Echo Company landing pad. "Where's Brody? Somebody find him. The Whoremonger's just *gotta* see this!"

Broken Arrow was just about to point in the direction of the Hell Hole when the Spec-4 rose slowly from the bunker, trying not to spill a VC skullcap full of beer. "*Who's* callin' the Emperor of Echo Company?" He spoke with a royal twang of dubious breeding.

"*Look!*" Lee pointed up at the clouds, and Brody dropped his bone mug in the dust. He started running toward the landing pads, whooping for joy.

A huge Chinook was descending from a black blanket of storm clouds. It was a downed-chopper retrieval craft, and *Pegasus* was suspended under its belly, her rotors disassembled, but the mural of a mythical winged horse across her snout was as beautiful as ever. A shaft of sunlight pierced the clouds as the Chinook gently set its cargo on the ground and mechanics hustled about disconnecting the cables as the monstrous Jolly Green CH-47 hovered overhead.

Brody would have liked to have pointed up at the ray of gold, claiming it was a magical sign, but they had all watched the sun slowly appear. There was nothing supernatural about what had just happened. It was all just coincidence, and few soldiers behind Brody didn't give the scene a second thought. But Brody could dream. And he believed in *Peg*. They had not lost her after all. He would supervise the clean-up job personally. The lady was back to stay.

350

He noticed the holes in her roof and belly as another dusty shaft from the sun highlighted them. An intense look of concern creased his features, and he asked a crew chief passing by if the damage looked serious to him, but the sergeant just walked on without stopping, shoulders drooping in an uninterested shrug.

"Your chopper there'll be all right, Treat." Lt. Vance was suddenly standing beside him, and Brody responded with a friendly, enthusiastic smile.

"You think so, sir?"

"Yah, no sweat. They used to come in from the field over in An Khe when I was in-processing looking much worse than that, but the mechanics always seemed to get 'em back in the air."

"Hey, Whoremonger!" Broken Arrow was walking up from the mess tent and constantly stumbling on the tarmac. Brody wasn't sure if he'd had some hundred-proof brew, or if it was really because he was so interested in the newspaper he was trying to read. "Check out what they got published here in the *Stars & Stripes,* dude! The dickheads in Hanoi released a list of American POW's they're considering negotiating over.

"Yah?"

"Yep. Seems they want to start talks to see if they can have a prisoner swap in the near future. Annnnnd . . ."

"You're kidding, Two-Step!"

"Nope. One Richard E. Fletcher is *Numba* One on the list, boy."

Brody hugged Lt. Vance and jumped for joy, yelling at the top of his lungs and waving his fist in the air. Vance seemed just as pleased to hear the good news, but both soldiers froze when they spotted Buchanan and one of his captains rushing from the CP in their direction.

"Lieutenant!" the colonel pointed at Vance.

"Aw, fuck me 'till it hurts." Brody frowned on the officer's behalf.

"Here comes trouble." Broken Arrow made a quick but silently graceful exit.

Vance snapped to the position of attention and saluted, and Brody swallowed hard. "Knock off all the military courtesy crap!" Buchanan grabbed the officer's trembling hand and

351

shook it. "The verdict's in, young man." He slapped a teletype in Vance's sweat-slick palm.

"The verdict, sir?" Brody had been unaware there'd even been a trial yet.

"The JAG representative just completed his investigation and has found evidence Lt. Vance called in the *correct* coordinates that day the mortars fell on your people, soldier. The trooper calling the shots relayed the wrong numbers to the mortar pit. The same trooper was KIA less than one hour later. End of Story."

It was Vance who wanted to lift Brody off *his* feet in a bear-hug this time around, but they were interrupted by a small, four-legged mobile alert siren.

Carrying Brody's squashed snakehead mask in his mouth, *Choi-oi* trotted through the dust, running circles around the group and trying to howl through clenched teeth.

"Oh-oh." Buchanan started running for the nearest bunker. "Speaking of mortars..."

But no barrage of projectiles descended on the men. No smoking shrapnel chased them to the trenches. *Choi-oi* raced over to the tree line at the edge of the landing-pad tarmac and dropped the mask. Pawing at it, he barked loud and long, nose pointed up at the dense branches.

"What the fu—" Brody unslung his M-16 and started to raise it to his shoulder. But the weapon wasn't needed.

There came a rustling in the branches, and then an AK-47 fell quietly to the ground, cracking the stock down the middle as it landed. A pair of thick eyeglasses followed it.

A couple of second later, a Vietnamese man crashed down through the branches and began thrashing about, screaming for help in a dialect even Truong Ju-ju didn't understand. He was wrapped, from neck to ankle, in the coils of a huge python that must have measured easily in excess of thirty feet.

"Take that...that...*egghead* into custody!" Buchanan slowly emerged from his bunker, dusting off his refractured arm.

Brody and Vance exchanged hesitant looks, then attached the bayonets to their rifles and slowly started toward the irritated reptile.

The man being smothered to death was their longtime friend, the sniper who couldn't shoot straight.

352

GLOSSARY

AA Antiaircraft weapon

AC Aircraft Commander

Acting Jack Acting NCO

AIT Advanced Individual Training

AJ Acting Jack

AK-47 Automatic rifle used by VC/NVA

Animal See Monster

AO Area of Operations

Ao Dai Traditional Vietnamese gown

APH-5 Helmet worn by gunship pilots

APO Army Post Office

Arc-Light B-52 bombing mission

ArCOM Army Commendation Medal

Article-15 Disciplinary action

Ash-'n'-Trash Relay flight

Bad Paper Dishonorable discharge

Ba Muoi Ba Vietnamese beer

Banana Clip Ammo magazine holding 30 bullets

Bao Chi Press or news media

Basic Boot camp

BCT Basic Combat Training (Boot)

Bic Vietnamese for "Understand?"

Big-20 Army career of 20 years

Bird Helicopter

BLA Black Liberation Army

Bloods Black soldiers

Blues An airmobile company

Body Count Number of enemy KIA

Bookoo Vietnamese for "many" (actually bastardization of French *beaucoup*)

Bought the Farm Died and life insurance policy paid for mortgage

Brass Monkey Interagency radio call for help

Brew Usually coffee, but sometimes beer

Bring Smoke To shoot someone

Broken-Down   Disassembled
Buddha Zone   Death
Bush ('Bush)   Ambush
Butter Bar   2nd Lieutenant

CA   Combat Assault
Cam Ong   Viet for "Thank you"
Cartridge   Shell casing for bullet
C&C   Command & Control chopper
Chao   Vietnamese greeting
Charlie   Viet Cong (from military phonetic: Victor Charlie)
Charlie Tango   Control Tower
Cherry   New man in unit
Cherry Boy   Virgin
Chicken Plate   Pilot's chest/groin armor
Chi-Com   Chinese Communist
Chieu Hoi   Program where communists can surrender and become scouts
Choi-oi   Viet exclamation
CIB   Combat Infantry Badge
CID   Criminal Investigation Division
Clip   Ammo magazine
CMOH   Congressional Medal of Honor
CO   Commanding Officer
Cobra   Helicopter gunship used for combat assaults/escorts only
Cockbang   Bangkok, Thailand
Conex   Shipping container (metal)
Coz   Short for Cozmoline
CP   Command Post
CSM   Command Sergeant Major
Cunt Cap   Green narrow cap worn with khakis

Dash-13   Helicopter maintenance report
Dau   Viet for pain
Deadlined   Down for repairs
Dep   Viet for beautiful
DEROS   Date of Estimated Return from Overseas
Deuce-and-a-Half   2½-ton truck
354

DFC   Distintushed Flying Cross

DI   Drill Instructor (Sgt.)

Di Di   Viet for "Leave or go!"

Dink   Derogatory term for Vietnamese national

Dinky Dau   Viet for "crazy"

Disneyland East   MACV complex including annex

DMZ   Demilitarized Zone

Dogtags   Small aluminum tag worn by soldiers with name, serial number, religion, and blood type imprinted on it

DOOM Pussy   Danang Officers Open Mess

Door gunner   Soldier who mans M-60 machine gun mounted in side hatch of Huey gunship

Dung Lai   Viet for "Halt!"

Dustoff   Medevac chopper

Early Out   Unscheduled ETS

EM   Enlisted Man

ER   Emergency Room (hospital)

ETS   End Tour of (military) Service

Field Phone   Hand-generated portable phones used in bunkers

Fini   Viet for "Stop" or "the End"

First Louie   1st Lieutenant

First Team   Motto of 1st Air Cav

Flak Jacket   Body armor

FNG   Fucking new guy

FOB   Fly over border mission

Foxtrot   Vietnamese female

Foxtrot Tosser   Flame thrower

Frag   Fragmentation grenade

FTA   Fuck the Army

Gaggle   Loose flight of slicks

Get Some   Kill someone

GI   Government Issue, or, a soldier

Greenbacks   U.S. currency

Green Machine   U.S. Army

Gunship   Attack helicopter armed with machine guns

and rockets
Gurney Stretcher with wheels

Ham & Motherfuckers C-rations serving of ham and
lima beans
Herpetologist One who studies reptiles and amphibians
HOG-60 M-60 machine gun
Hot LZ Landing zone under hostile fire
Housegirl Indigenous personnel hired to clean buildings,
wash laundry, etc.
Huey Primary troop-carrying helicopter

IC Instillation Commander
IG Inspector General
In-Country Within Vietnam
Intel Intelligence (military)
IP That point in a mission where descent toward target
begins

JAG Judge Advocate General
Jane Jane's Military Reference books
Jesus Nut The bolt that holds rotor blade to helicopter
Jody Any American girlfriends
Jolly Green Chinook helicopter

KIA Killed in Action
Kimchi Korean fish sauce salad
Klick Kilometer
KP Mess hall duty

Lai Day Viet for "come here"
LAW Light Anti-Tank Weapon
Lay Dog Lie low in jungle during recon patrol
LBFM Little Brown Fucking Machine
LBJ Long Binh Jail (main stockade)
Leg Infantryman not airborne qualified
Lifeline Straps holding gunny aboard chopper while he
fires M-60 out the hatch
Lifer Career soldier
Links Metal strip holding ammo belt together

Loach Small spotter/scout chopper

LP Listening Post

LRRP Long-Range Recon Patrol

LSA Gun oil

Lurp One who participates in LRRPs

LZ Landing Zone

M-14 American carbine

M-16 Primary U.S. Automatic Rifle

M-26 Fragmentation grenade

M-60 Primary U.S. Machine gun

M-79 Grenade launcher (rifle)

MACV Military Assistance Command, Vietnam

Magazine Metal container that feeds bullets into weapon. Holds 20 or 30 rounds per unit

Mag Pouch Magazine holder worn on web belt

MAST Mobile Army Surgical Team

Med-Evac Medical Evacuation Chopper

Mess Hall GI cafeteria

MG Machine gun

MI Military Intelligence

MIA Missing in Action

Mike-Mike Millimeters

Mike Papas Military Policemen

Mister Zippo Flame-thrower operator

Mjao Central Highlands witch doctor

Monkeyhouse Stockade or jail

Monkeystrap See **LIFELINE**

Monster 12–21 claymore antipersonnel mines jury-rigged to detonate simultaneously

Montagnarde Hill tribe people of Central Highlands, RVN

MPC Money Payment Certificates (scrip) issued to GIs in RVN in lieu of greenbacks

Muster A quick assemblage of soldiers with little or no warning

My Viet for "American"

Net Radio net

NETT New Equipment Training Team

Newby New GI in-country
Numba One Something very good
Numba Ten Something very bad
Nuoc Nam Viet fish sauce
NVA North Vietnamese Army

OD Olive Drab
OR Operating Room (Hospital)

P Piasters
PA Public Address system
PCS Permanent Change of (Duty) Station (transfer out of RVN)
Peter Pilot Copilot in training
PF Popular Forces (Vietnamese)
PFC Private First Class
Phantom Jet fighter plane
Phu Vietnamese noodle soup
Piaster Vietnamese Currency
PJ Photojournalist
Point The most dangerous position on patrol. The point man walks ahead and to the side of the others, acting as a lookout
PRG Provisional Revolutionary Govt. (the Communists)
Prang Land a helicopter roughly
Prick-25 PR-25 field radio
Profile Medical exemption
Psy-Ops Psychological operation
PT Physical Training
Puff Heavily armed aircraft
Purple Heart Medal given for wounds received in combat
Purple Vision Night vision
Puzzle Palace The MACV HQ building

Quad-50 Truck equipped with four 50-caliber MGs
QC Vietnamese MP

Rat Fuck Mission doomed from the start
Regular An enlistee or full-time soldier as opposed to

PFs and Reserves, NG, etc.
REMF Rear Echelon Motherfucker
R&R Rest and Relaxation
Re-Up Re-enlist
Rikky-Tik Quickly or fast
Rock 'N' Roll Automatic fire
Roger Affirmative
ROK Republic of Korea
Rotor Overhead helicopter blade
Round Bullet
RPG Rocket-propelled grenade
Ruck(Sack) GI's backpack
RVN Republic of (South) Vietnam

Saigon Capital of RVN
SAM Surface-to-Air Missile
Sapper Guerrilla terrorist equipped with satchel charge (explosives)
SAR Downed-chopper rescue mission
Scramble Alert reaction to call for help, CA or rescue operation.
Scrip See **MPC**
7.62 M-60 ammunition
Sierra Echo Southeast (Northwest is November Whiskey, etc.)
Single-Digit Fidget A nervous single-digit midget
Single-Digit Midget One with fewer than ten days remaining in Vietnam
SKS Russian-made carbine
Slick Helicopter
Slicksleeve Private E-1
Slug Bullet
SNAFU Situation normal: all fucked up
Soggy Frog Green Beret laying dog
SOP Standard Operating Procedure (also know as Shit Output)
Spiderhole Tunnel entrance
Strac Sharp appearance
Steel Pot Helmet
Striker Montagnarde hamlet defender

Sub-Gunny Substitute door gunner

TDY Temporary Duty Assignment
Terr Terrorist
"33" Local Vietnamese beer
Thumper See M-79
Ti Ti Viet for little
Tour 365 The year-long tour of duty a GI spends in
    RVN
Tower Rat Tower guard
Tracer Chemically treated bullet that gives off a glow
    en-route to its target
Triage That method in which medics determine which
    victims are most seriously hurt and therefore treated
    first
Trooper Soldier
201 File Personnel file
Two-Point-Five Gunship rockets

UCMJ Uniformed Code of Military Justice
Unass Leave seat quickly

VC Viet Cong
Victor Charlie VC
Viet Cong South Vietnamese Communists
VNP Vietnamese National Police
Void Vicious Final approach to a Hot LZ; or the jungle
    when hostile

Warrant Officer Pilots
Wasted Killed
Web Belt Utility belt GIs use to carry equipment,
    sidearms, etc.
Whiskey Military phonetic for "West"
WIA Wounded In Action
Wilco Will comply
Willie Peter White phosphorous
Wire Perimeter (trip wire sets off booby trap)
The World Any place outside Vietnam

Xin Loi Viet for "sorry about that" or "good-bye"

XM-21 Gunship mini-gun

XO Executive Officer

'Yarde Montagnarde

ZIP Derogatory term for Vietnamese National

Zulu Military phonetic for the letter Z (LZ or Landing Zone might be referred to as a Lima Zulu)

THE AUTHOR served with the United States Army in Southeast Asia from 1972 until shortly after the fall of Saigon in 1975. He alternates between homes in the Orient and Little Saigon USA, has written sixteen other adventure novels on the Vietnam war under several pseudonyms.